THE STONE SHIP

THE STONE SHIP

A NOCTURNE

IN THREE WATCHES

DUNSTAN MASSEY

RESOURCE *Publications* · Eugene, Oregon

THE STONE SHIP
A Nocturne in Three Watches

Resource Publications
An Imprint of Wipf and Stock Publishers
199 W. 8th Ave., Suite 3
Eugene, OR 97401

www.wipfandstock.com

ISBN 13: 978-1-62564-101-4

Manufactured in the U.S.A.

CONTENTS

ACKNOWLEDGEMENTS

Any monk who writes, knows his work is as much due to the support of his community, as to his own endeavour. Gratitude urges me to thank all of the members of the Abbey who have helped;

Rt. Rev. John Braganza, Abbot of Westminster at Mission, British Columbia, Canada, for his kind approval of this work for publication;

Fr. Basil Foote for composing musical settings for the songs, and for advice in selecting Gregorian Chants from the Antiphonale Monasticum, and Preces Cantatae;

Fr. Peter Nygren for a first typing of the chorus parts and the musical score; Fr. Alban Riley and Fr. Leo Barker for secretarial and E-mail assistance;

Fr. Joseph Park for digital photography of the book's illustrations, and of the set model and miniature figures designed for the Nocturne; also for Br. Gabriel Do's work on the choreographic diagrams, and on the cover of the book;

Miss Rhonda Wood, long a friend of the Abbey, for the first complete typescript of the manuscript which served as a reliable guide throughout the chaos of an extensive revision;

Barbara and David Mackay, my cousins in Medicine Hat for their professional and definitive word processing and printout of the book;

This play was typeset using open source tools. The prose was set using Leslie Lamport's LaTeX document preparation system.

The musical score was typeset using MusiXTeX, developed by Daniel Taupin, Ross Mitchell, and Andreas Egler.

The Gregorian chant was typset using tools from Élie Roux's Gregorio Project, developed for the monks of Sainte Madeleine du Barroux Abbey.

THE THIRD WATCH

DRAMATIS PERSONAE

DOM JEROME . . . . PORTER OF CLOISTERGARTH

WITH DOUBLING OF CHARACTERS

TOM BURNS . . . . 2 CALEB THORN
ROSE BURNS . . . . 2 MOTHER WICKS
. . . . 3 MARY SIMS
YOUNG TOM . . . . 2 WILLIE SIMS
AUNT HANNA . . . . 2 MRS. THOREAU
. . . . 2 SR. SUPERIOR
CAPT. CODROCKS . . . . .2 HARRY IBBS
. . . . 3 UNCLE REMUS
REGIS WICKS . . . .
NICK . . . . 2 JOB WICKS . . . . 3 NICHOLAS BURNS (SIMS)
. . . . 4 SANDY
FAY FLOSS . . . . 2 YOUNG WILLIE
FANNY FLOSS . . . . 2 JENNY WICKS
SR. JENNIFER . . . . .2 SUE
DAN WICKS . . . . 2 COURIER
BEN WICKS . . . .
MR. FROAR . . . . .2 BERT
MRS. WAGUARD . . . . .2 GRANNY OWEN
ANNABELLE PEW . . . . .2 MRS. THORN
MOLLY GREEN . . . .
AMY HEARTH . . . . 2 MCCORKERAN
ELI RENAIRE . . . .
OLRIG HAGAN . . . . 2 DR. MALLOY
LIBRARIAN . . . .
BUB . . . . 2 DRUGGIST
TAD MCFERGUSON . . . . .2 CAPT. HADDOCK
MISS MILLIE . . . .
MRS. CARP . . . .
MISS BRAYLORN . . . . .2 KATY
OPERATOR . . . . VOICE OFF STAGE U.C.
SPOKEN OR SUNG CHORUSES ARE LIVE OR TAPED
SUNG CHANTS BY CANTOR AND NOVICE, OFF S.D.L.
THE PSALMODY OF THE MONK'S CHOIR IS TAPED

THE FIRST WATCH

BUT LISTEN JEROME, P.20

THE FIRST WATCH

The theatre darkens as the sound of seas breaking, of gulls, fog horns, of numberless forgotten voices, ineluctable visions, nightmare realms, begin, commence their nocturnal emergence.

Taped sound

(Waves breaking on the shore at a distance . . . .
. . . . . (a single toned deep fog horn)
. . . . .

the sound of waves continues . . . .
. . . . (nearer a 'minor third' foghorn) . . . .
. . . . . (cries of a few seagulls) .

the seas gradually subsiding . . . .
. . (tug horn) . . . . . . (distant 'minor third' fog horn) . . . .
. . . . . (rousing a flurry of gulls) .

TENORS

Ere ghóstly fóg . . . . ship of stóne . . . .
. . . ghóst . . . . . from a Fáll . . . . be dríven . . . .
. . . . fóg . . . . . . Fáll ship of stóne . . . . or wráiths

BARITONES

. . . . .from . . . . . ship of stóne be dríven . . . .
. . . . a Fáll . . . . .be . . . . . . or wráiths
. . . . .of stóne . . dríven . . . .

Taped sound

the seas fade under into a murmuring . . . .
. . . . . (distant deep fog horn) . . . . . .
. . . . . a mysterious wind

TENORS

róuted, ráw . . . . . . north . . . .
. . . . . . ráw cutting . . . . . eásterly, . wínd . . . .
. . . . cutting north . . . . a wínd of wínter . . . .

BARITONES

. . . . . . ráw . . . . eásterly, a wínd of wínter . . . .
róuted, . . . cutting . . . . a wínd of . . . . . . is dúe . . .
róuted, ... northeást . . . . wínter . . dúe, as

Taped sound

the seas's murmur grows with the wind . . . .
. . . . . (cry of a single gull) . . . .
. . . . that moans with hollow flutings . . . . then rises

BARITONES

Dark . . . . mercúrial . . . .
Dark raínfall . . . . or sléets . . . . mercúrial elíxirs . .
. . . . . raínfall squalls, ... equanóxial, ... elíxirs . .

BASSES

. . . . or sléets . . . . mercúrial . . . .
. . . . raínfall squalls, ... equanóxial, ...
Dark raínfall . . . . or sléets . . . .

Taped sound

the sea, sighing on the shore, rises, as waves begin to break .
. . . . (a brief passing sound of rainfall) . . . .
gusting, the wind . . . . blows the rainfall past . . . .

(decrescendo)

BARITONES

. . . . léthal . . . . of your blóod[1] . . . .
flow . . . . . in the cóurses . . your blóod[1] . . . . wícked, our

BASSES

flow léthal . . . . . cóurses . . your . . . . while wícked . . . .
flow . . . . . in the cóurses of . . . . [1]ánd, while . . . .

(piano)   *(crescendo)*

SOPRANOS

flow léthal . . . . [1]ánd, while . . . .
. . . . the cóurses . . . . while wícked . . . .
. . . . léthal in . . . . of your blóod[1] . . . . wícked, our

Taped sound

the seas subside with a calm . . . .
. . . . as the wind dies . . . .
. . . . . followed by a humming of lines,

CONTRALTOS

. . . . chátter . . . .
[1]télephones . . . . . . [2]with híssing . . . . [3]gárbled . . . .
. . . . chátter . . . . . híssing gossip's . . . . gabble[4] . . . .

CONTRALTOS

[1]télephones . . . . . . [2]with híssing . . . . [3]gárbled . . . .
. . . . chátter . . . . . híssing gossip's . . . .
. . . . [3]gárbled gabble[4] . . . .

MILLIE

. . . . [2]'eló dear . . . .

BRAYLORN

. . . . [3]óh! . . . . [4]so glád you cáll'd .

Taped sound

[1]*(distant phone rings) humming of lines continues under . . . .*

SOPRANOS

    our náttering hótlines . . . .
    . . . . hótlines ¹ . . cráckle ² . . from . . . .
    our náttering . . . . ¹ . . cráckle . . . . póle . . . .

CONTRALTOS

    . . . náttering hótlines ¹ . . cráckle ² . . from póle . . . .
    our . . . . hót . . . . ¹ . . cráckle . . . . póle to póle³ . . .
    . . . náttering . . lines . . . . to póle³ . . .

MILLIE
Taped sound

    . . . . ¹Wir’ . . ²hávin’a chi’chat . . . . . . ³yes,
    humming of lines under . . . .
    . . . (soft sustained cymbal . . . . fades) . . . .

CONTRALTOS

    ¹recéivers all . . . . clútching . . . .
    ¹recéivers all dówn ²   the tówn ³ . . . . at the néws . . . . .
    . . . . all dówn . . . . clútching . . . . ⁴with

CONTRALTOS

    ¹recéivers . . dówn ² . the tówn ³ . . . . at the néws . . . . .
    ¹recéivers all . . . . the tówn . . clútching . . . . ⁴with
    . . . . dówn ² . . . . . tówn ³ . . . . at the néws . . . . .

MILLIE
BRAYLORN
Taped sound

    ¹t’night . . . .
    . . . . ²oh? . . . . . ³nó! . . . . ⁴ya dón’say! .
    humming . . . . (soft sustained cymbal . . . . fades)

SOPRANOS

    their . . . . coloured¹ . . . .
    . . . . góre- . . . . scrátching . . . .
    their góre-coloured¹ . . . . Tábby bloodied² cát . . . .

CONTRALTOS

    . . . . góre-coloured¹ scrátching . . . . . bloodied² cát claws! .
    their . . . . Tábby . . . . cát claws! .
    . . . . góre- . . . . scrátching . . . . . bloodied² . . . claws!³ .

MILLIE
BRAYLORN
Taped sound

    . . . . ¹o’córs dear . . . . ³tá Bray . . . .
    . . . . ²b’ríte ov’r! . . . .
    humming . . . . (soft sustained cymbal . . . . fades)

TENORS

[
¹Hey, Tád!. . . . .
¹Hey, . . . we'll gét ya a shót. . . . .
. . . . . Tád!. . . . . a shót a scótch, ...

BARITONES

¹Hey, . . . we'll gét ya . . . . . a scótch, ²a hót shot . . . .
. . . . . Tád!. . . . . a shót . . . . ²a hót shot t'cheér y'úp Tad!
. . . . gét ya . . . . . a scótch, ... t'cheér y'úp Tad!

Taped sound

¹*(foghorn 'minor third') . . . fade in cozy pub sound* . . . .
. . . . ²*(clinking of glasses)*. . . .
]

TENORS

[
a nóggin?. . . . .
. . . . ¹or a jígger . . . . . . or ryé?. . . . .
a nóggin?. . . . . a gín? . . . . . t'líght. . . . .

BARITONES

. . . . ¹or a jígger a gín? . . . . . t'líght yer líver! . . . . . a trý!. . . .
a nóggin? . . . . or ryé?. . . . yer líver! gíver . . . .
. . . . jígger a gín? . . . . . t'líght . . . . gíver a trý Tad!

Taped sound

. . . . ¹*(pouring liquor into glasses)* . . . .
. . . . *congenial pub murmur continues under* . . .
]

TENORS

[
a toást! ¹to the . . . . 'órrible. . . . .
. . . . ¹to the bleár- . . . . hórrible . . . .
a toást! . . . . . . bleár-eyed 'órrible . . . . mád. . . . .

BARITONES

. . . . ¹to the bleár-eyed . . . . . hórrible mád eyed . . . .
a toást! . . . . 'órrible . . . . mád eyed móon!. . . . . .
. . . . bleár-eyed . . . . . . hórrible . . . . móon Lad!

Taped sound

. . . . ¹*(clinking of glasses)*. . . . .
the pub murmur continues . . . modulates into combo brushes . . . .
]

(sung)   *(crescendo)*
SOPR. TEN.

[
¹deép . . . . inébriate . . . . drank deép . . . .
¹deép drank . . . . jázz-rash! Jámshyd . . . . an' . . . .
. . . . . drank inébriate jázz-rash! . . . . drank deép . . . .

Taped sound

¹*(fog horn moans)*. . . . .
. . . . *the combo brushes accelerate to the jazz tempo* . . . . .
]

13

(spoken)

SOPR. *(sung)* .... búrn-ing! .... -a-a-a-azzrásh! ..... gorge yáwns
TENOR .... búrn-ing!² ..... ³a-Já-a-a-a-azzrásh! héll's gorge ......
TENOR he- .... ¹búrn-ing!.Búrns³ ... -a-a-a-azz..⁴as héll's ..... yáwns

BASS *(spoken)* .. búrns¹ .... ²Tom Búrns ... -a-a-a-azzrásh! ..... gorge yáwns
BASS he búrns¹ ..... Tom .... ³a-Já-a-a-a-azzrásh! héll's gorge yáwns
BASS he- .... ¹búrn-ing!.Búrns³ .... ⁴as héll's ..... yáwns

Taped sound .... ²sustained cymbal crescendo ⁴subsides ....
.... light drum roll rises, is sustained then ⁴fades .... the combo

MONA *(sung)* Oh¹ .... ²smóke-eyed³ .... yóu ....

BASS *(spoken)* ¹for .... so² .... diúrnal ... slów time's etérnal
BASS ... yeárning so .... ³so .... yóu .... time's ....
BASS ¹for yeárning .... diúrnal ... slów ...... etérnal

Taped sound brushes move in a sultry blues tempo .... then

MONA *(sung)* .... ²Blue Móna³ .... the óna óne I'm gónná

BASS *(spoken)* túrning Tom só blue² .... Búrns ... óna .... gónná
BASS .... Tom .... ³Tom Búrns ... óna óne I'm ......
BASS túrning .... Tom ..... the ... óne ... gónná

Taped sound continues to smolder on, with soft drums to a hushed cymbal ....

MONA *(sung)* .... lóve¹ ....
ROSE *(spoken)* .... Thómas .. ²Tóm son³ ....
BASS *(spoken)* stíll Tom ... ¹retúrning Tom .... Búrns
BASS ... Tom .... Tom .... ²Tóm ...³búrning ....
BASS stíll .... túrning .... son³ ..... Búrns

(retard)

Taped sound the brushes begin to modulate into sea sounds................

TENORS *(chant)* Remémber.......... remémber .... remémber
FAY *(spoken)* .... Regis? .... where are you? ....

Taped sound of waves breaking on the shore. ....

FAY *(sung)*

       [1] . . . . yé will be láunchin' . . . .
. . . . sáfe under saíl,[2] . . . .

Taped sound

      [1]*(fog horn . . echoing off the headlands) . . . .*[2]*flurry of gulls*
. . . . sighing the seas withdraw, then rushing, return . . . . . .

FAY *(sung)*

      yóung laddie dréamin' . . . .
. . . . [1]tráde winds avail . . . *(fade)* . . . .

NOVICE *(sung)*

      . . . . Véni fíli aúdi me . . [2]

Taped sound

      the ebb and flow . . .[1]*rallies with wind . . . .*
. . . . . (a distant sound of a bell)[2]

Y. WILLIE

      [1]Fáther! . . . .
. . . . . . [2]come báck, father! . . . .
. . . . come báck, come báck- . . . .

Taped sound

      [1]*Waves thunder under a freshening wind, then fade . . . .*
. . . .[2]*as the boy descends his cries reecho . . . . . .*

SOPRANOS   . . . . but hów? dówn in the deép, ... can I . . . .
TENORS   Hów? . . . . dówn . . . . . deép, hów . . . .
CALEB   . . . . but hów? . . . . . in the deép, ... can I éxtricate . . . . . .
TENORS   . . . . dówn . . . . . deép, hów can I . . . .

Taped sound

      following the father under . . . .
. . . . swirling waters merge in deep sea sound . . . . . .

SOPRANOS

      . . . . Kélpied . . . . weeds . . . seá green seá?
cráwling . . . . flésh . . seáweeds in a . . green seá?
. . . . my Kélpied . . . . . as seáweeds . . . seá . . . .

TENORS   . . . . my . . . . flésh . . seáweed? . . . seá green seá?
CALEB   cráwling . . . . flésh as . . . . in a . . green seá?
TENORS   cráwl . . my . . . . as seáweeds . . . seá . . . .

Taped sound

      of a slow tympanic . . . .
. . . . thunder descending, pianissimo . . . .

CONTRALTOS

where . . . . déep, reéfs . . . . . . .the finned flócks
. . . . .down déep, ... pásture the finned . . . . . .
where córalline . . . . reéfs pásture . . . . flócks

BARITONES

. . . . . .córalline . . . . . déep, ...the finned . . . . . .
where . . . . .¹down . . . . . reéfs pásture . . . . flócks
. . . . . .córalline . . . . . déep, ...the finned flócks

Taped sound

the pulsating tympani descends ever deeper . . . .
. . . . .¹(with a school's shimmering sound) . . . . . .

BARITONES

. . . . in a green fóg far . . . .
. . . . .¹out of oóz . . . . .far fáthoms . . . .
. . . . stríve ¹out of . . . in a green fóg . . .fáthoms dówn . . .

TENORS

. . . . stríve . . . . . . oóz in a . . . . . fóg far . . . .
CALEB
and I . . . . . ¹out of . . . in a green . . . far fáthoms dówn . . .
TENORS
. . . . stríve ¹out of oóz . . . . .fóg . . . . dówn . . .

Taped sound

the deep sea sound grows ominous . . . .
. . . . .¹as tremulant strings build tension . . . .

TENORS

. . . . sílted excreméntal . . . . . slime, ...
CALEB
¹swím ²out of . . . . .méntal quíck slime, cráwl . . . . . .
TENORS
. . . . . . ²out of sílted excreméntal quíck . . . . . .cráwl . . . . . .

BASSES

. . . . . . ²out of sílted . . . . .slime, ...
¹swím . . . . .excreméntal quíck slime, cráwl . . . . . .
. . . . . . ²out of sílted . . . . méntal quíck . . . . . .cráwl . . . . . .

Taped sound

¹funeral drum beat (long, two short) as the roll continues
. . . . . . ²tremulant strings slide a half tone down . . . .

TENORS

. . . .blínkless . . . . . obsídian, malévolent, ...
CALEB
while . . . . éyes,²obsídian, ...hýpnotize . . . . .
TENORS
. . . .¹blínkless éyes, ... malévolent, ...

BASSES

. . . .blínkless . . . . . obsídian, malévolent, ...
while . . . . éyes,²obsídian, ...hýpnotize . . . . .
. . . .¹blínkless éyes, ... malévolent, ...

Taped sound

deep sea descends . .²yet another half tone . . . .
then a minor third to fade ²(sustained cymbal rises, falls)

TENORS

    . . . . tést, explóre . . abhórrent- . . . .
[1]their . . . . . [3]téntacles tést, explóre me . . . .
. . . . [2]coíling . . . . explóre . . abhórrent- . . . .

BASSES

[1]their . . . . . [3]téntacles tést, ... abhórrent- . . . .
. . . . [2]coíling . . . . tést, explóre me . . . .
. . . . [3]téntacles . . . . explóre . . abhórrent- . . . .

Taped sound

[1]*funeral drumbeat, as* [2]*tremulant cellos replace tymp.* . . .
. . . . [3]*(scaly sound with clicketing, threatens)* . . . . .

TENORS

. . . . [2]óctopi . . . . cupped súcking húg, ...
[1]these . . . . . in their cóld . . . . súcking . . . [3]dráwing . . .
. . . . [2]óctopi . . . . cóld cupped . . . . húg, ...

BASSES

. . . . [2]óctopi . . . . cupped súcking húg, ...
[1]these . . . . . in their cóld . . . . súcking . . . [3]dráwing . . .
. . . . [2]óctopi . . . . cóld cupped . . . . húg, ...

Taped sound

[1]*dropping a half tone, gathering intensity to a* [3]*stress* . . . .
. . . . [2]*a roll and crescendo on higher tympano* . . . .

TREB. SOPR.
CONTRALTOS

me, ... mángling me dówn, ... to its béak . . . .
. . . . mául mángling . . . . eách . . . . . béak pronged . .
. . . . mául . . . . me dówn, ... to its . . . . pronged . .

TENORS

me, mául . . . . dówn, ... to its béak . . . .
me, mául mángling . . . . eách . . . . . béak pronged . .
. . . . mángling me dówn, ... béak pronged . .

BAR. BASS.

. . . . [3]mángling . . . dówn, ... to its béak . . . .
[1]me,[2]mául[3]mángling me . . . . . eách to its . . . . pronged . .
[1]me,[2]mául . . . . me dówn, ... béak pronged . .

Taped sound

[1]*soften then* [3]*drop, continuing tremulant deep down* . . . . .
. . . . *dropping for funeral drum, then for a deeper roll* . . .
. . . . [3]*(soft sustained cymbal rising and falling)* . . .

TREB. SOPR.	órifice ....³devóuring ... digésting............
CONTRALTOS	órifice drówning, ... me, digésting me alíve!...
	..............³devóuring me, ...alíve!...
TENORS	......²drówning,³devóuring me, ...alíve!...
	¹órifice²drówning, ... me, digésting me ....
	¹órifice ....³devóuring ... digésting............
BAR. BASS.	¹órifice ....³devóuring ... digésting me ....
	......²drówning,³devóuring me, digésting me alíve!...
	¹órifice²drówning, ... me, ... me alíve!...
Taped sound	*......²tremulant cellos rise in a chrmatic assent ......*
	¹single deep drum, then steady crescendo to climax ....
	..............³sustained cymbal rises to climax ....

(The voices suddenly break off when the rising

CURTAIN

reveals DOM JEROME, *the monk, cringing under the onslaught, covering his ears. He is seated in a narrow circle of lamplight before open books, in the porter's cell at Cloistergarth. All else is plunged in darkness. Though vigorous, the monk appears aged. Long suffering years have taken their toll. Dazedly, he begins to lower his hands, with the cessation of the uproar. Sensing he is not alone, he turns tentatively toward the audience, though he can see no one. When he will speak, switching off the lamp, a blue haze will invade the scrim, followed by ghosts of house gables, and a haloed street light. Under his initial reactions, these gentler ambient sounds subside.)*

Taped sound	*(Sea murmur gradually ebbing away ....*
	echo of drum roll dying ....(distant fog horn) .
	....................(a few gull cries) ....

DOM JEROME   If one Jerome by your leave,
monk of Cloistergarth,
were to snap shut and puff
the dust out of his books,

*(which he does, while reaching
for the lamp to turn it off)*

if he were to switch out light
and look down into the town
across those shrouded lights
and out beyond them, what
would you say he would see?

*(as a projected wraith-like
cathedral emerges out of the fog,
like a tall ship, riding at anchor.)*

TENOR

A stóne grey . . . . . . veined . . . . . a shíp? of stóne? . . . .
. . . . grey márble . . . . . . shíp? a shíp? . . stóne? . . . .

BARITONE

A stóne . . . . márble veined shíp? . . . . of stóne? . . . .

BASS

. . . . grey márble . . . . . . shíp? a shíp? . . stóne? . . . .
A stóne grey . . . . . . veined . . . . . a shíp? of stóne? . . . .

TENOR

táll of . . . . ghóstly boned, ... in a míst . fóg . . . .
. . . of límestone, ghóstly . . . . . shróuded in a . . . of . . . .

BARITONE

in a slów . . . . of the seá wraith's . . . . steálth; . . . .
. . . slów smóther . . the seá . . . . dréaded . . . .

BASS

that lúring . . . . . . lóoms on the . . . . líghtless . . . . cápes . . .
. . . lúring dóom, ... on the síght- . . . less hóuse lost . . . .

TENOR

Whíle in the . . . . . . áll those streéts . . . rúnning run . . . .
. . . . . . in the hárbor áll . . . . . streéts rún, ... run dówn . . . .

TENOR

on the tówn . . . shore's . . . . glíding, tídal . . . . of gúlls . . . .
. . . . . . tówn fóreshore's ever . . . . tídal féstival of . . . .

BARITONE

ráucous reéking . . kélp above shéll- . . . . . . embárnacled . . . .
. . . . reéking of kélp . . . . . shéll-crusted . . . . whárves

BASS

and oút on the leáden straíts . . . the sláte . . . . seás of Novémber . .
. . . oút on . . . . straíts, of the . . . . grey seás . . . .

TEN.   ⌈   ... remémber ..... those móurnful freíghters ... moán ....
BAR. BASS. ⌊   you remémber them, those .... freíghters that moán ....

TEN.   ⌈   .... their horns, .. the shríll whistled plaínts .. seá tugs, lóst - ..
BAR. BASS. ⌊   with their ...... or the shríll .... plaínts of seá tugs, ...

DOM JEROME   But listen, Jerome, what
do you hear in your night wake?
What voices? So many mysterious
voices - some are real I'm sure,
others, I'm - not so sure.

Sometimes, when I'm listening
I speak - maybe I'm just
an old man talking to myself - but
I cannot escape a curious feeling
that others are listening -

If I am curious about them,
perhaps they are curious about me!
So if you are - whoever you are -
for the sake of a civilized conversation
perhaps we should get acquainted?

Apparently an old monk,
God bless'im, who was the porter then,
brought me in off the street -
a young man of about twenty.
I was dazed, they say.

Strangely, that very night
the porter passed away - so the monks
allowed me to stay. I inherited
his office and name. Though only a brother
I'm jocularly known as Dom Jerome.

Well, though it all happened
that November night a very long
time ago, I still listen. Perhaps
some voice will tell me - for years
I've been trying to remember.

I question myself - Jerome, I say,
you who can't even remember who you are -
(though many have tried to tell me)
what is it you really hear when you'r awake?
when you listen in silence - to the voices?

(As the scrim rises slowly)

SOPR.	In sílence on a . . . . móunt, a moúntain of . . . .
CONT.	. . . . on a soúndless móunt . . . . of sílence . . . .

SOPR.	what scríptures . . . . do you reád? or . . . . peniténtials . . .
CONT.	. . . . scrípt . . . glímpsed do you . . . . . or scrípted . . . .

SOPR.	. . . . . wrítten in . . . . fáded foótprints, ... prínted . .
CONT.	heéd? . . . . in a pálimpsest of . . . . . foót . . . . . on the prínted . .

SOPR.	streét? can stíllnes so stíll . . . . híde these quíckening . . . .
CONT.	. . . . . . can a stíllnes so . . . disguíse, híde these . . . .

SOPR.	. . . . rústling like a sígh . . . rising, ...
CONT.	múrmurs rústling . . . . . sígh éver . . . .

SOPR.	réstless, in the níght? . . . rúmour of the húman tíde? . . . .
CONT.	réstless, in . . . . this rúmour . . . . . húman . . . .

DOM JEROME	And one can use his eyes-

(CAPTAIN COD *appears briefly on the seawall
steps* U.C.4, *spreads nets over the end of the
parapet, and disappears down to the quay
again.* CALEB'*s voice offstage* D.L.13.)

DOM JEROME	Captain Códrocks . . . . spreáding his néts . . . .
CALEB	. . . . Cód . . . . old Cód there, ... his néts . . . .

(TAD MCFERGUSON *enters on the seawall* U.L.10
pauses by the lamp to light his pipe.)

DOM JEROME	and Tád . . . . seé? óld man, ...
CALEB	and . . . the dócker seé? . . . . once . . . .

DOM JEROME	our jánitor . . . . drúnken, míldly- . . . .
CALEB	our . . . . . . óne time drúnk . . . . but . . . .

DOM JEROME	. . . . too óften . . . . . and só - we lét him . . . .
CALEB	ónce too . . . . drúnk . . . só - . . . . . . him gó. . . . .

DOM JEROME	His face glows a moment, when he
thrusts an angry match in his briar,

DOM JEROME	like a dévil . . . caúght . . . . in the cóld. . . . .
CALEB	like a . . . . cold . . . . . . dévil . . . . . cóld. . . . .

DOM JEROME	God knows his thoughts -

(CAPTAIN COD *appears at the bottom step,* U.C.4.)

COD   Ahoy Tad, m' good man!
       lend us a hand, will ye?

TAD   Be glad ta, Capt'n Cod -
       wi' yon nets?

COD   Aye lad.
TAD   I'll come dohn.

(They disappear down the steps.)

DOM JEROME And if you listen you can hear
       the cantor with a novice -

(Cloistergarth) *(In the novitiate off-stage* D.L.13.*)*

CANTOR   Now, Frater, try the chant . . . .
       plus delicato - . . . .
NOVICE *(sung)* . . . . Véni, fíli, aúdi me - . . . .

CANTOR   Mais plus ritardando! . . . .
NOVICE   . . . . fíli, aúdi me - . . . .
CANTOR   Bene! . . . .

DOM JEROME And if you were to leap,
       Jerome,

TENORS ⎡ on this éve's . . . . of the vígil . . . Féast of the shíp - . . . . .
     ⎣ . . . . . . éve's évening of . . . vígil and Féast of . . . shíp - . . . . .

TENORS ⎡ . . . . . seáfaring Cathédral's Dedicátion, not . . . .
     ⎣ fáring seá . . . . . Cathédral's . . . . not leáping . . . .

TENORS ⎡ íf it pleáse you . . . of your tówer's . . . .
     ⎣ . . . pleáse you oút of your . . . . presúmption! . . . .

DOM JEROME No, not so - but into the moment of the hour -
       would you not see then, mysteriously

CONT. TEN. ⎡ The ólden . . . . . hóly . . . . ghóstly . . . . Bernárd, Priést . .
     ⎢ . . . . ólden aged, ... ancient, ... Pere . . . . Priést . .
     ⎣ . . . . aged, hóly ancient, ghóstly Pere Bernárd, Priést . .

TENORS   ⎡ nórthern steérs- . . . . stórmtossed Nórman Nóah . . . .
BARITONES ⎢ . . . . steérsman, old . . . . . tossed . . . . Nóah who . . . . .
BASSES   ⎣ . . . . -man, old stórm . . . . . . Nórman Nóah . . . .

TENORS   ⎡ . . . . límestone vaults, groíned in his . . . . ribbed húll?
BARITONES ⎢ rídes under . . . . stone . . . . . . groíned . . his náve ribbed . . . . .
BASSES   ⎣ . . . . under límestone vaults . . . . in his náve . . . .

TENORS	while the ...... granitic keél, lévels ...ghóstly shíp?..........
BARITONES	.....the crýpt's ....keél, ... his ghóstly ....
BASSES	while ...crýpt's granitic .... lévels his......................

DOM JEROME   where the sinner seeks
the confessor's feet,

TREB. SOPR.	where sheép ..... knów, ...seék the......................
CONT. TEN.	......sheép strays knów, soúls ....the feét..................
BAR. BASS	where ..... strays ......soúls seék ...feét.................

TREB. SOPR.	of a fólded ....peáce ....priést ...the shépherd,........
CONT. TEN.	....fólded sheép's ..... folding priést for the shépherd,........
BAR. BASS	of a fólded ....peáce folding ..... for ...shépherd,........

TREB. SOPR.	where bírds .. síng ......cáll .... in their .... áviaries
CONT. TEN.	......bírds all síng .... all túneful ....béstiaries or áviaries
BAR. BASS	..........all ....beasts cáll .... in their béstiaries..........

TREB. SOPR.	they cóme, óxen ..... fóxes finches..........and bírds ....the Árk,
CONT. TEN.	....cóme......asses, fóxes finches, béasts all and bírds ínto the Árk,
BAR. BASS	they cóme, óxen asses, fóxes ....béasts all .... ínto the Árk,

(Hearth Lodge)   *(Amber light fades in as* MRS. HEARTH *enters*
D.L.12 coming downstairs and seeing DOM JEROME,
she lifts an invisible sash window to listen.)

DOM JEROME   to the priest where he waits
a patient ear of God to forgive,

TREB. SOPR.	clear ....forgíveness.. guílt to wásh ... fóld awáy...
CONT. TEN.	.... cleánsing forgíveness.. guílt to wásh and fóld........
BAR. BASS	clear cleánsing ....of guílt ..wásh ... fóld........

TREB. SOPR.	the dárk ....the grief, and the heárt's.................
CONT. TEN.	...dárk despaír,... grief, ... the heárt's troúble..........
BAR. BASS	.... despaír,... grief, and .... troúble..........

DOM JEROME   .... into peáce. .

(Bell stroke.)

(Hearth Lodge)   *(As* AMY HEARTH *listens to the monk, one of the*
double doors, U.C.2, *opens of its own accord*
revealing MISS MILLIE *on the telphone.)*

AMY HEARTH   We've got t'differ with his
              Riverence up there - I doubts
              he hears the buzz hummin'
              and the ringin'o'bells -

              (Phone rings off-stage up left.)

AMY HEARTH   telephone bells, that is.
              Some people never answer
              church bells - only telephone
              bells that jangle -

DOM JEROME   Peace, good woman, I'm
              trying to hear! . . . .
AMY HEARTH   . . . . - them party wires . . . .
              hot enough, if the lines could hold 'em,
              t' sizzle storks! But a body wonders
              why those rows of tiny birds
              don't burn their feet!

              *(She leaves without lowering the window,
              disppearing upstairs,* D.L.12.*)*

OPERATOR   *(Voice from off-stage up centre.)*

              buzz clicking - line's busy -
              better call seven six, two three -

DOM JEROME   One hardly has to imagine
              voices coursing over the wires,

MISS MILLIE   Hello-hello! This is Miss Millie.
              Yes, Miss Braylorn please.

DOM JEROME   being on a party line with that
              interminable - . . . .
BRAYLORN   *(Voice from off-stage)*
              Oh hello, dear, ...
DOM JEROME   . . . . non-stop talker.

BRAYLORN   I'm so glad you called! . . . .

MISS MILLIE   Bray dear, I'm throwing . . . .
              a bit of a chit-chat tonight - . . . .
              Annabelle can't attend - I know . . . .
              the weather's dreadful - . . . .

BRAYLORN   Did you say Annabelle can't be there? ..

MISS MILLIE   That I did. . . . .
BRAYLORN   . . . . Oh what a pity! . . . .
                I'll be right over, dear! . . . .
MISS MILLIE   . . . . Ta Bray. . . . .

                (Fog horn off-stage up left centre.)

DOM JEROME   It can be trying when one must
                needs call the chancery, or the
                chaplain of the hospital,

                (Phone rings off-stage up left.)

MISS MILLIE   Hello - . . . .
DOM JEROME   . . . . . . or the local doctor - . . . .
                someone might be dying! . . . .
MISS MILLIE   . . . . - hello! . . . .

DOM JEROME   while she's mustering her hen fest,

MISS MILLIE   Mrs. Waguard? Millie here.

                (Voice from off-stage left.)

WAGUARD   Darling! I'm so glad. . . . .
                to hear your voice! . . . .

MISS MILLIE   Since Pew can't come, ...
                d'you care to join us tonight? . . . .

WAGUARD   I'm afraid my dear the weathe- . . . .
                did you say Annabelle can't be there? . . .

MISS MILLIE   I'm afraid I did. . . . .
WAGUARD   . . . . -Oh what a shame! . . . . .
                Yes! I'll be right over! . . . .
MISS MILLIE   . . . . Seeing you. . . . . . .

                *(Fog horn from the sea off-stage up
                left; Cathedral bell stroke up right)*

DOM JEROME   And yet, beginning from here
                while that lumbering

25

DOM JEROME bronze fellow, booms from his
        spiny gothic spears,

TENORS ⎡ whére up the . . . . whále back . . . . north eásterly
    ⎣ . . . . . . up the eástern whále . . . . nórthern . . . . . eásterly

TENORS ⎡ híll, eách . . . . its dímmed . . híll high stréet lamps . . . . .
    ⎣ híll, ... with its dímmed lit híll . . . . stréet . . . .

TENORS ⎡ vígil . . . lights, cándle . . . . . shímmering, like pílgrims
    ⎣ vígil like . . . . . . cándlelights shímmer . . . . like . . . .

TENORS ⎡ . . . Cándlemas that márch, ... into cathédral squáre,
    ⎣ for Cándlemas . . . márch, móve into cathédral . . . .

DOM JEROME being quite unaware
        of the telephonic rumpus . . . .

CONTRA. ⎡ cháttering phónes, hót . . . . from póle . . . .
     ⎢ cháttering . . . . hótlines . . . . póle to póle . . . .
     ⎣ . . . . phónes, . . lines from . . . . to póle . . . .

CONTRA. ⎡ rattle náttering . . . . áll the way . . . .
     ⎢ rattle . . . . the néws, áll . . . way dówn . . . .
     ⎣ . . . . . náttering . . . néws, ... dówn the tówn. . .

DOM JEROME Would you say, perhaps I'm
        only imagining these voices? . . . .

(Phone rings off-stage down left.)

DOM JEROME for they do seem a trifle
        should we say - . . . .
MISS MILLIE   . . . . Hello - hello! . . . .
        Is this the Carp residence? . . . .

(Voice off-stage down left.)

MRS. CARP This is the Carp residence,
        Mrs. Carp speaking. . . . .
DOM JEROME   . . . . - Yes, grotesque. . . . .

MISS MILLIE Oh! I didn't recognize you, dear!

MRS. CARP I'm not surprised - had a cold last week,
        in the larynx - bin livin' on lemons.

MISS MILLIE   Oh, I'm sorry dear - feeling better now?

MRS. CARP   Hoarse a bit, a little lemon-puckered
and sour as usual. . . . .

MISS MILLIE   Why don't you join us
for tea tonight? . . . .

MRS. CARP   Who's pouring - Pew? . . . .

MISS MILLIE   No dear, Annabelle can't be there - . . . .

MRS. CARP   Can't be there! No Pew? . . . .

MISS MILLIE   No dear. . . . .
MRS. CARP   . . . . Well now! there's a horse . . . .
of a different hue! Yes! of course, dear . . . . . .
I'll be right over! . . . .
MISS MILLIE   . . . . Ta Ta!

*(She hangs up and the door closes of
itself. Fog horn off-stage* U.L., CALEB
and CANTOR *speak off-stage* D.L.*)*

DOM JEROME   Yet while we dream them,
they're following lineaments
of the real as ideas phantasms do -
there must be mány . . . .

JEROME   of the . . . . flóck . . . wálk this níght . . . .
CALEB   . . . . . trúdging . . . . . that wálk . . . níght . . . .
CANTOR   . . the trúdging flóck that wálk this . . . .

JEROME   in sílences . . . . . míst into . . . . míst, mány . .
CALEB   . . sílences out of míst . . . . mystérious míst, ...
CANTOR   . . . . out of . . . . into mystérious . . . .

JEROME   clímbing . . . . . . dámp and . . . . lámp lit, stréets .
CALEB   . . . . on the . . . . . and spéctral lámp lit, ...
CANTOR   clímbing on the dámp . . . spéctral . . . .

JEROME   each . . . . . hálo'd by . . . . míst, . . . alóne . . . . .
CALEB   . . . . eérie, ... by shroúded míst, and . . . .
CANTOR   each eérie, hálo'd . . shroúded . . . .

27

JEROME   ⎡ pale . . . . like ghóstly sóuls . . . might sáy, . .
CALEB | . . . . phántoms like . . . . sóuls you might . . . .
CANTOR ⎣ pale phántoms . . . ghóstly sóuls you . . . .

DOM JEROME   like souls with thoughts of their own.

AMY HEARTH   So it's ghosts or dreams he's dreamin' -
well, I kin assure his Riverence
that Amy Hearth is no dream!
I've my wits about me, runnin'
a boardin' house for twenty years,
an' I may say as good a nose for news
as any - better'n Pew's for all her
clatter patterin' to church in her
religious high-heeled shoes -

     (At the sound of high-heels off-stage D.L.,
     HEARTH *gingerly lowers the sash and*
     disappears upstairs.)

MISS PEW   *(Entering* D.L.13, *she skirts outside the*
     bench as dim amber light fades in
     upon the lower platform.)

Och! such a dank night and chilly.
It's a shame to miss the cozy
bridge game at Millie's - . . . .

MILLIE, BRAY.   *(Off-stage up centre)*

the girls will be gay - . . . .

MISS PEW   must be to confession though, tonight -

MILLIE, BRAY.   Sodality tomorrow. . . . .

MISS PEW   I often wonder what they talk about . . . . . .
when I'm away - . . . .

MISS MILLIE   . . . . shouldn't be hard . . . . .
to ferret out

BRAYLORN   . . . . any indiscretions - . . . .

MRS. CARP   one can. . . . .
. . . . depend on Mrs. Waguard's . . . .
tongue!

MISS PEW   Oh! here's old Hearth's -
whyn't we just drop in a minute
'n' try the nose - for news! . . . .

CAPT. COD   *(Meanwhile, as* TAD *comes up the seawall*
U.C.4, COD *appears below on the steps.)*

That's good Tad - the nets'll
dry fine fer the lads - . . . .

TAD MC.FER.   Anytime Capt'n Cod. Aam g'n up
t' kirk now - guid night t'ye. . . . .

CAPT. COD   An' I'll be comin' later.
Thankee Tad. . . . .

(He disappears down to the quay.)

TAD MC.FER.   Aye, Tad laddie, I been thinkin' -
takin' stock a bi' aboht yerr soul.
If mither waire alive, she'd agree 'twaire
best ye tak' the pledge, lad.

orr whisky - drrunken
diels 'll hitherr come
wi' their yearrnin' houndin' ye
strait dohn t' hell!

like the auld hounds
bayin' ferr a rabbit ance,
alang Bannockburn fields -
an' ye waire a lad.

Aye, it's a forregone
conclusion - if a mickle thirst come
o'rr me, 'tis sairrten I'd be damned!
may th' Laird Almighty spare me -

*(A premonitory groan on the seawall
ushers a wintery chill from far out
on the straits as Tad, alerted, listens -)*

(A foghorn moans from the sea.)

HARRY IBBS   *(Voice at a distance off-stage up left.)*

        . . . . Aye . . . . Tad! . . . .

TAD MC.FER.   Aam afeared - . . . .
Is't the voice o' Harry Ibbs? . . . .

HARRY IBBS   . . . . . . Ahoy . . . . lad! . . . .

TAD MC.FER.   Nay - 'tis all i' the mind!
There's nay one here, nay soul
but me ain - sae wet wi' the mist!
shiverin' here in the street -

HARRY IBBS   *(First line off-stage on the seawall*
U.L.10, *then he appears, a drowned man*
brought back. TAD *shrinks from him*
under the lamppost. The dead man speaks.)

Nay - nary a soul Tad, but clammy
'Arry, ripe like a bloated sea corpse
an' ye without a stout or an ale t' warm
yer 'eart, an' make ye merry! . . . .

TAD MC.FER.   It's nae drrunken Harry, surely?
Ye as waire dead, sae lang ago 'twas,
an' buried far oot t' sea? . . . .

HARRY IBBS   That's hullucinátin' y' be, m' boy -
I'm n' more 'n a pineultimate stage -
of a dead, drunk! . . . .

(Meanwhile D.R.16 BERT *has entered,*
opening the bar. In a blue light, PADDY
and BUB, U.R.8, *with* DIEL *and* NICK, D.R.17
drift in, muttering about weather.)

PADDY   ⌈ Faúgh! fall fógs . . . . wi' the wínt'ry .
BUB   ⌊ . . . . fógs cómin' lads . . . the wínt'ry .

DIEL   ⌈ wínds an' the benúmbin' . . . . sleét! . . . .
NICK SIMS   ⌊ wínds an' . . . . shíverin' sleét! . . . .

(HARRY *staggers toward* TAD, *who backs down
the steps, keeping an eye on the ghost.*)

TAD MC.FER. 'Tis m' drrunken visions
come oot o' the mirk a nights
t' harry a man t' drink! . . . .

(*As* HARRY *stalks him to the door, Stew's
Tavern lights up with amber and
the drinkers, watching, call out.*)

HARRY   Tís damn . . . . . . ye'll bé, . . . in the déw . . . . stréets,
PAD. BUB . . . damn dámp . . . . Tad in the . . . . drippin' stréets,
DIE. NICK . . . . dámp ye'll bé, Tad . . . . . déw drippin' . . . .

HARRY   óvercast toó! . . . . . cóme on . . . láddie! . . . . we'll
PAD. BUB óvercast . . . . come . . . . Tad láddie! come ín, we'll
DIE. NICK . . . . toó! . . . . . cóme on Tad . . . . come ín, ...

HARRY   gét ya . . . . . a scótch, a hót . . . . t' cheér y' up, Tád! . .
PAD. BUB . . . . . . a shót a scótch, a . . . shot . . cheér y' up, ...
DIE. NICK gét ya a shót . . . . a hót shot t' cheér . . up, Tád! . .

HARRY IBBS Arrivin' wasn't a' that
difficult now was it Tad?
Ye knew all along t' git t' kirk
ye'd 'ave to pass by Stew's, so -
what'll it be Tad? . . . .

TAD MC.FER. (*As he shrinks away from the
tempter with a shudder of
revulsion.*)
     . . . . Nay nothin'! leave me . . . .
be, ye arrt niver a friend o' mine! . . . .

(*he backs into a circle of drinkers*)

HARRY IBBS   Just a nip - . . . .
TAD MC.FER.   . . . . Nay drink fer me! . . . .
HARRY   a lit'le swig? . . . .
               (*The tavern gathers around
in drunken hilarity.*)

HARRY   a lit'l . . . or a nóggin', ... a gín . . . . . t' líght yer .
PADDY   . . lit'l níp or a nóg . . . . a jíg . . . a gín or rýe t' líght . . . . .
BUB   . . . . . níp . . . . nóggin', . jígger . . . . . or rýe . . . . . . yer .

HARRY	. . . . ráscally éye! . . . . little . . . of a tincture 'll . . . . .
NICK	pleádin' . . . . éye! One . . . . tínt. . . . .
PADDY	. . . . ráscally . . . . One little tínt of. . tincture 'll . . . . .
BUB	. . . . ráscally éye! One . . . . of a tincture 'll . . . . .

NICK	dó, . . a twínge of a tínt . . . . so shóut . . . . . . to the . . .
PADDY	. . . or a twínge . . . . or twó, so . . . . . a toást . . . .
BUB	dó, ... of a tínt or twó, . . shóut a toást to the . . .

NICK	toẃn . . . . Díng . . . . me láds, ... the rábble . . . . .
PADDY	. . . . . Tad! Díng the gláss . . . . aroúse . . . .
BUB	toẃn . . . . gláss me láds, aroúse the rábble . . . . .

NICK	for a Héll's, héll . . . . Tad, táylors a mált . . roúnd . . .
PADDY	. . . . héll of a hót, ... táylors. . mált all . . . .
BUB	. . . a Héll's, ... hót, Tad, ... all roúnd . . .

NICK	Why the lad 's that lonely . . . .
HARRY	. . . . he's thirsty 'n' dry . . . .
PADDY	An' his gut's a-groanin' . . . .
BUB	. . . . fer a shot-a-rye - . . . .
HARRY	T' blaw 'is 'ead right up . . . .
PADDY	. . . . on 'ight t' the blear-eyed . . . . .

HARRY	'órrible . . . . lúna-. . mád man's . . . .
NICK	'órr-. . . hórrible . . . tic mád man's moón! . . . .
PADDY	. . rible hórr-. . . lúnatic mád . . . . . moón! . . . .
BUB	'órrible . . . rible lúnatic . . . . man's moón! . . . .

ALL *(on-stage)*	Ahoy boy! . . . .
HARRY	. . . . whiskies a'round! . . . .
ALL *(on-stage)*	'n' make 'em . . . .
	. . . . hot 'n' soon! . . . .

(As TAD *makes an attempt to escape*
HARRY *blocks his way - the lads lay*
hold of him.)

TAD MC.FER.	Fie, lads, leave me be! I'll nae more a yerr roarin' carousin' drunks - . . . .

(sung)

HARRY	Oh - we bín ya boón com-pánions Tád . . . .
PADDY, BUB	Oh - we bín . . boón com-pánions . . . .
DIEL, NICK	Oh - we bín ya . . . . . com-pánions Tád . . . .

HARRY   ⎡ an' típplin' típsy . . . . . toó . . . .
PADDY, BUB | an' . . . . típsy tópsy . . . .
DIEL, NICK   ⎣ . . . típplin' . . . . tópsy toó . . . .

HARRY   ⎡ Páddy . . . . an' Hárry . . . Níck . . . . . .
PADDY, BUB | . . . . . . an' Búb an' Hárry an' . . . .
DIEL, NICK   ⎣ Páddy . . . Búb . . . Hárry an' Níck . . . . . .

HARRY   ⎡ . . . á' yer drúnk . . créw, . . . há! . . . .
PADDY, BUB | an' á' yer drúnken . . . . . ah . . . .
DIEL, NICK   ⎣ an'. . . yer . . . . ken créw, ah, há! . . . .

(Amber light fades in D.L.12 *as* ANNABELLE,
*hearing the uproar, rushes downstairs
to the invisible window and peers through.
Outrage and a secret delight hold her.
By the end, righteousness wins. She will
march to the door with a mission.)*

HARRY   The lad's ha' stood ya. . . . .
           . . . . many a drink, Tad . . .
           when ye was broke . . . .
           . . . . an' blue - so . . . .
PADDY, BUB   here's t' Hades . . . .
DIEL, NICK   . . . . wi' the likes . . . .
           o' knaves what . . . .
PADDY, BUB   . . . . drinks 'emselves . . . .
           t' early graves, ...

HARRY   ⎡ like gróggily . . . . . . Mc Férgus . . . .
PADDY, BUB | . . . gróggily jóllied Mc . . . . . son . . . .
DIEL, NICK   ⎣ like gróg . . . . jóllied Mc Férguson . . . .

HARRY   ⎡ drúnken yóu Tad . . ha! há! . . . .
PADDY, BUB | . . . . ken yóu . . . áh ha! há! . . . .
DIEL, NICK   ⎣ drúnken yóu Tad . . ha! há! . . . .

*(When as his tormentors are convulsed
with laughter,* TAD *breaks free, and
runs up onto the seawall, where he
faces them. At that very moment,*

ANNABELLE, *flinging open the invisisble*
door, steps out to confront, bristling
with indignation, the intemperance
of the world. Seeing her, as Stew's
dims into blue, the bartender and the
drunks scatter - PADDY *and* BUB, U.R.8,
DIEL, NICK *and* BERT, D.R.17. HARRY, *the last to*
leave, scowls at TAD, *then disappears* U.R.8.
Overwhelmed by his deliverance, TAD
slumps to his knees by the lamppost.)

MISS PEW   *(Turning on* TAD*)*

So! Tad McFerguson - drunk again!
What a shame if you aren't
the scandal of the parish!

TAD MC.FER.   Aam verra grateful t' ye, ma'am
fer ye bein' m' guardian
angel after m' prayers.

MISS PEW   Who ever saw
a sober man praying
to a lamppost?

TAD MC.FER.   Aye Miss Annabelle, miracles
may still be softly comin' doon!
Aam takin' the pledge.

MISS PEW   Oh are you, now? Well, it looks
likely, though you've been good enough
at lying in ditches.

TAD MC.FER.   *(Rising with offended dignity.)*

Nay doubt the wurrd
of a Scotsman ma'am, fer aam
tellin' ye the truth.

MISS PEW   Well, tell it to the priest!
It may be he'll believe it.
Such a scandal! I must tell
Mrs. Hearth - the Temperance
Guild shall hear of it -

*(She stomps back into Hearth's and
disappears upstairs* D.L.12. *Dejectedly,*
TAD *sits on the parapet by the lamppost.)*

TAD MC.FER.   Aye, Ma'am Miss Annabelle.
Sainted women can nae be wrang
correctin' black sinners like me -

*(Dim amber light fades in on the lower
platform as* MISS MILLIE *enters* U.C.6
*with a miniature wheeled tea table
and service. Placing in the centre
she glances out the invisible window
on the left for her guests, but sees*
TAD *instead.* BRAYLORN, WAGUARD *and* CARP
enter D.L.13. *They notice* TAD *about
to come down the steps, but he
is turned back by their scathing
comments - so he sits down again.)*

BRAYLORN   That's McFerguson, is it not? . . . .

WAGUARD   Staggering in his cups? . . . .

MRS. CARP   About as sober as a boiled owl! . . . .

(They knock at the left invisible door.)

MISS MILLIE   *(Opening to them.)*

My dears, what a pleasure! . . . .

(They all glance back at TAD *with disdain.)*

MISS MILLIE   Oh yes, him - the usual inebriation. . . . .
Won't you come in? . . . .

(As they enter, MILLIE *takes the hats of*
WAGUARD *and* CARP, *and leads them off*
U.C.3, *while* BRAYLORN *crossing, takes
off her hat, and follows the others
off* U.C.6. *The lights have faded a dim blue.)*

(A fog horn sounds out at sea.)

DOM JEROME   Our docker looks meek -
              discouraged, I presume -

TAD MC.FER.   Help me, m' Father, m' wurrd
              t' keep, ferr a spirit's willin'
              but m' faint heart 's weak.

              (Suddenly, TAD *senses again the presence
              of the drowned fisherman. Terror siezes
              him as he backs away from the stone
              steps leading down to the quay. Though
              the ghost is invisible he hears a
              sibilant whisper* U.C.4.*)*

HARRY IBBS   So ye're affeared, Tad . . . .
              . . . . o' the drunken drowned one! . . . .

TAD MC.FER.   Go back Harry Ibbs! . . . .
              . . . . down t' yerr murky grave! . . . .

              Go back! an' leave me alone! . . . .

              *(*TAD *runs off on the seawall,* U.L.10.*)*

DOM JEROME   I would venture,
                        . . . . our lad's not defeated.

              *(The blue light melts into amber and
              brightens as* MISS MILLIE *and* BRAYLORN *enter*
              U.C.3 *and* U.C.6, *each carrying a delicate
              chair with* WAGUARD *and* CARP *following.
              The ladies gather at the tea service
              seating themselves on the bench
              and chairs.* MISS MILLIE *pours. During
              this entrance they speak the chorus
              in conversational tones under*
              DOM JEROME*'s laconic observations.)*

JEROME   ⎡ While híssing . . . . gábble . . . .
MILL., BRAY. ⎢ . . . . our góssiprey . . . . . . is gárbled by . . . .
WAG., CARP   ⎣ . . . . . . híssing our . . . . gábble is . . . . by flués!

JEROME   ⎡ spéwing the chímney's . . . . into the pátient eár
MILL., BRAY. ⎢ . . . . látest néws! . . . .
WAG., CARP   ⎣ spéwing the . . . . néws! . . . .

JEROME	..... of níght- ....
MILLIE	I was .... quíte at a lóss, what .... at teá. ....
WAG., CARP	.... quíte .... what to tálk about? ....

BRAY.	You don't ...... do you? .... Péw, again! toníght? ...
WAG.	.... meán, do you? to tálk about Péw, again! ....
CARP	You don't meán, ... tálk about Péw, ... toníght? ...

JEROME	with .... éven as Miss Péw's ...
MILLIE	.... of coúrse, my dear! ....
CARP	with Ánabelle awáy? .... éven as ....

JEROME	át her rúeful .... exámen of .... scrúple? ....
BRAY.	.... why Míllie, it's .... plupérfectly ...... cleár!
WAG., CARP	.... why ...... it's .... pérfectly ...... cleár!

MILLIE	Yés! lét's just tálk! .... about Ánnabelle!
BRAY.	.... lét's just .... we're tálkative .... tálk about ....
WAG.	.... just tálk! ..... tálk .... let's tálk ..... Ánnabelle!
CARP	.... we're tálkative .... tálk about Ánnabelle!

DOM JEROME   Is it not, Jerome
        ....the trivial, all too human tune?

(As ANNABELLE *comes downstairs, light
on the gossips fades to dim amber.
Light in Hearth Lodge fades out,
as she steps outside, moving into a
highlighting path of cold light.)*

MISS PEW   Have I been remiss
    in my duties? paid my dues
    to the C.W.A.? properly convened ....

MISS PEW   The Annual Auxiliary
    Bazaar, the Teas and the Ladies'
    Charities? - yes, I have. ....

(Majestically unaware, PEW*'s self-
righteous examination of conscience
rides over the background prattle
of the gossips.)*

MISS PEW	Évery Súnday............I've ....
MISS MILLIE	.... But ís it ríght? ....

MISS PEW	⌐ beén in my péw, ... and nót . . . .
MISS MILLIE	∟ . . . . sníping at hér . . . .

MISS PEW	⌐ a féw . . . . weékdays toó. . . . .
MISS MILLIE	∟ . . . . when shé's awáy? . . . .

BRAYLORN   Millie, do be gay! . . . .

MISS PEW	⌐ Gáve my álms . . . .
MRS. CARP	∟ . . . . Here's oné the revérse . . . .

MISS PEW	⌐ in the poór bóx, ... and hélped . . . .
MRS. CARP	∟ . . . . of dúll, ...

MISS PEW	⌐ the poór - . . . .
MISS MILLIE	. . . . of coúrse! . . . .
MRS. CARP	. . . . let's dó it in vérse! . . . . what fún! . .
BRAYLORN	. . . . of coúrse! . . . .
WAGUARD	∟ . . . . what fún! . .

MISS PEW   Made my Novena . . . .
             to Anthony of Padua, ...
             to Teresa of Lisieux, ...

MISS PEW	⌐ my Fírst Frídays, ... Hóly Hour . . . .
WAGUARD	∟ . . . . we bétter bé . . . .

MISS PEW	⌐ vígils on the . . . . Fírst Thúrsdays . . . . .
WAGUARD	∟ . . . . éver so cáreful, ...

MISS PEW	⌐ . . . . of the mónth . . . . althóugh. . .
WAGUARD	∟ her eárs . . . . are shárp enough, ...

MISS PEW	⌐ . . . . I míssed . . . . the fífth, ...
WAGUARD	∟ ánd able . . . . to píck up . . . . tálk of a . . . . . .

MISS PEW	⌐ . . . . I thínk it was . . . . yés, ...
WAGUARD	∟ chímney . . . . a blóck away . . . .

MISS PEW	⌐ with the flué. . . . .
MILLIE, WAG.	. . . . Oh háha . . . . hóho . . hoó! . . . .
CARP, BRAY.	. . . . hahí hiho . . . . hoó! . . . .
BRAYLORN	∟ . . . . How trúe!

MISS PEW   Now what was that? . . . .
          Coming from Miss Millie's chimney? . . . .
          Hmm - that hooing - . . . .

MISS PEW   I have my suspicions, but
          I can't hear a damn - oh! thing. . . . .
          Well it's just the wind, I suppose. . . . .

MISS PEW   I was a little sharp
          with Mrs. Carp the other day - . . . .
          but really! . . . .

MISS PEW   That woman had it
          coming to her, how could . . . .
          she be so rude? . . . .

MISS PEW   'Twas my duty
          to remonstrate, I'm sure, ...
          the nerve of her - . . . .
WAGUARD   . . . . - the nerve? . . . .

MISS PEW   [to slúr the . . . . Geneólogy . . . . . .
BRAYLORN   [. . . . . .her précious . . . .

MISS PEW   [of the Péws! . . . .
MRS. CARP   [. . . . . avúncular núncles! . . . .

MISS PEW   [There wóuld be sóme to dó . . . .
BRAYLORN   [. . . . to dó? . . . . . .

MISS PEW   [were Í to make remárks . . . .
MRS. CARP   [. . . . remárks? . . . . . .

MISS PEW   [aboút the cómmon . . . .
MRS. CARP   [. . . . . cómmon! . . . .

MISS PEW   [órigin of the Cárps! . . . .
MRS. CARP   [. . . . . That dóes it - . . . . . .

MRS. CARP   [Ánnabelle chátterwell wíll-bé-bléd! . . . .
ALL GOSSIPS   [. . . . wíll-bé-bléd! . . . .

MISS PEW   Of coúrse, to be súre, I hóld no grúdge.

MILL. BRA. ⌈ Her-góre-coloured . . . . Tábby bloodied cát claws
WAG.   ⎢ Her- . . . . coloured scrátching Tábby . . . . cát claws
CARP   ⌊ Her-góre-coloured scrátching . . . . . . bloodied . . . claws

*(Her voice rises to drown out the
mounting crescendo of gossiprey.)*

MISS PEW   Nor woúld I ráshly - . . . .

MILLIE, BRAY. ⌈ . . . . with a cat . . . eye . . . .
WAGUARD   ⎢ . . . . a cat cold . . . .
MRS. CARP   ⌊ . . . . with a cat . . . eye . . . .

MISS PEW   anóther júdge, but sóme there áre . . . .
              and not a féw I feár - . . . .

MILL. BRA. ⌈ . . límber bloód- . . . . . . leách tongue stíngin'em drý!
WAG.   ⎢ her . . . . . . bloód-letting leách . . . . . . stíngin' . . . drý!
CARP   ⌊ . . límber . . . . leách tongue stíngin'em drý!

MISS PEW   are fár less dútiful than yóu, my deár - . . . .

MISS PEW   ⌈ sóme that had bést . . . . nót be seén . . . . .
BRAYLORN   ⌊ . . . . ríling venom . . . .

MISS PEW   ⌈ in Móther Church - . . . . like thát . . .
WAGUARD   ⌊ . . . . our Á. Pew pliés, ...

MISS PEW   disgráceful Mólly Greén! . . . .

MRS. CARP   ⌈ till nó . . óne . . . . nót one neíghbour's . . . .
BRAYLORN   ⌊ . . . . . not . . . even . . . one neíghbour's . . . .

MISS MILLIE ⌈ alíve . . . . oh-háha! híhi! hóho . . hoó! . . . .
BRAYLORN   ⎢ . . . . t'díe! háha! híhi! hóho . . hoó! . . . .
WAGUARD   ⎢ alíve . . . . hahá! hihi! hohó hoó! . . . .
MRS. CARP   ⌊ . . . . t'díe! . . . . hahá! hihi! hohó hoó! . . . .

*(MILLIE rises, beckoning the ladies to follow.
She leads the way out U.C.6 with the tea
things. They follow with the chairs,
carrying soundlessly their mimed
merriment with them. The amber
lights dim and fade out.)*

MISS PEW   *(In the meantime* PEW *reacts to the hooing.)*

Hmm! that sound again! . . . .
would that I had some x-ray ears! . . . .
M'hearin's getting thin. . . . .

But now I'm fretting - I sometimes
think the sin my most
besetting is - . . . .

DOM JEROME   . . . . .Detraction? . . . .

MISS PEW   Detraction! Good heavens, no -
Whatever made me think of that? . . . .
Not detractioin - distraction! . . . .

(Bell sounds from the cathedral.)

And there's the half hour -
Three blocks to go and I've yet to tally
all my imperfections in a row. . . . .

(She exits up Campus Street U.R.9.*)*

DOM JEROME   I sometimes think dreams
are no stranger than the real.
They turn out in fact to be people -
strange, wonderful, bizarre people.
If I can be watchful enough,
I may sometimes entertain
angels unawares, fallen angels
sometimes, or demons incarnate,
those subterranean carriers
of tears, terrors, of nightmares
and fears that infest the hold
of this wintering ship, knocking
anchored, briefly here -

HAGAN   *(As the blacksmith enters his cellar* U.C.7,
*fire begins to gleam through the vents
in the iron door of his furnace. He
walks with the lurch of a cripple.)*

Me old woman called me
a deathwatch beetle - only once,
her Olrig Hagan stompin' 'ome, ...

41

HAGAN

'Twas m' little dance
fer that foundry spill
riddled me red hot. . . . .
t' the bone in m' boots! . . . .

(His invisible dog barks. HAGAN *turns on
the animal, his back to the open furnace.)*

HAGAN

Dance, ya dog! ya
crippled critter, come 'ere! . . . .

*(He makes several movements as if
cornering the dog. His voice grows
soft, but sinister.)*

HAGAN

Ya were a retriever once,
old huntin' hound, ...
Yer no use anymore;
d' ya hear? Biddy hound?
No use flushin' out . . . .
pheasants, anymore. . . . .

(There is a whimpering, another bark.)

HAGAN

We'll teach ya t' chase
firedogs instead. . . . .
Come out of it, ya rheumatic
bitch - come 'ere! . . . .

(There is a low growl as HAGAN *closes
in on the dog.)*

HAGAN

Yer the hunted now, ...
hound dog, come - come 'ere - . . . .

*(He lunges, grabs hold of the dog, then
lurches toward the furnace, his back
to the audience. He throws the animal
into the fire and slams the door shut.
There are several sharp barks, followed
by a prolonged eerie howl. The* LIBRARIAN
has entered on Campus Street U.R.9.
*He pauses, listening to the howl,
then knocks at the cellar's invisible door.)*

HAGAN

Must be the Librarian,
our rabid and dangerous
Corascene dog - for he's
always on time. . . . .

(He opens to him, cautiously.)

LIBRARIAN

Evening Blacksmith. . . . .

HAGAN

Have ya picked up
the scent? dogged his steps? . . . .

LIBRARIAN

That I have - on the quays . . . .
we've not yet *scored*, though. . . . .

HAGAN

Ya will - and our
fraternal Druggist? . . . .

LIBRARIAN

He comes later. . . . .

HAGAN

(Coming out, he closes the door.)

You suggest the quays - why? . . . .

LIBRARIAN

Our quarry walks there nightly, ...
Come, you'll see - . . . .

*(They move stealthily toward the
centre of the lower platform, where
they peer around the invisible corner
of the house. The sound of the sea
begins to be heard.)*

LIBRARIAN

Time was street boys
were in scant supply. . . . .

HAGAN

Aye, but now they're had
fer a dime-a-dozen. . . . .
You've spied on 'im? . . . .
probed his bent? . . . .

LIBRARIAN

He was out there, praying. . . . .
Mist had ears - look! . . . .
there's the boy - he's the one. . . . .

43

(TOM BURNS, *a young adolescent, enters on
the seawall,* U.L.10. *He pauses by the streetlight
and gazes out to sea.* HAGAN *makes a sign
to the* LIBRARIAN, *and they retreat further
out of sight by the cellar, where they watch.*)

DOM JEROME

Who could he be? This vagrant
who has turned himself about
out on the mournful wharves?
A prodigal? of some house? . . . .

(DAN, BEN - *chanted;* RENAIRE - *spoken,
off-stage up left.*)

DAN   Tóm - Tom Búrns - . . . .
DOM JEROME   . . . . Tóm? Who is Tóm? . . . . . .

DAN, BEN   Túrning, Tom Búrns - . . . .
DOM JEROME   . . . . Some poór boy . . . .

DOM JEROME   perháps? from the párish schoól? . . . .
DAN, BEN   . . . .- búrning - . .

(TOM *turns his back to the sea. Stress is
written in his whole demeanour. He
places his hand on the lamppost
for a moment as if steadying himself.*)

RENAIRE
(*off-*S.U.L.)

You have talked yourself alone
out of the lust in you - smoulder
and gnaw of the raw-nerved
spine - to end it! Sinking stomach,
clam cold sweat, this qualm
of a long and submerged regret -

(As TOM *comes down the steps the sound
of the sea subsides.*)

LIBRARIAN

Now's the time
to make a play for'im!

HAGAN

You're the seducer,
but - I catch the prey - . . . .
you'll wait. . . . .
DOM JEROME   . . . . Poor child - . . . .

HAGAN   Draw back!
we'll watch awhile - . . . .

(They watch briefly, then disappear U.R.8.*)*

DOM JEROME   Though the sea noise dies
in the quiet street, he'll
not so easily forget - . . . .

DAN, BEN   You remémber? . . . .
DOM JEROME   . . . . those shúdder-plucking . . . . .

DOM JEROME   whíspers - . . . .
DAN, BEN   . . . . Tom Búrns? . . . .

*(The voices calling rivet him at the bottom
of the steps as the doors* U.C.1 *and* 2 *slowly
open on their own revealing* ROSE BURNS
in a blue ghostly light behind scrim.)

RENAIRE   You were the only son,
her only one . . . .
what she said, ...
she that's dead. . . . .

ROSE BURNS   Tóm? . . . .
DAN   . . . . . you trémble . . . .
BEN   . . . . trémble when remémbering - . . .
DAN   . . . . remémbering - . . .

ROSE BURNS   Tóm son! . . . .

TOM BURNS   *(Seeing the ghost of his mother, it's
a moment before he can speak.)*

. . . . Yes Mom? . . . .

ROSE   When you begin
to be a man, remember . . . .
your mother said, ...

I'd rather have you dead
I'd rather nail down . . . .
the lid of your coffin . . . .
than have you do evil. . . . .
TOM   . . . . Yes Mom. . . . .

ROSE

I'd rather throw ground
on the lid, have the diggers . . . .
smack their spades on the grave, ...

than know my boy grown up
had soiled his soul . . . .
with any sin - . . . .

TOM

         . . . . Yes Mom. . . . .

ROSE

Remember this
when you begin
to be a man. . . . .

TOM

         . . . . I will, Mom - . . . .
         . . . . I *do* remember. . . . .

ROSE

*(The blue light moves, leaving only
her silhouette. She begins to sing.)*

Hów - when Tómmy
         . . . . was a weé boy
   . . he jóyed in the
         . . . . jólliest spríng time,
        . . . . jólly as a beé . . . .
         . . . . in the bloóm . . . .

Hé was a lárk of a lád
         . . . . néver bad
         . . . . néver sad hé;
   . . . . his sóul could síng . . . .
         . . . . like the míschief . . . .
         . . . . of a línnet on the wíng -

(She begins gradually to fade away.)

TOM

Mother - Oh God!
once - once I was . . . .
your ten-year-old . . . .
with time enough
to become, what . . . .
I've become, ...

but I heard
the gravel rattle on
your coffin, not mine. . . . .

TOM   Can you see? can you
                       see now through . . . .
                       all your tears? . . . .

                       *(As the doors close slowly, pale-tinted
                       daylight begins to fade in on the seawall
                       and Hearth Lodge.)*

                       I guess Mom
                       you must know - but it
                       was different then - then . . . .
                       I was just a child. . . . .

YOUNG TOM   *(Darting in on the seawall* U.L.10, *he runs
                       down the steps, bouncing his ball.)*

                       Auntie Hanna! . . . .
                       Auntie Hanna! . . . .

                       *(*TOM, *seeing this flash-back of his child-
                       hood, backs away, unnoticed by* YOUNG TOM,
                       *and seats himself on the far side
                       of the platform, watching.)*

HANNA   *(Comes out* D.L.13, *followed by* REMUS. *Her
                       mood makes the little boy momentarily
                       grave.)*

                       O Tommy boy, Tom
                       run 'ome quick! Yer
                       mother's ill agin, an' . . . .
                       papa he's - well, ...

REMUS   Out - out cold on his
                       ale! But it's late now, ...
                       run along son. . . . .

YOUNG TOM   Bye Uncle, bye Auntie
                       Hanna! . . . .
HANNA   . . . . Bye Tommy. . . . .

                       *(He darts off, disappearing through
                       the door* U.C.3. *Turning inside
                       HANNA and REMUS weigh the situation.)*

HANNA   O Remus,
                we'll 'ave to take the boy.
                Jock's drinkin' fer sure
                and Doctor Mallory
                says 'is mother is sinkin'
                and goes in a month, ...
                poor Rose! . . . .
REMUS   . . . . What I want
                t'know is, where's our
                Jock when 'e's needed? . . . .

HANNA   On 'is fishboat, maybe? . . . .

REMUS   O poppycock, Hanna!
                Rose'll rally, we hope,
                but that drunken
                brother o'me, never! . . . .

                (He goes back in D.L.13 *while* HANNA
                remains behind.)

TOM   So Auntie Hanna cried. . . . .

HANNA   *(She walks slowly down stage and
                pauses before the invisible window.)*

                An' a' that was only
                a month ago -
                when she succumbed - . . . .
                an' Tommy tried to hold
                'is quiverin' chin
                stiff like a tin soldier . . . .
                at the funeral - . . . .

                    *(Her voice breaks. She wipes her eyes
                and leaves* D.L.13, *as* TOM *completes
                her thoughts.)*

TOM   and the priest at the grave
                threw the ground in like
                thunder - that morning. . . . .

                (A foghorn sounds out at sea.)

TAD MC.FER.   *(His first three words are heard off-stage
                   as he rushes in on the seawall* U.L.10,
                   and down the steps.)

                   Nay nip orr noggin
                   Harry Ibbs! nay, nay morre - . . . .
                                          *(Glancing
                   back, he almost runs into* TOM.*)*

                   Why - shades o' the rrood! . . . .
                   Jock Burns' boy 'tis! . . . .
                                          (He quickly puts TOM
                   between himself and the invisible HARRY.*)*

                   Ye'll be rememb'rrin' me Tom?
                   at old St. Mary's stokin' fires
                   all the whiles ye waire lairnin'? . . . .

TOM   Why it's old Mister Tad! . . . .

TAD   Yea - Tad McFairrgeson. . . . .
                                          *(His reminiscences
                   come quickly, banishing the spectre.)*

                   The auld days were verra
                   dearr, Tom - D'ye recall
                   the cross school bell . . . .
                   clangerrin' oot o' the earrly haze
                   bangin' the bad boys in? Aye - . . . .
                   t' the last reluctant urrchin? . . . .

                   Remember shinkickin' Currley?
                   that ragamuffin spitter an'
                   bachelorr o' baitin'? just . . . .
                   waitin' ferr a chance . . . .
                   t' paste some blackeyed
                   bully in the yairrd? . . . .

                   Rran the rroost he - those
                   slickerrs waire no hookey
                   rookies - Jerry Maloney an'
                   cockeyed Tim McKay, Nails
                   McEwen, Jimmy 'Iggins an' . . . .
                   Buster Owen the rred! . . . .

Bad lot they waire, fumin’
cigarrette butts in their haunted
shed, an’ scrrawlin’ bad wurrds
on walls - ye remember....................

TOM BURNS   Yes, Tad, I do - I can
              hear their talk still - ....

TAD MC.FER.   Well, laddie, I’ll nay hold ye.
              Pray ferr an auld man, will ye?

TOM BURNS   Yes, sir. I will.............................

TAD MC.FER.   An’ Tom - be warry o’ the divils -
              G’night laddie.............................

TOM BURNS   Goodnight Mister Tad. ....

(TAD *leaves, hurrying up Campus Street*
U.R.9, *while* TOM *stands listening intently.
A distant foghorn sounds. He does not
see the* LIBRARIAN *stealthily emerge* U.R.8,
nor HAGAN *coming up on the seawall
from below,* U.C.4. *They close in slowly
on their reminiscent prey. The voices
are speaking off-stage down left.*)

TOM BURNS   Their tálk that húng
              like stíllness, that - ....
DAN (*off*-S.D.L.)   ....that clúng like ....
              víscous threáds, ...
RENAIRE   .... like wébs that ....
(*off*-S.D.L.)   caúght and spún the móth ....
DAN, BEN   before a wíng ....
(*off*-S.D.L.)   ....could be freé - ....

(*As* YOUNG TOM *enters his bedroom,* D.L.11,
*amber light for a moment floods
the room, then with the door closing,
darkness. Blue light falls through
the window. The boy kneels and
prays, then lies down to sleep.*)

TOM BURNS   He’s at peace - how little he knows
              what he will suffer ....

(*As he meditates on the past, voices off-stage begin their onslaught* D.L..)

TOM BURNS

It was só with me -

DAN, BEN

. . . . by their . . . .
luxúrious tríckery . . . .

D., B., CAN., REN.

no sún, no moón broke ín,

CAN., DRUG., REN.

for the dark . . . .'. . . . .
. . . . sín you . . . .

DAN, BEN, CAN.

feáred to be doómed with -

RENAIRE

scówled on you! . . . .

HAGAN

(*Behind unseen*)
So you *do* remember -

TOM

(*Startled*)
Who's there?

HAGAN

the way you
began to be torn with your tortures!
Your Blacksmith's here.

TOM

What do you want?

HAGAN

What do *you* want? You with your
vices demanding to be born!

(*To the* DRUGGIST *entering* D.L.13.)

Our Apothecary is tardy tonight,
is he not?

DRUGGIST

I'm just in the nick of time!
Cannabis anyone?

(*Lighting a cigarette, he sits on the
bench. The* LIBRARIAN *intrudes
with his commisioned seduction.*)

LIBRARIAN

Allow me to share some
pictorial literature might
whet your slumbering
appetite -

TOM

. . . . You get away from me!

LIBRARIAN

(*Pulling out a magazine.*)

What d'ya think?

TOM   . . . . You're a pornpeddler!
               That's a filthy rag -
LIBRARIAN   . . . . Oh come now,
               centrefold's the height of taste
               luscious photography -
               don't ya think?
                         *(He opens the book
                    with a sardonic leer -* TOM *recoils.)*

TOM   Go away!
                         (HAGAN *closes in on the boy.)*

HAGAN   He's only attemptin'
               t' remind ya, you've kindled
               yer own tinder and stoked yer
               fire box - all on yer own!
TOM   . . . . Leave me alone!

HAGAN   Very well - a respite
               for thinkin' and rememberin'
               the way ye were torn -

                         *(As the furnace flares up they
                         draw back. Moonlight has fallen
                         through the window on* YOUNG TOM*'s*
DRUG., HAG., LIB.   *restless sleep as* TOM BURNS *gazes back*
(on-stage   *into the time of his lost innocence.*
with chorus   *The three tempters draw near again.)*
off-stage D.L.)
LIBRARIAN   When you wóke, aroúsed,
DAN, BEN   . . . . do you stíll
               remémber? . . . .
DAN, BEN, CAN. . . . . the moón, the líght, ...
DRUGGIST   wét from your . . . .
               . . . . níght-drowsed . . . .
               dreáms in a . . . .
HAGAN   . . . . sweát and strúggle . . . .
               of fríght? . . . .
                         (YOUNG TOM *starts from sleep.)*
DAN, BEN, CAN.,
RENAIRE   . . . . alármed and forlórn! . . . .
HAGAN   all that . . . .
               . . . . . . tórn and hórrified . . . .
LIBRARIAN   nócturn, ...
DRUGGIST   . . . . níght time, ...

*(chorus off-*S.D.L.*)*
D., B., CANT., REN.
DRUG., HAG., LIBR.   . . . . góred on the hórn . . .
(on-stage)   of your cónscience's . . . .
     . . . . indíctment! . . . .

TOM BURNS   Go away! Leave me alone-

     *(*HAGAN *and* LIBRARIAN *withdraw to
the low wall enclosing the cellar,
where they perch with predatory
attention; the* DRUGGIST *mounts the
seawall-steps and sits wreathed
and drugged in smoke.* TOM BURNS
*slumps on the edge of the platform,
buries his face in his hands, while*
YOUNG TOM *shoving aside his covers
slides to his knees, resting his elbows
on the bed - his prayer is just audible.)*

YOUNG TOM   Help me Rose - . . . .
     . . . . Mary, mother . . . .
     . . . . hear me! . . . .

     *(A cloud obscures the moonlight
while dim amber fades in below.*
TOM *and the tempters, meanwhile
become shadows in darkness.)*

HANNA   *(Entering* D.L.13 *with her knitting,
followed by* REMUS *with his pipe.
They talk in loud stage whispers
so the boy will not overhear.)*

     Remus, you'll 'ave
     to talk t' Tom
     I'm afraid it's ruffians
     is runnin' 'im wrong.

REMUS   Oh, be calm, Hanna!
     Every boy's got
     t' sow oats of 'is own
     sooner or later.

MRS. HEARTH   *(Having entered upstairs* D.L.12, *and
tiptoed to the very edge of the landing,*

53

I'm not listenin' fer sure - but
who can help hearin'
in this house?

HANNA   The lad has gone
from bad t' worse, ye kin
see 'is face as long an'
glum as a hearse.

REMUS   Somehow it don't 'elp 'im
bein' ignorant o' the 'who'
an' the 'how', so it's now
I'd - best be tellin' 'im?

*(HANNA nods solemnly and follows him
out D.L.13. MRS. HEARTH skips downstairs,
pretends to look out the window, while
cocking her head the better to hear.
REMUS speaks off-stage D.L.11.)*

Tom? Yer not asleep, lad?
I want t' talk with ye.

YOUNG TOM   Yes Uncle?

*(Amber light spills into the room
through the opening door as YOUNG
TOM jumps up and sits on the bed.
REMUS enters closing the door and
pulling up a stool where he sits
facing the lad, his back to the
audience. They are both defined in
the moonlight. MRS. HEARTH scuttles
to a better listening post with her
ear glued to the wall.)*

MRS. HEARTH   If orphaned nephews
must be told, their greying
uncles must be bold about it,
an' screw their courage up,
cough an' talk solemn or breezy an' -
bless us! - he's bunglin' the facts!

MRS. HEARTH   Well, so they must, poor dears.
         They doubtless cast their queasy
         second thoughts behind 'em
         tellin' 'emselves, oh - 'twas easy.

         (Overcome for a moment with her own
         qualms for snooping, MRS. HEARTH *retreats*
         as invisibly and quickly as she can D.L.12.
         The amber light fades out as REMUS
         stands up, anxious to beat a hasty
         retreat. He opens the door allowing
         the amber light to enter.)

REMUS   So Tommy boy - . . . .
             (Not knowing how to
         finish, he turns to leave, but thinking
         better of it, he comes back -)
         . . . . now ya knows
         all that's t' be known, an' I've told y'
         all that's t' be told. You'll be a man,
         soon, strong as a bull, eh? an' a
         proud eye under yer tow 'ead!

YOUNG TOM   Yes, Uncle Remus.

REMUS   For now you'll not
         be scruplin' every cockle
         that ya felt, eh? an' not
         be bein' glum agin
         t' worry yer Aunt Hanna
         wi' thinkin ya bin bad.

YOUNG TOM   No Uncle Remus, I'll not -

         *(*REMUS *goes out* D.L.11, *closing the*
         door on the amber light, leaving
         only the bluish light as the boy
         lies down to sleep. The light grows
(chorus off-   *brighter on* TOM *where he still sits*
stage D.L.*)*   *brooding on the past.)*

RENAIRE   Deép waters flów now
         ténebrous with elíxirs. . . . .
(with CANTOR,   in the rívers . . . .
DAN, BEN, DIEL, ... of your bloód . . . .
NICK, PADDY*)*

DAN, BEN   as the héllish clócks
DAN *(chorus*   contínuously tálk - . . . .
off-stage D.L.*)*
DRUGGIST   *(Stubbing out his cigarette, and coming*
(on-stage)   *down the steps, he approaches* TOM
                exuding friendliness and sitting
                down beside him.)
           . . . . Be reminded, Tom - . . . .
you remember me? your old time
family druggist?
DAN, BEN   . . . . mercúrial . . . .
                évil's anaesthésia . . . .
DRUGGIST   . . . . Used to get . . . .
sugar maple candy an'
camphor oil for your Granny
and lavender . . . .
DAN, BEN   . . . . for her slúmbrous . . . .
                línen préss in the háll . . . .
DAN   you remember? . . . .
DRUGGIST   . . . . Now with your Mom . . . . . .
gone and all, my friends here and I
are makin' a modest proposal
t' bring a little money in - . . . .
                . . . . in trust! . . . .
DAN, BEN, CANT.   . . though lécherous . . . .
DRUGGIST   for a poor orphan.
REN., JOB., CANT.   . . . . we're lethal! . . . .

                (Growing more intimate as HAGAN
                and the LIBRARIAN *close in.)*

DRUGGIST   . . . . But see there, now . . . .
don't ya become frightened -
they're attemptin' t' scare some
sense into ya - you're only young
once, ya know when -
DAN, BEN, CANT.   . . . . .the clócks . . . .
(with DRUGG.*)*   of héll struck wéll the hour . . . .
RENAIRE   of dárkness, ...
DRUGGIST   . . . . and your . . . .
yoúthful desíres neéd some reliéf, ...
surceáse, a little, releáse,
some peáce - . . . .

                (The DRUGGIST *puts his hand on* TOM*'s knee -*

the boy shrinks, jumps up, as HAGAN
and the LIBRARIAN emerge from darkness.
The moon silvers once more YOUNG TOM's
restless bed, riveting TOM's attention, as
the tempters seem bent on rushing him
over the terrible precipice of despair.)

LIBRARIAN	Sin conceíved in a wómb was
HAGAN	fórged into a mólten áct,
DRUGGIST	undertówed by tídes
DAN, BEN	. . . . of a heárt's . . . .
D., B., CANT., REN.	búrning blood of fíre!
HAGAN	. . . . wríthed . . . .
	on the ráck of the níght's . . . .
DAN, BEN, CAN.	. . . . delírium, ...
HAGAN / REN.	ráved, criéd
DRUGGIST	. . . . till the áshes . . . .
DAN, BEN, CAN.	. . . . of pássion . . . .
LIBRARIAN	. . . . tásted . . . .
DAN, BEN	. . . . despaír! . . . .

(Meanwhile blue light has shone
down through the transom above
the central doors. TOM looks toward
the light - at the sound of Rose's
voice all are struck motionless.)

ROSE BURNS	Thomas! Tom, son! . . . .
	(YOUNG TOM sits up)
ROSE	Your mother, Tom - . . . .
	(then putting his
feet down he sits on the edge of
his bed. He shakes with silent
sobs, his face buried in his hands.)
ROSE	. . . Thomas? . . . your mother . . . .
	(TOM
turns to see the shadow of his
younger self fleeing the darkened
horror of his room.)
TOM BURNS	Then I was aware - . . . .
	(Turning to the tempters.)
TOM BURNS	even knew as I fled -
what it was to have sinned.

HAGAN   *(Centre - with ferocious mock pity.)*

                       Ah yes. . . . .
                       He was sick, with a trickle
                       of sweat down 'is ribs,
                       where the caged 'eart, cringed
                       poor kid,
                       . . . . . shudderin' under the air . . . .
                       clutchin' 'is 'ead for an abhorrent
                       skull, where the serpent
                       skulked, ...
                       . . . . . and grinned. . . . .

TOM BURNS   *(Confronting his tormentors, he
                       does not see the* LIBRARIAN *circling
                       behind, drawing near on the left.*
                       TOM *speaks as if he were young
                       again, reliving the past.)*

TOM   I was afraid. . . . .
                       . . . . I was afraid . . . .
                       of the priest, so I crept next day
                       to church, as a snail goes,
                       preparin' for penance.

LIBRARIAN   You crawled, frail wrestler,
                       counting every street, ...
                                             *(dogging
                       his steps as* TOM *backs away
                       from him.)*
LIBRARIAN   . . . . distraught,
                       you numbered the innumerable
                       demons who would deride
                       what you had lost - ah, lost!

                       (Seeing HAGAN, TOM *stands still
                       as if frozen, while the* LIBRARIAN
                       and DRUGGIST *pace like caged
                       beasts behind him. The first
                       now to the right the other to
                       the left.)*

DRUGGIST   as they deride you, even
                       now, mock what you desire,
                       what you yearn for in your travail.

HAGAN

(*Crossing in front of* TOM *to the left.*)

Perhaps you've wondered
who we really are? and why
we're really here? Because you say
we're queer, we're Sodomites? nay
much more, we're the brimstone
whores of Gomorrah, stormed
Lot's doors t' know his angels? nay
not men at all - Executives
rather - of Hell Fire!

LIBRARIAN

(*Holding a small pocket Bible,
he approaches from the right.*)

If you won't read pornography,
read Sophonias instead -
'Moab shall be as Sodom . . . .
and Ammon as Gomorrah -' . . . .

(TOM *steps downstage to get away,
only to be met by the* DRUGGIST.)

DRUGGIST

Once you have tasted your own
sweetness, TOM, it's too late,
too late - . . . .

LIBRARIAN

(*Darting in from behind to finish
his quotation on the left.*)

. . . For the scriptures go on -
'Dryness of thorns and heaps
of salt - and deserts, forever -'

HAGAN

(*As* TOM *backs away from the devil
quoting scripture* HAGAN *clutches
his sleeve drawing him back.*)

What good did it do ya
trotting t' the priest
t' be confessed of a sin
ya went a week clear of
and did again?

(TOM *wrenches himself free, and
turns to face* HAGAN.)

TOM   I - I couldn't. I -
                I couldn't ever have done it
                if I hadn't tried!

HAGAN   *(Still holding him with blazing eyes
                       and an accusing finger.)*

                What good does it do ya trying?

TOM   Can't you see?
                can't you see that I had to?

HAGAN   Your mettle's already tried -
(off-stage D.L.*)*
REN., CANT., JOB   . . . . Búrning - Tom Búrns!
TOM   Go away, you!
HAGAN   . . . . Yer sóul is scória, impúre
                       . . . . slág-a-hell slúices! . . . .
TOM   I - I can't -
HAGAN   . . . . fornicátion's off-scoúrin' -
                       . . . . a scúm of abúses!
TOM   leave me alone!

                       *(The tempters stream up onto the
                       seawall, where they stand, motionless,
                       staring at* TOM. *A faint light grows
                       in the transom.)*
REN., CANT., JOB   . . . . Héll's gorge. . . . .
                       yáwns, it yeárns . . . .
HAGAN, REN., ... for the etérnal . . . .
(with LIB., CANT.*)* túrning, Tom - . . . .
                       *(By the steps to the
                       quay, his tormentors go down, below.)*
HAGAN, LIBR.,
DRUG. -   . . . . búrning . . . .
*(off-*S.U.C.*)*   . . . . burning . . . .
ROSE BURNS   Thómas . . . .
HAGAN, LIBR., DRUG.   . . . . búrning . . . .
ROSE *(off-*S.U.C.*)* . . Tóm son! . . . .
DAN, BEN   . . . . remémber . . . .
*(chant, off-*S.U.L.*)* . . . . remember . . . .
FAY *(off-*S.U.L.*)*   . . . . . . Régis? . . . .
DAN, BEN   . . . . rémember . . . .
FAY   . . . . where áre you? . . . .
DAN, BEN   . . . . remémber . . . .

TOM

May God deliver me!
from the vice of this slavery.
May he help me pay, whatever
price I may, for his favour.

> (REGIS WICKS, *a young boy about
> twelve, enters on the seawall* U.L.10.
> *Seeing* TOM, *he stops and watches
> curiously by the lightpost.*)

TOM

I was not always this way.
There was a time when I was still a child,
it was different then - I had a dream.
My name was Regis Wicks.

I was a good boy then - I had no evil
thoughts; and my father wasn't
a drunken seaman who's hardly ever home -
he was a good man.

He ran a garage on Campus
Street, and I never heard him curse -
But he died - I had two brothers and
a sister in the dream - . . . .

REGIS

. . . . Tom Burns? . . . .

TOM

(Not hearing)
. . . . then - the dream died. . . .

(Cathedral bell - TOM exits U.R.9.)

REGIS

What did he mean sayin'
I'm only his dream? I'm the real me!
an' my name is Regis Thomas Wicks.

(Coming down the steps.)

Perhaps when he was young
I was real to 'im, an' Tom Burns
was only a sad future.
But I do have two brothers
an' a sister an' two small
cousins -

> *(Off-stage* U.L. *but closer.)*

FAY

. . . . Regis - where are you?

REGIS   There they are - Fay! Fanny!
don't run in the fog!

(He listens for an answer.)

FANNY   . . . . We're comin', Regis
. . . . we're singin' a song!

*(Satisfied, he sits on the left side
of the bench to wait for them.
Dim amber light fades in on the
right of the lower platform as*
GRANNY OWEN *enters* U.C.6. *When the
song begins she pauses to listen,
then settles herself on the platform
bench. She watches and listens.
The song grows as the children
approach.)*

FAY *(sung)*   . . . . Lífe is a joúrney . . . . .
. . . . oút to the seá . . . .
. . . . lábourin' bírthday . . .
. . . . shípwright Mageé. . .

FAY *(sung)*   . . . . Yé will be laúnchin' . . . .
. . . . sáfe under saíl . . . .
FAY, FANNY *(sung)* . . . . yoúng laddie dreámin' . . . .
. . . . tráde winds avaíl. . . . .

FAY *(spoken)* *(Entering with* FANNY *on the seawall* U.L.10.*)*

. . . . . I know! I know . . . .
. . . . . how it goes - it goes . . . .

FAY *(sung)*   Mánning the rúdder . . . .
stróng in the stórm . . . .
lóngin' for lándfall . . . .
the dáy ye were bórn. . . . .

FAY *(spoken)* Doesn't it?
FANNY   . . . . Yes it does -
          (Running down)
Regis, what's it do next? . . . .

REGIS   Not sure Fanny,
but I think it goes - . . . .
        (Standing to sing.)

REGIS   Old ship and áged
leéward the Isles,

ALL   lánded on góldstrand
seáman Mageé.

FANNY   I do like that song!
FAY   . . . . It's jolly!

REGIS   Well now, Fay, you've
had your fun. It's time to pray -

*(*FAY *and* FANNY *sit on the 'seaside'
of the bench, facing each other
so they can keep an eye on* REGIS.*)*

you've got to think of all
the wicked things you've done.
Disobeyed your mother, fought
your sister almost every day -
FAY   . . . . Yes Regis.

REGIS   You can't be noisy when you pray.
You must be still 'cause that's
the way it's done - so hush now,
you two -
FANNY   . . . . . We will, Regis.
FAY   . . . . We'll be still.

*(*REGIS, *pulling out his prayer book,
goes around and sits on the other
side of the bench behind the twins,
becoming instantly absorbed. A
dim light has faded in on* DOM
JEROME.*)*
DOM JEROME . . . . You see, he's tethered their
frolic; grave little nuns now, and
solemn, they seek for a moment
their faults, the mischief they've done.
Who could this young boy be?
He seems, somehow, familiar,
but one can never be sure -
who knows - a cousin? a nephew?
Impossible to say. He's won his
silence though, searching perhaps
for the remembered days?

(The light on DOM JEROME *fades away
while that on* GRANNY OWEN *grows brighter.)*

G. OWEN

*(As she recalls her memories, the twins
nudge one another, suppress giggles,
flirt and dart their way with mischievous
solemnity on to the seawall.)*

Oh, I remember when Dan,
Regis, Jenny and Ben,
all of them played at a game
called 'sacristy' - though his
brothers and sister all were
older, he was always the pastor,
always the priest -

*(*DR. MALLOY *comes up from the quay
in time to watch for a moment the
humorous antics of* FAY *and* FANNY
as they disappear on the seawall.)

G. OWEN

Ben now studies for the bar while
Dan joined the navy and went to sea,
and across the way his sister
Jenny is becoming a nun, merciful
white angel, in the convent there -

*(*SR. JENNIFER *appears on the convent
porch and closes one of the gates.)*

FAY

(Off-stage U.L.*)*
. . . . Regis!

SR. JENNIFER

(Noticing him.)
. . . . Why, there's Regis!

*(She remains discreetly withdrawn,
while* REGIS, *coming out of his reverie,
notices the twins have gone. He
listens intently.)*

REGIS

. . . . Fay! where are you?

SR. JENNIFER

He must be with our cousins -
Oh! how I would love to call out,
but I mustn't. We young nuns
are supposed to learn detachment.

(*Meanwhile* DR. MALLOY, *shaking his head,*
comes down to the left entrance.)

SR. SUPERIOR (*Off-stage* D.R.)
. . . . .Sister could you spare
me a moment please?
. . . . .Yes Mother!

(*She hurries in, not closing the gate.*)

REGIS Fanny? come back - . . . .

DR. MALLOY (*He glances at* REGIS, *but the boy*
is already absorbed in his book.
Knocking on the invisible door,
he lets himself in.)

Well, grandmother Owen,
I see you observe the Flosses.

G. OWEN Yes Doctor Malloy, come in.
They're a joy for an old woman.

DR. MALLOY (*Humouring the old lady, he opens*
his bag and makes a few routine
checks. He's an old-fashioned doctor.)

One doesn't really know what
to think of them - ghosts? elves? fairies?

G. OWEN You'll notice they've burst the bonds
of gravity - . . . .
DR. MALLOY . . . . and run every which way
in the mist - . . . .
G. OWEN . . . . . . .quite invisible, behind
the lamposts - . . . .
 (*The lights dim a little as*
conversation continues inaudibly.)

FAY (*Voice off-stage* U.L.)

. . . . Regis, I've disappeared!
. . . . I'm a fairy - can you find me?

REGIS (*Deliberately he pockets his prayer book*
and waits for the novelty to wear off.)

Come, Fay, don't run
in the fog, Fay -
do you hear me? . . . .

FAY
. . . . I'm appearing -

(Darting in on the seawall U.L.10,
she skips down the steps to REGIS.)

here I am!

REGIS
. . . . . . Where's Fanny gone now?

FAY
She's hiding - . . . .

REGIS
. . . . Fanny! - Fanny, come back!

FANNY
(Immediately she appears on the seawall.)

FAY
There she is - see her? . . . .

FANNY
. . . . Fay can't catch me!

FAY
I can too!

*(*FANNY *quickly vanishes
with* FAY *running after her.* REGIS
*bounds up the steps, calling after
them.)*

REGIS
. . . . All right you two - come back!
Do you hear me? . . . .

*(There being no sound
of an answer, he sits on the parapet
by the lightpost to wait for them.)*

DR. MALLOY
*(He puts his stethoscope back
in his bag as the lights grow
stronger. He rises, goes to the window.)*

Our shepherd has only
two lambs, but how they frisk.

G. OWEN
Mist on cornsilk hair 'minds me
of the veils o' their First Communion.

DR. MALLOY
Well, the two of them
avoid his crook, I'm afraid.

G. OWEN
My poor Regis - he's quick,
but he'll never catch those two!

*(The doctor sits by the old lady, as
lights dim; they continue with silent talk.)*

FAY   *(Off-stage* U.L.*)*
       . . . . Regis - we've vanished -
REGIS   come find us!
      (Unheeding, he sits
      on the parapet, lost in his own thoughts.)

      Sometimes when I begin
      to think, I begin to wonder
      what I should be - . . . .

      Maybe a missioner
      in Africa or India
      in the east - . . . .

REGIS   Or a priest maybe
      like Pere Bernard?
      a holy confessor - . . . .

      Or a monk, perhaps
      at Cloistergarth
      like Dom Jerome? . . . .
FAY   . . . . Where are you?

REGIS   I don't know, I can't
      quite tell. Whenever I
      ask myself that question
      It's there, deep inside
      like a bell -
CANTOR   *(Off-stage* D.L. *with* NOVICE -
      (sung). Dim aura fades in on JEROME.*)*

      . . . . Véni - fíli, aúdi me.
REGIS   A sound like words
      from somewhere - . . . .
CANTOR   . . . . Timórem Dómini
          docébo te.
REGIS   like music I once heard.
      What it means
      I can never tell - . . . .
NOVICE   . . . . Véni - fíli, aúdi me.

REGIS   It's so strange -
FAY   *(Off-stage* U.L.*)*
      . . . . Regis!
REGIS   I can't remember.

*(*DOM JEROME*'s aura fades while the*
platform light grows brighter.)

G. OWEN

Whenever she goes, he'll not
forget the calm eyes of his mother,
in their haven of quietness,
poor soul, she'e not well.

REGIS

     (The boy is listening.)
. . . . But she's ready -

DR. MALLOY

Tragic Job's disappearance
and all - must trouble the boy.

G. OWEN

He used to watch him for hours
in his oily work clothes - vestments
o' the trade - says he never went to sea -
says he never died.

REGIS

. . . . He never did -
he never went to sea.

DR. MALLOY

. . . . Dangerous fantasy
we must watch the lad.

*(*REGIS *is attentive. Quietly he comes*
foreward and sits on the top step.)

DR. MALLOY

I knew his father well - a man
of car parts; his whole dingy
garage was filled with the ruins
and wreckage of engines!

Those disembowelled reeking
gas pungent anatomies - motors,
he was a diagnostician of the ills of
heaven knows what, crankcases, gears,

he could resurrect an engine
shaft and bolt like an intrigued
paleontologist wiring vertebrae -
he could have been a surgeon!

G. OWEN

Now, Dr. Malloy ha! you're
goin' t' have me dyin' o' laughter!

*(*REGIS *comes down; sits on the bench.)*

DR. MALLOY   It's a good way to die - but he was
                a quiet man of good deeds and
                few words. In town they called him
                'Job' Wicks, because he was convinced

                anything that could be taken apart,
                could be fixed!
REGIS   . . . . My dad could fix any
                jallopy, even old Frosty's -

G. OWEN   Ah yes, he could fix 'em -
                despite his faults, doctor, he was
                a good man, and a fine engineer.

                *(As the furnace transforms
                itself into a frosted window
                in the old garage, the shadows
                of* WICKS *and* FROAR *move
                about behind it.* REGIS *strains
                to see more than shadows.)*

G. OWEN   Remember him wrestlin'
                year after year with old Froar's
                conking car?
DR. MALLOY   . . . . To keep it on the road
                somehow - who knows why!

G. OWEN   They always came back,
                peppery old man, truculent
                as ever -
DR. MALLOY   . . . . . and his chronic car-ill
                with distemper somewhere inside!

                *(The lights fade dim on the platform
                as they come up in the office of
                the garage (* HAGAN'*s cellar).* FROSTY
                FROAR *emerges from the garage* U.R.
                *gesticulating and stomping into
                the office.* JOB WICKS *follows, after
                surveying the ancient car with
                misgiving.)*

MR. FROAR   Now Mister Wicks, I've had ye
                service this automobile before! and
                futhermore the balking crate
                is, evidently, in distress!

JOB WICKS   What seems to be the trouble
Mister Froar, do you know?

MR. FROAR   Trouble? with a stallin', knockin'
rattletrap? Well first the brakes
won't take, then the clutch won't
go, even the horn won't blow! It's
shocking!

JOB WICKS   ...... 'Tis indeed - I'm afraid she's
ready for the rubble, but, who'd deny
were one to pry awhile inside,
she might be fixed -

(SR. JENNIFER *returns to the porch to close
the other gate; seeing* REGIS *she pauses
to watch. She is unaware of* JOB *and* FROAR.)

MR. FROAR   I'll need it, Wicks, by Monday next.

JOB WICKS   I'll do the best I can
and let you know on Sunday.

MR. FROAR   Thank you Wicks. What's more, sir -
good day sir!
            (shaking hands.)

JOB WICKS   Good day Mr. Froar.

MR. FROAR   *(The truculent* FROAR *stomps off* U.R.9
while WICKS, *amazed at having 'done it
again', returns to his garage. The light
in the office fades out as* DOCTOR MALLOY
assists GRANNY OWEN *to rise, takes his
leave by the invisible door and exits* U.R.9.
GRANNY *goes in* U.C.6, *and the dim lights
fade out. Only the window remains
with* WICKS' *shadow at work. The sound
of his tinkering and the light in the
window gradually fade away.
The furnace returns, supplanting the
past.* REGIS *is left standing, staring
at the place where his father was.)*

S. JENNIFER   I know we're not supposed
to daydream, but Mother'll not
object, if it's only a moment.

(REGIS *turns from the garage and
walks listlessly around the bench
and sits down facing Cloistergarth.*)

S. JENNIFER   I wonder if Regis remembers
our Dad on Communion days?
with his grimy hands scrubbed white
as pumice could scrub 'em,
like an altar boy's - poor Dad,
it hurts to remember.

(REGIS *buries his face in his hands.
An aura of dim light just defines
*DOM JEROME *during the play within the
play.*)

(*off*-S.U.L.)
FAY *(spoken)*   Regis! where are you?
NOV. *(sung)*   Véni -
FANNY *(spoken)*   Where are you, Regis?
NOV. *(sung)*   Fíli, aúdi me.
(*off*-S.D.L.)

(*Slanting afternoon sunlight breaking
out floods the bench with the boy,
the steps and the seawall, with
a flush of light in the sky over the sea.*)

S. JENNIFER   Who could forget our squabbling
brothers Dan and Ben, when
we were small those long afternoons
when we played the play?

(DAN *and* BEN *burst through the right
hand door on the upper platform* U.C.1
and run down the steps, arguing.
REGIS *jumps up, throws off his jacket,
and after a moment's hesitation,
runs over to join the game.*)

DAN   But I'm always Pontius Pilate!
Can't I be a soldier or a centurion
just this once?

BEN   But I'm one, we
don't need two!

DAN   Yes, but if you were
Pilate, I could be -

BEN   Regis, I want the sword!

REGIS   *(Conciliatory.)*

                   You be the soldier, Dan.
                   Ben'll be Pilate, won't you, Ben?

BEN   Well - all right. *This* time.

                   *(He reluctantly gives up his wooden
                   sword.* JENNY *comes out* U.C.1, *closes
                   the door and comes down the steps
                   tying her blue kerechief under her chin.)*

REGIS   Jenny'll be Mary again
                   won't you, Jenny?

JENNY   I'm always his Mother, an' I'm
                   Mary Magdalene, too.

REGIS   All right then, Jenny's
                   Our Lady an' I'm Our Lord. Ben,
                   you're Pilate, an' you've the sword, Dan
                   so you're the soldier. An' let's not
                   be talkin' all the time - it's God's dyin'!
                   Crucifixion 's a very solemn thing.

JENNY   We will, Regis. We'll be quiet.

DAN   But we haven't any thorns
                   at all, or a cross yet -

REGIS   I know what, we'll weave 'em
                   from the vines on the wall!

BEN   *(Entering suddenly into the spirit,
                   he jumps up on the bench and barks
                   commands, while* DAN *stands at
                   ramrod attention.)*

BEN   See here now, I'm
                             Pilate - centurion!
DAN   . . . . Aye, sir?
BEN   A cross can be made
                             with a saw and a pole.
DAN   . . . . Aye, sir!

BEN	Fetch me thorns and whips of the wall vines!
DAN	. . . . Aye, sir!
BEN	I'm overseer of Roman lands
S. JENNIFER	. . . . Jésus Nazarénus -
ALL	His blood on us and on our children be!
DOM JEROME	. . . . Réx Judaeórum!
BEN	Bring me water to wash my hands.
DAN	. . . . Aye, sir!
BEN	Hail Caesar!
ALL	. . . . Yea! All Hail!

>   JENNY *pours invisible water over*
>   BEN*'s hands. Then they all run off*
>   *hustling the condemned with them,*
>   *disappearing* U.C.3.*)*

S. JENNIFER
       So the Passion was our play -
       blood on us and on our children -
       a thornless crown of thorns, a cross
       of sticks and string - and my brother,
       was a very image - of the King -

(As the afternoon darkens toward
sundown a small procession enters
U.C.8. BEN *leads dragging* REGIS *after him*
secured by a rope. Over his grey pants
and white shirt, REGIS *wears a long*
cloak the colour of old ivory. His head
is circled by a crown of plaited vines.
He manages to make the slender
black cross he shoulders, appear
heavier than it is. JENNY*'s kerchief is*
now worn as a veil, while DAN *follows*
with sword and hammer in belt and
a wooden spear. On reaching centre
stage he forgets himself and prompts.)

DAN
       You're s'posed to fall here, Regis!

*(*REGIS, *absorbed in his role is silent, he*
staggers and falls as if under the weight
of the cross. JENNY *tries to reach him.)*

JENNY

He's my son! let me through!

DAN

......................Stand back, lady!

*(He thrusts the butt of his
spear between them as* BEN *turns with
a commanding gesture.)*

BEN

Make room for the condemned!

DAN

.......................Haul 'im up!

*(*BEN *pulls on the rope as*
REGIS *struggles to rise.* DAN *prods him
the shaft of his spear.)*

BEN

Forward now - march! ....

S. JENNIFER

And wasn't Calvary at the back
of the yard? under the lampost there,
where the apple tree was - ....

(When BEN *has climbed the steps to the
seawall, he turns abruptly and barks
his command.)*

BEN

.... Prisoner, halt!

*(*REGIS *sinks to his
knees on the second step, while* DAN
and JENNY *are still at the bottom.)*

BEN

Erect the cross, soldier. ....

DAN

.... Aye aye, sir.

*(*BEN *takes the spear
while* DAN *uncinches the rope and
takes the cross. He drags it up the
steps, and standing it in front
of the lightpost, ties it up with the rope.)*

BEN

Give me your cloak, you! ....

(As REGIS *unclasps and surrenders it,*
DAN *snatches it roughly.)*

BEN

Hm, good homespun - ....
.................we'll see who gets it.

JENNY

He's my only son, ...
.............I wove it for him.

*(*BEN *tosses the cloak on the parapet.)*

BEN   Prisoner, come forward!

DAN   . . . . You there - move!

> *(REGIS rises unsteadily;*
> *he ascends the steps to the seawall,*
> *and turning, stretches out his hands on*
> *the cross.)*

S. JENNIFER And I was always terrified -
. . . . at that part.

BEN   The nails now, soldier! . . . .

DAN   . . . . Aye aye, sir!

> *(Drawing a hammer*
> *out of his belt, and spikes out of his*
> *pocket, he places one against the*
> *palm of his brother's outstretched hand.)*

JENNY   Oh no! not there Dan, ...
. . . . between the fingers!

DAN   I knows 'xactly, what
. . . . I'm doin', cause
I'm the centurion! . . . .

BEN   . . . . I'd draw that hand
back, if I were you - . . . .
. . . . just in case!

REGIS   Can't do that, 'tisn't . . . .
. . . . right! - He didn't.

JENNY   Be careful!

> *(As DAN hammers the spikes*
> *into the prepared holes between the*
> *fingers, accompanied by off-stage*
> *sound, REGIS winces at each blow.*
> *The light on the bench fades away,*
> *while that on the seawall turns*
> *gradually bluish as if clouds*
> *are obscuring the sun. DAN and*
> *BEN throw dice then for the cloak.)*

REGIS   Father, forgive them
for they know not what they do.

BEN   Ah ha! the cloak's mine!
So there; Stand guard, soldier.

DAN   Aye aye, sir. . . . .

> *(He stands with the spear U.C.3.*
> *BEN assumes a new role as John.)*

BEN   I'm John the Apostle, Jenny -
              come up - stand by the cross.

JENNY   John! I'm *Mary!*
BEN   . . . . Oh yes - Mary.
                 *(*JENNY *comes up,*
                 takes her place by the right hand
                 of REGIS, *while* BEN *stands at the left.*
REGIS   REGIS *says to* JENNY *-)*
                    . . . . Woman, behold your son -
                 (then he turns to BEN *-*
                    . . . . behold your mother.
                 (As shadows gather
                 on the seawall, the lighting grows
                 more dramatic on the figures in
                 the passion and on SR. JENNIFER *and*
                 DOM JEROME.*)*
S. JENNIFER   . . . . Anyone who does
              the will of my Father, ...
DOM JEROME   . . . . is my sister, my
              brother, my mother.

              'Twas over soon, his mother given,
              with his seventh word - said.

REGIS   I thirst - . . . .
DOM JEROME   . . . . . The dark blood came welling
                    slowly, till the ghost was spent.

REGIS   Father -
                 . . . It is finished. . . . .

                 *(*REGIS *expires as darkness falls,*
                 leaving the figures stark in
                 silhouette against the sky;
                 in Cloistergarth the NOVICE *begins*
                 singing -)
*(off-*S.D.L.*)*
NOVICE *(sung)*   Stábat Máter dólorósa
                 júxta crúcem lácrimósa . . . .
                                 *(*JENNY *crosses*
                 slowly to the left where she stands with BEN.*)*

NOVICE *(sung)*   dúm pendébat Fílius
                 Cújus ánimam geméntem . . . .
                                 *(*DAN *steps forward*

with the spear, and stands on the right.)

NOVICE
(sung off-S.D.L.*)* cóntristátam et doléntem . . . .
*(DAN lunges with the
spear, holds it there, a motionless tableau.)*

pértransívit gládius. . . . .
*(Pulling out the spear,
he returns, leaving it at the door* U.C.3. *He
assumes a new role as Arimathea.)*

*(Twilight relieves the starkness, as an
incoming tide brings the sound of waves
breaking on the seawall.)*

S. JENNIFER Our Deposition was undignified -
work for full grown men, but
carried out by children -

Dan was a clumsy Arimathea
and Ben a rough and ready John,
but even then, the moment, was solemn.

*(DAN and BEN remove the nails, draw
REGIS's arms over their shoulders, and
supporting him step away from the cross.
They lower him, his knees buckling, as he
slides to the ground. The monk and
nun repeat spoken fragments of
the hymn.)*

(spoken)
DOM JEROME júxta crúcem - . . . .
(Coming from behind JENNY
*receives her slain son, supporting his
shoulder over her left knee while
she kneels on the other.* DAN *and* BEN
stand back before this Pieta.)

(spoken)
S. JENNIFER Máter dólorósa - . . . .
*(BEN at the head and
DAN at the feet raise* REGIS *and carry
him down from the seawall
with* JENNY *following with her
son's discarded cloak.)*

DOM JEROME   lácrimósa - ....
                    (They lay him on top of the
                    bench, with his head to the right.
                    DAN *mounts guard at the foot while*
                    BEN *being John for a moment -*
                    covers REGIS *with the cloak.)*

S. JENNIFER   cóntristátam - ....
                    (BEN *leads* JENNY *away*
                    as the principal mourner, where
                    she exits U.C.3, *and soldier again*
                    he returns with the spear standing
                    guard at the head opposite DAN.)

DOM JEROME   et doléntem - ....
                    ....and having sealed
                    the stone before the tomb,
                    they must have waited, breathless
                    for the Resurrection! ....
                    (A cathedral bell
                    sounds the first stroke of six, when
                    white light rolls in like a wave
                    over REGIS. *He sits up, dropping*
                    his feet on the 'seaside' of the bench.
                    The cloak falls over his right
                    arm. The guards stumble back
                    in terror. He turns, jumping
                    up onto the bench and throwing
                    his arms into the air.)

REGIS   I'm alive! I've risen!
                    I'm alive Father! ....
                    (Bell stroke the second.
                    The sea sound is suddenly filled
                    with gull cries answering his
                    exclamation. He turns to the
                    guards. They are backing up the
                    steps onto the seawall.)

DAN   Run for your lives! ....
                    (Bell stroke the third.)

BEN   It's a ghost! it's -
                    it's a spectre - run! ....
                    (Bell stroke the fourth.
                    They run in panic down the steps U.C.4
                    to the quay. Then from off-stage U.C.)

DAN (*off*-S.U.C.)	Run Ben! . . . .
BEN (*off*-S.U.C.)	run for your life!

> *(Bell stroke the fifth.*
> *The white light fades into pale blue,*
> *as* REGIS *jumps down and drops his cloak*
> *on the bench. He runs to the right of the*
> *lower platform where he hides with*
> *back against the invisible wall of the*
> *house. He watches as* JENNY *comes out*
> U.C.3 *where she pauses to listen. She*
> *does not see* REGIS. SR. JENNIFER *also -*
> *stands listening.)*
>
> *(Bell stroke the sixth.*
> *The sea sounds have subsided until*
> *now it is perfectly quiet.)*

S. JENNIFER	And Magdalene came with a tall
	glass vase; it was early dawn - . . . .

> (JENNY *glides*
> *down the steps with her vase of ointment,*
> *kneels to examine the empty tomb. She*
> *picks up the fallen cloak reverently.*
> *The flush fades from the sky. It is*
> *evening. Then a child's voice is heard*
> *in the distance.)*

FAY (*off*-S.U.L.)	. . . . Regis, where are you?

MOTHER WICKS	*(Opening the door* U.C.1, *which spills amber*
	light down the steps -)

Come in, children, it's time
for supper. . . . .

> *(Answering from the below.)*

DAN (*off*-S.U.C.)	Here we are, Mom!
BEN (*off*-S.U.C.)	We're coming! . . . .

> *(They come running up from*
> *the quay* U.C.4, *and follow her into the*
> *house. Picking up her vase,* JENNY
> *hurries to follow them, but pauses*
> *on the steps to call* REGIS.)

JENNY	Hurry, Regis, you'll be late. . . . .

(She goes in - the door closes.)

S. SUPERIOR   *(A voice of authority)*
(off-S.D.R.*)*   . . . . .Sister Jennifer?
S. JENNIFER   Yes, Mother, I'm coming.

> *(She hurries in, this
> time remembering to close the other
> gate. The porch light fades as a foghorn
> is heard out at sea.)*

REGIS   *(Staying hidden for a moment, he steps
                   away from the wall.)*

It was strange - they were
always the same - those days.
Now they've all grown up,
they've flown away, like the
swallows - I'm the only one left.

> *(Suddenly aware of the cold, he walks
> over to the bench and sits down.
> He puts on his jacket, and pulls out
> his prayer book as amber light
> gathers in the porter's cell.)*

DOM JEROME   There is no loneliness
like a child's. But an old man
reduced to a child, who's unable
to remember who he was - that's
the essence of loneliness.

Some say it was amnesia -
this lad may be my nephew
if I had brothers, a cousin
if I had uncles or aunts.
Some have said they were -
but they were strangers -

FAY   *(A child's voice far away.)*
(off-S.U.L.*)*   . . . . Regis!

DOM JEROME   To be a missioner? a priest?
or a monk? brave little boy!
Anguished arrows pierce his
trembling conscience with a hail
of questions he may never answer!
God alone knows what will be -
Tabor - or Gethsemane.

(The amber light dims while the children
are heard again and the novice -)

FAY *(off*-S.U.L.*)*	. . . . Regis - where are you?
NOVICE *(sung)*	Véni, fíli, aúdi me,
(off-S.D.L.*)*	. . . . Timórem Dómini
	. . . . docébo te.

REGIS Almighty God, teach me,
and show me the way -

FANNY . . . . We're coming, Regis -
(off-S.U.L.*)* *(*FAY *runs in on the seawall*
U.L.10, *waits a moment for* FANNY.*)*

FAY Here we are, Fanny!
we were near -
*(*FANNY *enters* U.L.10, *and they*
both run down to REGIS.*)*

REGIS Fanny and Fay! you two've
been running in the fog again.

FANNY It's not too dark
FAY . . . . there's streetlights!
REGIS There's other lights too,
. . . . that some never see -
FANNY *(Drawing him by*
the hand to the right of the platform.)

Regis, can we light
. . . . candles?
FAY in the cathedral?
FANNY . . . . can we, Regis?
REGIS When we get there.
. . . . But you've got to say
your prayers now.
FANNY . . . . I know, let's say
the rosary on the
. . . . streetlamps!
REGIS On the streetlamps?
FANNY . . . . There's ten on the hill,
I counted them once.
FAY . . . . Can we, Regis?
FANNY It's a decade!
REGIS . . . . Well, alright - but don't run.

FAY   We won't run.

REGIS   . . . . And meet me in the square -
on the 'Glory be'.

FANNY   . . . . We will, Regis.

*(Starting up Campus street, they exit
U.R.9. Then, from a distance -)*

FANNY   First myst'ry

(off-S.U.R.)   . . . . 'nunciation -

DOM JEROME   For God's children, prayer
is a game they can play with their
Father and their Mother -

*(WILLIE SIMS, a small boy about eight
years old, enters on the seawall U.L.10.
He stands looking at REGIS.)*

REGIS   Dear Father in Heaven - I've never
spoken to anyone about this before,
but since you already know,
it won't hurt my telling you.

*(WILLIE comes down the steps very
quietly, moves like a shadow toward
the bench, and stops to listen.)*

REGIS   I had a nightmare once, when
I was very young - they called me
Willie then. And my father, he -
he was a ghost.

he came back - but it couldn't
have been real - my real father was
a garageman - he wasn't a fisherman.
Willie was only a dream -

Save me Father from ghostly
visitations - it was only a dream -

*(As he leaves up Campus street U.R.9,
a deep mournful fog horn sounds.
WILLIE gives vent to his thoughts, as if
REGIS were able to hear him.)*

WILLIE SIMS   But it wasn't no dream,
no nightmare. My father was
a fisherman - he worked on Macrae's
schooner before he bought the garage.
He'd disappear from time to time.

WILLIE   Nobody knew where he was - an' then
he just didn't come back.

WILLIE   Doctor Malloy was my friend
at the time - he looked after my Grandma.
He thought my dad was gone too when
Macrae's schooner foundered.

*(Sitting down on the bench, he looks
at the old house.)*

WILLIE   Even my Mom told me a lie -
she didn't want to! But it wasn't no
ghost that came back. . . . .
*(A deep bell and
distant, begins to toll six fathoms deep.)*

WILLIE   And I'm no nightmare -
I'm the real me! . . . .
*(Bell stroke the second.
The scrim begins to fall slowly.)*

DOM JEROME   Poor little boy - another orphan?
of some broken house? Well I must
nap on it I think, for a spell -

(Bell stroke the third.)
JEROME   He seems to know Regis,
But Regis *dreams* of him? . . . .

(Bell stroke the fourth.)
JEROME   There grows herein, some
strangeness - . . . .
(He rises bemused with thought.)
JEROME   a mystery - . . . .
(Bell stroke the fifth.)

CURTAIN

*(DOM JEROME goes into his cell, the lights fade.
Bell stroke the sixth.)*

THE SECOND WATCH

UNDER THE WAVES TUMULT, P.98

THE SECOND WATCH

HADDOCK   Weel, Codrocks, seinin'
fer herrin' off Barkley Sound
was no picnic,
like slavin'-a-nights
in a big swell, makin'
a water haul!

COD   Fer sure. An' nay radar.

HADDOCK   An' ye in a big run
in a floatin' village of boat lights!

COD   Sure - fore an' aft
we'd load 'em - dangerous,
down t' the gunnels

HADDOCK   bulkheads springin'
full of five tons
o' herrin' an' water -

COD   Ye better pump out!

HADDOCK   I'll say! eyein' the swell
or she'll shift on ye
like as not - take
the whole catch an' ye
down t' Davy Jones!

COD   Well I'm glad
t' be in m' moorin's
mendin' nets fer the lads -
did I ever tell 'e
Haddock about one Russian
priest I met in Anchorage?

HADDOCK Nay. What about 'im?

COD There's a Russian sayin'
says 'e - 'Come Judgement Day
Orthodox Churches 'll
fly away home.'
What ya think o' that?

HADDOCK Home t' heaven?
COD . . . . Aye.
HADDOCK Russians in 'em?
COD . . . . Aye.
HADDOCK He's daft!
COD . . . . . . So thought I -

'till I thought on it.
Can't ye imagine a stone
fleet on a fiery flood?

HADDOCK Why, ye daft
man, ye'll have a time
keepin' 'em afloat!

COD Ye want t' be caught
in a wooden ship that'll burn?
I'll be takin' a stone one.

HADDOCK Will ya now -

COD Aye, up yonder - she's a stone ship.
I've known it fer quite some while.

HADDOCK Have ye now -

COD Any fool seaman can see
That's no spire - it's a spar!
shrouds reefed up inside -
stern t' the east an' prow t' the west of 'er -

HADDOCK Now Codrocks, yer off yer rocker!

COD *(Beginning to put away his mending.)*

It's plain t' see - all them
riggin's-a-buttresses, an' crypts
fore an' aft full-a-souls!

HADDOCK   Weel, Codrocks, I'm
                   fer a carousal - I'll nay board
                   yer ship tonight.

COD   At yer own peril, Haddock,
                   but I'm off t' see the man o' God -

                        (He goes down several steps U.C.4,
                        still talking as he stows his nets.)

                   'e keeps a straight course!

HADDOCK   Oh, yea - sure, Cod.
                              *(*DR. MALLOY *enters*
                        U.R.9, *as dim amber fades in on the*
                        right lower platform. GRANNY OWEN
                        has entered U.C.6 *and is about to sit*
                        when the doctor knocks. She rises
                        to answer the knock. COD *has come*
                        back up.)
COD   . . . . Well - goodnight t' ye.

HADDOCK   Goodnight, Codrocks, an' -
                   let me know when she sails.

COD   Oh ho! nay need! Ye'll know
                   when she sails -
                              *(*COD *exits* U.R.9, *while*
                        HADDOCK *goes down to the quay* U.C.4
                        and GRANNY *opens to the doctor.)*

DR. MALLOY   Well, Mrs. Owen, I've
                   brought you your prescription.
                   This should help with those
                   old arthritic bones of yours.

                        (Light begins to fade in on WILLIE
                        where he sits on the bench.)

G. OWEN   I surely hope it will, for they
                   do complain so. Good night, Doctor
                   and thank you for going
                   out of your way.
DR. MALLOY   . . . . 'Twas my pleasure,
                   Ma'am. Good night.

(GRANNY OWEN returns to her
room U.C.6. The amber light fades
as DR. MALLOY comes down the steps.
He sees WILLIE sitting on the bench.
A fog horn sounds.)

DR. MALLOY   Is that you there, Willie Sims?
Isn't it late at night for a
small boy t' be out?

WILLIE   *(Standing up
as* DR. MALLOY *approaches.)*

Yes, sir - I'm goin'
t' church with my Mom.

DR. MALLOY   And where is she?

WILLIE   I ran ahead, sir. I wanted
t' look at the old house.

DR. MALLOY   Ah yes, I remember, above
the Wicks - I brought you
into the world in that house -
don't you remember?

WILLIE   No, sir.

DR. MALLOY   I'm not surprised - you were
makin' a big howl at the time.
Well, let's sit down and look at it
so you can wait for your Mom.

WILLIE   Yes, sir.
(They sit on the bench.)

DR. MALLOY   So you like the old house
better 'n the shanty, eh?

WILLIE   Oh yes, sir!

DR. MALLOY   It's a bit more grand I suppose
but the shanty has its points -

WILLIE   Does it, sir?

DR. MALLOY   Yes - yes, those damp
                    lowlands of town still
                    have fields, outlying gardens,
                    railroad tracks, eh?
                    where the rails sing
                    at night, and the freights
                    wake up the dog yowls of town!

WILLIE   And they howl, sir,
                    just like wolves!

DR. MALLOY   Aye, while that ramshackle
                    shanty of yours, rattles
                    a few boards loose!

WILLIE   The train knocked
                    a bowl off our shelf once.

DR. MALLOY   Did it now? Well, Willie,
                    while the whistlin' steam
                    wails all night long
                    and shunting engines
                    batter away at boxcars,

                    what does it matter
                    if a yellow blind flaps
                    in a broken pane?

                    or a chimney leans
                    like a tired tombstone
                    on a mouldy roof?

                        (Noting the boy's abstraction.)

                    Are you dreamin', Willie?

WILLIE   Just thinkin' -
DR. MALLOY   . . . . That's dreaming -
                    Just like that
                            . . . . of any old man -
                    Penny for your
                            . . . . thoughts!
WILLIE   Just rememb'rin' -
                            . . . . *(Playing a game.)*
                    Can you guess
                    what I'm thinkin'?

DR. MALLOY   (Playing along)
                                              Well now,
                              that's a hard one, but let me try -
                              were you thinkin' of the old garden
                              they tore up here? three years ago?
                              when they laid the street?

WILLIE   How'd you guess?

DR. MALLOY   Horse sense I suppose -
                              was thinkin' of it myself.
                              There was somethin' else too -

WILLIE   What else was I thinkin' of?

DR. MALLOY   Ah ha I remember -
                                              *(Reminding him
                                      of some of his early pranks.)*

                              how when Willie was
                              young once and a boy
                                  . . . . ya pillaged
                              our raspberry bushes
                                  . . . . and rifled
                              our chestnut burs, ya
                                  . . . . shook
                              the pelting apples on
                                  . . . . heads
                              of helpmate robbers
                                  . . . . eh? and
                              whipped, but no, ...
                                  . . . . unrepentant
                              chased with slings

                              those fat and saucy robins
                              in our cherry trees,
                                  . . . . remember?
WILLIE   And the bags
                              of crabapples my Granny
                              stewed and twisted -

DR. MALLOY   till all the jelly juice
                              had oozed, simmering,
                              scenting the house.

WILLIE   Remember our cellar?
                Hagan lives there now.

DR. MALLOY   How could I forget it?
                those earthen crocks
                where Granny's excellent
                liquor reeked of dandelion
                heads, snapped off milky stems
                by my friend here
                in vacant lots!

WILLIE   And the cat, sir,
                climbing the tree!

DR. MALLOY   Ah yes, I almost forgot,
                they called 'im an' called 'im.
                That cat in his catnip madness was
                wilder than wonderland -
                But tell me now, what else
                do you remember?

WILLIE   Walkin' on the rails
                teeterin' like acrobats,
                and on the fences of the yards!

DR. MALLOY   Or say, rustlin' hide-and-seek
                in Miss Braylorn's corn
                and bein' scolded home again,
                and warned!
WILLIE   . . . . Yes, sir.

DR. MALLOY   But then, in the softness of dusk
                when it fell -
WILLIE   . . . . we'd be kneelin'
                a' nights for prayer.
DR. MALLOY   . . . . Aye, an' for a
                change, bein' an angel there
                at your mother's knees -

WILLIE   Cause the Virgin's image
                was flickerin' in the
                vigil light!. . . . .
DR. MALLOY   . . . . *(Struck)*
                And all was holy and right -

                (A pause - then seriously.)

DR. MALLOY	Where does your dream go from there, Willie?
WILLIE	I don't know where it goes. That's when my dad went t' work on the fishin' boat.
DR. MALLOY	Macrae's schooner?
WILLIE	*(Nodding.)* It happened about then -

     (Amber light
grows gradually on the upper plat-
form as a distraught MARY SIMS
enters U.C.3, *closing the door after her -*
She stands against it.)

WILLIE	When I was rakin' some maple leaves in the fall. They was always scurryin' away in the wind - an' I kept worryin' about my dad.

     (During WILLIE*'s*
narrative MARY *goes upstairs. She*
slumps to the floor by the bedside
and buries her face in her arms.
YOUNG WILLIE *appears, coming up,* U.C.4.
He lets himself in by the invisible door.)

WILLIE	He'd never been away that long on his herring boat before, an' when I - I came in, my -

     *(*YOUNG WILLIE *sees her.)*

WILLIE	my Mom was on the floor -
YOUNG WILLIE	. . . . . . Mom? oh Mom!

     (He runs
upstairs and throws himself down
beside her, trying to comfort her.)

YOUNG WILLIE	Don't cry, Mom - . . . . don't cry!
MARY	Is there no one . . . . to spare us - In heaven, Lord?

Y. WILLIE   Don't cry, Mom -
               . . . . don't cry!
MARY   I'll try not, son -
Y. WILLIE   . . . . Don't cry -
MARY   I'm all right now,
               child - here,
               . . . . *(She sits on the bed.)*
               come up on my knee.
               . . . . *(Lifting him up.)*
               You're a big boy now
               for seven - listen to me -

Y. WILLIE   Where's Dad?

MARY   Your father's gone away now,
               so we must shift - the two of us
               somehow - as best we may.

Y. WILLIE   Gone where?

MARY   *(Aside)* How? how can I
               . . . . tell him?
Y. WILLIE   Gone where, Mom?
MARY   *(Sitting him
               on the side of the bed facing her,
               she removes his coat and scarf.)*

               You know the herring boats
               were dangerous, Willie?

Y. WILLIE   Yes, Mom.
MARY   . . . . Well Captain Macrae
               overloaded the ship in a big swell
               Willie -
               . . . . *(Aside.)* It's no worse
               . . . . than the truth.
YOUNG WILLIE   Mom?
MARY   . . . She rolled over and foundered -
               your father was drowned, son!

Y. WILLIE   Dad - drowned?
               . . . . *(Deliberately.)*
MARY   Yes son - drowned.

               *(A foghorn moans as they sit
               motionless for a moment. Then,*

DR. MALLOY

So you wept and were sad
and never heard no more
about your dad - well
he's gone, Willie. . . . .

WILLIE

He's not gone.
I don't know where he is -
he's not dead! . . . .

DR. MALLOY

Not dead! whatever
do you mean, son? . . . .

WILLIE

It was late one night.
I was lyin' awake
an' list'nin' t' the wind - . . . .

DR. MALLOY

To the wind? you mean
something you heard? . . . .

WILLIE

(Spoken during their entry.)

A soft step
stoppin' on the stair,
some whisperin' -
it was my Mom.
She came on tiptoe
with a shaded taper.
Then someone followed
in the shiftin' shadow,
an' the lit candlelight - . . . .
caught his face! . . . .

DR. MALLOY   Your father?

                              (WILLIE *nods.*)

DR. MALLOY   and you dared not breathe
                  for thought of the breathing
                  dead, or see, but shut your eyes
                  the tighter, when the ghost
                  began to talk -

NICHOLAS   (*In stage whispers so as
                          not to wake the boy.*)

                  Mary, he sleeps
                  like a skipper aboard ship.
                  Is he always so quiet
                  when he sleeps? . . . .

MARY   Like any old sailor. . . . .

NICHOLAS   Poor skipper Willie!
                  S'pose ya told 'im what I done?

MARY   I lied. I told him you were drowned
                  when the ship foundered.

NICHOLAS   You told him what? . . . .

MARY   Keep your voice down,
                  you'll wake him!
                  I couldn't tell him the truth -
                  how his father left those men
                  to save his own skin!
                  how he's drowning his
                  cowardice in drink. . . . .

NICHOLAS   Oh my God! . . . .

MARY   Does it really trouble you
                  that much? If you had a heart
                  you'd return for your son's sake.

NICHOLAS   Perhaps you're right, Mary,
                  haven't any heart left,
                  it's lost at sea - that night
                  finished me off. It would have
                  been better if I'd drowned.

MARY

Oh Nicholas, that's all past -
just try to remember what you're
doing to your son! - but come now,
quickly, before he wakes.

NICHOLAS

It's too late - to try.
Skipper Willie? goodnight
son - goodbye.
*(They move in the
candlelight quietly down the stairs
to exit* U.C.6 *while* DR. MALLOY *is saying.)*

DR. MALLOY

And the ghost was gone
with the light, creaking down
the stairs into night, ...
*(As bartender
BERT enters the tavern D.R.16 with SUE
and serves the lady . . .)*

DR. MALLOY

. . . . And you heard
the retreating steps dying
in the wind, ...
*(As the blue light in the
bar fades into amber,* NICHLAS *enters
U.R.8, and goes in . . .)*

DR. MALLOY

. . . . and once, alone
you cried your grief asleep!

*(*WILLIE*'s head has fallen against
DR. MALLOY*'s shoulder.)*

DR. MALLOY

I say - Willie?
why the lad's fast asleep!

*(*NICHOLAS *is served a double scotch.
He pulls out a tattered book
and is soon feverishly reading
and drinking.)*

SUE

You're weepin' in yer whisky,
Nick, what ya readin'?

NICHOLAS

Poem 'bout some
drowned sailors,
like the ones I knew -
wanna hear it?

BERT   Sounds like clammy 'Arry.
                        any other poor devil.
                        Read 'er out, Nick.

SUE   Come on Nick, read it out.

NICHOLAS   Called 'Threnody' - it begins
                        with a wreck that goes

(reading)   'Down to the deep reef
                        green-sea-where-'
                                            *(He breaks down.
                        As the chorus repeats the line, the
                        doors* U.C.1 *and* 2 *open slowly. The
                        hall's window flat is gone. An under-
                        water sea projection engulfs the sky.)*

TENORS   ⌈ Dówn to the déep reéf . . . . . seá, where . . . .
                │ . . . . . . to the déep . . . . green seá, ... únder . . .
                ⌊ . . . . the déep reéf green . . . . where únder . . .

TENORS   ⌈ the waves túmult, . . . breáking . . . . thúnder, ...
                │ . . . waves . . . . the breáking seá's . . . .
                ⌊ . . . . túmult, the . . . . seá's thúnder, ...

BARITONES   ⌈ périlous rócks . . snáre the . . . . shíp's hold . . .
                │ . . . . rócks ensnáre . . . unwáry . . . . . hold . . .
                ⌊ périlous . . . . the unwáry shíp's . . . .

Y. WILLIE   . *(tremulous)* . . . . Father!

BASSES   ⌈ dówn to the . . . . seámen long . . . .
                │ . . . . to the drówned . . . . long súnken . . . .
                ⌊ dówn . . . . . drówned seámen . . . . súnken . . . .

BASSES   ⌈ In their . . . . húlks . . . . . . shíp bells knéll, . .
                │ . . their hóllowed . . . . . where . . . . bells . . . .
                ⌊ In . . . . hóllowed húlks . . . . . . shíp . . . . knéll, . .

TENORS   ⌈ téll of the . . . . wrecks . . . . a wráck . . ruin-
                │ . . . of the shíp . . . . stréwn in a wráck of . . . . . .
                ⌊ téll . . . . wrecks stréwn . . . . of ruin-

Y. WILLIE   . *(fearfully)* . . . . Where are you?

TENORS   ⌈ Down . . . . banks pásture the . . . . . . flócks,
    | Down deép . . . . . . the seá . . . . . pásture . . . fínned . . . .
   ⌊ . . . . . . deép where . . . seá banks . . . . the . . . . . . flócks,

BARITONES ⌈ in a gréen fóg far . . . . únder where . . . dímness . . . .
    | . . . gréen . . . far fáthoms . . . . . where the . . . .
   ⌊ in a . . . . . fóg . . . fáthoms únder . . . . . . the dímness . . . .

BASSES   ⌈ dróps dárk and . . . . sífting . . . . . drífted, ...
    | dróps . . . . and abýsmal . . . . . . down . . . .
   ⌊ dróps dárk . . . abýsmal sífting down drífted, ...

TENORS   ⌈ to the efflúvial ríft, ... for his . . . . . wreáth - . . .
BARITONES | . . . . . efflúvial . . . as a rhýme . . . his búrial . . . .
   ⌊ to the . . . . ríft, . . a rhýme for . . . búrial wreáth - . . .

Y. WILLIE   . *(quavering)* . . . . It's me father -

NICHOLAS   Is that you, Willie?
               I'm down deep in the sea, son.
               I've drunk boy, deep of the brine -
               my eyes are filled with sand.
               Clawing I - I'm going down -
Y. WILLIE   . . . . .Father!
NICHOLAS   she's founderin' Willie, we're
               goin' down, down -

TENORS   ⌈ to the búrial . . . . of tíme's sílt . . . slíme. . . . .
BARITONES | . . . . . búrial moúnds . . . . sílt and . . . .
BASSES   ⌊ to the . . . . . moúnds of tíme's . . . and slíme. . . . .

Y. WILLIE   . . . . Come back! come back father - come back!

                    (NICHOLAS stumbles off like a blind
                    man, D.R.17. *BERT and* SUE *leave* D.R.16 *as*
                    the bar lights having faded into
                    blue, lapse into darkness. MARY
                    enters U.C.R.1, *finds* YOUNG WILLIE
                    sitting up in terror. She gathers
                    him up in his bed clothes, and
                    carries him out. The doors close
                    of their own accord - projections
                    fade as WILLIE, *asleep by the doctor*
                    repeats under his breath while
                    still asleep the cries of his younger
                    self.)
WILLIE   . . . . Come back - come back father -

MARY   *(Approaching off-stage* U.L.10.*)*
.........................Willie!
.. Where are you, Willie?
                          (Entering)
Oh, Doctor Malloy, you've
found him! I was so worried -
he ran ahead.

DR. MALLOY   He's asleep, Ma'am, dreams
of his father. He cried out -

MARY   It's one of them nightmares.
He hasn't been sleeping -

DR. MALLOY   He's living in a world,
Ma'am, belongs to old men
like me, in the past,
but a little boy?
You must tell your son
the truth, Mrs. Sims!

MARY   That's impossible! I -

DR. MALLOY   I'm sorry I - wait
he's waking - Well sir!
I'd say you bin dreamin' -

WILLIE   Yes, sir,
                   (Rubbing his eyes.)
I was sir.
DR. MALLOY   You were talkin' out.

WILLIE   It was a thinkin' dream, sir.

DR. MALLOY   A thinkin' dream?
MARY   ....And what were
you thinking about son?

WILLIE   Nothin' Mom, just thinking.

MARY   Come, tell your mother, Will -
WILLIE   ....Just
thinkin', Mom, how strange
the sea was -
MARY   ....Well think no more
upon it! ....

MARY   . . . . And thank you, Doctor,
for watching Willie.

DR. MALLOY   . . . . My pleasure.
Good night, Mrs. Sims -
             . . . . good night Willie.

WILLIE   G'night Doctor Malloy.

(As a foghorn sounds MARY SIMS *and*
WILLIE *exit* U.R.9. DR. MALLOY *stands for a
moment looking after them. He turns
and walks slowly toward the seawall.
The scrim begins to fall. Nocturnal
light has faded in on the porter's cell
and rakes the apron, without light
touching the scrim.* DOM JEROME *enters
in some bewilderment -* D.L.14.*)*

DOM JEROME   I must have slept longer
than I thought - and what
a strange dream! I do seem
to have known that doctor;
but where? and when? Could
this faint echo of the familiar
be the initial turning of a key?

*(Catching sight of the Doctor 'in the
dream', he impulsively runs down
his steps outside the scrim.)*

Is it you? Doctor Malloy?

DR. MALLOY   *(Stopping on the steps, he turns.)*

Who calls? yes? Oh, it's you,
Brother Jerome - I see you're
taking the air -
        *(As he comes down
the scrim lends him a ghostly
unreality, though his acting is
perfectly natural.)*

DOM JEROME   Yes, I thought I would step out,
though it's foggy tonight -

DR. MALLOY   Well, you know how it is with
us old doctors - out at all hours.

S'pose I'm the only doctor in
town still makes house calls

*(Approaching the scrim he enters
into a pool of light.)*

DOM JEROME   Do you really! The last
house call we had in cloister
was a good twenty years ago,
when Abbot Gilbert died.

DR. MALLOY   Makes me a prime
fossil eh? extinct species!
Well, this dinosaur's about
done for. Talk to myself about it,
Brother, over and over -

DOM JEROME   I take it there's something wrong,
something serious, Doctor?

DR. MALLOY   Early fall he did the exploratory -
Old Gillies was decent about it.
'It's most distressing, dear colleague,'
say he, so I shot back,
'for God's sake, Gillies, don't hedge!
I've seen your diagnostic.'
You know it's hard to keep a secret
from a doctor - so then he broke
down - 'It's a malignancy, John,
metastasized. You were riddled
with it -'
    So I asked him - 'how long?'

'Oh I'd say from six to eight
months at most,' says he,
'but one never knows.'

DOM JEROME   I'm sorry to hear that,
doctor, it's a hard blow -

*(A slight pause, then urgently
with strong curiosity.)*
    I wonder
if you could tell me one thing?

DR. MALLOY   What would like to know?

DOM JEROME	Was it old J.B.Gillies did the exploratory? He attended Abbot Gilbert, you know.
DR. MALLOY	Yes - old J.B. did it - best diagnostician in the city. May I ask you a favour? Though I'm not a believer, Brother, I want you to pray for me.
DOM JEROME	Yes - yes, of course I will.
DR. MALLOY	Old Grandmother Owen would know how to, but we dissimulate - we're adept at putting it off. At the old art of dying we're rank amateurs.
DOM JEROME	*(Sensing the strangeness of their encounter, he backs away.)*

I understand, and I will
pray for you -

| DR. MALLOY | Well, good night, Brother, and
thank you for your prayers. |

*(He steps back, bowing slightly,
and departs on the seawall* U.L.10.
A foghorn sounds.)

| DOM JEROME | It's impossible! How can it be?
Old J.B. he says, did an exploratory
three months ago? Yet I know
for a fact, after the Abbot's death -
old Gillies died - a year to the day!
twenty years ago - |

        (Returning to his cell.)
I must be going mad!
Could it be eternity invading
this temporal sphere? or the ghostly
illusion of a diseased mind?

Malloy must have died
years ago - so who is this

DOM JEROME I was speaking with? so considerate,
kind, asking my prayers?
         (Perturbed,
     he sinks wearily into his chair.)

Is it possible that memory
could come roaring back, a dangerous
presage of derangement?
a floodtide of the long forgotten?

     DOM JEROME*'s light grows dimmer when*
     BERT *enters the tavern* D.R.16. *Blue light*
     comes up as he opens the Bar. PADDY,
     BUB, DIEL *and* HARRY *drift in from* U.R.8.
     BERT *serves them. The scrim begins*
     to rise.)

DOM JEROME . . . . . . .Perhaps amnesia
was a grace of God - for I'm
beginning to be afraid -
       (A faint light
     remains, defining his presence,
     while amber light comes up on the
     right of the lower platform with
     the entrance of GRANNY OWEN, U.C.6.*)*

G. OWEN Doctor Malloy did not
look well tonight. When you
get to be as old as I am
you come to read behind
the eyes, sometimes -

*(off-*S.D.R.*)*
CHORUS 1 . . . . .ráge, ráge
G. OWEN the startled thoughts.
CHORUS 2 . . . . .a rágin' fíre!
CHORUS 1 . . . . .ráge, ráge
G. OWEN Tavern's so noisy,
CHORUS 2 . . . . .a rágin' wráckin'
     . . . . and a rágin' fíre!

G. OWEN begin to worry . . .
    about poor Molly
     . . . if only she were
      . . . out of there
    (The blue light has
    been growing amber
    as the combo crescendos.)

(*off*-S.D.R.)

SOLO   Thrów on the náptha
                           . . . . and the búrnin' ⌈tów!

CHORUS 3   . . . . ⌊tów!

SOLO   Thrów on the pítch
                           . . . . and the tínder ⌈só and

CHORUS 3   . . . . ⌊só and

CHORUS 1   . . . . ráge, ráge

DIEL   (*Seeing* MOLLY *appear* D.L.16, *and*
                           coming down stairs, trying to be unnoticed.)

                           Hey, it's bawdy, batty
                           . . . . Molly Green,

CHORUS 2   . . . . a rágin' ráge,

DIEL   Brawltown Harlot
                           . . . . turned Magdalene!

ALL   Ha há! ahá aa há!

CHORUS 4   . . . . . . a rágin' wráckin'
                           . . . . and a rágin'
                           . . . . róck! and
                           (MOLLY *retreats, dismayed,*
                                      to the convent steps.)

BUB   Hey Moll, gal,
                           . . . . give us a roll, eh?

SOLO   The óna gód we're
                           . . . . . . gónna knów is
                           . . . . ón'y the Nálucho -
                           . . . . dónosor's
                           . . . Bábylónian mólten
                           . . . . gólden gód!

CHORUS 1   . . . . ráge, ráge,
                           (MOLLY *darts across the*
                           street to the lower platform's
                           left side where she knocks
                           at the invisible door, and opens it.)

MOLLY   Granny, it's me,
                           . . . . . Molly - can I come in?

CHORUS 2   . . . . a rágin' ráge

G. OWEN   Of course - come
                           . . . . in, child!

CHORUS 1   . . . . ráge, ráge -
                           (*The light in the Bar*
                           shrinks to a dim amber and the chorus
                           breaks off as MOLLY *closes the door.*)

MOLLY   I had to get away, I can't
stand that place any longer.

G. OWEN   *(Rising to greet her.)*

Here, child, come sit down,
calm yourself,
            (She settles MOLLY
*on the bench beside her, as the
lights narrow into a pool on
the two of them.)*

G. OWEN   . . . . there now, that's
better - tell me all about it.

MOLLY   It's all the old story,
Granny, you've heard it
over and over - I just
can't go on that way.

G. OWEN   . . . . I know dear -

MOLLY   You heard what they were
shouting after me
when I came out! just you
ask them, tenement dwellers,
fish-wife gossips
on the quays.
            (In tearful outrage)

MOLLY   Ask any such!
mascara'd crooners
in shody cabarets, pushers,
poolroom slickers
idlers 'n' thieves -
            (Bitterly)

MOLLY   they'll tell you
all you want t' know
about bawdy Molly, your
brawl-town harlot - . . . .

G. OWEN   There, now, my dear,
let them laugh - you just
set your face in flint.

Your soul's a crucible,
Molly, burns out the slag
of these low taunts!

MOLLY   But even in church! . . . .

G. OWEN   I know. The cast
stone, the curling sneer of
contemptible pharisees!

But remember, dear,
it's your conscience's cost of
smeltering away the temporal
pangs for sin - you're still
determined, aren't you?

MOLLY   Oh yes, Granny!
ever since that trembling boy
knocked on my door, I've
kept it locked. You saw
that letter. He's coming tonight -
I'm so afraid!

G. OWEN   You must promise me,
Molly, on no account will you
give your consent to that -
do you promise?

MOLLY   Oh God help me, yes I do!

G. OWEN   And you've spoken
to Sister Jennifer? . . . .

MOLLY   Oh yes, she was so sweet.

G. OWEN   So it's all arranged? . . . .

MOLLY   Yes, Granny. . . . .

G. OWEN   Well then, God be praised!
there's nothing left to fear, child.

MOLLY   Except my horrible
dreams. . . . .
           (The pantomine of PADDY
           and BUB*'s intoxication has*
           progressed till they drift out of
           the Bar, supporting each other.)

MOLLY   They say it was seven
devils came out of Magdalene.

MOLLY   How many out of me?
                What if they return? with
                seven more? the last state
                will be worse -
PADDY   *(Pausing unsteadily*
                                 before the invisible door on
                                 the right.)
                                 . . . . Molly Green!

                                 (They circumnavigate the
                                 inhospitable household.)

G. OWEN   After confession, dear
                 your house will be swept
                 clean and guiltless.
BUB   *(Pausing*
                                 before the invisible window
                                 on the right.)
                                 . . . . We see you Molly!

                                 (DIEL *and* HARRY *stagger out of the*
                                 tavern pausing by the invisible
                                 door on the right.)

MOLLY   If I could stop my
                 ears and not hear -
DIEL   *(Trying the steps*
                                 he pounds on the door, sound U.C.
                                 off-stage.)
                                 . . . . Come on Moll,
                                 . . . . love us again, girl -
MOLLY   Oh God, Granny! . . . .

G. OWEN   It's only drunken sailors
                 dear, from the Tavern -
BUB   *(Pounding on*
                                 the invisible door on the left, sound
                                 U.C. *off-stage.)*
                                 . . . . D'ya hear a knockin'
                                 . . . . Molly Green?
                                 (Rapping.)
PADDY   . . . . 'pon yer door,
                                 . . . . Molly Girl?

                                 (As from a whoreless port, they
                                 heave off from the offending house.)

MOLLY

If I could brick up
the window, barricade the door,
build some defence against the
battery, the violence!

PADDY

     (Negotiating
with BUB *the stairs to the seawall*
with difficulty.)
. . . . By the devil!
. . . . the harlot's shy!

DIEL

(Following.)
. . . . but we'll abide awhile, girl,
. . . . till dead of night'll jar
. . . . the door aspell!

MOLLY

Hold me tight, Granny!

HARRY

     (Passing last
in his undersea shroud by the door
on the left.)
. . . . We'll be panting there,
. . . . all the hungry growlin'
. . . . pack of us from hell!

ALL

. . . Há ha há!

HARRY

. . . . Now what ya say, another day?

ALL

. . . . some other time.
(He follows the others
as they lurch down to the quay U.C.4.*)*

MOLLY

Oh, my Jesus! the dreams -
the sleepless nights! . . . .

G. OWEN

There now, my dear,
fear not, be calm - It's only
a bad dream -
   (A foghorn sounds
as GRANNY OWEN *leads* MOLLY *off* U.C.6,
while the amber light fades out,
and the Bar light grows dim blue.)

(HAGAN *appears from behind the*
cellar, U.R.8 *with* ELI RENAIRE *who*
impresses us by a certain sinister
elegance - both station themselves
watching.)
   (On the upper platform
the right door U.C.1 *opens, spilling*
bright light down the stairs.)

RENAIRE   See there? that thin wedge of white
                           light in the half closed doorway?
HAGAN   . . . . Aye!
                                (CALEB THORN *comes down the steps,*
                                stops at the bottom.)
RENAIRE   . . . . how the lanky
                           shadow there hesitates, to listen?

(*off*-S.U.C.)
MRS. THORN   Caleb dear?
HAGAN   . . . That's 'is stepmother -
                                    . . . . . . she had me forge firedogs
RENAIRE   . . . . Quiet!
MRS. THORN   Where are you going dear?
CALEB   . . . To the cathedral mother -
                                    . . . . I'll be back shortly.
HAGAN   . . . . The old lies -
                           (*In their eagerness to*
                           hear, they have been creeping
                           along the platform, their backs
                           to the invisible wall.)

MRS. THORN   Be sure you're warmly
                                    . . wrapped, dear - it's chilly out -
CALEB   . . . . Yes mother.
                           (*Irritably shutting the*
                           invisible door, he walks onto
                           the seawall, where he stands
                           staring out to sea.)

HAGAN   lies he had t' tell.
RENAIRE   . . I'm afraid he goes
                                    . . . . . . to the cathedral this time.

HAGAN   Ha! he need not
                                    . . . . ever reach it!
RENAIRE   (*Suddenly snarling.*)
                           Blackmonger you!
                                    . . . . I'm running this caper!
                                    . . . . He'll come around.
HAGAN   (*Backing off.*)
                                    . . . . Fer a surety -
                                    . . . . Aye, that he will.
                           (*As* MOLLY *comes out* U.C.6,
                           she leaves by the invisible door, crosses
                           quickly entering McCorkeran's D.R.16.)

RENAIRE   Ah now, there's a comely
        ...wench! Is that our harlot?

HAGAN   Aye, she's Molly Green,
        ...now known as 'The Magdalene'.

RENAIRE   *(As* CALEB *turns around.)*
        ....Wait! he's coming.
        ....Make yourself scarce.
        (They retreat,
        RENAIRE *into the alley* U.R.8, *and* HAGAN
        into his cellar, where he sits watching.)

CALEB   Are some souls given over
        ...to him for destruction?
        ..... but to confess! Dear God -
        .... how can I go through with it?

        (As the doors U.C.1 *and* 2 *open fully,*
        amber light on the upper platform
        fades in. Entering with her guest
        MRS. THORN *carries two demitasse.)*

MRS. THORN   .... Caleb always
        .... was a very delicate child.

        (Handing MRS. THOREAU *her coffee, they*
        sit on the bed, now a settee.)

CALEB   How could I tell her? when she
        wouldn't understand -

MRS. THORN   .... We worried about him
        ...... terribly, sleeping in those cold
        .... damp dormitories -

CALEB   I could have told my real mother,

MRS. THORN   .... Nor could we see
        ...... the need for all that regimented
        .... rigidity - ....

CALEB   only - if she hadn't -
        if it hadn't happened
        the way it did - ....

MRS. THOREAU   . . .For all your trials
                   . . . . . you've a fine boy now preparin'
                   . . . . for the priesthood.
CALEB   Preparing?

MRS. THOREAU   . . .He must be grateful
                   . . . . now, to his mother!

CALEB   Yes, born to the call,
                   but it all went wrong -

MRS. THORN   . . .I bent, you must
                   . . . . . know, every possible
                   . . . . influence, on his interest
                   . . . . to that end.
                   . . . . . Indeed, I
                   . . . . knew what he would be
                   . . . . before Nicholas drowned,

CALEB   Never lets me forget that
                   horror of Barclay Sound!

MRS. THORN   . . .and now at last
                   . . . . . it's bearing fruit!

                   *(The amber light dims so that the two
                   women become inaudible silhouettes.)*

CALEB   Reminds me of my
                   lost dreams - prods me
                   like a snarling beast
                   in a trap - snares me!
                   But no,
                   . . . . that's wrong -
                   I was never worthy of it, ever.
                   Why blame her,
                   poor woman - when father
                   came back
                   . . . . we were strangers.
                   He was away too long.
                   Not even stepmother
                   knows - how he
                   drowned,
                              *(After a moment's
                              hesitation.)*
                   . . . . the *second* time!

CALEB	Some even

CALEB

     . . . . say that he - no! not
that! blot it out! bury it -
forget it.

(Distant foghorns moan,
MRS. THORN *and* MRS. THOREAU *rise
and leave the sitting room. The doors*
U.C.1 *and* 2 *close after them. As the
lights fade out, those in Hearth Lodge
fade in.)*

CALEB

       Perhaps I should
call on Aunt Hanna - it's been
a while since I've seen her.
There's no one else now.

*(He knocks - sound off-*S.U.L. MRS.
HEARTH *enters* D.L.12, *crosses and opens
the invisible door. She looks*
CALEB *up and down.)*

HEARTH

Oh! Tommy Burns it is.
  . . I take it ye want t' see yer aunt.

CALEB

    . . . . If I may, please.

HEARTH

Step in, but mind
  . . ye wipe your feet.

CALEB

    . . . . Yes, ma'am.

HEARTH

(Top of her voice.)
    . . . . Hanna! ye've got
    . . . . a visitor -
(She exits D.L.12,
as AUNT HANNA *enters* D.L.13.*)*

HANNA

    . . . . Why Tommy!

CALEB

Hello, Aunt Hanna.

*(She kisses him, then holds
him back to look at him.)*

HANNA

Since yer dad disappeared
an' yer livin' wi' that stepmother a' yers
we see nay hide nor hair a' ya -
how are ye, lad?

CALEB

Oh, I'm fine, Auntie Hanna.

HANNA   What's this I hear she's remarried?
             an' a banker too!

CALEB   Yes - Jamison wants
             to name me in his will.

HANNA   Ah - there'll be an inheritance, Tom!

CALEB   They made me change my name
             a year and a half ago - you'd
             think there was something wrong
             with Tom Burns.

HANNA   Or Regis Wicks or Willie Sims
             you used to pretend to be?
             But what's the name?

CALEB   Those may have been dreams
             but they're closer to me than Caleb -
             that's Jamison's father. They've
             insisted on calling me Caleb Thorn.
             I'm beginning to wonder
             who I really am.

HANNA   Well ye better go along with 'em, lad,
             or you'll end a penniless orphan
             the rest of yer days.

             *(The blue light in the Bar fades to
             dim amber as* BERT *puts out a small
             table and two stools - then he wipes
             glasses.)*

CALEB   I've got to hurry along, Hanna,
             I'm going to church tonight.

HANNA   Ah, that's a good lad -
             I'll be goin' m'self a little later.
             Thanks fer stoppin' in Tom.

CALEB   Good night Auntie Hanna.

             *(Comng out, he stands watching
             in the street. As* HANNA *leaves* D.L.13,
             the Lodge lights fade out while

*those in the Bar expand and grow
brighter as people drift in -* HAL
and KATY *from* U.R.8, SANDY *and* SUE
from the seawall U.L.10, JAKE *from*
D.R.17. HAGAN, *seeing* CALEB, *disappears
through the door* U.C.7.*)*

CALEB You remember the night?
you tried to escape the vortex
of boredom that was spun
of a Saturday afternoon?

*(Hesitantly, he moves out toward
the bench, as* HAGAN *emerges* U.C.3
*on the seawall. As the spell of
reminiscence draws him back
to that fatal evening* CALEB *lives
it all over again. He sits on the
bench, listening.)*

*(off-*S.D.R.*)*
CHORUS 4 Jázz-rash Jámshyd
. . . . inebríate deép dránk
CHORUS 2 . *(fade under)* . . . . . dránk deep inébriate

CALEB Bearing fruit, she said?
CHORUS 1 . . . . neát deep inébriate
. . . . inébriate neát deép
CALEB I'll say it did,
. . . . in Stew's Tavern,
. . . . off Campus Street,
CHORUS 2 Jámshyd he
. . . . deép dránk inébriate
CALEB . . . . where you went
. . . . remember?
CHORUS 1 . . . . neát inébriate
CALEB to down the glooms
. . . . with a couple of drinks
. . . . and new tunes.
CHORUS 2 *(crescendo)*
. . . . as ránkle dránk
CHORUS 4 Jázz-rash Jámshyd he
. . . . deép dránk
. . . . inébriate
Jázz-rash! Jámshyd
. . . . dránk deép
. . . . Já-aaa-azzrásh!

115

(CALEB *has risen with the crescendo and
enticed by the party hovers midstage
undecided. Meanwhile, unnoticed,*
HAGAN *stalks his prey at a distance.
Shrugging off hesitation,* CALEB *skirts
the dancers upstage and works his way
down to the Bar.*)

SOLO   Thrów on Sídrach,
         . . . . ólden Mísach
         . . . . the ólden Abednégo
         of the lóng ago
         . . . . óld embóldenin'
         . . . . Hébrew Gód!

CHORUS 2   Bámboom bímbam!
CHORUS 1   . . . . rimadímrim
HAL   *(In his gyrations)* -
         . . . . Why crackle
         my joints - look who
         . . . . blew in!

KATY-SUE   . . . . Caleb! - Hello, dearie -
CHORUS 2   Bímbam
CHORUS 1   . . . . bámbim rímadim
CHORUS 4   . . . . bímbám boóm!

JAKE   *(Drunkenly convivial)*

JAKE   Cóme on . . . . Cábe, joín the . . . . gáng!
CHORUS 3   . . . . Bámadim . . . . the bímbam . . . . .

JAKE   We're hávin' a . . . . whále of a . . . rippin' . .
CHORUS 3   . . . . a rímadin . . . . a rímrippin' . .

JAKE   Jám boozin' Ráttle
CHORUS 2   Jám boozin' - . . . . dam Bám
CHORUS 4   . . . . Ráttle dam
         . . . . Bámboóm bám!
JAKE   Damn good time!
         . . . . *(Dragging* CALEB *to the bar.*)
ALL   Há ha! ahá ha há!
CHORUS 1   . . . . It's a ráge, ráge,
CHORUS 2   . . . . a rágin' fíre!
JAKE   Toss up a beer, Bert,
         . . . . come on, Cabe!
CHORUS 1   . . . . ráge, ráge,

CALEB   *(Irritably.)*
        . . . . Don't jolly me Jake!
I'm in no mood now -
CHORUS 2   . . . . it's a rágin'
*(off-*S.D.R.*)*   . . . . wréck and a
JAKE   Héy now . . . . tálk about . . . .
CHORUS 2   . . . . róck . . . .
CHORUS 3   . . . . bím bam . . . .

JAKE   your deád . . freéze . . . .
CHORUS 3   . . . . rag . . . . . and a rágin' fíre!
CHORUS 1   . . . . deád . . freéze . . . .
CHORUS 2   . . . . and a rágin' fíre!

         *(*HAGAN *enters up stage, and stands watching.*
         Dance becomes perfunctory as remarks
         focus on CALEB. *Feigning indifference,*
         he drifts downstage with drink in hand,
         sits at the table, his back to the revellers.)

SANDY   What gives with Cabe?
CHORUS 1   . . . . it's a rágin' ráge
JAKE   Oh, he's got the glooms
         again - the usual.
CHORUS 2   . . . . and a rágin' wráckin'
CHORUS 4   . . . . and a rágin' róck!
CHORUS 1   . . . . and ráge
HAGAN   *(Accosting* HAL *and* KATY.*)*
         . . . . That's your Theologue,
         . . . . . . ya say?
HAL   That's him.
CHORUS 1   . . . . ráge, ráge, it's a
CHORUS 2   . . . . it's a rágin' ráge
KATY   *(For* CALEB*'s benfit.)*
         . . . . We oughta call 'im
         . . . . little lovelorn Thorn!
CHORUS 1   . . . . it's a rágin' ráge
SUE   *(Purposely loud.)*
He just needs t' get
         . . good 'n' stoned, that's all!
CHORUS 2   . . . . and a rágin' fíre!

         *(*SANDY *pointedly picks up the theme*
         while the others, dancing forgotten,
         eagerly gather for the baiting.

(CALEB*'s face becomes a battlefield
of brooding injury and smouldering
anger. His attempts to appear
indifferent are pitiful.)*

SANDY	What a life for the likes
	of a nice guy like Cabe -
CHORUS 4	. . . . a Bámbim
SANDY	nó games, nó chance
CHORUS 2	. . . . a bímbam
SANDY	nó dice, nó dance and -
CHORUS 3	. . . . a rímadima
	. . . . . . dímbam
SANDY	nó dámes!
ALL	. . . . . . Ha há ha há ahá ha há!
CHORUS 4	básh wráckin'
	. . . . and a rágin' róck!
CHORUS 1	. . . . and ráge, ráge -
CALEB	*(Suddenly lashing out)*
	All right, you fellows -
	. . . . lay off me, will you?
SANDY	*(Mocking deference.)*
	Oh sure, Cabe.
CHORUS 1	. . . . a rágin' ráge -
SANDY	Hey Bert, nickel
	. . . . . Blue Mona next, will ya?

(Behind CALEB *dancing resumes,
becoming progressively, for his
benefit, all the more outlandish.)*

CHORUS 2	. . . . . . a rágin' wráckin' and a
SOLO	Thrów on the náphtha
	. . . . and the búrnin' ⌈tów!
CHORUS 4	. . . . ⌊tów!
SOLO	Thrów on the pítch
	. . . . and the tínder ⌈só and
CHORUS 4	. . . . ⌊só and
CHORUS 1	. . . . ráge, ráge -
HAGAN	*(Sidling in for the siege.)*
	You fellows oughta
	. . . . cheer 'im up.
CHORUS 1	. . . . ráge, ráge -

JAKE Ya, we oughta

CHORUS 2 .... a rágin' fire! .... ráge -

JAKE .... poor devil ....

HAGAN Now that I've
...mentioned it, whatta ya
.... think of this?

CHORUS 1 .... a rágin' ráge -
(HAGAN *whispers his
proposal to* JAKE *who passes it on
to others - it spreads like wild fire,
all dancing instantly stops. When
someone laughs, they all begin
to chime in -*)

ALL Há ha!..... ahóho! ... há ... hoó!
...hí hihi... hi híha...ho!
.... hahá!...hoó!

CHORUS 2 .... a rag rágin' fíre!

JAKE Molly'll do?
.... oh boy that's rich!

CHORUS 1 .... ráge, ráge -

HAGAN *(Egging them on.)*
Well ya kin dare 'im
.... but I doubts
.... his itch!

ALL Há ha! háha ahá ha há!

CHORUS 2 .... a rándy stítchin'
.... in pítch

HAGAN Pretty cold fish!

ALL ....Ha há! ahá ha há há!

CHORUS 3 .... stítchin' in pítch

SANDY Hey Cabe!
(Grinning lewdly)

CHORUS 3 .... stítchin' in pítch

SANDY ....Come 'ere

CHORUS 3 .... stítchin' in pítch

(CALEB *looks, sees the leer and turns
abruptly away.* SANDY *circles the
table left to right - his sinuous
movement and elaborate pantomime
of seduction as he draws up the stool
and sits, facing* CALEB. *Leaning forward
close by his ear, and playing to the
crowd, he hisses the dare.* ....

CHORUS 4   and a wráckin' wréckin'
            . . . . and a rágin'
            . . . . róck! and
SOLO   The óna gód we're
            . . . . gónna knów
            . . . . is ón'y the Nábucho -
            . . . . dónosor's
            . . . . . . Bábylónian mólten
            . . . . gólden gód!

            (CALEB stiffens at the proposal,
            when SANDY rasps aloud -)

SANDY   So it figures - ya gotta
            . . . . prove yer a man!
CHORUS 4   . . . . Bám-a-dam!
            (They all crowd around
            in a mounting crescendo of mockery.)

HAL   Lookit lady lavender
JAKE   . . . . clench 'er fists!
CHORUS 4   . . . . Rák-a-dam!
HAL   Lookit 'im grow red
JAKE   . . . . cheap dud of a coward!
CHORUS 2   . . . . rímadim bím bam!

SANDY   Well, Cabe? whatsa matter?
HAGAN   . . . . What dya say, theologue?
CHORUS 4   . . . . bám bim rímadim -
HAGAN   Fling it back at 'em
            . . . their dare into their teeth!
CHORUS 3   . . . . bím bam!
KATY   Mother's little coddler
SUE   . . . . Poor little pip-squeak
CHORUS 3   . . . . dím bam!
CHORUS 2   . . . . bám bim
SANDY   Swear like a man if ya be one!
HAGAN   . . . Fling the proof back if ya can!
CHORUS 2   . . . . ríma dim -
CHORUS 4   . . . . bím bam!
ALL   Há ha! ha há ahá há!
HAGAN   (Lunging with savage derision,

120

	his barbed shaft goes home.)
HAGAN	If ya dare!
	. . . . . . Bím! Bám! Básh!

| CALEB | *(In a paroxysm of rage, his control snaps. He jumps up, his words come tumbling out, his voice breaks, but he ends defiantly.)* |

CALEB	. . . . You - you devils
	. . . . dare me then, do you?
	All right then I - I'll show you -
	I'll do it!
CHORUS 4	. . Tlángorásh!
	. . . . Já aa aa aa aa azz -
ALL	. . . . Há ha há háa ahá!
CHORUS 4	. . . . Rásh!

(Suddenly silence. Nobody moves; eyes devour his horrified face. He backs away from them, feels for the staircase. As he goes up, he cannot tear his eyes from his tormentors; they remain motionless staring at him. With the solo, the lights fade blue.)

SOLO	Oh smóke-eyed yóu
	. . . . Blue Móna
	. . . . the óna óne I'm
	. . . . gó-nná-lóve.

(CALEB disappears upstairs D.R.16. The scrim begins to fall slowly while the revellers drift away U.R.8, but BERT stays. The Bar's blue light fades, as silvery light comes upon DOM JEROME in his cell and on the apron as he paces.)

| DOM JEROME | Tragic youth - somehow our paths have crossed - somewhere. But where? His conscience remembering is painfully searching, for he wants to confess. He must live through it all, all over again - retrace his steps. |

DOM JEROME And if ever I'm to retrieve
that lost key to the past, I too
must retrace my steps, try
to remember the people I have seen,
the voices I have heard - where they
came from - where they go.

Lonely Tom, adolescent in his struggle,
tormented by tempters, haunted
by the memory of his mother, poor Rose,
of his drunken father, dazed - and lost.

DOM JEROME Is Regis only an imagined innocence
that is gone, or a pius childhood
dreamed? Or could it be, he's a strong
little boy with a mind of his own?

who worships the magisterial mechanic
who is Dad? Why does he fear
young Willie, poor boy from the other
side of the tracks? because his father

DOM JEROME is a failure, perhaps? disappears?
comes back as a ghost, yet alive,
to be lost again out at sea?
Mary Sims, Mother Wicks, who are these?

Rose Burns? these mothers of mysterious
progeny?
   (A dim blue light comes up as
  HAGAN *enters the cellar* U.C.7, *where*
  he checks the furnace and sits down
  to watch.)

DOM JEROME . . . . Are Jock Burns and Job
Wicks the same? and who pray tell,
is Nicholas Sims?
    (Bluish light fades in
  on the Tavern, as CALEB *crosses from*
  U.R.8, *receives coffee and sits gloomily*
  at the table.)

DOM JEROME . . . . And Caleb?
who claims to be the son of all three,
who is he?
    (RENAIRE *enters on the seawall* U.L.10,
  and disappears down the steps U.C.4

In bewilderment, DOM JEROME *returns to his cell where he sits pensively, opening a book, while the scrim rises.)*

DOM JEROME

Questions beleaguer me -
like hornets out of honey.
Taste, and you will see.
                    *(The silver
light grows dim on* DOM JEROME, *while
gathering itself sharply on* CALEB.
*Red light from the furnace, plays
on* HAGAN.*)*

HAGAN

. . . . Fer three nights now 'e
creeps over there - scene-a-the-crime.
Wonders how the devil 'e fell!
huddled over black steaming
coffee, coffined in 'is thoughts.

*(*RENAIRE *reappears,* U.R.8, *crosses and
enters the bar.)*

HAGAN

Your play, Eli - go fer 'im old
Blacktalon soul-slayer!

*(The blue light fades from the cellar
while* RENAIRE *stands observing* CALEB
*for a moment. Then he addresses him
with the utmost urbanity.)*

RENAIRE

You'll pardon me if I'm
intruding - do you mind
if I join you?

CALEB

No, of course not,
why should I mind?

RENAIRE

I'm Professor Renaire,
Eli Renaire - medievalist.
You're a student, I presume?

CALEB

You could say that, though
God knows why -
                    (Embarrassed, he rises.)
but forgive me, I'm
Caleb Thorn. Won't you sit down?

123

(*As they sit,* RENAIRE *offers cigarettes
which are declined, then lights
one for himself, while scrutinizing*
CALEB *with an appraising eye.*)

RENAIRE

You're a bit under the weather,
I take it?

CALEB

    . . . . . You'd be under the weather, too,
. . . . if you were in my shoes -

RENAIRE

(dryly)
        Why, what's wrong?
your favourite girl friend jilt you?

CALEB

Not likely. I haven't any 'favourite
girl friends.'

RENAIRE

. . . . Oh - unusual I'd say,
for a young fellow your age.

CALEB

Do you really think so? well -
. . . . you may be right.

(RENAIRE *draws deeply
on his cigarette, he holds his smoke
thoughtfully, as if weighing the
younger.*)

RENAIRE

. . . . You appear to be a very
unhappy young man, am I right?
perhaps talking about it
might help?

CALEB

. . . . Maybe. It's my own private
affair. It's hard to talk about things
when you've made a fool of yourself.

RENAIRE

(with casual jocularity.)
. . . . We've all had our
little affairs - what's wrong, you
patronized the establishment upstairs?

CALEB

(Caught off guard.)
. . . . Who told you that?
I mean - how did you find out?

RENAIRE

Oh, just a shot in the dark
I assure you!

(Stubbing out his cigarette with
careful amusement.)

RENAIRE

Whatever you've done is no concern
of mine, but I am curious
why it troubles you so.

CALEB

(Earnestly.)
. . . . Well, it's because
I'm studying theology, you see -

RENAIRE

Extraordinary! we're at opposite
ends of the spectrum - your field
theology, my field demonology!

(Sensing shock, he's instantly
reassuring.)
. . . . There's no need to be
alarmed - I'm speaking academically.

CALEB

(Blurting out his tortured thoughts.)

You don't think, do you,
that demons might force a man
into evil, against his will?

RENAIRE

(Reasonably.)
. . . . Why force? the serpent
is subtle enough, one would suppose,
to persuade with suggestion,
enticement - don't you think?

CALEB

(Suddenly withdrawn.)
. . . . That's right -
our dark desiring blood conspires,
he needs only to arouse it.

RENAIRE

But your studies, do they not
divert or distract you?

CALEB

(Agitated.)
My books are dry,
unpalatable, arcane; so that even
at lectures my focused attention
dissembles. Under the Rector's
probing gaze, I -

125

RENAIRE   *(Finishing for him the hard truth.)*

You find yourself wearing
your own face so open, innocent,
like a mask - the perfect lie!

CALEB   If you say so - but it's
probably true.

RENAIRE   I'm sure the father of lies
has a measure of sympathy
for the likes of you.

CALEB   *(Despairingly.)*
. . . . Yes. I suppose
he has - he knows his own.

                              *(In a hoarse whisper,
                     his voice edged with hysteria and
                     horror.)*
                     . . . . I feared the severity of
the confessors, their commands.

I dared not broach my sin
under even the absolving hands.
It was sacrilege! Stepmother's
wishes were whips scourged me to it!

RENAIRE   *(Hard, menacing.)*
                     . . . . Don't blame her,
or anyone else - you've made your
choice. It's over and done with.
There's no going back on it!

CALEB   *(Unheeding and distant.)*
                     . . . . I'm afraid
my faith is comatose, like a child
long kept in a sick bed,
but no longer alive -

RENAIRE   *(Standing, he rouses* CALEB.*)*

Come, we'll walk down
to the docks - perhaps some air,
a little traffic of curious
talk may divert us.

(RENAIRE *pays* BERT *who takes away the coffee cup and a stool.* CALEB *stands.*)

CALEB
Yes, that would be good -
some sea air. You could tell me
about your studies - this
demonology.

(BERT *removes the
other stool and the table behind
the Bar, wipes the counter - it's
time to close. Oblivious to his
importunities, they still stand
in the pool of light.*)

RENAIRE
You haven't heard of the Kurd
Yezidis of Iblis?

(*As they leave,*
BERT *exits* D.R.17. *The light fades.*)

CALEB
Not that I recall -

RENAIRE
. . . . Well, they're
beyond the two seas called
Caspian and Black, an ancient
people - let's go by the alley,
it's shorter - they've retained
what must be the most
remarkable . . . .

(*His voice fades as
they disappear in the alley* U.R.8.
*Suddenly, the furnace door
opens with a clang, revealing*
HAGAN *in a fiery light. He has
split wood in his arms.*)

HAGAN
Tell 'im, Eli, how the gods
of Canaan cower an' smile,
how old Solomon, Astaroth
beguiled, hauls fuel t' Gehenna,
Haha ha aha!

(*Throwing in wood.*)
How he steams
with a stench of incence, his
female demons, too old, wise and deaf
to hear in a gum-burning Moloch of
bronze - his children, screaming!
Haha ha aha!

127

*(Throwing in the rest of the wood,
he slams the door shut, disappearing
in the dark* U.C.7. *The ghost of a dog
howls to the moon in the distance.
Meanwhile* RENAIRE *and* CALEB *come up
from below,* U.C.4, *to stand under
the streetlight.)*

RENAIRE   . . . and so, being held high -
'elevated', Satannael's grail wine
was flung to the flagstones
from a cup full of curses!

CALEB   *(Shuddering.)*
a most horrible, sacrilegious -

RENAIRE   . . . . Is it so? you -
perchance have already
             . . . . flung it!

CALEB   *(Visibly shaken.)*
            . . . . No! I've - I've never -

RENAIRE   *(Holding him with
glittering eyes, the voice, silky, sinister.)*

But you will, my lad, oh yes,
you will. This wine-stain of guilt
spreads residual in the traits
of the mind -

CALEB   . . . . Renaire - go away,
I'm afraid to hear any more
of this now!

RENAIRE   . . . . Of course, another time.
          (All suavity.)
            . . . . I might tell you even
stranger things - at a suitable
hour -
   . . like the withering sick witchery
of Saint Secair, or say when storms
are breaking ships - the Norman
mass of the hallowed ghost, but
another time -
           . . . . Good night Caleb Thorn.
          *(A slight bow,
and he walks away in the mist
on the seawall,* U.L.10.*)*

CALEB   *(Pondering.)*
A wine stain's - residual guilt?

(*Meanwhile dim light reveals* MOLLY
*standing by the invisible window that
faces the seawall. She sees* CALEB *enter
his house* U.C.3. *Turning she goes to
the other window, facing the convent
porch. As she does early light fades in.*)

MOLLY
Not only does he remember,
he must - but I remember too
waiting at this window
and wondering -
(*She opens the window.*)
Perhaps she'll come -
onto the porch. She does
on many mornings.
(MRS. HEARTH *enters*
D.L.12, *comes down to her invisible
window where she spies* MOLLY.
Raising the sash, AMY *stands aside
where she can listen undetected.*)

MOLLY
She has a kind face - perhaps
she'll listen. Someone will -

(SR. JENNIFER *appears with a small
carpet. Opening the left hand
gate she comes out on the porch.*
MOLLY *draws back out ot sight.*)

SR. JENNIFER
There now! Oh, I love
the fresh morning air! It's
so clean and good -
(*She vigorously
shakes out the carpet, while* MOLLY,
still out ot sight, raises her voice.)

MOLLY
. . . . Sister!

SR. JENNIFER
Did someone call?
. . . . - is someone there?

(MOLLY *shows herself timidly, as if
ashamed to be seen in daylight.*)

MOLLY
Sister, it's me, Molly Green.
They call me the Brawltown
Harlot - please!

SR. JENNIFER   *(Awkwardly, but not wanting to be
                      unkind.)*

                      Oh - why, hello, Molly -
                      We're not supposed to talk
                      to anyone in the tavern,

MOLLY   I know, but I need
                      help, Sister.
SR. JENNIFER   . . . . .Mother would be
                      very displeased.
MOLLY   *(Urgently.)*
                      Please, Sister!
SR. JENNIFER   *(Relenting.)*
                      Well - if it's only
                      a few moments.

MOLLY   It's about a seminarist
                      who came to me.
SR. JENNIFER   *(Taken aback.)*
                      Oh, Miss Green -
MOLLY   . . . . .He kept loitering
                      about this den of ours, where the old
                      sorcery makes swine of men.

                      You have no idea, Sister -
                      all sweating hands in their
                      grovelling lechery -
SR. JENNIFER   *(Her carpet drops.)*
MOLLY   Oh - how I loath them!
SR. JENNIFER   *(Turning to go.)*
                      Why - how horrible! I -
                      really I must go now.
MOLLY   . . . . No Sister, listen!
                      *(The desperation in the
                      girl's voice holds the nun.)*

                      He was the first repulsed,
                      shrank from me, averted
                      his face -
                      . . . . . and he was muttering
                      all the time, 'He who looks
                      on a woman
                      . . . . to lust after
                      her has committed, already
                      in his heart' -

MOLLY   *(Quavering perilously,*
                          her voice breaks. She begins to cry.)

                          Oh, I'm so ashamed!
                                            (MRS. HEARTH *having*
                          heard enough, runs upstairs.)

SR. JENNIFER   *(Moved and sympathetic.)*

                          There now, poor child,
                          don't cry. God is good.
                          he loves you, Molly.

MOLLY   How could He love me?
                          the worst sinner ever lived -

SR. JENNIFER   He loves everyone, no matter how
                          terrible the things they've done.

MOLLY   *(Pulling herself together.)*

                          Do you thinks so?
                          then you *must* listen!
                          I asked him, 'why did you
                          come here?'
                          . . . . and he said,
                          'They dared me - I did not mean
                          to deny him - didn't mean
                          to betray him!'
                          . . . . 'But we've done
                          no wrong,' I said, 'we've only
                          talked!' 'Yes, he said, but it's
                          written about a certain
                          betrayer- . . .
                                            (Awed, in a small voice.)
                          It were better
                          he had never been born!'
                                                 (Urgently.)
                          Oh Sister - what can I do?
                          he may do himself
                          some harm!
SR. JENNIFER   *(Gently.)*
                          Just pray for him,
                          Molly, and for yourself too -
                          for the Brawltown Harlot
                          turned Magdalene -

(CALEB *comes out* U.C.3 *catching a glimpse
of* SR. JENNIFER *and of* MOLLY *at the window.*)

SR. SUPERIOR

(*Off-stage* D.R.)
Sister Jennifer?

SR. JENNIFER

(*Snatching up the carpet.*)
Yes, mother, I'm
coming - remember, Molly - pray!

(*Going in* D.R.18, *she closes the gate.*)

MOLLY

(*Savouring a new hope.*)
Yes! oh, yes!
the Brawltown Harlot
turned Magdalene -
(*Reminiscent.*)
All this I do remember.
(*She closes
the window and leaves* D.R.15.)

CALEB

And I too remember the folly
of that afternoon. It measures
the weight of my guilt.
(*The daylight
has declined swiftly as in winter
toward sundown.*)
(MRS. HEARTH
appears D.L.12, *and descends putting
on her hat. A glance at the tavern
confirms her suspicions.*)

MRS. HEARTH

Well! the things
an innocent body hears!

(*At the door she spies* CALEB *on the
seawall and primes herself for
an encounter, then hurries
up the steps to accost him.*)

MRS. HEARTH

Why, young master Thorn!
I heard somethin' this mornin'
but I really couldn't repeat it -

(*A significant pause, with her
confidential hand on his arm,
and then -*)

CALEB
(aside)

Though she couldn't -
she did - and I burned
enraged in my own quiet hell -

MRS. HEARTH

But of course,
one doesn't believe
a word of it - does one?

>   (CALEB *stares*
> *at her. She bustles off* U.L.10.
> *Hearing voices from Campus*
> *Street, he steps back out of sight.)*

WAGUARD

>   (*Off-stage* U.R.9.)

No, you don't mean it?

BRAYLORN

. . . . But I do,
I saw her plainly!

WAGUARD

>   (*As they appear.*)

Surely, not in church,
my dear?

CARP

. . . . . Before the altar
of the Virgin - I saw her myself.

> *(They gather in a tight group by the*
> *right hand steps.)*

WAGUARD

You don't say so -

CARP

. . . . and what's more,
lighting a candle, please you -

WAGUARD

The hussy!

CARP

. . . . and genuflectin', before
the high altar -

BRAYLORN

. . . . and not ashamed!

WAGUARD

Didn't that old priest there
know her name?

CARP

>   (*As she knocks.*)

Don't look now,
but I think she's comin' -

> *(Meanwhile,* MILLIE *has entered* U.C.6
> *with a tall backed chair. This she*
> *places, as amber light fades in.*
> *At the knock she opens to the*
> *ladies.)*

MILLIE   My dears, you're just in time!
I've waited so long -

> *(As* MOLLY *comes
> in sight, all turn their heads in
> unison to stare after her as she walks
> quickly past into McCorkeran's* D.R.16.*)*

MILLIE   Oh, the saint! ... Come along -

> *(All enter
> to a conversational murmur as
> MILLIE runs upstairs and knocks on
> the door* U.C.1. RENAIRE *comes out, and
> a hush falls as he is led down.)*

MILLIE   Ladies, the Professor has consented
to continue his account of the most
remarkable experiences of his life -

> *(General applause and excited
> murmur. At that moment* CALEB
> *knocks on the left side invisible door.)*

MILLIE   Excuse me for a minute -

> *(Opening to him.)*

Ah, Caleb Thorn! Professor
Renaire was expecting you;
won't you come in?

> *(*MILLIE *delays their
> entrance, lest the narrative be
> interrupted. They stand a little
> aside, listening.)*

RENAIRE   As I hinted in our last
conversation about a certain
shipwright, you remember?
in the naval docks in Brest?

BRAYLORN   Your father, wasn't it?

RENAIRE   Yes, my sombre papá, how he
never once talked or laughed
with me again, as I recounted,
after my mother's death.

WAGUARD   But how sad -
BRAYLORN   .... how truly tragic!

RENAIRE   So at seven I was sent
                 to grandpapá where he
                 manned the lighthouse
                 on the Atlantic Finisterre.
                 My childhood there was
                 lonely and even strange.

CARP   In what way?
RENAIRE   . . . . I was what one
                 might call a model - arsonist.
                 My instinct for destruction
                 developed early.
BRAYLORN   . . . . .Really! and -
                 What did you burn?
RENAIRE   . . . . In my gandfather's
                 stone basement, I set whole towns
                 and villages afire,
WAGUARD   . . . . You don't say!
RENAIRE   that I had cunningly
                 made of cardboard and matchboxes
                 so they burned like the very
                 world-pyre on doomsday!

CARP   I do declare, unusual -
BRAYLORN   . . . . and then?
RENAIRE   My uncle at Saint Owen,
                 Canon Duschene, fetched me
                 to study - petite seminaire,
                 Saint Gabriel, Rue du Bec.
                 I was a good student.

BRAYLORN   But of course -
                                 *(Beginning to suspect
                         the mother lode.)*
BRAYLORN   . . . . where you then?
RENAIRE   Baccalaureated; later
                 in grim old Saint Sulpice, with it's
                 spartan fare and mouldy walls.
                 Studied the perennial philosophy,
                 theology, and at the end of it all,
                 a doctoral thesis, Demonology
                 in the Heresiarchs. It was
                 orthodox enough.
WAGUARD   *(Attempting to pry out
                         the vital statistics.)*
                         . . . . So then you-

| BRAYLORN | you must have been? |
| RENAIRE | *(Adroitly discreet.)* |

Yes. A chaplaincy at
Saint Brieuc with time enough
to write my three black books.

| MILLIE | *(Stepping forward as* CALEB *crosses* |
| | *to* RENAIRE.*)* |

. . . . Professor? your guest.

| RENAIRE | Ah, Mr. Thorn, |

I was expecting you.

(They shake hands.)

If you'll excuse me. ladies -

| MILLIE | Perhaps we could arrange |

another séance? Your last
was simply intriguing!

| RENAIRE | But of course, Madam, if our |

fee does not impede, I should
be happy to oblige.

*(*CALEB *and* RENAIRE *withdraw
by the left invisible entrance.)*

WAGUARD	Well! what can one say?
BRAYLORN	. . . . . I'd never have guessed
CARP	. . . . Unbelievable!

| MILLIE | *(Carrying the chair as if it* |
| | *were a relic.)* |

. . . . Come along, girls!

*(Aglow with the revelation, as the
amber lights fade, they all exit* U.C.6.
*Outside the last light of sunset
is touching the housetops. Darkness
falls steadily during the following
conversation.)*

| CALEB | . . . . So it seems |

you were ordained?

| RENAIRE | . . . . Of course - |

why do you ask?

| CALEB | . . . . Just curious. |

*(Silence divides
them as they walk down to the bench.)*

CALEB   *(Then tentatively -)*
          . . . . You were dispensed,
I take it?

RENAIRE   *(With amused incredulity.)*
Of course not -
an apostate is not dispensed.

CALEB   *(Apologetic.)*
But I thought - I mean -

RENAIRE   *(Bitterly.)*
You can say whatever
you think - the medieval phrases -
degraded, defrocked, pariah
of the pius.
          . . . . Yes, metaphorically
my hands were scraped
by Bishop d'Hervé!

CALEB   *(Shocked.)*
And you feel no shame?
No twinge of regret?

RENAIRE   *(Flippantly.)*
Not yet, why should I?
The Gardener's to blame.
No good tree bears bad apples;
evil roots, evil fruits.
I can't do good,
          . . . . *(Pointedly.)* can you
Caleb Thorn?

CALEB   *(After a pause.)*
No - *(Brokenly.)*
          . . . . I can't say I can.

RENAIRE   *(Slyly insinuating.)*
          . . . . Tell me,
is it true? I've heard it rumoured
a certain renegade harlot
has shocked the town
by being converted?

CALEB   *(Warily.)*
You mean Molly Green,
don't you?

RENAIRE   *(Mocking.)*
Fancy, you've hit 'er -
beginner's luck!

CALEB   *(Coldly.)*
You're not funny.
What do you want with her?

RENAIRE
                              (*With a buried hatred.*)
Oh, perhaps I feel
some unpriestly subterranean
urge to desecrate this vestal
virgin of the confessor -

CALEB
                              (*At once outraged.*)
Now look, I saw her
laughed at today - you
leave her alone!

RENAIRE
                    (*A threat creeps in.*)
Your pity touches
me, especially as I'm aware -

CALEB
Aware? . . . . . . (*Sensing danger.*)
aware of what?

RENAIRE
                         (*Playing with him.*)
Your misfortune;
remember McCorkeran's
little joke about
                         (*Mimicking her.*)
'Signing the register,
Sir?'

CALEB
        .. Are you? . . . (*As it dawns on him.*)
Renaire! are you
trying to say?

RENAIRE
                     (*Cold as steel.*)
Pray, let's not
go into the sordid details -
all that remains for
you, is to do evil.
                      (*Abruptly.*)
You'll prevail on this
'Magdalene' penitent to accept
my employ.
If you fail,
                 (*A sinister pause.*)
or betray my
trust, I'll scribble a little
Latin missive to your
                      (*Snarling it.*)
Rector Seminarii -
        . . . . good night Caleb Thorn.
    (*Turning curtly,
    he strides up the steps to the seawall.*)

CALEB   Seminary? Rector? Renaire,
                         Come back!
                                   (As CALEB *runs up to him*
                                   RENAIRE *turns on him a cold stare.)*

RENAIRE   Oh yes, you'll
                         hack her a note, at once -
                         immediately!

CALEB   . . . . But I can't!

RENAIRE   *(A crooked smile.)*
                         Oh - but you will, you'll
                         be my protegé, my apprentice -
                         So stick to your studies -
                                             (Darkly.)
                         There's no way back.
                                       *(He turns and
                         disappears on the seawall* U.L.10.
                         A fog horn moans out of the mist.)

                         *(*CALEB *enters by the left invisible
                         door. He runs upstairs as a pool
                         of light gathers on the bed where
                         he sits. Snatching up a pad and
                         pulling out his pen he begins to
                         write, saying the feverish words
                         aloud as he does so.)*

CALEB   Dear - Molly Green,
                         I'm very ashamed - to write this
                         note - do you remember - the seminarist -
                         they dared to visit you? You were good
                         enough - not to entice - me further -

                         (As CALEB*'s light dwindles into a deep
                         darkness,* MOLLY*'s subtly fades in
                         as she enters,* D.R.15, *in night dress, and
                         reading the opened letter aloud -)*

MOLLY   'than my peers - my evil thoughts -
                         had already done -'
                                       *(She sits on the edge
                         of the bed. The letter she is holding
                         trembles slightly -)*
                                             '- I know your life
                         has been different from mine - perhaps
                         to you it doesn't' . . . . . *(Brokenly.)*

MOLLY   . . . . 'seem so bad.
This demonologist
discovered how I foolishly signed
McCorkeran's register.

He's trying to blackmail me.
He's even commandeered me
to procure your services'
                              (Taking fright.)
'for some satanic rite!
          . . . . Could you find
the book and tear out the page for me?
It was Saturday, October tenth -'

No Caleb Thorn, I looked before -
It was just as I expected,
the whole page torn out - It's
McCorkeran's cut -
                              (Taking up the letter.)
MOLLY   'He threatens to reveal
my shameful fall to the Rector
of my college,
          . . . . If that page is gone -
it sticks in my throat to ask it -
could you pretend to do
what he asks?'
                              (The letter falls in her lap.)
MOLLY   Oh God, no!
                    I - I could never!
                (Reading again.)
                              'I'll come tomorrow
late - pray God you find it.
                              Caleb Thorn'
                *(As the light fades,
                MOLLY remains motionless. In the
                dark the scrim falls and a fog
                horn sounds. She takes a pillow
                and lying down draws up the coverlet.
                In the same blackout CALEB stows
                his day clothes, and in the pyjamas
                worn under them, with a pillow
                lies down pulling the covers over him.)*

                *(Darkness and shifting moonlight
                become a troubling weather obscuring
                and revealing those who are asleep.)*

(DOM JEROME *has also fallen asleep
at his desk. As the streetlight dims
and expires a dog howls in the distance.*)

(HAGAN *stealthily enters the cellar* U.C.7.
*He speaks menacing phrases,
being answered by the choral echo.*)

HAGAN	Nính's fóg,
CHORUS 1	. . . . nính's fog nính's fog
CHORUS 2	. . . . nính's fog nính's fog

(DOM JEROME *rouses,
awakened by the echoes.*)

HAGAN	Drífting éddy,
CHORUS 1	. . . . eddy éddy eddy
CHORUS 2	. . . . éddy éddy

(HAGAN *is creeping up
the cellar stairs, crouching
like a wild thing, scenting its prey.*)

HAGAN	Múffle ány -
CHORUS 1	. . . . any ány any
HAGAN	. . . . Stép,
CHORUS 2	. . . . step stép stép

(DOM JEROME *rises, gropes
to the head of the stairs like a
sleepwalker, listening, frozen with fear.*)

HAGAN	Ány écho,
CHORUS 1	. . . . . . echo écho echo
CHORUS 2	. . . . écho echo

(HAGAN *is gliding
without sound to the bench
below the bed, shadowy, crouching.*)

HAGAN	Ón the staír.
CHORUS 1	. . . . stair staír stair
CHORUS 2	. . . . staír staír

(HAGAN *hovers for a
moment, then retreats with the
prowling gait of a lame panther.*)

(*He watches from the side* U.C.6,
as the doors behind the bed U.C.1
and 2 *begin opening slowly.*

*Moonlight falls through them on
the bed.* CALEB *sits suddenly bolt
upright, staring terrified into the
moonlit hall, while* DOM JEROME *moves
hesitantly down his steps by the scrim.)*

HAGAN	Moónstruck, aré you?
CHORUS 1	. . . . . strúck áre you? struck áre you?
CHORUS 2	. . . . struck áre you? struck áre you?
HAGAN	Stártled?
CHORUS 2	. . . . . . stártled? 'artled? 'ártled?
CHORUS 4	. . . . 'artled? 'ártled?

                  *(*DOM JEROME *freezes,
sensing suddenly, the presence
of danger. A shadow slides across
the wall outside the open doors.* CALEB
is motionless his voice vibrant with fear.)

CALEB	Is sómeone thére?
CHORUS 3	. . . . . . sómeone thére? sómonere?
CHORUS 4	. . . . sómonere? sómonere?

                  *(*RENAIRE, *entering
from the left, is wearing a long
dark cape. He speaks in a sepulchral
stage whisper -)*

RENAIRE   . . . . Come with me
to the Mesa, it is midnight, Caleb.
Under the milky moon, a dog's
howls are lost on the faults
of the shifting air -

                        *(A distant howl
trails from the heights.)*

RENAIRE   Listen! . . . .

                       *(A horn sounds a
rousing distant summons.)*

RENAIRE   Like the call
    . . . of a ram's horn
        . . . . from the vap'rous steeps -

                       *(The bourdon bell
of the Cathedral tolls
the first stroke of twelve.)*

RENAIRE   Come quickly!
                   *(They leave through the
open doors, which close after them.)*

(Bell stroke the second.)

> *(*HAGAN *springs
> up the steps, runs on the bench around the
> bed, drawing off the pillow and cover, gaining
> the upper platform, he stows the bedclothes,
> lifts the left hinged side of the bed over
> onto the right, and rolls what is now
> an altar, to the centre.)*

(Bell stroke the third.)

CHORUS 1

Hów? . . . . stríve to? . . elúde . . . . . . hórrent stálker?
. . . . . How- . . . . to elúde this, abhórrent . . . .
Hów? . . . . stríve to? . . . . this, ... stálker?

> *(*HAGAN, *as the chorus above is spoken, takes
> up a lantern and ignites the flame. He
> passes in front of the altar over to the steps
> and descends to the seawall where he
> signals to the quay below.)*

(Bell stroke the fourth.)

CHORUS 2

Whére . . . . a béstial trápp'd . . . . maúled, hówling escápe?
. . . . . . does a . . . . . trápp'd man maúled, ...escápe?
Whére does . béstial . . . . . . .man . . . . hówling escápe?

> *(At the fourth stroke,* HAGAN *has turned and
> is signaling toward the west. He runs
> off then on the seawall. We hear him
> knocking several times off stage* U.L.10.*)*

(Bell stroke the fifth.)

CHORUS 2

Aríd . . thís . . hígh . . . snárl- . . rávagement
. . . . in . . . his . . . . dry snárling rávage . . . .
Aríd . . thís his . . . . dry . . . . rávagement

> *(With his lantern* HAGAN *looks in through
> TOM BURNS's window - then comes out on the
> seawall, and darts down to* AMY HEARTH's
> *invisible door,* U.C.3.*)*

(Bell stroke the sixth.)

CHORUS 1
> .... he .... cráwls .. the .... ríot of his ísolátion!
> ríled ... gróvels, cráwls in the wíld ríot ..... ísolátion!
> .... he gróvels, ... in ... wíld ... of his ísolátion!

(where he knocks, causing AMY HEARTH *to appear
briefly at the head of the stairs* D.L.12. *Surveying
the street he crosses to the centre where he
stops suddenly to listen and spying the
door* U.C.3 *opening, he scurries on across the street.)*

(Bell stroke the seventh.)

*(*RENAIRE *comes out in his sweeping cape
followed by* CALEB *in his night clothes,
barefoot. He seems insensible of the
night air, as if sleep walking. They stand
for several moments watching* HAGAN'*s
furtive rallying of the votaries as he
raps on the invisible door at the right
and* MILLIE *opens slightly, the inner door*
U.C.6, *peers out and closes it again.)*

(Bell stroke the eighth.)

(As HAGAN *crosses to McCorkeran's* D.R.16, *he
knocks, then goes off* D.R.17.*)*

RENAIRE
See, our infernal
blacksmith has tapped
at doors, all the long centuries
back, while the steeple
tolls eternal twelve.

(Bell stroke the ninth.)

CHORUS 1
> Fúrtive, móst
> .... móst fúrtive, most fúrtive,
> .... most fúrtive

(Tapping at doors off-stage D.R.; MOLLY'*s
window blind goes up as* HAGAN *peers in
with his lantern, then comes down,
while* MOLLY *turns in her sleep.)*

(Bell stroke the tenth.)

(CALEB *has become aware of the chill
air. He hugs himself with a shiver.*
RENAIRE *noticing, throws a part of
his voluminous cape over him, quite
engulfing him.*)

CALEB   Why is the blacksmith gathering
all these hooded people?

RENAIRE   They are the votaries - at the hour
of the new moon they come together.

CALEB   But why have you brought me here?

RENAIRE   The time is not yet propitious
for explanation - but soon you will see.

(RENAIRE *indicates the parapet where
they both sit to watch, enrapped
in the same nocturnal cape.*)

CHORUS 2   Creák of staír
. . . . . of staír, creák a staír,
. . . . creák a staír, creák-

(*The entrances accompany the choruses
in a gradual accelerando.* MILLIE *comes
out* U.C.6, *wearing a hooded cape, while*
BRAYLORN *appears* U.L.10 *in similar garb.
As* MILLIE *crosses,* BRAYLORN *descends from
the seawall to join her -*)

CHORUS 2   . . . . a staír a staír-
(*Bell stroke the eleventh.*)

CHORUS 3   Clánk a bólt
. . . . . a bólt, clánk a bólt,
. . . . clánk a bólt, clíck-

(HAGAN *glides across Campus Street to
disappear* U.R.8. *His tapping is heard
off-stage* U.C. SANDY *and* SUE *enter* D.R.16, *cross
to the right entrance and sit near the steps.*)

CHORUS 4   Únbared pórts
. . . . pórts that knów,
. . (*crescendo*) . . . . pórts a knów, anon

CHORUS 5   A knów, anon
. . . . anon a knów
. . . . a knów, anón, anón, anón -

*(*BEN *appears* D.R.17, *loiters by the Bar.*
WAGUARD *and* CARP *enter* D.L.13 *to join* MILLIE
and BRAYLORN*'s group, while* MCCORKERAN
BRAYLORN *appears* U.L.10 *in similar garb.*
comes out D.R.16, *watching from the head*
of the stairs - all in hooded capes.)

CHORUS 6   Jár open jár,
Jár . . . . Ópen jar ópen -
. . . . Ópen . . . . Jár Ópen!

(The cellar door U.C.7 *swings open,*
revealing HAGAN *with his lantern.)*

(Bell stroke the twelfth.)

(Suddenly he darts in, sending
SANDY *and* SUE *scurrying to the Tavern.*
Jumping up on the steps, he thrusts
his lantern aloft, shouting -)

HAGAN   Benedicámus!
CHORUS 6   . . . .'dicámus!
. . . .'dicámus! 'dicámus 'dicámus!

HAGAN   Diábolo!
CHORUS 5   . . . .'ábolo . . . . . Mal-'ábolo
CHORUS 4   . . . . 'ábolo . . . .'ábolo-ménte!

CHORUS 2   While wé withín, híss out
CHORUS 3   . . . . withín, ...the rábblemént
CHORUS 1   . . . . híss out . . . . of sín!

*(*HAGAN *returns his lantern to the cellar,*
where he fires up his furnace; during
these choruses the DRUGGIST *has entered*
D.L.13, *languidly smoking narcotics. He*
sits on the bench. The LIBRARIAN *has also*
entered D.R.17 *where he engages* SANDY
and BEN *in a whispered conversation,*
while D.R.16, MCCORKERAN *at the conclusion*
of the 'invocation' shuffles back inside.
In the meantime JAKE *has clambered up*

*on the low wall on Campus Street. He
looks down at* HAL *on the far side.)*

JAKE

Wake up, ya snorin'
carbuncular cowherd, . . . Hal!

(His sleep-drugged head appears.)

HAL

What? the Caprid, Jake?

JAKE

Aye. Crawl out - yer not afeared?

HAL

I said no prayers.

JAKE

'E's near - best cross yerself!

*(*HAL *does. They drop into the street
and disappear* U.R.8. *The* LIBRARIAN
has crossed over to the DRUGGIST.
*Their veiled speech is subversive -
their works stupefy, to corrupt.)*

LIBRARIAN

Seeking night poisons,
hypnotic herbs? Apothecary?

DRUGGIST

                                        (Rising)

Drugs under a flight
of herons, rooks and kites -
and you, Scrivener?

LIBRARIAN

I stir with liberotic tales,
novelistic nightmares, dreams -
yes! . . . reams of fantasy!

*(*DOM JEROME *steps toward them as if to
speak, but hesitates when the dog's
howl again trails on the air. Seeing*
JEROME*'s movement,* HAGAN *darts up to
the* LIBRARIAN, *pointing out the monk.)*

HAGAN

Look there - an alien!

DRUGGIST

Could it be? approaching
our circled arcanum -

LIBRARIAN

. . . . Odd hour
for the monk to be abroad - let him
enter that he may see -

(As the scrim rises, the DRGGIST *circles
behind the bench, coming up on*
DOM JEROME*'s left while the* LIBRARIAN
approaches him on the right.)

LIBRARIAN Remember me?
      *(Continuing the
encirclement, the* DRUGGIST *crosses
behind to the right while the*
LIBRARIAN *passes in front of* JEROME
to his left.
. . . . your pictorial
purveyor of rituals for the
whetting of appetite?

DOM JEROME   *(Bewildered.)*
Whose drowsed dreams
were they in the night - this Tom?
the remembered struggles?
the fright?

DRUGGIST   *(A hand on his arm.)*
Be remindeed, Tom -
don't you remember me?
your old time family
druggist?

DOM JEROME   *(Drawing away.)*
I don't know you -
though I begin to recall
all the troubles your
voices have caused me!
    *(*HAGAN *has
been edging in closer. He darts in
from behind on* DOM JEROME*'s left.)*

HAGAN We three - we're the brimstone
whores of Gomorrah, your very
own tortuers - soon you'll see.

(Turning to face him, DOM JEROME
*backs away from them. They dog
his footsteps back to Cloistergarth.)*

DRUG. LIB. HAG. Áll your iníquities
CHORUS 2 . . . fóllow and hówl,
DRUG. LIB. HAG. . . . . wé will recáll them
CHORUS 2 . . . . númber them áll -

(A distant sound of thunder diverts
their attention to CALEB whom RENAIRE
is leading to the edge of the steps. As
he addresses him, he summons his
minions the Tavern people and the
gossips on his left into two flanking
semicircles.)

RENAIRE
Come, Caleb Thorn,
you must run with all such
sleepwalkers, underworld rakes,
such awakened minions -
                    (The LIBRARIAN
          scurries behind the bench, HAGAN in
          front of it to below the steps while
          the DRUGGIST stays watchful near it.)

LIBRARIAN
Pánsexuánalysts!
DRUGGIST
          . . . . pócked homosýphilates!
HAGAN
          . . . . áll such háters of the sún!
RENAIRE
Their thín-lipped
wíves fóllow, glíde
          . . . out of eýries as háwks
          . . . . from broóds of múrdered chíldren!

LIBRARIAN
Chíld corrúptors
DRUGGIST
          . . . . bátterers, abórters!
HAGAN
          . . . . bástardízers! With áll
RENAIRE
          . . . . such míseries rún!
          (HAGAN bounds up
          onto the seawall, but CALEB, eluding
          his grasps, runs down the steps. The
          LIBRARIAN and DRUGGIST block his escape.
          RENAIRE, consigning him to the torturers,
          moves along the lower platform's
          bench to centre stage where, with signs,
          he orchestrates the votaries' nightmarish
          molestations. With the action above,
          another roll of distant thunder is heard.
          The choruses that follow form a continuous
          recitation.)

CHORUS 1
Hów can I . . . . my cráwling flésh . . . .
Hów . . . . éxtricate . . . . flésh from thése
. . . . can I . . . . my cráwling . . . . thése

CHORUS 2

   oleáginous múd . . . . the crócodílian . . .
   . . . . múd rucks, of . . . crócodílian Níle
   oleáginous . . . . rucks, of the . . . . Níle

RENAIRE

(So signaled from RENAIRE, *all suddenly
meld, moving as a single organism
inching* CALEB *backwards to the bench
with reptilian slowness.* HAGAN *crouches,
coiled for a spring.* DOM JEROME *makes a
tentative move but a glare from* HAGAN
arrests him.)

CHORUS 3

   this míre blácker . . . . bíle . . . . ínk of squíds
   . . . míre . . . . than bíle is greén or . . . . . squíds
   this míre blácker than . . . . . . greén . . ínk of . . . . .

CHORUS 3

   is bláck while . . . . éyes malígnant . . . .
   . . . . while blínkless éyes . . . . hýpnotize,
   . . bláck . . . . . blínkless . . . . malígnant . . . .

(On 'blacker', the slow hand of HAGAN, *with
a sudden strike nails the boy catching
his foot.* CALEB, *convulsed, as if a shock
passes through him, falls back on
the bench. Shaking loose his captor,
he scrambles on top where he crouches.
All are startled back, quite motionless
for a moment.* HAGAN's *blazing eyes hold him.)*

CHORUS

   Hów? . . . . oóz out . . éxcrem . . . . quíck slime cráwl?
   . . . . . to cráwl, . . . out of éxcerémental . . . . . slime . . . . . .
   Hów? . . cráwl, oóz . . . . méntal quíck . . . .

*(On the words 'to crawl' all lunge at him
with clutching hands. Flailing he
struggles to escape but faints after
the word 'crawl?'. Thunder rolls as
the three tortuers catch him. All
the others let go, scattering in panic -
the Tavern people to the right, the
gossips to the left. Lowered to the
floor, and supported by the* DRUGGIST,
he gradually revives.)

(Then, coming up the steps U.C.4,
DIEL *discovers dead drunk* HARRY, *but*

hurries by so that NEIL *who follows*
will have to wake him - he calls out.)

DIEL

Clammy 'Arry's 'ere -
wake 'im up, Niel!

NIEL

(Unwilling to touch him.)

Nay! not that corpse
with 'is keelhaul eyes an' bloated sea legs!

HADDOCK

(Barking a command off-stage U.C.*)*

All out, ya calloused rawboned
Saturday drunken seadogs!
Capt'n 'Addock 'ere!

DIEL

(Startled by Capt'n.)

Wake 'im up Neil -
we're in fer Sainte Secaire -

*(*DIEL *relents,*
and the two of them haul HARRY *up*
to the seawall depositing him by
the parapet where he slides down
asleep. The Sabat horn resounds
reproaching the drunkard. In the
meantime MCCORKERAN *has crept into*
MOLLY*'s room, roused and given her,*
still half asleep, a potion to drink.)

MCCORKERAN

Yer madam maculator's 'ere -
McCorkeran'll walk ya unawake
while ya sleep in your
pretty nighty, dear -

(They appear D.R.16
and descend the steps MOLLY *walking*
like a sleepwalker. She is clutching
an unlit church candle. HAGAN *who*
is watching, darts over snatches the
candle from her, scuttles into his
cellar and lights it at the furnace.
MOLLY *suddenly faints.)*

MCCORKERAN

(Peremptory.)

Give a hand, ya dapper
botchin' whore aborter - come!

*(*SANDY *runs up.)*

MCCORKERAN

Lift 'er lightly! M' pretty Jill.

*(*MOLLY *revives*
is bewildered as HAGAN *returns with*

151

MCCORKERAN

*the candle lit with hell fire and
thrusts it at* MCCORKERAN, *who forces it
into the girl's hand.)*

.... So Miss Moll,
this harelipped crone o' the wizened
moon says come t' the Sabat - come -
come t' the Seer.

(But MOLLY *resists her
persistent urgings toward the steps.
CALEB is coming to, through the* DRUGGIST*'s
ministrations. The gossips, curious
about* MOLLY, *surge back to look, then
drift to the left of* DOM JEROME *who now is
standing by the bench.*

CARP

.....................*(CARP sees* MOLLY.*)*
Don't look now, but I think
she's the one -

BRAYLORN

..........*(Eagerly.)* You mean
the Sabat Queen?

WAGUARD

............*(Disdainfully.)* She's bearin'
a candle, please you.

BRAYLORN

................*(Feigned shock.)*
Why it's - Molly Green!

WAGUARD

...................I suppose
the professor knows what's needed.

CARP

.....*(Heavy sarcasm.)* Something
brazen, I believe.

MILLIE

...........*(Very superior.)*
But of course. It's
a ritual requirement, you see.

*(But now the gossip's curiosity has
noticed the presence of* DOM JEROME.
*They begin very casually circling
the scrutinized monk, pretending
to be not looking, but seeing everything.
They swing back to the platform in
a semicircle.)*
(Meanwhile RENAIRE
*having stepped down from the
bench, walks slowly downstage
to the edge of the platform,
intoning the follies and the
iniquities for the worldly wise with
ironic relish.)*

RENAIRE	Ladies' auxiliaries,
	.. on whom batten their
	.... gnostic gurus
	..... of absurd philosophies -
	.... every liar and cheater,
	.... every dishonest eater
	.... of the poorest poor -
	..... See! each risen
	.... sleeper leers blood,
	.... with a redshot eye!

(As CALEB *has
regained his feet, his many
tormentors close in, circling him,
continuing the litany.)*

HAGAN	Hog snouted grafters,
LIBRARIAN	.... bribers
DRUGGIST	.. thieving chimpanzees
HAGAN	.... lead gutted
LIBRARIAN	..... racketeers, pimps and
DRUGGIST	.... pretty pushers
HAGAN	.... addicts, and derelicts
LIBRARIAN	.... of seven seas -

*(In the meantime,
during this encirclement,* FROAR
glides in U.R.9, *followed by* BEN *from
the Tavern,* DIEL, NEIL *and* HARRY *from
the seawall. As* RENAIRE *speaks again,
they pass through the inner circle
of* HAGAN, LIBRARIAN *and* DRUGGIST
*who fall back to their outposts,
observant with* RENAIRE.*)*

RENAIRE	Shadows of three,
	.. five, nine of them,
	.... out of the night, under
	.... the moon, materialize.

(FROAR *leads
his 'ancients' slowly counterclockwise
about* CALEB, *each naming for his
benefit their poisonous offerings.)*

FROAR	Have ye the 'erbs?
HARRY	..... 'emlock, nightshade,
BEN	.. and mandrágora,
DIEL	.... black turnip too -

NEIL	Aye, and janicot!
HARRY	.. I've a green 'orned toad -
FROAR	. . . . 'tis well - we go!

            *(The echoing
Sabat horn resounds;* BRAYLORN *as*
KATY, *and* DIEL *as* JAKE *with* BEN *and* FROAR
*stream to the right in a semicircle
with* SUE *joining them. To the left,*
NEIL *and* HARRY *circle the bench to
apprehend* DOM JEROME *but he moves
ahead, almost within reach of*
CALEB. *The boy and the monk are
facing each other.)*

CALEB	Only in a dream can I
	.. walk and seem innocent
	. . . . in my guilt - . . . .
DOM JEROME	. . . . In *my* guilt
	. . . . can I still seem
	. . . . innocent, still
	walk as in a dream?

            *(He reaches out and the boy responds.
As their hands are about to meet,*
HAGAN, LIBRARIAN, *and* DRUGGIST *swirl in
drawing* CALEB *away to the right in
a clockwise whirlwind.* NEIL *and*
HARRY *restrain* DOM JEROME *drawing him
to the left.* RENAIRE *also drifts to the
left, ever watchful. In their careening
abduction of the boy,* HAGAN *slows
allowing the* LIBRARIAN *to coast past
him, and the* DRUGGIST *past the* LIBRARIAN.
*The vortex spent, they are motionless
for a moment.*

              Then HAGAN *begins
to draw the others slowly creeping
counter-clockwise in a predatory
circling, as of some tentacled
organism.* CALEB, *in his pool of light,
turns intermittently, rigidly clockwise, shrinking and horrified.)*

CHORUS 1	⎡ . . . . . víle . . . . detéstable, feél . . . and explóre . . .
CALEB	While . . . téntacles . . . . feél for . . . . explóre me
CHORUS 1	⎣ . . . . . víle . . . . detéstable . . . . . for, and explóre . . .

*(As before, the choruses are a continuous
recitation over the stage action.)*

CHORUS 2	... quáking nákedness máking .... my légs
CALEB	my quáking ..... ness máking immóbilized my ...
CHORUS 2	.... nákedness .... immóbilized ... légs

(Following HAGAN *on the inner circle
the* LIBRARIAN *and* DRUGGIST *fuse as a
first tentacle, while* KATY *streaming
in from the right with* SUE *and* SANDY
meld into a second.)

CHORUS 3	..... my hánds, ... thíghs, maul .... me so
CALEB	árms, my ...... and thíghs, ... haúling ... so
CHORUS 3	.... hánds, and ...... maul haúling me ..

(The symbiosis is completed as JAKE
with BEN *and* FROAR *following* SANDY
transform themselves into a third.)

CHORUS 4	...... in a rúck of .... cupped súcking ... of óctopí,
CALEB	slímed in a rúck of the cóld .... súcking húg ....
CHORUS 4	slímed in .... the cóld cupped .... húg of óctopí,

*(Slowing almost to a crawl, they
close in with a convulsive spasm
at the words 'hug of octopi', by
sliding down on one knee, they
clutch at him with their hands.*
CALEB *struggles as in a knot of thrashing
tentacles. They subdue him, drag
him down, resisting inch by inch.)*

CHORUS 5	...... they mángle me ...... eách to its .... pronged
CALEB	a thráll, ... me dówn, ... to its beák ....
CHORUS 5	...... they mángle ... dówn, eách ..... beák pronged

*(As his hand is drawn down, last of
all, like that of a drowning man.)*

CHORUS 5	órifice .... devoúring ... digésting me .....
CALEB	...... drówning, devoúring me .... me alíve!
CHORUS 5	órifice drówning, ... me digésting me alíve!

DOM JEROME	Caleb - break away! ....

DRUM ROLL

*(A drum roll roars
as the Votaries recoil, throwing
back their whiplashed arms.
Released, the boy leaps up, lifted
from behind by* HAGAN. *They lunge
to another tympanic roll when*

SIGNUM

CRUCIS

*he transfixes them with a sword-
slashing sign of the cross. Instantly
they all shrink back into a wide,
glaring, crouching circle.*

CALEB

STANDS

CALEB *drops
to his feet, his hands still raised
while the drums descend to a
hushed ominous rumble. A flurry
of simultaneous movement ensues,*

HAGAN THE

HELLSTOKER

as HAGAN *scuttles down to his furnace,
flinging open the door to the flames
where he stands.*

DRUGGIST

LIBRARIAN

INFERNAL

ACOLYTES

The DRUGGIST *and*
LIBRARIAN *glide through the doors*
U.C.6 *and* 3, *reappearing hooded and
cloaked, the* DRUGGIST *bearing with
ceremonial decorum a cup and paten,
the* LIBRARIAN *a folded vestment.
They stand in readiness.*

BESIEGED

ONCE AGAIN

*Meanwhile the crouching Votaries
have circled* CALEB *coming up behind
him hurling the old taunts. They
drift in on the right and the left.)*

KATY

Mother's little Levite - ....

SUE

.................Poor little Priestling -

SANDY

Whatdya say Prester

.................Cabe? ....

JAKE

Ya gotta prove

.... yer a man! ....

SANDY

If ya can!

JAKE

......Ya gotta prove ....

yer a Priest!

*(*CALEB *backs away from
the onslaught, while* KATY, SUE *and*
SANDY *stream to the Tavern,* JAKE,
BEN *and* FROAR *go up on the steps to
the seawall, and the gossips
widen the circle to the left.*

(CALEB *has retreated up the steps on the*
right where HAGAN *challenges him*
from the furnace.)

HAGAN Sweár t' the Cáprid, Clérk
HAGAN ...if ya dáre!   *(decrescendo.)*
CHORUS 7 .... dáre! Sweár .... dáre if ya .... if ya ....
       ....Sweár if ya dáre .... dáre .... dáre

CALEB You dévils have
CALEB ...dáred me! have dóne ... befóre!
CHORUS 8 .... me! .... dóne this ...... this ......
       ....have .... this befóre .... befóre!

HAGAN So swear t' the Caprid, Caleb
            t' the Caprid's ingot iconic,
               to the idolized Angel swear!

CHORUS 9 Sweár .... to the íngot ..... sweár!
       ..... if ya dáre .... icónic ......

(When HAGAN *has stirred up the flames*
and closed the furnace, it's as if
a summons has been given.
With subterranean rumbles the
central doors begin slowly opening
on the emptiness beyond. CALEB *is*
alarmed. He sits huddled on the
steps as RENAIRE *summons the orgy.)*

RENAIRE Arouse! ye Votaries
            .... arouse! arouse! All demons
            .... demoniacs and devils, awaken!
            .... Orgiastic carousal arouses the dance
            .... dythrambic of the graveyard
            .... dead, and the damned!
            *(*RENAIRE *drawing them in,*
                    as SANDY, SUE *and* KATY,
              MILLIE, WAGUARD *and* CARP *stream in along*
              the sides of the platform, from right and left.)

CHORUS 10 Aróuse! aróuse! .... the deádliest .. traúma- ....
       .... aróuse! awáken! the deád .... of traúmatized dreáms!
       .... awáken! ... deádliest of traúma- ... dreáms!

(The dancers throw up their arms, then

CHORUS 11

Of démons adváncing . . . . with stálking the deménted!
. . . . adváncing, entránced . . . . stálking . . . .
Of démons . . . . entránced with . . . . the deménted!

*(Then dropping to one knee, they rise and
stride forward with measured steps,
forming an open 'v' before the altar.)*

CHORUS 12

Whírling dythrámbic . . . tántric . . . . rávening . . . .
. . . . dythrámbic to a . . . . . . delírium's ráven . . ráve!
Whírling . . . . to a tántric delírium's . . . . ráve!

*(With a complete whirl the dancers throw
up their arms, then lower them slowly
extended with palms up, as they glide
backwards to the 'open doors' position.)*

CHORUS 13

Pándemónium's . . . . to th' . . . . dárkening of . . . .
. . . demónium's Intróitus to . . . Sabát's, dárk- . . . . . . th' dámned!
Pán- . . . . 'tróitus . . th' Sabát's, ... of th' dámned!

*(When they begin to bend the knee a low
tympanic roll rises from the deep.
They rush to the edge of the platform cowering.
The emptiness beyond the transom and
the open doors is now flushed with a
fiery red. As RENAIRE declaims, crossing
over to CALEB, a great headless torso
like an ingot cooling from the abyss.)*

RENAIRE

Revere th' Caprid's iconic ingot rising
. . . . uplifted, on the caryatids of hell,
. . . . ruined architrave of a temple destroyed
. . . . of the idolized angel enraged beware!

*(The Votaries, terrorized stream in panic
right and left as the idol lifts a severed
goat's head with great horns, and settles
it upon its own headless shoulders. The
fire immediately takes possession of the
eye sockets, nostrils and opening mouth.
CALEB having turned, stares as if compelled.)*

CALEB

What's this - this Idol, phallic,
hoofed and black?

RENAIRE

It's th' mystic mockery of Lumen Christi
come burning five hundred years hither,
from an owl lit blink and pitch
smoked flaring of torches!

> *(A far distant wolfish howl is heard,
> drifting down, while CALEB climbs
> the steps as if in a trance. A shifting
> of light has thrown the Caprid into
> darkness against the flames, save
> the eyes which continue to blaze.
> With smoke and light he is
> rendered more immaterial. At the altar
> CALEB places his hands upon the mensa
> but quickly withdraws them. The
> DRUGGIST and LIBRARIAN are ascending
> the steps from right and left bearing
> sacerdotal insignia for the Sabat.)*

LIBRARIAN

Receive the vesture, ghostly Pater.

> *(He places it over his shoulders. It
> entirely envelops his night clothes.
> Turning around, CALEB, bewildered,
> looks from one to the other. The
> DRUGGIST passes the paten to the
> LIBRARIAN. The boy's face is dark
> with foreboding.*

CALEB

. . . . What chalice is here?
what altar is this?

> *(JEROME struggling.)*

JEROME

No don't! you must'nt -

> *(MOLLY to MCCORKERAN.)*

MOLLY

Why have you brought
. . . . me here?
What do they want with me?
. . . . all these people?

CORKERAN

Hush, m' dear - come near
. . . . come, come near -
(dragging her up steps.)

DRUGGIST

> *(Showing the chalice.)*

Revered Officiant,
. . . . the anodyne cup
with tincture of wine!

LIBRARIAN   *(Showing the paten.)*
                    . . . . Bread of affliction
                 black manna make!
DRUG. LIBR.   *(Placing them in his hands.)*
RENAIRE   Redeem the time!
(left of C.S.*)*   *(With the sign of an occult*
                 malediction, he prostrates the Votaries.
                 The tympanum begins an ominous roll,
                 while the eyes of the satanic goat glare
                 down on CALEB. *The* DRUGGIST *and* LIBRARIAN
                 raise his arms, then step away leaving
                 him alone with the demonic.)

CHORUS 14   Bláck élevátion! greén . . . . . fráctio!
                 . . . . élevátion! . . . . . toad's fráctio!
                 Bláck . . . . greén toad's . . . . . .
                 . . . . élevátion! . . . . . toad's fráctio!
                 Bláck élevátion! greén . . . . . fráctio!

CHORUS 15   And wáken, . . . come! . . . . . t' the . . . . éxecrátion!
                 . . . . come! . . . . . t' the Válois' éxecrátion!
1 MCCOR-   . . ¹wáken-²Nó! . . . . . ²néver! . . . . .¹Válois' . . . .
2 MOLLY
CHORUS 15   And . . . . come! . . . . . t' the Válois' éxecrátion!
                 . . wáken, . . . come! . . . . . t' the . . . . éxecrátion!

                 (Lucifer's miasmal penumbra, glinting
                 with sparks, broods over the rooftops.)

DOM JEROME   Too late! it's -
                                 *(*CALEB *comes out of his*
                     trance with a sickening realization.)

CALEB   What am I - what am I doing?
                 . . . . What have I done?
MOLLY   *(Screaming.)*
                 . . . . They have come!
CALEB   . . . . Oh - my - God!
                 (Horrified, he stands
                 for a moment frozen, then convulsively
                 throws down the cup and paten to a
                 tympanic drum roar that rolls into
                 an awe-struck silence. MOLLY *breaks*
                 free, runs down from the steps, but
                 is restained by SANDY.*)*
RENAIRE   *(With solemnity.)*
                 The umbrageous deed is done.

THE DUMB WILL SHOUT, P.62

*(Lucifer's penumbra fades as the Idol
descends leaving behind only a green
luminescence.* CALEB *buries his face in
his hands. Light grows on* JEROME *who
struggles to free himself from an astonished
tongue-tied silence - he has remembered!)*

DOM JEROME   Who is there? Who?   *(lunging forward.)*
    .. who among you? will grasp this
    ..... mandrake scream down the throat of me
    .. and tear it out with shrieks of an uprooted tongue!
    ...... The dumb will shout!
    .... the words will out!
                                *(Breaking free
of his captors he runs up the steps, is barred
by* RENAIRE, *stumbles to his knees by the
bench, reaches imploringly to* CALEB.*)*

DOM JEROME   It is you! you are the one!
    .. Now that I see it I know it now -
    ..... you are the son, the one
    .... that was lost and is found.

DOM JEROME   You, Caleb - you are my youth,
    .. my sole self lost these long years gone
    ..... We are one - we with Willie,
    .... Regis, Tom 'tis so - it is true.

*(*CALEB *is now staring at* JEROME, *and suddenly
racked by deep sobs, he frantically
tears off the vestment. Swaying, his
overstrung nerves undone by the
strangeness of the revelation he begins
to fall.* RENAIRE *runs up the steps,
catching him just as the sound of
a distant angelus is heard.)*

RENAIRE   The bell of Sainte Eustace!
    the eastern lucifer trembles -
                        (Dismissing the Votaries.)
RENAIRE   Cower all shadows!
    ...... melt! fly away!
    .... *(Gathering up* CALEB *in his cape.)*
RENAIRE   Each bears with his
    ..... burdens a conscience
    .... he must quell!

(*As* RENAIRE *runs down the steps carrying
the unconscious* CALEB *to disappear* U.C.3,
JEROME *follows them but the door
is already closed. The* DRUGGIST *has
descended to retrieve the cup and
paten while the* LIBRARIAN *follows
to gather up the vestment; they
go out* U.C.6. *The green luminescence has faded into the moonlight
while the double doors have been
slowly closing.* HAGAN *in the dark
glides up to the altar, transforms
it again into a bed. He leaves* U.C.7
by way of the cellar.)

BEN   'Must conscience quell',
              . . . . I think 'e said -
FROAR   . . . . Who's conscience?
                              (*turning to leave*)
JAKE   What the hell's that?
FROAR   . . . What we must quell.
BEN   . . . . A voice we must quench.

JAKE   Naw, mine's dead -
              . . . . maybe Corkeran's!
                      (FROAR, BEN *exit* U.C.10.)

MCCORK.   Hell no - I've none.
MOLLY   . . . I've one - but I'm afraid.
                      (MCCORKERAN *comes
              down, leads* MOLLY
              *to her doorstep where thay pause
              to look at* DOM JEROME. WAGUARD,
              MILLIE *and* CARP *huddle together
              whispering.*)

WAGUARD   Quell? really?
MILLIE   . . . . . He said we must.
CARP   . . . . and burdens bear.
                      (*They exit* D.L.13.)
SUE   But where?
SANDY   . . . . . God knows where -
                      (HARRY *staring at* JEROME
              answers SANDY.)
HARRY   . . . . I know where -
                      (SUE, SANDY *exit* U.R.8.)

(HARRY *drifts toward the seawall. He
pauses at the foot of the steps watching*
DOM JEROME *descend the steps. Still in
the shock of his nocturnal revelation
he moves slowly neither seeing nor
hearing anyone. Entering a pool of
light by the bench, he stands there
quite motionless, again.)*

MCCORK.   Come girl! . . . . . come!

MOLLY   . . . . . How can we quell
           . . . . the unquenchable?
           . . . . the remorseless conscience?

*(Immediately the chorus picks up
very softly the refrain 'must quell'.
Gradually it will grow louder.*
HARRY *leaves the seawall* U.L.10,
and NEIL D.L.13, *while* MCCORKERAN
goes in with MOLLY D.R.16. DOM JEROME
remains alone on stage.)

(Stealthily, the central doors U.C.1,2
*are opened, revealing in the moon-
lit hall the shadow of* RENAIRE,
carrying CALEB. *He enters, lays
the boy on the bed and draws the
coverlet over him. Departing he
goes out as silently as he came.
The doors remain open. As the
muted chorus gathers strength it
becomes reverberant.)*

CHORUS   . . . . must quell!
        Conscience - must quell!
           . . Conscience - must quell!
           . . . . Conscience - must quell!
        Conscience - must quell!
           . . Conscience - must quell!
           . . . . Conscience - must quell!
           . . Conscience - must quell!
          Conscience - must quell!
           . . . Conscience - must quell!
           . . . . Conscience - must quell!
           . . . . Conscience - must quell!

CHORUS

Conscience - must quell!
...Conscience - must quell!
........Conscience - must quell!
.... Conscience - must quell!

*(Sitting up suddenly in bed, CALEB's
strangled cry, distorted by sleep,
breaks through the choral climax.)*

CALEB

..... A-a-a-a-a-a-a-a-a-A-A-A-A-Ah!
...........................Conscience!

*(DOM JEROME convulsively covers his
ears, his mouth. There is a moment
of dreadful silence - he lowers his
hands slightly, listening intensely.
An amber light switches on in the
hallway outside the door.)*

MRS. THORN

(Off-stage up centre.)
..... Caleb, dear, is there
.... anything wrong, dear?

CALEB

..... No - Mother, nothing wrong -
.... Just nightmares -

*(The amber light in the hallway
fades into moonlight. A deep
distant foghorn moans out
at sea as the scrim begins to
drift down. Then the boy falls
asleep while JEROME remains
standing exalted, motionless,
in his own relentless light.)*

CURTAIN

THE THIRD WATCH

ON A SEA OF SORROWS, P.168

THE THIRD WATCH

(During a brief blackout a sound of
waves can be heard gently breaking
on the seawall. It continues for a
while, receding gradually as the
CURTAIN *rises. The scrim is down.*
Amber lamp light fades in on
DOM JEROME *who is seated in his cell.)*

DOM JEROME   I've asked myself, do you think Jerome
that dream was only a nightmare?
Clearly, I'm unable to decide, because
when I woke I found myself, alone,
standing in the street, weeping -

When all those memories came
flooding back like tides on a sea of sorrows
I knew I had been there before,
and I knew that the voices would not
leave me, would continue to speak,

as if really they were living lives
of their own, separate from my
remembering. I've become a prophet
of their peace - bewildering surmises
are sheer knowledge now, of what will be!

(The amber light fades into a
bluish dimness merely defining
his presence. Then behind the
scrim, light comes up on the
bench, where CALEB *is seated.*
The scrim rises slowly.)

CALEB   Remembering all that long
nightmare, somehow tonight
the reality - the thought of it
appals me!

How can I go through with it?
To confess? I'm afraid I'd -
I'd have to leave
I'd be ruined!
        (Rising nervously.)

There's no escaping him - I've
got to ask her -
> *(Crossing over resolutely
> to* MCCORKERAN*'s invisible door at the foot
> of the stairs, he hesitantly raises his
> hand to knock - then drops it.)*

It's a frightful thing!
but there's no way out -
no other way left.
> *(He knocks on
> the door - sound off stage* D.R.*)*

MCCORKERAN   Have patience!
> *(An amber light switches
> on, flooding the steps and* CALEB*.
> He knocks again as she comes out*
> D.R.16, *descending the stairs.)*

Let a body come before ya
tear the door down!
> *(Opening irritably.)*
Oh, it's you again! - well
if yer lookin' fer Molly Green
she's not receivin' callers,
and her door's locked
and she'll not be glad t' see ya!

CALEB   McCorkeran, listen! I'll
pay you well for that page
I signed in your Register -

MCCORKERAN   Register? what Register?
Ha! Anyone signin' a Register
on my premises would be
a pretty precious fool, eh?
A Register - imagine!

CALEB   But I signed it!
you asked me, you -

MCCORKERAN   Don't be absurd, boy!
I runs a discreet establishment.

> *(As* MOLLY *appears* D.R.16.*)*

MCCORKERAN   Well, Miss Green! ye've unlocked
              yer door. I've told 'im yer
              not receivin' callers.
                         *(From the top
              of the stairs, as she comes down.)*

MOLLY   It's alright Mrs. McCorkeran,
              I will only be a moment.

MCCORKERAN   I tell ya, I'll let m' room
              if yer not i' the convent soon.

                   (As CALEB *steps forward.)*

              Don't come in! Talk there.
              Yer not a payin' customer.
              With me nay th' richer fer it
              I'll not be battlin' every
              bastard knocks m' door.
              I'm at the end o' m' tether soon!

MOLLY   Yes, Mrs. McCorkeran,
              you'll have your room -

                   (MCCORKERAN *stomps up the stairs,*
                   goes in D.R.16, *without closing*
                   the door. MOLLY *comes outside.)*

CALEB   Molly! . . . .
MOLLY   . . . . What's the meaning
              of this wild note? . . . .
CALEB   . . . . The Register!
              did you get the page? . . . .
MOLLY   . . . . It was torn out -
CALEB   Oh God, no! what'll I do? . . . .
MOLLY   . . . . I'm so sorry -
CALEB   That McCorkeran she -
                   . . . . she's in league with him!
MOLLY   With whom? . . . .
CALEB   . . . . Eli Renaire!
              Molly, listen to me -
                   . . . . that man's no -
              demonologist he - . . . .
                   . . . . he's a demon, he'll
              denounce me to the Rector, yes
              and to my step-parents!

CALEB   At any breath of scandal, they'd
           disown me. I'd be ruined.
           I'm afraid it's too late,
           being sorry -
MOLLY   . . . . It seems like
           another of my molestations, my
           terrible dreams -

CALEB   . . . . All my worst ones
           revive with the daylight - Molly, you've
           got to help me! . . . .
MOLLY   . . . . How can I help you?
           should I haunt the churches for you?
           and I have - I've prayed for you.

CALEB   *Prayed* for me? No, Molly,
           listen - I came here -
           how can I put it -
           to beg you - . . . .
MOLLY   . . . . He really did
           commandeer you to procure
           me for his vile rites -
           didn't he? . . . .
CALEB   . . . . . . Molly, if you would
           just consent to - . . . .
MOLLY   . . . . *Consent*? Oh my God,
           no! I can't, he's a devil worshipper!
           There's something you should know -
           I had a dream last night - a nightmare
           It was frightful Caleb -

CALEB   . . . . You did? I did too,
           we were both there! . . . .
MOLLY   . . . . We were?
CALEB   Somehow the two of us -
                . . . . were demented!
           That ritual was hypnotic. . . . .

MOLLY   . . . . Our dreams
           then, *were* the same -
           Caleb, what you did, that sacrilege,
           was a horrible thing!
CALEB   . . . . I know, and I'm
           still not sure whether it was -
           you know, *real*.

171

CALEB   . . . . But that's impossible!
I was in bed when I awoke.
            . . . . Renaire's
blackmail threat, however -
            . . . . *that's* real!
I'm only asking that you
pretend Molly, tell him you'll
think about it - back out later
if you wish.

MOLLY   . . . . That's impossible

CALEB   What do you mean?
            . . . . what's the matter
with you?

MOLLY   . . . . . . Caleb, listen to me!

You've got to change your life,
you've got to repent! Those oils -
what do they call them? no matter -
for anointing a priest.
            . . . . For anyone
unworthy, they'd become - how
to say it? a fuel? like naptha!
to ignite and destroy you!

Save yourself while you can -
abandon theology, and
set your soul straight!

CALEB   You *preach* to me?
It's rumoured you've repented.
Are you a hypocrite too?
What do you mean, impossible?
You're living in a whorehouse,
aren't you? - *well*,
answer me!

MOLLY   . . . . I have no answer
to your accusations -
what could I say?

CALEB   Intercourse incorporated,
that's your business, isn't it?
selling yourself to every
drunken sailor comes along!
Would a lie defile your lips?
Their former scarlet on that
Saturday night, made me blush -

MOLLY   Oh Caleb, don't go on!
You've shot me full of arrows
straight to the quick -

CALEB   Arrows? but I thought,
how have I -?
MOLLY   . . . . It's *true*!
It's the truth, the cruel things
you've said - it's what I saw!
what I read in your face.
It fairly shone with horrified
shame! It was a merciless
mirror to my life! It was then
I couldn't go on anymore -

CALEB   Are you saying you've -
that the rumours are true? Molly?
that you've really repented?

MOLLY   That's why my door is locked -
against any further molestation.

CALEB   You've given up this
sordid traffic? . . . .

MOLLY   Oh God, yes - over and over!
Caleb - I'm entering the convent
tonight, after I make my confession -
not as a nun - as a Magdalene.

CALEB   *(Suddenly repentant.)*

I'm sorry, my poor sister.
I've been unjust, Molly -
forgive me if you can.

MOLLY   *(Walking donwstage toward
the convent,* CALEB *following her.)*

There's nothing to forgive,
but there's another I must forgive.
All my life I've been alone,
I've always been afraid -
         *(She sits on
the edge of the convent porch.)*

MOLLY   Often as a child I dreamt
of my father as of a man possessed.
Startled, I would cringe when he
thundered home in a drunken rage!
With foul oaths, alcoholic threats
he forced me with abuse - sent me
on the streets when I was
only thirteen -

CALEB   *(Sitting down beside her.)*
Poor child!
       . . . . it's all over, Molly.

MOLLY   Yes it's all over -
        . . . . .But you Caleb, what are
you going to do?

CALEB   . . . . God alone knows!
and I'm still afraid - I keep
seeing his glittering eyes
knifing into me like steel.

MOLLY   Do you remember, Caleb,
I asked you why you had come?

CALEB   Could I easily forget it?

MOLLY   You were sick with remorse,
you said you were a betrayer,
and it would have been better
for you if you'd never been born!

CALEB   I still say it!

MOLLY   . . . . Yet you climbed
those stairs, and faced that horrible
McCorkeran with her register,
which you *signed*!
            (She rises, walking
a few paces away, reliving the scene.)

MOLLY   . . . . And you - *forced*
yourself to open that door,
where you stood as if waiting
for God to strike you!
           (Returning to
CALEB, *confronting him.)*

MOLLY   Why? why in God's name did you
do it, Caleb - *why?*

CALEB

          (Brooding, almost
as if talking to himself.)

It's no use pretending,
I see it now - I wasn't forced.
There was no trap my stepmother set,
that's a lie.
        . . . . It was there - a call,
all the time, and I allowed it to die,
I set all my own traps,
and now -
       . . . . . . I cannot escape
or stand up, Molly, like a man
on these water weak knees.
What a fool -
     . . . . ashamed at being
laughed at, sober in that den, hauled
before a hotel jury of hot rod kids
to prove I was a man -
    . . . . had to be
as good as they, just as hot-blooded,
drunken, whoring and as wild -
I don't *know* why!
             (Stifling his grief.)

MOLLY

         (Compassionately.)
    . . . . .Just listen to your
heart, where it moans, all alone,
like some dove on a housetop.

CALEB

           (Looking up at her.)
Maybe I do -
           (He stands up facing her.)
maybe I've
been alone, Molly, just like you
all these years -
            (As they walk back.)

CALEB

bereft by death
or circumstance of brother, sister,
father, mother, not seeing them
in my only Friend -
          (Pacing in his
anguished agitation.)

CALEB

the One I so cruelly
betrayed! Oh how I rue it I did
what those damned devils dared me -

175

CALEB   green fool of a kid! Perhaps that's
the reason why -
(Turning to MOLLY.*)*
Renaire's right -
there's nothing left.
(MCCORKERAN *comes*
out D.R.16 *to the head of the stairs.)*

MCCORKERAN Well, ye better hurry up
yer moanin' - I got t' lock
the door. I'll not be
settin' here all the night!

MOLLY   Yes, Mrs. McCorkeran, just
a moment -
(MCCORKERAN *goes back in.)*

Caleb, listen to me!
There's still a way left open for you -
the only one.

CALEB   . . . . A way? open for me?
what possible way?

MOLLY   . . . . You must
go up there to the confessor,
Pere Bernard -

CALEB   . . . . He'd make me *leave*!

MOLLY   You *must* leave!
It's your only way to unbarb
the blackmail - this venomed hook!
Can't you see? There's time yet
to unburden your heart - the confessor
will know a way out with honour -
why are you afraid?
(MCCORKERAN *reappears.)*
Though your sins
may be leprous, or scarlet like
arteries, throbbing your wounded
life away, he'll wash you
clean new - as the snow!

MCCORKERAN   *(Impatiently.)*
Away with ya now!
Do ye ken ye keep a body waitin'
a' the night t' lock the door?

CALEB   *(To* MOLLY.*)*
You make me want it so!

MOLLY   . . . . . Then go! The time is getting late.

176

CALEB   I promise, Molly, I will try.
MOLLY   . . . . And pray for a Magdalene.

                   (She hurries upstairs. MCCORKERAN
                   has already come down.)
CALEB   *(To* MOLLY.*)*
               Goodnight -
MCCORKERAN   *(Glaring at* CALEB.*)*
               . . . . All right! goodbye with ya,
               . . . . and goodnight!

                   (She slams the door - sound off-
                   stage D.R. *and marching off* D.R.16,
                   slams another.)

CALEB   Goodnight - Molly Green.
                             (A fog horn
                   sounds as he exits up Campus Street U.R.9.*)*

                   (Down the same street we hear MISS PEW*'s*
                   heels returning from the cathedral.)

MISS PEW   Pere Bernard was severe -
                   . . . . I really must mend my
                   . . . . ways, it appears - my
                   . . . . gossipy, uncharitable
                   . . . . talk, that I scarcely
                   . . . . thought of as a fault.

                   (Passing the centre of the platform
                   she pauses, savouring her new found
                   resolution.)

MISS PEW   Mrs. Carp is the key -
                   . . . . I really must give up
                   . . . . my antipathy.

                   (Unnoticed behind her back dim
                   amber light fades in as BRAYLORN,
                   WAGUARD *and* CARP *enter* U.C.6 *carrying*
                   tea cups, MISS MILLIE *follows with the*
                   miniature tea table and service.)

MISS PEW   Whyn't we just
                   . . . . drop in a minute 'n'
                   . . . . say a kind word or two -

(MISS PEW *goes around to the entrance on
the left, pauses weighing the possibilities.*)

(*As* TAD MCFERGUSON *is entering* U.R.9, *on
Campus Street we hear him speaking.*)

TAD The faither was guid t' me,
sae langsufferrin', murrciful.
An' a am verra grrateful
t' the Lairrd for my prromised
pledge - a Scotsman's wurrd!

A' am aye sae feer'd
I'll gae astray again - but
fie Harry Ibbs! nae more a that
I pray! Yer roarrin'
drunks - nae more!

(TAD *crosses to the bench, where he sits
to light his pipe. The lights on him
fade to dim while on the platform they
grow brighter as* MISS PEW *decides.*)

MISS PEW Millie won't mind -
. . . . we'll make it a scandal
. . . . monger's surprise!

(*As she quietly lets herself in the
chorus grows louder; she halts and
listens, just outside the circle of light.*)

BRAYLORN her gore . . . . cat claws with a cat . . . eye,
WAGUARD . . . gore-coloured . . . . with . . cat cold . . . .
MRS. CARP her . . . . colour . . cat claws with a cat . . . eye,

BRAYLORN her blood . . . . . . leech . . . . . . stingin' em dry!
WAGUARD her . . . . . letting leech tongue stingin' . . . dry!
MRS. CARP . . . blood letting . . . . . tongue stingin' em dry!

(MISS PEW, *still unnoticed, but beginning
to understand, moves in closer to
the very edge of the light.*)

BRAYLORN . . riling . . . . . . our A. Pew . . . . till - . . . .
WAGUARD as . . . . . venom our . . . Pew plies till - . . . .
MRS. CARP . . riling venom . . . A. Pew plies . . . .

MILLIE	not ... neighbour's alive - t'die! ....
BRAYLORN	... one neigh- ... 's alive - t'die! ....
WAGUARD	not one neighbour's .... - t'die! ....
MRS. CARP	not ... neighbour's alive - t'die! ....

MILLIE	oh-ha ha .. hi hi .. ho ...... oooh-no! ....
BRAYLORN	...ha ha .. hi hi .. ho ho ... oooh-no! ....
WAGUARD	oh- .. ha ha .. hi hi .. ho ... oooh-no! ....
MRS. CARP	oh- ..... ha ha .. hi hi .. ho - oooh-no! ....

(Becoming suddenly aware of MISS PEW*'s presence as she steps into the light, their suspended tea cups are all lowered together with an indrawn oh!)*

MISS PEW   So! That's what you
talk about, when I'm away!

MISS MILLIE   *(Utterly dismayed.)*
It's - it's Annabelle. ....

*(*MISS PEW *stands for a moment glaring at them - then with revolted disdain -)*

MISS PEW   Oh - what a fool I've been!

(As the imagined conviviality of MILLIE*'s circle collapses,* MILLIE *herself wheels off the ruins of her party with the tea things* U.C.6, *while the others drift away* U.R.8, *unaware that they have carried off their tea cups with them.* MISS PEW *closes the door behind her as she comes out, with a quiet finality. She is greeted by the drunken chorus of a carousal somewhere on the quay below.)*

NICK	Oh - we bin ya boon com-panions Tad ....
PADDY	Oh - we bin .. boon com-panions ....
BUB	Oh - we bin ya ..... com-panions Tad ....

NICK	an' tipplin' dipsy ..... doo! ....
PADDY	an' .... dipsy dopsy ....
BUB	... tipplin' ..... dopsy doo! ....

(While ANNABELLE, *with her back to the
door, ponders the futility of her life*
MISS MILLIE*'s salon darkens. Light
touches* TAD *as he hears the old siren
enticing him.)*

NICK	Paddy an' .... drinkin' Nick.....
PADDY	...... an' Harry an' drinkin' ....
BUB	Paddy ... Harry an' .... Nick.....

NICK	... a' yer drunken .... ah, ha! ....
PADDY	an' a' yer .... crew ah, ha! ....
BUB	an' a' ... drunken crew ah, ha! ....

*(*TAD *is beginning to weaken - he
shuffles up the steps to the seawall.)*

HARRY   The lads ha' stood ya
               .... many a drink, Tad
               when ye was broke
               .... an' blue - so

PADDY, BUB   here's t' Hades
DIEL, NICK   .... wi' the likes
               o' knaves what

PADDY, BUB   .... drinks 'emselves
               t' early graves. ....

HARRY	like groggily ...... McFergus ....
PADDY, BUB	... groggily jollied Mc..... son ......
DIEL, NICK	like grog....jollied McFerguson ......

HARRY	drunken you Tad ..... ha! ha! ....
PADDY, BUB	....ken you .... ha! ha.........
DIEL, NICK	drunken you Tad ..... ha! ha! ....

(By now collected, MISS PEW *has
noticed* TAD. *She is suddenly
aware of his peril.)*

MISS PEW   Tad McFerguson! don't
              go that way! Come along here -

TAD MCFER.   *(Chastened.)*
               .... I'll nae go dohn, indeed,
               Miss Annabelle, ma'am, ferr ye've
               hitherr come -

MISS PEW   *(With gentle irony.)*
. . . . In the nick of time?

TAD   Aye! In a manner-o-sayin' Miss
t' become m' guarrdian
angel agin -

MISS PEW   *(Pleased in spite of herself.)*
. . . . .Now Mr. Tad!

TAD   Could it be an auld man
may hae the honorr t' escorrt ye
hame, ma'am?

MISS PEW   *(Completely won over.)*
. . . . . . Why, Mr. McFerguson!
. . . . I should be very pleased -

TAD   *(His most courtly.)*
. . . . . . The hahppiness t' be sure
. . . . is all mine, Ma'am!

(Offering his arm, they exit D.L.13,
as TOM BURNS *a moment later, also
enters* U.R.9, *returning from the
cathedral.)*

TOM BURNS   Life's returned again for me, Mother,
I feel it! It's like when I was ten,
when all was new, had just begun -
though I didn't know it then
how hopes and dreams are
realized - so soon. . . . .

*(As a blue light suffuses the transom,
he goes up on the seawall and
gazes at the old house.)*

TOM   Weep no more for me, Mother
I've just begun to be your son!
Your prayers your tears when I
despaired, have won for me
such solace, such
blessed peace - . . . .

(As if answering, ROSE *begins to sing
her voice floating down from a distance.)*

ROSE   He was a lark of a lad
(sung as   . . . . never bad
she recedes -   . . . . never sad he;
                   . . . . his soul could sing
with   . . . . like the mischief
reverberance)   . . . . of a linnet on the wing -

*(MOLLY has come out D.R.16, and paused
at the foot of the stairs, hearing the song.
She leaves on her way to confession, U.R.9.
TOM BURNS, with the fading of the blue light
in the transom, turns to walk away
on the seawall U.L.10.)*

*(Meanwhile MISS MILLIE has entered in the
dark, seating herself on the bench.
Presently the door U.C.1 opens spilling
light into the darkness. RENAIRE enters.)*

RENAIRE   Millicent - are you there?
                        *(Amber light
              comes up revealing MISS MILLIE, seated.)*

RENAIRE   Oh there you are.
MISS MILLIE   . . . . *(Rising)* Oh! Professor -

RENAIRE   I heard your guests leave early -
                  I was wondering, might we
                  continue our discussion?

MISS MILLIE   Why, of course! Just a moment
                  while I take out my glasses -

                  *(RENAIRE comes down the right
                  hand steps carrying a briefcase.
                  He takes out legal papers and
                  searches among them.)*

RENAIRE   Ah! here we are -
                        *(As MISS MILLIE sits down
                  he presents several documents,
                  in turn, while he reviews the
                  contents.)*
RENAIRE   . . . . I assume you feel no
                  need to reconsider our previous
                  negotiations before the notary?

MISS MILLIE   Of course not, Professor!

RENAIRE   Then everything is determined
                   as agreed - except for the - uh -

MISS MILLIE   Why, yes! of course - the cheque
                   for the seances; here let me
                   write it now -
                             *(Taking her cheque book,
                        she writes as* RENAIRE *cranes to check
                        the number of zeros. She hands it
                        to him with a flourish.)*

MISS MILLIE   There you are, Professor!
                   and may it serve our
                   noble cause!
RENAIRE   . . . . My gratitude
                   knows no bounds - but of course,
                   your generous endowment of our
                   Foundation, my dear Miss Millie,
                   your promotion of study and research
                   into the parapsychological arcana
                   of the occult, is an humanitarian
                   venture of profound significance!

MISS MILLIE   My dear Professor, your
                   lectures have convinced me
                   of the importance of your discoveries!
                   Why, everyone says -

RENAIRE   But you are too kind - I doubt
                   if you realize the *extent*
                   of your benefaction. Think of it!
                   For ages to come, the name of Millicent
                   Brainborough shall be held
                   in benediction!

MISS MILLIE   Oh now, Professor Renaire,
                   I think you are exaggerating
                   my small contribution!

RENAIRE   Oh, I think not. But now
                   our business is complete; your
                   signatures upon these documents
                   for the liquidation of the several
                   securities and assets - in favour

RENAIRE	of the Foundatioin - and these important instruments of transfer - especially your generous according of Power of Attorney - will expediate our rapid progress!
MISS MILLIE	Professor, you've given me so much pleasure - to think that at last I can do something significant with my life.
RENAIRE	On the contrary, my dear Millie Brainborough! the pleasure is all mine.

(Bowing, he goes upstairs, leaving
MISS MILLIE *entranced. She rises*
and exits U.C.6. *As her lights fade out,*
those on the upper platform fade in.
RENAIRE *is sitting on the bed, leafing*
through the documents with obvious
satisfaction. He stows them in the
briefcase, closes it, and laying it
tenderly on the bed, briskly leaves U.C.1.)

(As his light fades out, that in the
cellar fades in. HAGAN, *seated on*
the steps, is shuffling through old
newspapers for the fire. Dim
light fades in across the way as
BERT *enters* D.R.16, *coming down*
to open the bar, RENAIRE *suddenly*
enters the cellar U.C.7.)

RENAIRE	Oh, by the way, Hagan, the Burns boy seems to have escaped our entaglement, while the Green-Thorn caper may possibly have failed - however, other not insubstantial emoluments have been realized upstairs -
HAGAN	An' how long d' ya keep us in suspense waitin' fer our cut? We're nay workin' fer a mere tupence!

RENAIRE   We'll divide the loot
as soon as I cash in - I'll
give Thorn a final try tonight.
Keep your eyes open -

(As RENAIRE *crosses the way.)*

HAGAN   Keep my eyes open 'e says?
Aye, that I will, ya may be sure -

(The lights fade out as he leaves U.C.7,
*with a sheaf of old newspapers under
his arm.* RENAIRE *has entered the bar
where he passes the time with* BERT,
waiting for CALEB *to appear.)*

*(On the upper platform a muted
blue light fades in, as the door* U.C.1
*opens stealthily. A flashlight beam
intrudes as* HAGAN *enters. The beam
searches - falls on the briefcase.)*

HAGAN   Ahha! Now what would 'e be stowin'
in a briefcase? Some monuments,
did 'e say? Let's see -
*(Sitting, he removes
the documents, leafing through them.)*

HAGAN   so that's 'is little game!
*(In their place
he inserts folded newspapers.
Closing the briefcase, he lays it
exactly as it was before.)*

HAGAN   Old news'll do - there now,
a bit of a surprise -
*(Tearing off the
back page of a document, he
writes on it. His hoarse stage
whisper is full of gloating satisfaction.)*

HAGAN   fer Mr. Renaire, this
little warnin' note t' Millie'll scotch
that snake fer awhile.

(He places the note carefully on the

topmost step of the left hand stairs.
Then gathering up the documents
and snapping off his flashlight,
he exits U.C.1, *as the blue light fades out.)*

*(*CALEB *enters* U.R.9, *walking slowly*
down Campus Street as if burdened
by the weight of his ponderous thoughts.)

*(off-*S.U.R.*)*

CHORUS 1   Whére now? . . . . drágged, ...
CHORUS 2   . . . . hoóked one, ... haúled? . .

CHORUS 1   lónely . . . . do you stágger? . . . .
CHORUS 2   and lóst one, ... fáll? . . .

CHORUS 1   dó you . . . . quíckslime . . . .
CHORUS 2   . . . . . . swím in this . . . . cráwl? . . . . . .

(Absorbed in painful introspection
he pauses, fails to notice RENAIRE
coming out of the tavern, approaching
behind him, listening.)

CHORUS 1   Whíther now? . . . . . and lóst one? . . . .
CHORUS 2   . . . . lónely . . . . whére? . .

CALEB   I couldn't. My water-weak
              . . . courage gave way. I - I couldn't

              bring myself to say those things,
              . . . . . those thoughts, those
              . . . . unforgiven crimes,

              . . . . . so I loitered in the porch
              . . . . in the atrium - I was afraid
              . . . . of another sacrilege -
              . . . . so I came away.

RENAIRE   *(Cutting in, jolting*
              him out of his reverie.)

So you failed, didn't you
. . . . in your commission!

CALEB   *(Swinging around.)*
              . . . . Renaire! you - you startled me!

RENAIRE   You have good reason to be startled.
                 My threats are never in vain - I've
                 written my letters to the Rector,
                 and Jamison Thorn enclosing
                 the damning evidence. I'm about
                 to hand them over to a courier
                 for personal delivery.

CALEB   Renaire, please! don't send.
                 those letters - they'd destroy me!
                 Can't you see, I couldn't
                 Molly Green's joining the convent - I

RENAIRE   Unfortunate for you, I would say -

CALEB   Is there *anything* I can do?

RENAIRE   An alternative ransom
                 for your reputation?
                                    (Slight pause.)
                 Yes - seventy grand
                 In Stew's, within the next two hours.

CALEB   But Renaire! I *can't* do that!
                 I'd have to tell my stepfather -

RENAIRE   You'll find a way - you *may*
                 have to open his strongbox -

                 (CALEB *backs away from* RENAIRE,
                 then turns and runs up on the seawall.
                 He stops before the door U.C.3, *looks*
                 back at his tormentor, then lets
                 himself in.)
                          (RENAIRE *on returning*
                 to the tavern, sees the LIBRARIAN *and*
                 DRUGGIST *coming around from* U.R.8.
                 He steps back out of sight as they
                 enter the cellar and disappear
                 through the door U.C.7; *then running*
                 quickly, he lets himself in at the right,
                 darts upstairs and snatches up the
                 briefcase. On returning to the tavern,
                 he goes upstairs and knocks at D.R.16.
                 He is let in by MCCORKERAN.)

(We hear CAPTAIN COD*'s voice as he comes down Campus Street* U.R.9.*)*

CODROCKS Aye - the man o' God
sure 'n' he said t' me,
       (Appearing.)
yer stone ship, m' boy,
is surely Payter's Bark -

e'en the little un o' the parish
an' the grand one o' the town,
all are after bein' one ship
i' the moorin's o' the world -

> *(While* COD *rambles on, the door opens cautiously* U.C.3, *and* CALEB *comes out on the seawall. He stands looking out to sea for a moment, then climbs carefully up on the parapet to the left of the lamppost, and steadying himself, turns around with his back to the sea. Wavering he stands, balancing himself with his right hand, then covering his eyes with the left.* COD *meanwhile has continued his theme.)*

COD - same as knocks 'ere
now, an' is even now departed,
is surely sailin' o'er the sea
an' soon comin' into haven -

> *(Rounding the platform, he sees* CALEB.*)*

COD Now what's that lad about?
tryin' t' drown hisself? ahoy!
it's slippery there - come down!

> *(*CALEB *throws up his hands.)*

COD He's gonna jump!
> *(Stepping back, with both arms raised.* CALEB *falls out of sight.* COD *runs up on the seawall and looks over the parapet.)*

COD	Why, God Almighty - may the dead be raised! *(He runs around to the steps U.C.4, and begins vigorously hauling in the nets.)*
COD	. . . . Well Cod, m' boy, we've landed sockeye, halibut an' chum - but never t'ought I'd see the day I'd be landin' a man! *(Reaching down.)*
COD	Here, lad - give us yer hand. *(He hauls up CALEB, all entangled in fishnets.)*
COD	There now - well, young man, what ya got t' say fer yerself? Here - let's take off the nets -
CALEB	I wanted to die.
COD	. . . . Ye wanted t' die - that's foul weather i' the sky o' the sun! Now why should a stappin' fellow like ye be wishin' t' end yer life when ye're so young?
CALEB	It's crimes I've done that some one found out -
COD	. . . . Crimes?
CALEB	. . . . My sins I mean, the deeds I've done, and my black ingratitude.
COD	. . . . We're all rank sinners son, there's time t' repent.
CALEB	There's no time! there's a devil out there -
COD	. . . . . . Yes?
CALEB	. . . . a blackmailing criminal! He's about to destroy the little that is left of my life -
COD	Now look 'ere, lad, there's no doubt about it, ye're in some deep trouble - so go up there, t' the man o' God, Pere Bernard, for he's kind, like a father -

COD   an' he'll help ye.
CALEB   . . . . You think he would?
COD   I'm sure of it, son.
CALEB   . . . . He'll not condemn me?

COD   He's not there fer that - he counsels,
                an' forgives, an' he 'elps ye
                t' forget.
CALEB   . . . . . I'll do as you say, and
                thank you Capt'n Cod - you've
                helped me to make up my mind.

COD   God go with ye, lad, an'
                don't be afeared.

                        As COD *rearranges his nets over
                        the end of the parapet and goes
                        down the steps to the quay,* U.C.4,
                        CALEB *descends from the seawall
                        and pauses, then sits on the
                        bottom steps. He prepares
                        himself for what he must do.*
                        MOLLY, *returning from the cathedral,
                        enters* U.R.9. *She does not notice* CALEB.)

MOLLY   Oh! to be free at last!
                . . . it's like air, the bright
                . . . . fresh morning air!
                        *(She goes
                        directly to the convent.)*

MOLLY   but in the evening of my life,
                . . . strange evening! beyond
                . . . . belief - all joy and peace -
                        *(She rings
                        the convent bell.* CALEB *seeing her,
                        has risen - he comes downstage.)*

CALEB   Is that you, Molly?
MOLLY   . . . . Why, Caleb!
                        (She runs over to him.)
                . . . . I thought
                you had already gone - have you
                seen the confessor yet?

CALEB   I tried but I couldn't, Molly -

CALEB but I am going now. 'Twas the
old fisherman, Capt'n, Cod who
convinced me.
MOLLY . . . . Praise God Caleb!
Go up there quickly now, before it's
too late - Pere Bernard's a saint,
he'll show you the way -
CALEB . . . . And you Molly?
MOLLY I'm entering the convent
tonight, I just rang, and I'm
so happy! I'll pray for you Caleb.

CALEB And I for you. I'll
need your prayers now,
as never before -
(Amber light
comes up in the convent
porch. CALEB *steps back out of*
sight by the platform as MOLLY
runs back to the steps.
SR. JENNIFER *appears* D.R.18, *and*
opens the gate.)

SR. JENNIFER You're here!
. . . everyone's glad, Molly -
(She calls inside.)
Mother, it's Molly!
(She comes out
with dignified formality.)

M. SUPERIOR My daughter, do you come
hither to do penance, and to
amend your life?
MOLLY . . . . I do, Mother.
M. SUPERIOR Welcome then among
the Magdalenes, my child, and may
Christ strengthen your resolve -
Come in, my dear.

MOLLY *(As the sisters turn to lead* MOLLY *in,*
she glances back at CALEB. *They*
go in, the gate is closed, and the
amber light fades out. At the
same time the light comes up
in the bar. Only BERT *is there,*
polishing glasses.)

191

CHORUS   (*As* CALEB *approaches the tavern,*
(*off*-S.D.R.)   *the memory of that night revives.*)

CHORUS 4   Jazz-rash Jamshyd he
                         . . . . deep drank
                         . . . . inebriate
                         Jazzrash! Jamshyd
                         . . . . drank deep,

CHORUS 2   . . . . a há ha há ha . . . . . rásh!
CHORUS 4   Já-a-a-a-a-a-a-a-a azz rásh!

                         (*The blind going up,* CALEB *suddenly
                         sees* RENAIRE *staring at him through*
                         MOLLY'*s window. The boy shrinks
                         back fearfully.* RENAIRE *disappears.*)

CHORUS 1   Rage, rage
CHORUS 3   . . . . a ragin' fire!
CHORUS 1   . . . . rage, rage,

                         (*Walking out onto Campus Street*
                         RENAIRE *approaches, blocking the way.*)

RENAIRE   You have the ransom,
                         . . . . Caleb Thorn?
CHORUS 1   . . . . rage, rage,
CALEB   No! no Renaire!
                         . . . you'll never have it!
                         . . . . and you'll never get me!

                         (*Gathering his courage, he suddenly
                         bolts past* RENAIRE, *knocking him
                         down, and running up Campus Street.*)

CHORUS 4   Tlángorásh!
CHORUS 4   . . . . Já-a-a-a-a-a-a-a-aazz rásh!
CHORUS 2   . . . . a há ha há ha. . . rásh!

RENAIRE   Wait! Come back,
                         . . . . you fool! you'll
                         . . . . pay for it!
                         (*Scrambling for his
                         briefcase he jumps up, and strides
                         furiously into the tavern.*)

CHORUS 3   a rágin' wráckin'
                . . . . and a rágin' róck!

CHORUS 1   . . . . and ráge, ráge,

RENAIRE   Gimme a
                whisky 'n' soda, Bert.

COURIER   *(Entering the tavern.)*
                . . . . . You called for courier
                . . . . service, sir?

CHORUS 1   . . . . ráge, ráge,

RENAIRE   Oh - oh yes!
                here - deliver these letters
                to the addresses indicated -
                you can keep the change.

COURIER   . . . . . Thank you sir!
                                (As he leaves U.R.9.)

CHORUS 2   . . . . a rágin' ráge! rage

CHORUS 1   . . . . ráge, rage, ráge,

                *(The light in the bar fades dim,
                while in the cellar a ruddy glow
                of the furnace grows. Then three
                conspriators enter stealthily, U.C.7.)*

LIBRARIAN   So you think he's planning
                to trick us out of our cut?

DRUGGIST   You said he's laid hands
                on some upstairs 'monuments'?

HAGAN   Aye, that's what 'e said,
                an'e sounded slippery as an eel.

                *(He silences the conspirators as
                a bright amber light fades in
                on the upper platform and
                MISS MILLIE enters U.C.6 with tea service
                murmuring to herself as she goes
                upstairs.)*

MISS MILLIE   . . . . Millicent Brainborough -
                benefactress of humanity!

                                (At doors U.C.1-2.)

MISS MILLIE   Professor Renaire, I'm
                bringing in your tea, if you'll
                excuse me . . . Professor?

193

*(MILLIE knocks, but receiving no answer
she opens the door* U.C.2, *and looks in.)*

MISS MILLIE   Hum - must have stepped out
for a moment - .....
*(Seeing no one, she
enters to set out the tea things.
In the cellar the conspirators confer.)*

LIBRARIAN   These so-called 'monuments' must
have been emoluments!

DRUGGIST   Might we possess ourselves
of the same? .....

HAGAN   .... An hour ago ya might.
I've already took possession o' the
contents - stuffed 'is case with
old newsprint. Surprise fer 'im!

LIBRARIAN   Well let's see it! May be of value -

HAGAN   Went through the whole thing -
just old legal forms.

LIBRARIAN   What did you do with it?

HAGAN   Do with it? I threw it in the furnace -
there weren't no money in it!

DRUGGIST   You what? you destroyed it?

LIBRARIAN   Threw it in the furnace? .....

DRUGGIST   Of all the idiots! .....

LIBRARIAN   .... Blitherin'
benighted son of a bastard!

DRUGGIST   Let me explain somethin' Hagan -

HAGAN   Ya don' mean it were worth
somethin', do you? .....

(They groan in unison. HAGAN,
*expecting something silences
the others. They all begin to
listen intently. Then off-stage*

                                    up centre - the door U.C.2 *is still open.)*

MISS MILLIE   Professor Renaire? . . . . .
                                    (As she comes out.)
                     That's strange - he was here
                     a short while ago - probably
                     called away on business -
                     . . . . . well, we'll have tea later.

                                    (About to go down on the left, she
                                    notices the note on the top step.)

MISS MILLIE   Now what's this?
                     . . . . . A note? *(Snatching it up.)*
                     . . . . To M. Brainborough?
                     . . . .*(Opening it hastliy.)*

MISS MILLIE   'So-called 'Professor' . . . well known
                     . . . to Police . . . . . did time for
                     . . . . extortion . . . . . embezzlement!'
                     . . . . . Eli? Oh no! - no! I've -
                     . . . . I've been robbed! my money -
                     . . . . my securities - call the Police!

                                    (MISS MILLIE *rushes through the open*
                                    door U.C.2, *takes the phone in*
                                    trembling hands.)

MISS MILLIE   Operator! give me the police!
                     I've - I've been robbed -
                     I live at . . . Oh! oooh . . . . .
                                    (She faints,
                                    and slumps to the floor - the
                                    operator answers off-stage U.C.)

OPERATOR   Hello - hello! is there anyone
                     on the line? Answer me, please -
                     is there anyone on the line?

                                    (The door closes of itself as the lights
                                    fade out. The conspirators are
                                    alarmed by MILLIE*'s outcry.)*

DRUGGIST   We'd better get out of here -
                     someone may come!

(The LIBRARIAN *and* DRUGGIST *disappear
into the alley* U.R.8. RENAIRE *also has
heard* MILLIE. *Anxiously he pays for
his drink. As* BERT *closes the bar,
he exits* D.R.16 *and the lights fade
out.* RENAIRE *has come out into the
street.* HAGAN *is watching in his lair.)*

RENAIRE

That screaming! Something's gone
wrong - sounded like Millie!
Must get t' the bank - cash in
before it's too late!
(He rushes off D.R.17,
*clutching his precious briefcase,
stuffed with stale news.)*

(Crouching by his furnace, HAGAN
*appears to be gloating over the
discomfiture of all concerned.
With immense satisfaction, he
draws out the documents from
an inner pocket. Opening the
furnace, he flings the lot of them
contemptuously into the flames.)*

HAGAN

Too late! háha há hahá!
Ya see - every devil is a cheat
while I'm the past master-a-lies!
háha há hahá!
(Wheezing breath drawn in.)
. . . . fools!

They think they've lost
a fortune - haha! an' they have -
háha há hahá!
(Wheezing breath in.)
. . . . their souls!

Ha ha! they've lost 'em -
háha há! - an' their minds!
(Wheezing breath in.)
háha há hahá!
*(He crawls into the
furnace, feet first - looking out,
the face in the fire is demonic.)*

HAGAN

*(Begining to slump in agony, he
snatches breath in staccato
gasps -)*
. . . . Ah! . . . ah! . . . aah! . . . aaagh!
*(And exhales in a harsh
hissing gargle.)*
      *(Shaking hands
take hold of the iron door
and slam it shut.)*
        *(Loud inhuman
laughter ricochetes up the chimney
followed by a dog's howl.)*

DOM JEROME

The voices are terrible!
(Rising unsteadily.)
. . . . . I cannot hear anymore,
. . . . I must go in and pray -

*(He goes in, but the dim blue light
remains in the Porter's cell.
A single bell stroke of the bourdon
sounds from the cathedral.
MARY SIMS and WILLIE enter on Campus
Street U.R.9.)*

MARY

. . . . and then when
they foundered, your father
abandoned ship on a life raft,
but the others - the other
fishermen, weren't so fortunate,
and that's why your father
wasn't lost at sea, son.

WILLIE

Why didn't you
. . . . tell me Mom?

MARY

I just couldn't -
. . . . I didn't want you
to think bad of your father.
He blames himself for
the loss of the others -

WILLIE

. . . . But I knew
dad wasn't drowned!

MARY

. . . . You knew?
but how could you?
      (She comes to a stop.)

WILLIE

You remember
that night he came home? I . . . . .

WILLIE   I wasn't asleep - I thought
he was a ghost at first,
but he wasn't dead -

MARY   *(She drops to*
her knee beside the boy, clasping
him by the shoulders.)
. . . . Oh Willie!
your father's become a hopeless
drinker, and that's why he hides,
because he loves you,
and he's so ashamed -

G. OWEN   *(Entering* U.R.9, *she moves with*
arthritic slowness down the street.)

Thank God the dear girl
got to confession! Now she'll be
safe in the convent, God bless 'er.

     (As she sees her daughter and WILLIE,
she stops for a breath, leaning
on her cane.)
. . . . Is that you, Rosemary?

MARY   Mother! what are you doing out
at an hour like this?

G. OWEN   . . . . I've come
a little too far today - I'm out of
breath - besides havin' my
usual pain -

MARY   . . . . You're looking poorly.
I'll send Willie - hurry over son, an'
call Dr. Malloy -
      (He runs off
U.L.10, *on the seawall.)*

G. OWEN   Don't disturb the good man,
he's not well.

MARY   . . . . *You're* not well
Mother, now come along.

     (She helps her around to the left
entrance. As they go in, amber
light comes up on the lower
platform. The old woman
seats herself wearily on the bench.

MARY *takes her coat and hat into the hall* U.C.6.)

    (Singing sounds in the distance, off-stage U.R. *The song grows louder as* REGIS *and his cousins approach.)*

FAY
    . . . . Mánning the rúdder
    . . . . stróng in the stórm

FANNY
    . . . . lóngin' for lándfall
    . . . . . the dáy ye were bórn

FAY, FANNY
    . . . . Old ship and áged
    . . . . leéward the Isles,

FAY, FAN., REG.
    . . . . . lánded on góld strand
    . . . seáman Mageé.

    (Entering U.R.9, *they appear on Campus Street.)*

FANNY
Regis, let's stop to see Granny Owen.

REGIS
    . . . . Alright Fanny, we'll see if she's in.

FAY
    . . . . Her light's burnin' I'll bet she's in!

    (They run around to the left entrance where they knock - sound U.C. MARY *answers.)*

MARY
Good evening, children.

REGIS
Good evening - can we see Granny Mrs. Sims?

MARY
Well, only for a moment, Regis. Mrs. Owen is not well -

    (As they troop in.)

G. OWEN
    . . . . Why it's my grandson, Regis!

MARY
    . . . . No Mother, it's the Wicks boy -

G. OWEN
    . . . . Well Mary, every little boy I see is my grandson - Fay and Fanny

G. OWEN   are my granddaughters too -
                   aren't you?
FAY, FANNY   . . . . Yes, Granny Owen.

G. OWEN   You see? Now Regis, since
                   you've come, be a good lad -
                   run across to Cloistergarth
                   and get the porter, Dom Jerome.
                   He tends my furnace, and I
                   need to talk to him -

REGIS   I'll get him, Granny!

                   (He goes with FAY *and* FANNY
                   *trailing after. They ring the
                   bell at Cloistergarth, but not
                   seeing the porter, they enter.)*

                   (COD *comes up from the quay,* U.C.4.)

CODROCKS   Well, that's all spread agin -
                   one never knows what one's gonna
                   catch - aye an the stone ship -
                   shouldn't be surprised she takes
                   a soul or two, tonight.

                   *(He lights his pipe. A foghorn
                   sounds, as* WILLIE *returns on the
                   seawall* U.L.10 *with* DR. MALLOY.)

COD   G' evenin', Doctor.
DR. MALLOY   . . . .'Evenin' Capt'n Cod.

                   (MARY *is watcing and opens to
                   them.)*
DR. MALLOY   . . . . Good evening, Mrs. Sims.

MARY   Thank you for coming,Doctor,
                   it's Mother again.
                             *(They go in -
                   DR. MALLOY takes out his stethoscope.)*

DR. MALLOY   Well, Mrs. Owen, been
                   overdoing it again, have you?

                   (He listens.)

G. OWEN
Well, it's the Feast
of the Dedication, you know -

DR. MALLOY
I know, Mrs. Owen,
but still, I hear a murmur,
a rustle of the heart -
(Taking her pulse.)
I'm afraid you must
sleep a little more, and
walk a little less.

G. OWEN
We do not have too much
time for the world.

DR. MALLOY
No - not too much.

G. OWEN
Is Regis bringing my
grandson from Cloistergarth?

MARY
Yes, Mother, he's coming.

DR. MALLOY
Take one of these with a cup of hot
tea, before bed tonight.

G. OWEN
Thank you, Doctor Malloy.

DR. MALLOY
Good night, Mrs. Owen.
(To Mary.)
She'll be alright tonight.

MARY
Doctor, Mother's getting senile -
she's talking about the *Wicks* boy
being her grandson, and now
it's the *porter* of Cloistergarth!

DR. MALLOY
I shouldn't worry about
that, Mrs. Sims - your Mother
is a very, very wise old lady.

MARY
I suppose she is - I told Willie
about his father.

DR. MALLOY
.... Those nightmares
will stop. *(To* WILLIE.*)*
.... You're not afraid
of the sea anymore, are you, Willie!

WILLIE   No, sir.

DR. MALLOY   . . . . Ah, that's good - I think
I'll light a pipe with the Captain
before I walk home - there's
a good boy!
        . . . . Goodnight Mrs. Sims.

(He goes out, joining COD. *They sit
on the parapet, smoking.* MARY
returns to her mother.)

MARY   Don't stay up too late, Mother.

G. OWEN   Thank you, dear. Goodnight
Willie, my little grandson -
               (She hugs him.)

WILLIE   How can you have three
grandsons, Granny?

G. OWEN   . . . . What a question!
Now, when you grow up,
then you'll see -
             (She kisses him.)

*(*MARY SIMS *and* WILLIE *leave; the boy
waves to the doctor as they come
out on the seawall.* DOM JEROME *comes
down the steps of Cloistergarth at
the same moment with* REGIS, FAY
and FANNY. *Seeing the two on the
seawall he instantly stops, and
the children become quiet. As* MARY
stoops to button WILLIE*'s coat,* JEROME
is lost in thought, remembering.)

DOM JEROME   Goodbye, Mother, with your
manifold names - Mary, Rose,
Rosemary - with your fabled
widowhood, fading with the
summer of my youth, gone -
goodbye my childhood - Willie -

*(*MARY *and* WILLIE *leave on the seawall
                    U.L.10.)*

REGIS   They used to call me Willie.

DOM JEROME   . . . . I know, Regis.

REGIS   I want to be a monk too,
at Cloistergarth - just like you!

DOM JEROME   Ah yes - I remember. You're
a little young as yet, I'm afraid,
to become a monk - so we'll
pray over it a while,
shall we?

REGIS   . . . . . Yes Dom Jerome.

DOM JEROME   But remember this
as you grow up: no matter
how dark or difficult your
life becomes - no matter what
terrible things might happen
to you, God is your Father,
and you will be one day,
happy - just as I am.

Now, children, it's getting late!
You had better be running along.

REGIS, FAY   Goodnight, Dom Jerome!
FANNY

DOM JEROME   Goodnight, children -
*(They skip
up the steps and disappear
on the seawall* U.L.10.*)*

DOM JEROME   . . . . and goodbye -
(From a distance.)

FAY   . . . . . We're disappearin' -
. . . . where are you, Regis?

(Crossing over to GRANNY OWEN*'s,* DOM
JEROME *knocks - sound off stage* U.C. -
he opens the door.)

DOM JEROME   Grandmother? are you sleeping?

G. OWEN   No, I am not asleep - come in,
Dom Jerome, I want to talk to you.

*(*DOM JEROME *enters, comes over to the
old woman, kisses her on the
forehead, and sits beside her.*

G. OWEN   So you remember now, after
all these years, your Grandmother,
and Rosemary your Mother - and
Nicholas, your poor Father gone.

You remember young Willie,
orphaned, and Regis the young dreamer,
and Tom the tormented, but at
peace now - you remember them all
because they are you.

DOM JEROME   Yes, Grandmother, I remember
them all - they were separate
dreams on a dark river.

G. OWEN   One more ghostdream comes
freighted with your darkest hour.
When Caleb went to confession
tonight, and the confessor's hand
was raised in absolution,
the dark river of forgetfulness
descended on his mind - 'twas
a merciful healing of his soul.

But protect him - he is bewildered!
His step-parents have disowned him.
They received a letter, and a message
from the Rector, and word was sent
to the cathedral, that he need
not bother coming home -

DOM JEROME   Don't worry, Grandmother,
it is all over, everything is
all right now, for all this has
happened a very long time ago.
It's all a memorial - of the past.

G. OWEN   Ah - that is well. I'll have
a little peace now - and a good
night's sleep. Good night,
my child -

DOM JEROME   ...... Good night, Grandmother -

DOM JEROME

*(As he rises to leave, G. OWEN seems
to be already receding into a
dream. He stops in the doorway
to whisper softly -)*
..................and goodbye -
*(He closes the door
very carefully. G. OWEN retires
leaning on her cane U.C.6; then
as the lights fade away, the
bourdon sounds from the
cathedral.)*

COD   Ahha! ship's bell!

DR. MALLOY   ....Haha - no, it's
..............the tower clock.

DOM JEROME   I say, Capt'n! keep
.....an eye on the hauling
..............of the anchor, eh?

COD   ....Aye, that I will
................yer Riverence!

DOM JEROME   Well, goodnight t' you.

DR. MALLOY   .....goodnight, Dom Jerome.

DOM JEROME   ....Goodnight, Doctor.

*(CAPTAIN COD and DR. MALLOY now go
down to the boats U.C.4. A fog horn
wails in the harbour as DOM JEROME
comes down the steps.*

*(HANNA enters U.C.9. Anxiously
she leads a dazed and bewildered
CALEB down Campus Street.)*

AUNT HANNA   Oh! what will I do?
The boy's lost 'is mind,
he don't even know
'is own auntie! .....

DOM JEROME   *(answering)*
Is that you, Hanna? ....

AUNT HANNA   ....Ah! Dom Jerome!
thank the Lord ye're here! ....

HANNA   What will we do? poor
                   Master Thorn - I mean
                   Tom! An'e don't remember
                   a thing - ye recall yer
                   auld Aunt Hanna? . . . . .
                        . . . . don't ya Tommy? . .

CALEB   Aunt Hanna? I don't
                        . . . . know I - I can't tell -

HANNA   But yer uncle - ye
                        . . . . recall Remus, surely?

CALEB   My uncle? no, I - . . . . .
                        . . . . I don't know if I have one.

HANNA   Now lad, yer Grandma,
                        . . . . she lives across the
                        . . . . way there - O Tom!

CALEB   Grandma - I don't
                        . . . . have a grandmother -

HANNA   Don't say that, Tom!

CALEB   I've no brother or
                        . . . . sister - I've

                   no father or mother -
                   I've . . . . . I've none I've -
                        . . . . forgotten them all -

HANNA   Oh, what's t' be done?

DOM JEROME   Now Hanna - pull
                        yourself together, there's
                             nothing you can do.

AUNT HANNA   Will 'e need a doctor
                        . . . . do ye think? . . . . .

DOM JEROME   We'll see - but believe me,
                   his cure has already begun.
                   It's a matter of time, I should
                   know, for I suffered the same
                   affliction - years ago.

HANNA

Well if ye think so
. . . . I'll try to be calm -
but 'is step-parents
. . . . disowned 'im - won't
let 'im come 'ome!

DOM JEROME

Leave that to me, we'll
. . . . . . take good care of the boy.
In the peace of Cloistergarth
. . . . his mind will mend.

HANNA

Oh, I do hope so. . . . . .

DOM JEROME

Good night now, Hanna,
. . . . and don't worry.

HANNA

I'll try not, yer
Riverence - Good night, an'
goodbye my poor Tom -

(HANNA *enters Hearth Lodge by the
invisible door, and disappears upstairs,*
D.L.12. *The bourdon sounds a single
bell stroke as* DOM JEROME *leads* CALEB
to the bench where they sit.)

(*Inside Cloistergarth the* CANTOR *and
the* MONASTIC CHOIR *begin chanting for
the Feast of the morrow.*)

CANTOR

Angularis fundamentum -

CHOIR

. . . . . Lapis Christus missus est
. . . . Qui parietum compage -

(*The chanting fades just under*
CALEB *and* JEROME*'s converstation;
their muted phrases, fall in with
with the rhythm of the chant. The
doors* U.C.1 *and* 2 *open slowly upon
the sky where the shadowy form
of the cathedral begins to dissolve
in the mist, almost imperceptibly,
into a rainbow semblance of sails.*)

CHOIR   In utroque nectitur,
CALEB   ....What is that?
DOM JEROME   ....It's the hymn

CHOIR   Quem Sion sancta suscepit,
DOM JEROME   ....for the cathedral's
                     ....Dedication.
CHOIR   In quo credens permanet
CALEB   .... It is beautiful

CHOIR   Omnis illa Deo sacra
DOM JEROME   .... Will you come?
                     .... my younger but
CHOIR   Et dilecta civitas
DOM JEROME   .... bewildered youth?
CALEB   ....to go? but where?

CHOIR   Plena modulis in laude
DOM JEROME   .... We will be going
                     ....on a voyage
CHOIR   Et canore jubilo,
DOM JEROME   ....of final discovery,
                     ....a sea voyage
CHOIR   Trinum Deum unicumque
DOM JEROME   ....embarked on a
                     .... Ship of Stone.
CHOIR   Cum fervore praedicat
CALEB   .... Why are we alone
                     ....when sailing?
CHOIR   Gloria et honor Deo
DOM JEROME   .... We're alone
                     .... because we've forgotten

CHOIR   Usquequaqu(e) altissimo
DOM JEROME   .... the sorrows
                     ....of the world -
                     (DOM JEROME *stands, takes*
                                  CALEB *by the hand -*
CHOIR   Una Patri, Filioque   *he rises.)*
CALEB   .... Will we ever
                     .... remember them?
CHOIR   Inclyto Paraclito
CALEB   ....the sorrows,
                     ....I mean -
                     (They walk to Cloistergarth.)

CHOIR	Cui laus set et potestas
DOM JEROME	. . . . Sorrows? . . . when we do
	. . . . remember them

(They pause at the steps.)

CHOIR	Per aeterna saecula
DOM JEROME	. . . . they will no longer be
	. . . . sorrows -
CHOIR	Amen.

*(DOM JEROME leads CALEB into
Cloistergarth. The cathedral
bourdon is heard to strike again.
Waves beyond the seawall
accompany the stone ship under
her rainbow sail, as she slides
from the slipway into the aerial
ocean.)*

*(The monk's chanting grows
louder for a spell, then recedes as
if the church doors had just been
opened and someone had entered.)*

CANTOR	Haec est domus Domini
	. . . . firmiter aedificata.

CHOIR	Bene fundata est
	. . . . supra firmam petram.

(Off-stage U.C.)

COD	. . . . Look, look up there,
	. . . . Doctor Malloy!

*(As COD runs up the stairs
              onto the seawall.)*

CANTOR	Domum tuam Domine,
COD	. . . . Come up on the wall!

CHOIR	decet sanctitudo . . . . .
DR. MALLOY	. . . . I'm coming
CHOIR	. . . . in longitudinem dierum -

(Off-stage U.C.)

DR. MALLOY	. . . . What is it, Captain?

NOVICE	Dominus regnavit
	. . . . decorum indutus est,
CHOIR	indutus est Dominus
	• . . . . fortitudinem, et
	. . . . praecinxit se -

LOOK! THE SAIL - THE BOWSPRIT!, P.211

(*The psalmody continues,*
gradually growing more distant, as if
the choir were being carried off
in the stone ship.)
(*Then as* DR. MALLOY
reaches the seawall, the fisherman
cries out -)

COD   Look! She's
  . . . stirrin' in a ghostly
  . . . . manner out-a-the moorin's! see!
  . . . 'er spirit's movin'er even if stone walls
  . . . . still be anchored
  . . . . under 'er - look!

(SR. JENNIFER *enters*
in the moonlight D.R.18,
and kneels.)

COD   She's - she's
  . . . unfurlin'er sails there out-a
  . . . . yon spire! The spar, doctor! See?

DR. MALLOY . . . I can't see a thing -

COD   Ya can't? Why, she's - ya can see 'er
  . . . . *slidin'* there, the ghost of a dreamin'
  . . . ship of stone! as if she's longin'
  . . . . . fer a storm-a-seaspray!
  . . . . . . don't ya see 'er?

(DOM JEROME *comes out of*
his cell D.L.14, *and also kneels.*)

DR. MALLOY You *do* see it, don't you -

COD   Ya mean ya can't see 'er?
  . . . why man, ya must be plumb *blind* -
  Look! There! The sail - the bowsprit -
  . . . . . . the wake of 'er - look man!

(*As the ship sails directly overhead,*
he rushes back down off the seawall.
His triumphant shout echoes
below from the quay -)

COD   . . . . There she goes!

(*A flurry of gulls answers him from*
the harbour. Although the doctor
scans the heavens he sees nothing.

*The last trace of the ghostly ship
has disappeared into the sky - the
psalmody is still - only the sound
of the sea remains.* DR. MALLOY *reflects.)*

DR. MALLOY   Perhaps I am blind -
        . . . . It would good to see.
        . . .Beautiful - if one could believe.

*(The earthly cathedral hovers still
moored in the mist as* DR. MALLOY
leaves on the seawall. SR. JENNIFER
*has returned into the convent
closing the gate, while* DOM JEROME *who
has been kneeling, seeing what few
can see, is now sunk back upon
his heels, his clasped hands have
slipped into his lap, his head has
dropped forward as if in meditation.
The bourdon booms mournfully
out of the mist.* JEROME *is so without
motion, one must wonder if he breathes
yet, or has already taken his departure.*

*With the scrim descending, darkness
engulfs convent and cloister, as
the sound of the sea recedes.)*

THE CURTAIN FALLS

AFTERWORD

SYNOPSIS, INTERPRETATION, AESTHETIC
OF ALL THREE WATCHES.

WITH TIMBRE ORCHESTRATION OF CHORUSES,
CHOREOGRAPHY OF VOTARIES IN THE SABAT,
AND MUSIC FOR THE SONGS.

NOTES ARE APPENDED FOR
STAGE SET, LIGHTING,
AND COSTUME.

EARLY STUDY FOR THE SET

When the first sketches for this dramatic nocturne were written thirty-four years ago, they were more in the nature of poetic narratives. I began by snatching some fifteen characters off the street. The only thing they had in common was that they were going to confession - a little band of pilgrims, one might say, like Chaucer's going to Canterbury. Each was a separate story. The Narrator threaded them together.

Unfortunately for the writer, the Narrator proved to be a fascinating conversationalist, and had to be silenced for a while, lest his loquacity inhibit the others. The results of this interdict were remarkable. The other characters began to live their own lives with abandon, all betraying a remarkable ability to remember. Their dossiers began to swell as gourds do on a compost. Like a gardener, I was struggling to control exuberant vegetables gone wild!

The hardy ones - those who survived the competition - began to develop complexities of plot, interacting with the others. It was inevitable that Annabelle should confront Tad, and that Granny Owen should delight in watching Regis and his two small elves. Nor was it possible to prevent the conjunction of Tom and Caleb. Their mothers were complementary - one dead but real, the other alive but unreal. That Molly and Caleb should have met was providential. Something unexpected - a seduction supplanted by conversion - had to occur. And Reniare's machinations had to turn against him. It could only be the blackmail fulcrum that would catapult Caleb from his suicidal sea-leap into the blessed amnesia of absolution. But all that came later. In the early writing a logic was at work, but it was a hidden one. Writers often sail blind by intuition, like the ships that used to bounce their fog horns off the invisible. To resolve the ambiguities and contradictions required some final illumination, which had not as yet been given. And so the writing ground to a halt. The play was to lay fallow for almost ten years.

When I resumed writing, the problem was still there - what to do with Dom Jerome. Having cut him off from the others, he had pined away and lost interset in living. Yet I felt he was important, being, perhaps, the only character in the play who might prove to be a source of unity.

But was he? There was the confessor, Père Bernárd, one of the first to appear, living in the shadow of an Abbey I mistakenly transported from Brittany to the north. The following was among my notes, and is important not only for Père Bernárd, but also for the mise en scène of the entire play.

'Père Bernárd, wise,
Ancient, Norman priest
of olden stock, from fisher-folk
who dared the sea tides racing
over the man-trapping sands
of Saint-Michel,
long-known, with his
white wisped head and benign
time-scored face, like the scarp
of his native place . . .'

Mont-Saint-Michel! How that sea-girt rock-clinging gothic pile haunted my early imagination! I had read Cram's book 'Mont-Saint-Michel and Chartres' several times, and also Montalembert's 'Monks of the West'. This stream of romantic medievalism is apparent in the present work, and of course provided the main metaphor of the cathedral as a Stone Ship.

Regarding Père Bernárd: no matter how evocative he was in the beginning, he soon withdrew from any visible appearance in the play, no doubt because of his fidelity to the sacred seal of silence.

'The consciences of men
are gone into the ghostly ears.
Forgotten now every whisper
heard, every face blurred,
and gone beyond the grill
into the waters of Lethe,
washed and healed.
Ask me not how
the granite grace of stillness
seals the pastoral lips -
they cannot speak.'

And since they cannot speak, the penitents themselves must speak through the eloboration of flash-backs, which they did with a vengeance. Parents, step-parents, a grandparent, an aunt and uncle, a sister, brothers and cousins all clamouring for recognition. And along with these an undergrowth; the brambly spines of gossipry, the poisonous toxification of drunkards, and the even more sinister designs of the aberrant and criminal. In a jungle growth like that, one has to belabour with the machete, which I did. Characters vanished, subplots disappeared, elaborations were lopped, but still the intangible key to the unity of the play eluded me.

So I deepened my search, pondering anew the theological ramifications of the sacrament; all those penitents were gathering as Christ's bride - an Ecclesia withour stain or wrinkle, yet penitent. For the philosopher Jacques Maritain, the mysterious conjunction was 'the most troubling enigma, and the most magnificent - a church not without sinners, but without sin.' Any elucidation of that mystery will only be found in her twofold nature; human, in that her numbers are drawn from the seething mass of man's paranoia; divine, in that Christ, who draws them, is the all-holy who expiates in his own blood all the world's evil. He's able to forgive them and forget, because he loves them. The forgiving and the fogetting are closely linked.

And it was then that the inspiration struck - Lethe! That river of forgetfulness imagined by the Florentine poet, on top of his purgatorial mountain! My Bernárd knew of it, for the sins of his penitents vanished into it forever. What about Jerome? I did not know what he was to forget - just that forgetting was the key. So I gave myself to psychological study, reading a number of works, Carl Jung among them, and began to see the distinct possibility that I had written a memory play. The voices, the separate stories were not only outside, they were inside the mind of Jerome as well. They became interpretations of his own life, constructed subconciously and gradually emerging into the light.

> 'Go to the heart, poet,
> know this grace of state - read
> there the fable of every fashioned fate.
> See there the shame, the scalding
> of Abel's anguish on the branded
> sons of Cain - and sing
> such fiction will be true -
> your brother's image
> in the heart of you!'

Now as I wrote, Jerome's interventions were no longer hobbles to the play's momentum. They became curiously alive and full of suspense, spurring on the action. He too was hastening toward the inevitable reconciliation. In the horror and nightmare of the Sabat, when Christ and Satan stuggle for the possession of the soul, he discovers his own.

And so it comes about that the psychological theme meets and fuses within the sacramental one. Caleb forgets and Jerome remembers. The denouement works itself out, untangling the skeins of guilt and grace, in a tranquil going-home; all saints and souls, all beasts and birds, into the Ark.

Dunstan Massey
Westminster Abbey
Mission, B.C. 2010

ERE GHOSTLY FOG; CHORUS, P.10

SYNOPSIS, CHORUSES FOR THE THREE WATCHES
WITH MUSIC FOR THE SONGS

NOTE: All choruses within single or connected brackets are vertically simultaneous as are MUSIC when bracketed with sung or spoken text. Taped SOUND is also similarly coordinated.

SPOKEN VOICE TIMBRES for chorus speakers are indicated by the use of vocal terms such as TREBLES for children, SOPRANOS or CONTRAL-TOS for women, TENORS, BARITONES and BASSES for men. When persons in the play are introduced into the choruses, they speak or sing in character, except when they may serve to fill out some chorus in need.

THE FIRST WATCH

PAGE 10   Each Chorus consists of words and phrases, clustered like a flotilla of boats riding a sea of sound under them. The theatre is dark. Voices draw out fragments of the past, and of the Cathedral now, weathering in its fog bound anchorage, the immanence of winter -

PAGE 11   The Chorus shifts from the seasonal, to a darkening melancholy of mind which is banished in turn by a female chattering of gossips on phone lines -

PAGE 12   as they snatch with slanderous anticipation at the latest news of the town. Though vociferous they are supplanted by a carousel of roister-

PAGE 13   ous sailors at the bar. The clinking of glasses modulates into a quick tempo, with combo brushes for the Tavern's campus clientele, while a jazz chorus is sung, praising Omar's persian inebriate in the Rubaiyat.

PAGE 13

PAGE 13

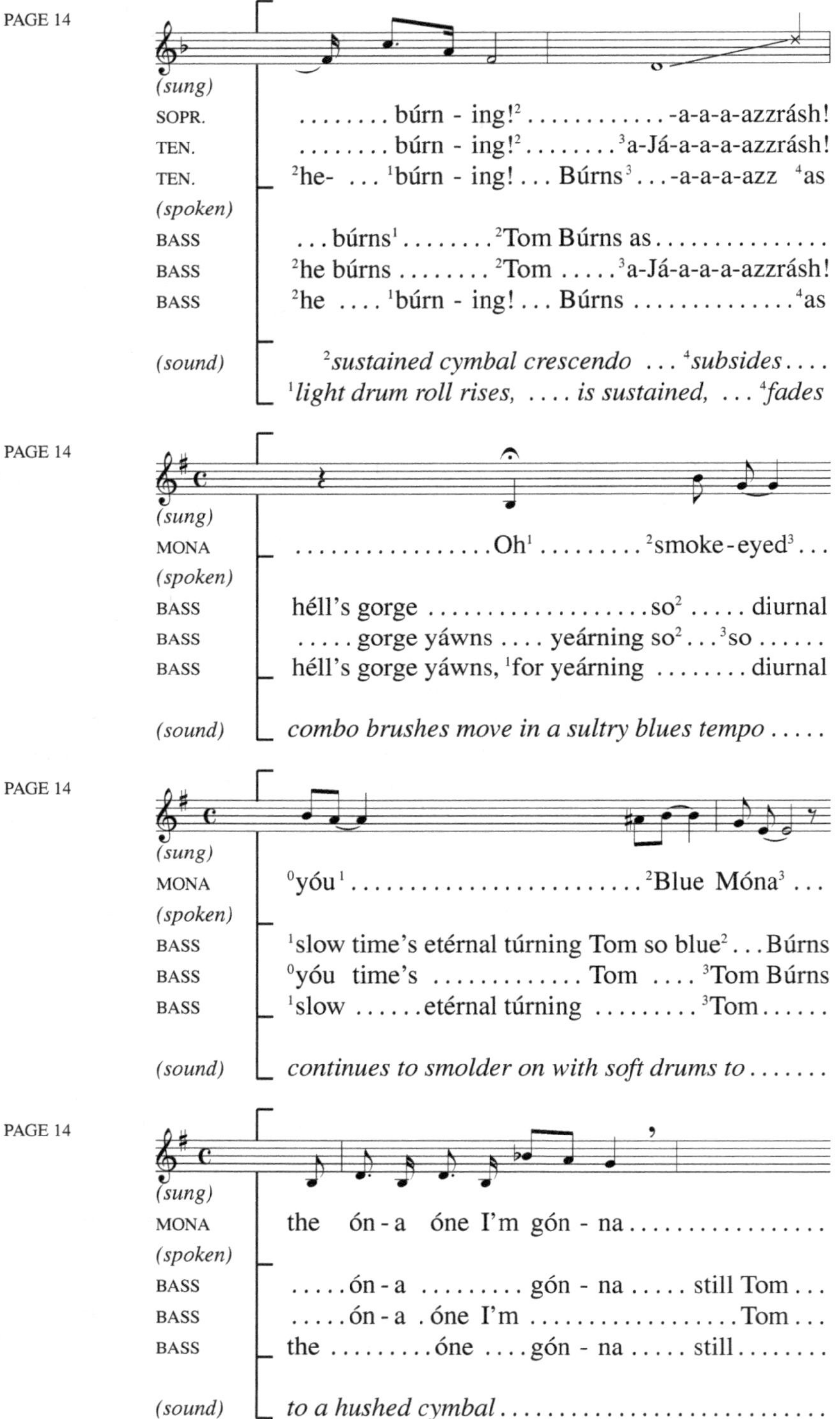

(sung)
SOPR. . . . . búrn - ing![2] . . . . -a-a-a-azzrásh!
TEN. . . . . búrn - ing![2] . . . . [3]a-Já-a-a-a-azzrásh!
TEN. [2]he- . . . [1]búrn - ing! . . . Búrns[3] . . . -a-a-a-azz [4]as
(spoken)
BASS . . . búrns[1] . . . . [2]Tom Búrns as . . . .
BASS [2]he búrns . . . . [2]Tom . . . . . [3]a-Já-a-a-a-azzrásh!
BASS [2]he . . . . [1]búrn - ing! . . . Búrns . . . . [4]as

(sound) [2]sustained cymbal crescendo . . . [4]subsides . . . .
[1]light drum roll rises, ... is sustained, . . . [4]fades

(sung)
MONA . . . . Oh[1] . . . . [2]smoke-eyed[3] . . .
(spoken)
BASS héll's gorge . . . . so[2] . . . . . diurnal
BASS . . . . . gorge yáwns . . . . yeárning so[2] . . . [3]so . . . . . .
BASS héll's gorge yáwns, [1]for yeárning . . . . diurnal

(sound) combo brushes move in a sultry blues tempo . . . . .

(sung)
MONA [0]yóu[1] . . . . [2]Blue Móna[3] . . .
(spoken)
BASS [1]slow time's etérnal túrning Tom so blue[2] . . . Búrns
BASS [0]yóu time's . . . . Tom . . . . [3]Tom Búrns
BASS [1]slow . . . . . . etérnal túrning . . . . [3]Tom . . . . . .

(sound) continues to smolder on with soft drums to . . . .

(sung)
MONA the   ón - a   óne I'm gón - na . . . .
(spoken)
BASS . . . . . ón - a . . . . gón - na . . . . . still Tom . . .
BASS . . . . . ón - a . óne I'm . . . . Tom . . .
BASS the . . . . óne . . . . gón - na . . . . . still . . . .

(sound) to a hushed cymbal . . . .

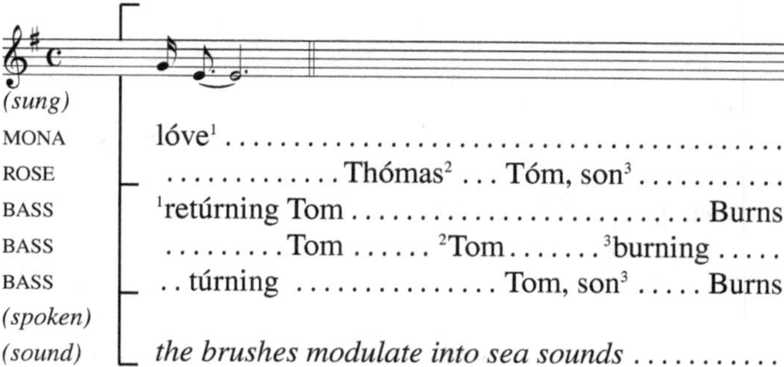

The Jazz Chorus had scarcely ended with its orgiastic shout when it was transmuted into the blues by Mona the torch singing Idol of adolescents, while deep sounding voices hurl their threats of infernal retribution. These alluring torments are swept away with a fresh sound of the sea, with enchanted remembering, and the children calling to each other.

They sing a sea shanty which is carried off in the wind; the cry of a child to his father, is lost in the depths of the sea.

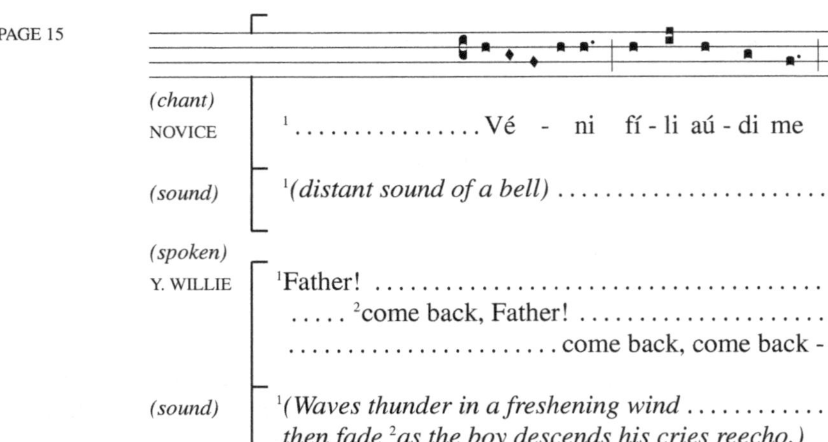

Until now, the voices have been the fragmented remembering of times past - Now they begin circling in a vortex drawing down the dreamer into the sea's slumbrous lulling, as if drowning were as natural as breathing. CALEB's voice, as yet unknown to us intrudes, edged with a nascent fear.

PAGE 16

He succumbes to a sense of perilous lassitude, takes alarm at the dragging weight and slime of the sea's mud rucks, he struggles vainly to free himself, but the cold cruel eyes of his own obsessions transfix him, seeming subliminal, monstrous, irresistable.

PAGE 17

The doubled Choruses are soon tripled. They assume a terrifying momentum as tentacles encoil his immobilized limbs, drawing him into the

PAGE 18

maw of an insatiable orifice, engulfing, swallowing him down a maelstrom of voices! Instantly the nightmare dies - he's startled awake in a sudden silence.

CURTAIN RISES

PAGE 19

When DOM JEREOME's soliloquies begin the chorus extends his train of thought, articulates the measure of his watchfulness, the intensity of his

PAGE 20

listening. If their voices speak to him, they also must be listening. When he questions them they will answer with a question of their own. They also contemplate the mystery of the town, the sea and the cathedral.

PAGE 21

With the scrim rising, the cobblestones echo with the cloistered compassion of nuns for their sorrowful sisters on the streets, (Good Shepherd nuns, whom JENNIFER will join and later MOLLY GREEN as a Magdalene.)

PAGE 21

When COD the fisherman appears whom DOM JEROME does recognize - "Captain Codrocks ... spreading his nets" while the younger voice of

PAGE 22

CALEB under him echoes his sympathetic thought - so also the same echoed chorus, with the entrance of TAD the docker, janitor and drunkard.

(In the novitiate off-stage D.L.13.*)*

CANTOR Now, Frater, try the chant
    plus delicato -

CANTOR Mais plus ritardando!

CANTOR .... bene!

JEROME And if you were to leap,
    Jerome, ...

Voices of tenors, with other timbres later, commence an antiphonal response to his few tentative words; giving voice to his unspoken train of
thought - Dedication of a Cathedral, his leaping 'into the moment of the
 hour' - to grapple with the mystery - where the saintly confessor aligns
his ship of souls as they stream, penitent to his feet for the cleansing
forgiveness of peace.

 The solemnity is broken with the salty observations of AMY HEARTH and
MISS MILLY's telephone mustering of the lady gossips.

 Tenor voices evoke the northeast hill with its candlelike procession of
street lights climbing to the cathedral square, while the contralto's phone
lines buzz with rumourous exchange. On MILLIE's telephone conversation with MRS. CARP, DOM JEROME questions himself whether they are only
imaginary, but comments laconically, nevertheless.

 Pondering the apparent reality of what he hears, he does accept that
the souls of those penitents have thoughts of their own. His musings
 mingle with the voices of CALEB and the CANTOR in a chorus of the mysterious multitude. AMY HEARTH again interrupts the meditative mood of his
'Riverence' with sundry observations, introducing ANNABELLE PEW on her
way to church, who stops by to exchange the news. Note the device of
an antiphonal chorus when she enters; two lines of disparate talk running concurrently, her own private thoughts, with an off-stage gossip's
chorus.

PAGE 30   TAD MCFERGUSON reappears, resolved to take the pledge, and going to church to fortify his defences. He meets HARRY IBBS unfortunately, the supposed ghost of a dead drunk. The boys gathering in the Bar mutter briefly, in chorus, about the weather. Then -

PAGE 31   A choral assault in made on poor TAD's resolution. They invite him in out of the damp and cold of the street - they offer him a shot of scotch to cheer 'im up. In a growing chorus of drunken conviviality they offer him every inducement to quench his thirst. When he stubbornly resists they

PAGE 32   redouble their efforts. Here an acknowledgement is due for the colourful tavern talk of Joyce's Dubliners - that irresistable Irish eloquence!

PAGE 32   The boys finally resort to song.

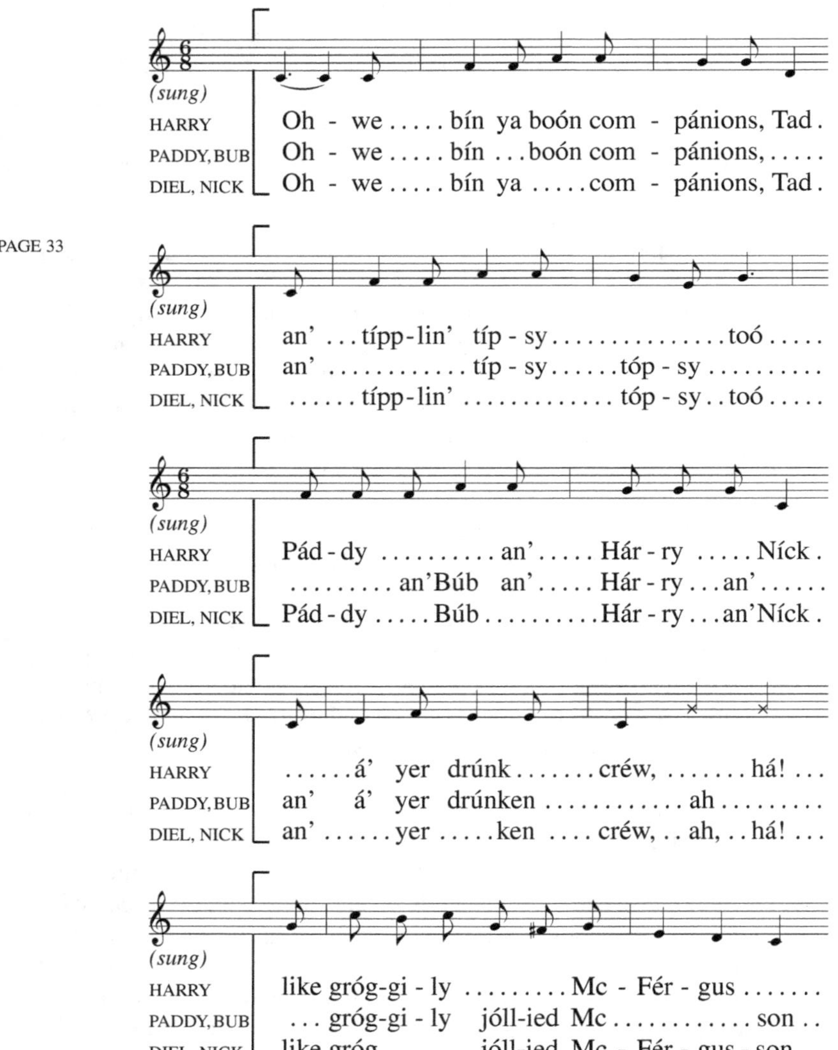

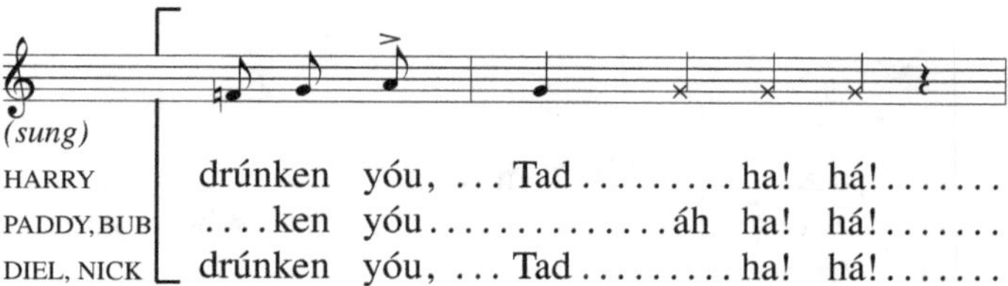

PAGE 33
PAGE 34
PAGE 35

PAGE 36

The singers are convulsed with laughter as TAD breaks free and runs up onto the seawall, where he will be confronted by MISS PEW, indignant at his supposed intoxication. She returns to AMY HEARTH with a full account of the scandal. When TAD runs into MISS MILLIE's guests, the gossips, he is again the subject of disdainful comments. He retreats and sits down on the parapet, only to be driven off on the seawall by hearing again the drowned voice of HARRY IBBS. The entrance of MISS MILLIE and her guests BRAYLORN, WAGUARD and CARP is accompanied by DOM JEROME's comment and the gossip's murmured conversational chorus.

PAGE 37

PAGE 38-39
PAGE 40-41

The antiphonal choruses are again used on pages 38 to 41. They consist of JEROME's occasionally appalled or amused observations; ANNABELLE PEW's self-righteous examination of conscience in contrast with the gossip's malicious demolition of her character. Neither party hears what the other is saying but their suspicions are not infrequently verified.

PAGE 41

PAGE 42

DOM JEROME's musings about his dreams turning out to be strange, wonderful, bizarre people will be evident - even angels in disguise, or demons incarnate. There are some good souls who do not know they are angels of a kind, for the good spirits have much to do with them, while others are sulphurous clearly, but think of themselves as cunning clever entrepreneurs, taking their rightful advantage of fools. This is true of ELI RENAIRE who's voice is heard, but who does not appear till the SECOND WATCH. The demonic, will often assume some human semblance like the DRUGGIST who tries to subvert by posing as a kindly friend of the family, or the LIBRARIAN who panders his salacious wares in the guise of sophistication and taste. No demon, being totally repellant, dares to show his true face. OLRIG HAGAN however is disturbingly different. Known as the blacksmith, crippled in a foundry spill, he currently tends a metaphoric furnace in MISS BRAINBOROUGH's basement. At his first entry, he burns his old hunting dog - alive. Gleefully he outwits his fellow conspirators. His horrific exit suitably demonstrates the essence of his problematic nature.

PAGE 43

PAGE 44

HAGAN consults with the LIBRARIAN about the latest prospect in their street-trafficking business. With the entrance of a young adolescent, TOM BURNS, JEROME wonders who this young prodigal could be -

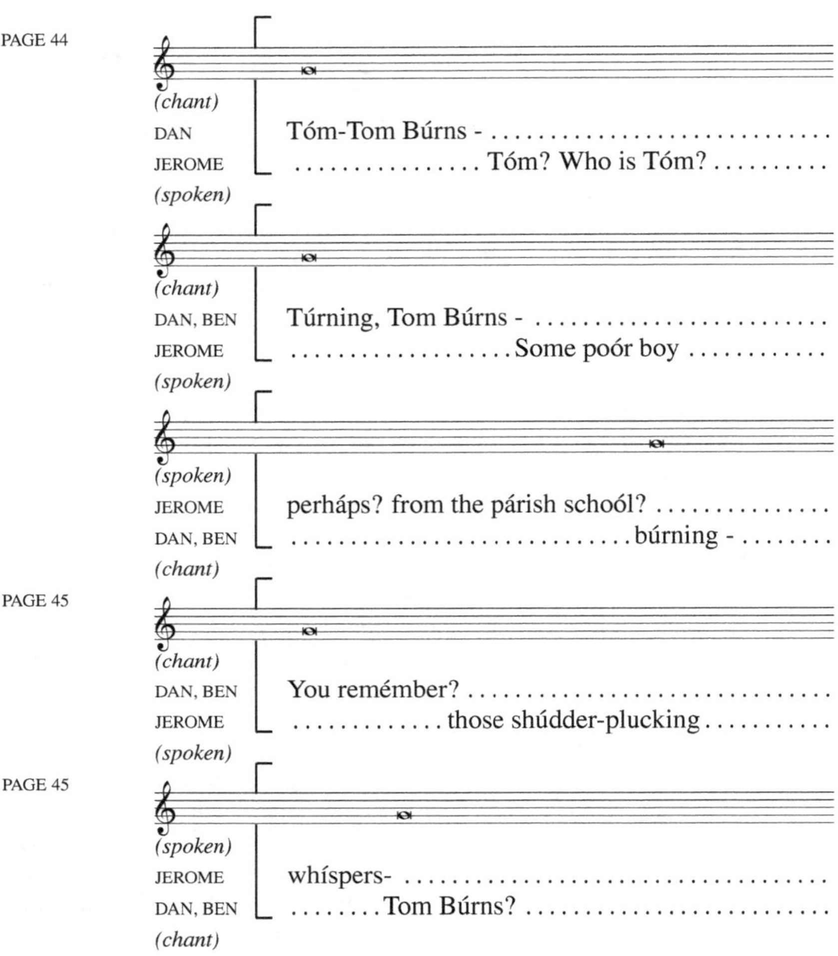

PAGE 45

PAGE 45

The ghost of TOM's mother ROSE BURNS appears
and the voice of RENAIRE reminds him -

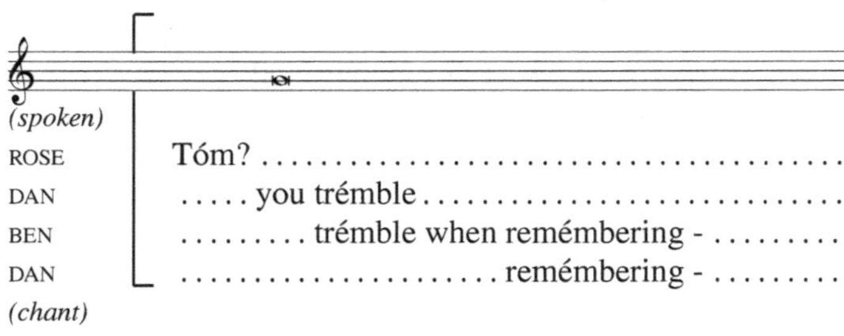

PAGE 45ROSE admonishes her son, and as she
begins to fade away, she sings a song.

227

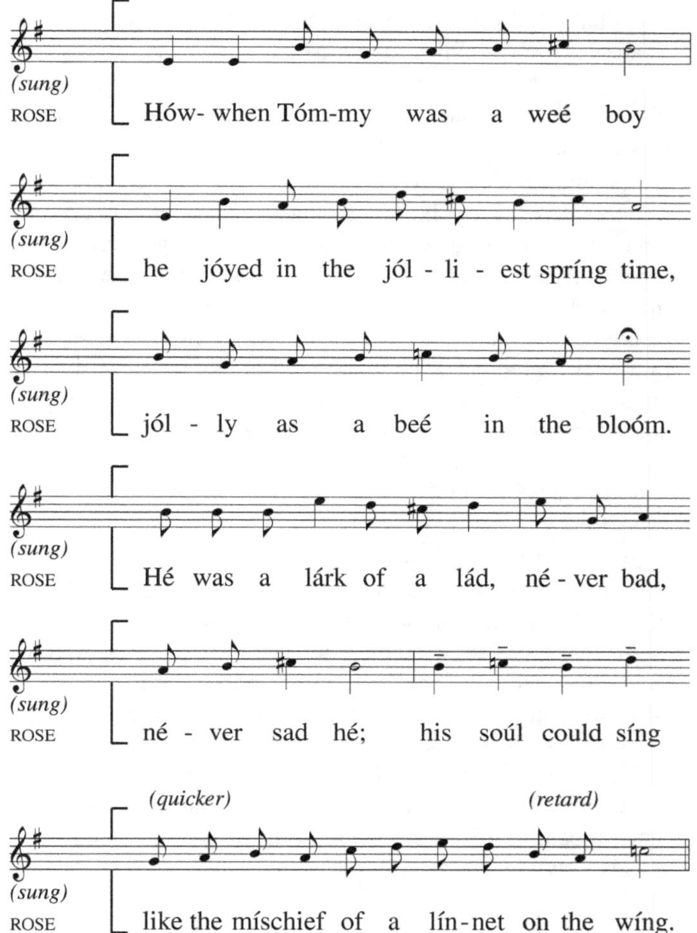

PAGE 47 TOM remembers the time when he was young and his mother ROSE was
PAGE 48 dying. Frequently he stayed with aunt HANNA and uncle REMUS. Then,
PAGE 49 ROSE dies - TOM encounters TAD MCFERGUSON who recalls the early school
days as janitor at old St. Mary's when TOM was in school.

PAGE 50 During TOM's reminiscence, memory evokes his long struggle to
be master of the flesh. In a sequential chorus, he is drawn back to the
PAGE 51 past to his earliest defeat and his recurrent resurrection. HAGAN cuts
sharply into his reverie and startles him awake to his present peril. The
DRUGGIST arrives all suave insouciance, while the LIBRARIAN presses with
unpleasant eagerness his lewd 'literature'.

PAGE 52 Having rejected their overtures, the chorus of tempters lures him back
again to the darkness of YOUNG TOM's lost innocence.

PAGE 53   Light fades on TOM and the tempters, while coming up on REMUS and HANNA, as she is exhorting him to talk to the boy. Uncle REMUS has no idea how
PAGE 54   to talk to his nephew but HANNA insists. We do not hear YOUNG TOM and his Uncle's conversation. Instead, AMY HEARTH, the eavesdropping landlady gives her account of poor uncle's ineptitude.

PAGE 55   REMUS, about to leave gives YOUNG TOM his final admonition before closing the door leaving the boy in darkness. Light comes up on the older TOM
PAGE 56   where he still broods on the past. The off-stage sound of a chorus again lures him as the DRUGGIST tries to win the boy's trust with affability but
PAGE 57   the chorus instills a dread of hidden implications. Augmented with the LIBRARIAN, HAGAN and the DRUGGIST, the chorus grows intensely as if rushing him over a precipice. The voice of his mother is suddenly heard; all fall silent. YOUNG TOM sits up. At another call he rushes from his room. TOM
PAGE 58   BURNS turns to face his three tempters - 'I knew I had sinned.' HAGAN describes with mock pity his anguish - TOM owns he was afraid to confess - the LIBRARIAN reminds him of the innumerable demons who deride him, even now.

PAGE 59   HAGAN raises the question torturing TOM's mind - why are these men tormenting me? Maybe they are perverts, queer ones - will they kill me? The blacksmith insinuates 'nay - were much more' - whoredom is human, but we're the pure fire of hate! The LIBRARIAN quotes scripture's threatening Sophonias while the DRUGGIST commiserates the lost one; it's too late now TOM - too late! HAGAN launches a tirade of abuse at TOM's useless 'trotting
PAGE 60   to the priest', yet weakly succumbing again and again. TOM's stammered defences crumble before the onslaught. When his tormenters leave him carrying away their imprecations down to the sea, he hears ROSE in the distance repeating his name while he hears a distant child's voice calling - 'Regis? - where are you?'

PAGE 60

PAGE 61   TOM BURNS prays. A twelve year old boy, REGIS WICKS enters on the seawall. He stands by the lightpost to listen. TOM describes a dream he had as a child. In his dream TOM called himself REGIS WICKS. This boy remembers his father as a good man who owned a garage - he wasn't a drunken seaman. REGIS had two brothers (DAN and BEN) and a sister (JENNIE). However TOM's deepest memories have not yet surfaced. They will only be revealed when WILLIE SIMS has appeared at the beginning of the SECOND WATCH. To interpret these ambiguities and convergences one could attribute them to the fragmentation of JEROME's memory, or perhaps with an equal plausibility that his voices were 'having lives of their own.' So REGIS insists that he's nobody's mere dream 'I'm the real me!'

229

PAGE 45   As FAY and FANNY are returning they sing.

PAGE 62

PAGE 63

PAGE 63

SUMMARY   In his very first soliloquy when DOM JEROME, sitting late over his books, is assaulted by the terrifying chaos of voices, he questions himself about their reality - 'some are real I'm sure, others, I'm - not so sure.' He yearns to unravel the stirrings in his long dormant amnesia -

SUMMARY   He recognizes some he has come to know after the loss of his early life; TAD the docker, the town drunkards, the gossips, the selfrighteous - are they not always with us?

But with TOM BURNS' last words on going up to the cathedral, and REGIS WICKS' puzzlement on hearing them, we too share the perplexity of the monk. Perhaps he will only discover his own identity in the 'others'. Does not every person's uniqueness share in the mysterious unity of our common humanity? the very nature we share with the Logos? And does not He share his own nature with us as well?

PAGE 63   REGIS is kept busy trying to moderate the exuberance of his small charges. They must be quiet to tally up their faults for confession, but the next moment they have slipped away on another lark of hide and seek.

PAGE 64   Meanwhile GRANNY OWEN reminisces about the family. S. JENNIFER has come out on the convent porch. Seeing her brother REGIS she has to

PAGE 65   restrain her impulse to call out. But SR. SUPERIOR calls her, and she disappears into the convent. DR. MALLOY makes a house call on G. OWEN and while making a few routine checks, they talk about the children, FAY'S

PAGE 66   voice is heard off-stage. REGIS calls her back. FAY appears on the seawall followed by FANNY, but they both run off again. REGIS bounds up the steps calling after them. Only silence answers. Patiently REGIS sits on the parapet to wait for them. The doctor returns from the window to sit with the old lady continuing their conversation silently.

PAGE 67   REGIS ponders what he should do with his life - a missionary? a priest like Pere Bernard? or maybe a monk like Dom Jerome? The CANTOR sings:

mode VIII
CANTOR   ... Vé - ni ..... fí - li aú - di me
(chant)

REGIS   A sound like words from somewhere -
(spoken)

CANTOR   Ti - mó - rem Dó - mi - ni do - cé - bo te
(chant)

REGIS   like music I once heard.
(spoken)   What it means I can never tell -

The NOVICE is heard in the Novitiate repeating the verse after the CANTOR:

PAGE 67

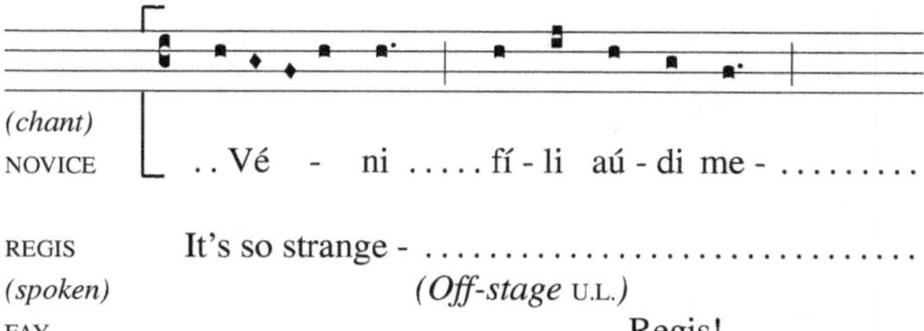

REGIS It's so strange - ....
(spoken) *(Off-stage* U.L.*)*
FAY ....Regis!..........

PAGE 68
PAGE 69
PAGE 70

As REGIS listens, G. OWEN and DR. MALLOY talk of ROSE, her illness, and of JOB's disappearance. The doctor's description of JOB WICKS' work in his garage evokes a long forgotten memory of old FROAR's jallopy brought in to be repaired yet again.

PAGE 71

S. JENNIFER remembers their father also and the play they improvised as children - her younger self as JENNY and their brothers DAN and BEN. REGIS joins them to relive those times when make believe was real. REGIS as-

PAGE 72
PAGE 73

signs the parts. When they all run off to prepare the props S. JENNIFER remembers how seriously REGIS would act the part of Christ. As the children return, they play the roles with a guileless simplicity - they do not

PAGE 74

seem to be acting - it is real to them. A bit of quarreling about how it should be done is not excluded. The crucifixion however seems to

PAGE 75

transfigure them - it's the way it was!

PAGE 76

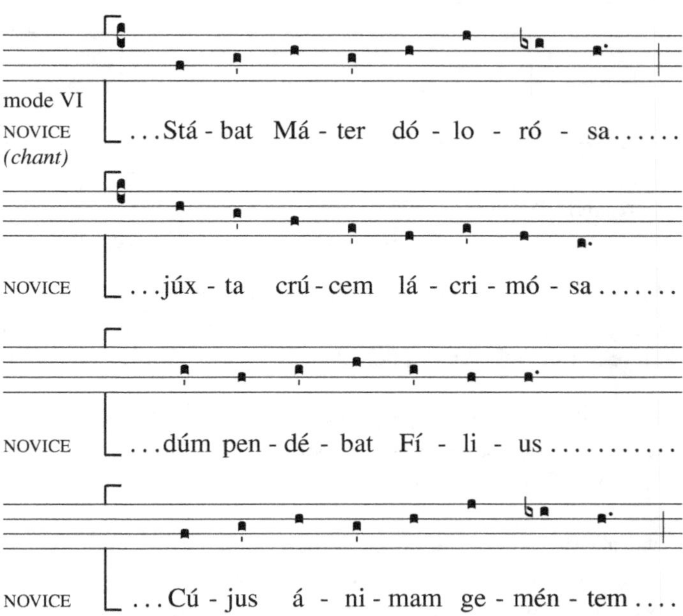

During this singing the Crucifixion continues on stage; Jesus gives Mary into the keeping of John. He dies - his side is pierced - he is taken down -

PAGE 77

PAGE 78, 79 buried and rises. MOTHER WICKS calls the children in and REGIS is alone.

PAGE 77

During the Deposition, characterized by S. JENNIFER as 'clumsy but solemn' the monk and the nun repeat some spoken phrases of the hymn. PAGE 78 PAGE 79 When REGIS rises, exclaiming from the top of the bench 'I'm alive Father!' youthful exuberance has the guards running off in gleeful terror. After JENNY returns to find the tomb empty, MOTHER WICKS calls the PAGE 80 children in for supper leaving REGIS alone again with his thoughts. DOM JEROME wonders who this boy might be - searching for his vocation. He seems familiar.

PAGE 81

FAY   Regis! where are you? . . . .
(spoken)

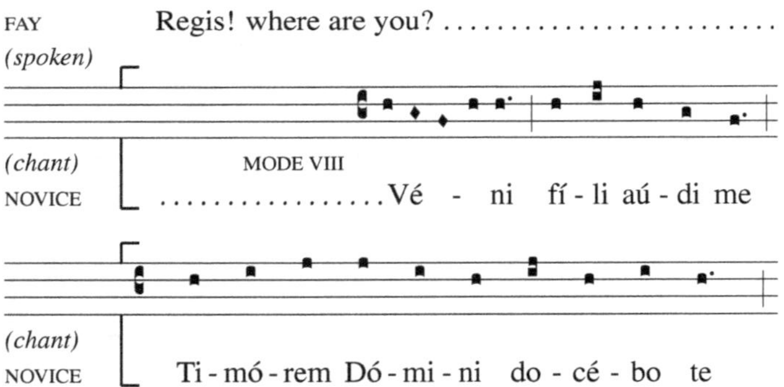

PAGE 81 When FAY and FANNY return REGIS advises them they should begin their prayers. FANNY suggests they say the rosary on the street lights because there are ten of them - a decade! they agree to meet REGIS in the square.

PAGE 82 When the twins have gone, REGIS speaks to God about his nightmare when he was young, when it seemed his father came back as a ghost - but he quickly banishes the idea because 'Willie was only a dream'.

PAGE 83 WILLIE SIMS has entered and overheard what REGIS said. He tells his own side of the story after REGIS leaves. 'My father was a fisherman,' and 'it wasn't no ghost that came back.' He ends echoing REGIS' words 'I'm the real me!'

The CURTAIN will rise on the SECOND WATCH after the INTERVAL with another interpretation of the Protagonist, DOM JEROME, and of his identity.

<table>
<tr><td>PAGE 86</td><td rowspan="2">The captains CoD and HADDOCK, seated on the seawall's parapet, are engaged in conversation. They talk about the dangers encountered in 'her-</td></tr>
</table>

PAGE 86 The captains CoD and HADDOCK, seated on the seawall's parapet, are engaged in conversation. They talk about the dangers encountered in 'her-
PAGE 87 rin' fishin'. CoD is mending fish nets while HADDOCK smokes. CoD brings up an idea he has heard about the church as a stone ship. HADDOCK receives this revelation with genial skepticism so CoD defends the idea with warmth. He points out the cathedral as readying itself for embarcation
PAGE 88 - it's full of souls ye know, heaven-bound! The nets stowed, they part amicably, HADDOCK to his carousal, CoD to 'is cathedral. DR. MALLOY, having entered, makes a house call upon GRANDMOTHER OWEN with medicine for her arthritis. Satisfied the the old lady will find some rest without
PAGE 89 pain, he takes his leave. On coming out he sees young WILLIE SIMS sitting
PAGE 89 on the bench in the dark. The doctor greets the boy who has run ahead of his mother to look at the old house. The doctor knows of MARY SIMS' straitened circumstances since the disappearance of NICHOLAS. So he is
PAGE 90 careful in comparing the old house with the shanty in which WILLIE and his mother now live. After all, there are outlying gardens, fruit trees and
PAGE 91 the railroad tracks. He reminds the boy of his early pranks, and the boy supplies memories of his own, like kneeling at night with his mother for
PAGE 92 prayer by vigil light.

PAGE 93 The boy grows serious when he recounts how he worried about his dad's long absence on Macrae's fishing boat - and how he came in one afternoon to find his mother on the floor - At this point an enactment occurs when YOUNG WILLIE appears (his younger self) and hearing his mother crying, runs upstairs to console her. MARY regains her composure and sits on the bed with the child. She tells him his father has gone away. But YOUNG WILLIE's questions are insistent - 'gone where?' MARY tries to satisfy him - her asides, however, indicate there is something she's unable to say. So finally she tells him, the ship foundered - 'your father was drowned,
PAGE 95 son!' YOUNG WILLIE slides down at her knees flinging his arms about her. After a moment she joins his hands for prayer, then puts him to bed. After kissing him she leaves, closing the door after her. When DR. MALLOY says 'he's gone, Willie' the boy instantly gives the reply 'He's not gone ... he's not dead! This so startled the doctor that WILLIE continues his story describing the nocturnal visit (enacted again) when MARY leads NICHOLAS by candle light to the foot of YOUNG WILLIE's bed.

PAGE 96 Catching a glimpse of his father's face, the child keeps his eyes tightly
PAGE 97 closed but he listens to his parent's hushed conversation. The 'ghost' takes his leave as DR. MALLOY reflects on what that must have meant to WILLIE when he discovers the boy has fallen asleep beside him. NICHOLAS enters the bar where hs is served his usual double scotch. Pulling out a tattered book he is soon feverishly reading and drinking. Asked what he

PAGE 97

is reading he answers 'Poem 'bout some drowned sailors, like the ones I knew' - SUE and BERT coax him to read out a bit. He attempts to do so but his voice breaks - a chorus of deep voices pronounce the elegy for him, evocative of the terror on him, that night on Barclay Sound - The dou-

PAGE 98

ble doors behind YOUNG WILLIE open slowly revealing the sky engulfed by the sea. The intonations from the deep are pierced by Y. WILLIE's tremulous voice, 'Father! ... Where are you?' and later, ... It's me, father -'

PAGE 99

NICHOLAS looks toward the old house. 'Is that you, Willie? I'm down deep ... she's founderin' Willie, we're goin' down' ... the boy cries out, 'come back! come back father -' NICHOLAS leaves, the bar lapses into darkness, as MARY enters, gathers the child up and carries him out.

PAGE 100

MARY SIMS is calling out for the boy, off-stage 'Willie! ... Where are you Willie?' ... When she enters, seeing the boy with the doctor, she is relieved. The ensuing conversation allows the doctor to suggest ... 'You must tell your son the truth, Mrs. Sims!' Before MARY can explain why for her it's impossible, the boy awakes. DR. MALLOY says, 'Well sir! you bin dreamin' the boy replies, 'It was a thinkin' dream, sir.' MARY asks 'What were you thinking about son?'

PAGE 101

'Just thinkin' he replies, 'how strange the sea was -' ... 'Well think no more upon it' his mother cautions. They take their leave of the doctor. When DOM JEROME reappears having had a strange dream - 'I seem to have known that doctor;' catching sight of him on the seawall, he runs out calling after him, 'Is it you? Doctor Malloy?' The doctor recognizing brother, comes down the steps. Their conversation on opposite sides of the scrim lends to the doctor a strangeness as if he were from some bygone age.

PAGE 102

I must be 'the only doctor in town still makes house calls.' JEROME observes the last call we had in cloister was 'a good twenty years ago -' 'That makes me an extinct species! ... about done for;' his serious tone prompts JEROME to ask 'Is something wrong, doctor?' DR. MALLOY replies that old Gillies did an exploratory early in the fall. 'Found me riddled with cancer - gives me six to eight months.' JEROME replies 'I'm sorry to hear that, doctor ...' His commiseration, however is cut short by an urgent need to know something - he asks, 'Was it old J. B. Gillies did the exploratory? He attended Abbot Gilbert's passing.' DR. MALLOY answers,

PAGE 103

'Yes - old J. B. did it - best dignostician in the city.' Then the doctor asks for prayers, '- though I'm not a believer.' Old Grandmother Owen, he adds, knows how to die - 'we're rank amateurs'. Then thanking JEROME for his prayers he takes his leave. DOM JEROME is left bewildered. 'How can it be? - an exploratory three months ago? Yet I know after Abbot Gilbert's death, old Gillies died - 'a year to the day! twenty years ago' -

 DOM JEROME's faint but incoherent memory of the doctor frightens him - is it only a presage of his own derangement? Perhaps his amnesia was a grace of God. GRANDMOTHER OWEN also reflects on DR.MALLOY who 'did not look well tonight' - what she 'read behind the eyes'. She hears the noise of the Tavern, and thinks about Molly Green.

Numbered choruses are introduced during the scene between MOLLY and G. OWEN as below: CHORUS 1 - DAN, BEN. 2 - DAN, BEN, CANTOR, LIBRARIAN. 3 - DAN, BEN MISS PEW, MISS MILLIE, MARY, SUE. 4 - DAN, BEN, CANTOR, LIBRARIAN, PEW, MILLIE, MARY, SUE. SOLO - CANTOR. (These voices are not in character they sing off-stage down right.) PADDY, BUB, DIEL and HARRY are at the bar.

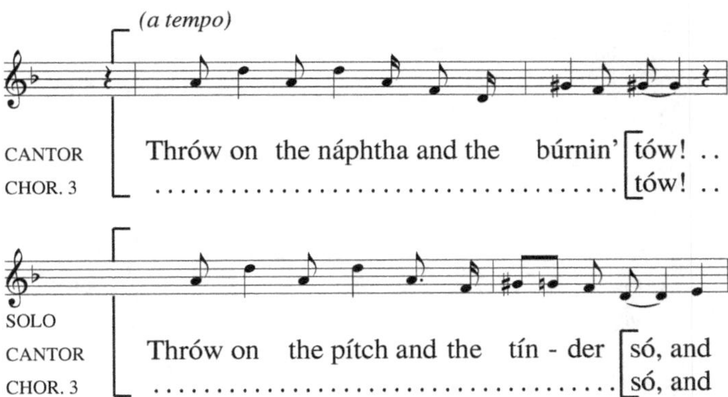

236

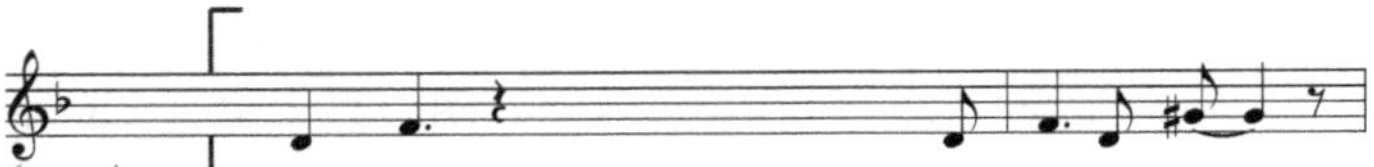

(sung)
CHOR. 1   ráge, ráge, ...
CHOR. 2   . . . . a . . rá-gin' ráge . . .
DIEL   . . . . Hey, it's bawdy
(spoken)   batty Molly Green, ...

DIEL   Brawltown Harlot turned Magdalene!
ALL   Ha há! aháaahá!
(spoken)

(twice as fast) 
(sung)
CHOR. 4   a   rá-gin' wráckin' and a   rá - gin' róck! and

(a tempo) 
SOLO
CANTOR   The   ón - a gód we're gón-na   knów   is . .

CANTOR   ón'-y the Ná-bu-cho - dó - no - sor's   Ba - by -

ló - ni - an mólten góld- . . . . -en gód! . . .

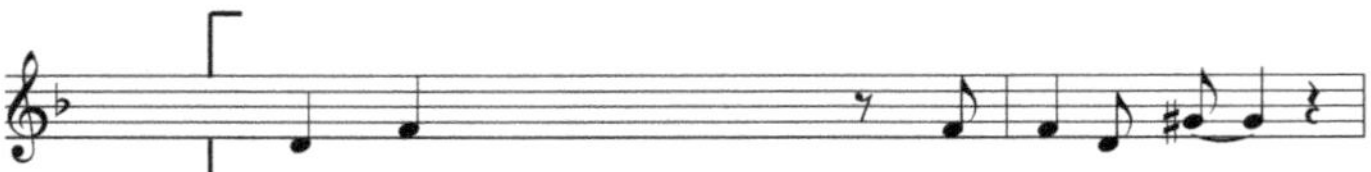

CHOR. 1   ráge, ráge, ...
CHOR. 2   . . . . 1a . . rá-gin' ráge, . .
MOLLY   . . . . Granny, it's me,
(spoken)   Molly, can I come in? 1 . . . .

G. OWEN   Of course - come
(spoken)   . . . . in, child! . . . . . 
CHOR. 1   . . . . .ráge, ráge,
(sung)

  MOLLY GREEN, a young 'fallen woman of the streets' as she was labeled by all the town's better people, might have been more accurately described as a child thrown out into the gutter by an alcoholic and abusive parent. She was 'rescued' for the trade by the scheming MCCORKERAN. MOLLY however, escapes periodically across the street to visit an old lady who has shown kindness to her. She rehearses the story of her troubled life again because GRANNY OWEN listens.

                                   Now that MOLLY has been trying to reform herself with help from her friend, she finds that she is shunned even in church. GRANNY dismisses the pharisees and questions her about her plans to become a Magdalene with the Good Shepherd nuns. The drunken sailors from the Tavern navigate their unsteady course, making overtures by pounding on the doors or leering in at the windows with loud shouts. MOLLY is terrified. GRANNY takes her into a quieter place, but not before HARRY makes his diabolical threat to return in the dead of night.

  Unlike HAGAN's smouldering bent, RENAIRE is the crafty sophisticate. His motives are not easily discerned, but obviously he directs the surveil- lance of one clerical student, CALEB THORN. The youth is about to step out when his stepmother calls out 'Where are you going dear?' his answer 'To the cathedral, mother -' betrays his irritation. He goes up on the seawall to stare gloomily at the harbour. The overheard conversation between MRS. THORN and her visitor, MRS. THOREAU, runs concurrently with CALEB's brooding train of thought. His ironic, bitter and sometimes re- pentant interjections are spoken asides. CALEB's soliloquy reveals how conflicted his emotions are about the prolonged absence of his father and especially about 'how he drowned - the *second* time.'

CALEB calls on AUNT HANNA since there's no one else he's close to. AMY HEARTH recognizes him as the Burns boy and his AUNT greets him as TOMMY. REMUS and NICHOLAS were brothers. After NICHOLAS disappeared ROSEMARY began using her family name of SIMS. Was she not after all a virtual widow? After the death of ROSE BURNS, when the young TOMMY lived with his aunt and uncle, NICHOLAS returned home to his empty house, changed his family name to WICKS, opened his garage and assumed the nickname JOB. (Must not everything of the past be wiped out?) Remar- rying, he brought TOM home. The boy's stepmother began calling him by his first name REGIS. He did not mind - his real mother had called him WILLIE for a while - the new mother is referred to in the play as mother Wicks. DAN and BEN his brothers and his sister JENNY who had been farmed out to other relatives were also brought home. These were the years when his vocation began to grow. Then the inconceivable happened again. His father sold the garage, went to sea on a trawler. His drowning was never satisfactorily explained. Later his stepmother remarried the banker Jamison Thorn. The boy is renamed once more after Caleb, Jamison's father.

PAGE 114   A real solution of JEROME's dilemma as he tries to solve it, lies not above - but in one mystical struggle of souls united in a common journey - and he saw!

PAGE 114   Since there was no preconceived plot, the characters grew intuitively. I sensed their mysterious inner connection, which surfaced in clues or hints rather than exposition. The gradual awakening of JEROME's identity was better seen through the bewildering filter of his amnesia. So one could interpret WILLIE, REGIS, TOM and CALEB as stages in his own life, but there is a meaning on a deeper level as well. He discovers they are not mere phantoms or illusions but real persons too, with lives of their own. Both WILLIE and REGIS insisted 'I'm the real me.' JEROME also discovers himself through encounter with the others. It takes a family to make a child, and whole town to remake a shattered man.

PAGE 115   On leaving AUNT HANNA, CALEB sits on the bench for a spell. Reminiscence draws him back to live that fatal evening all over again. The Tavern begins to brighten with the arrival of young people he knew. Numbered choruses: CHORUS 1 - DAN, BEN. 2 - DAN, BEN, CANTOR, LIBRARIAN. 3 - MISS PEW, MISS MILLIE, MARY, SUE. 4 - DAN, BEN, CANTOR, LIBRARIAN, PEW, MILLIE, MARY, MOLLY, (joining with those on stage). These 4 choruses along with the solo sung by the CANTOR and the blues singer by MONA are off-stage D.R.

These sung CHORUSES, while allowing space for the speaker's lines, sustain under them a ground gradually accelerating to a silent climax at the end.

PAGE 115

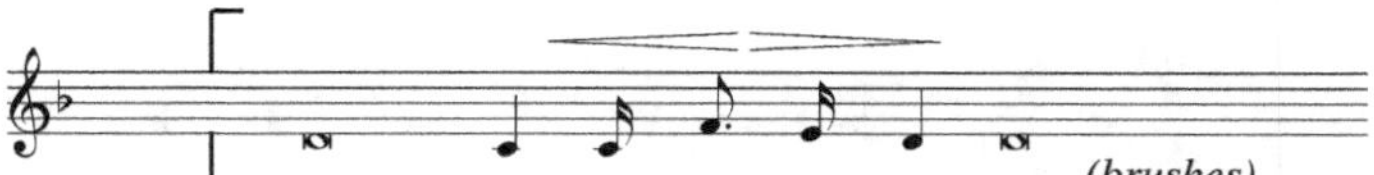

(brushes) . . . .

CHOR. 2 he deép dránk in - é - bri - ate . . . .
CALEB . . . . Where you went
(spoken) remember?

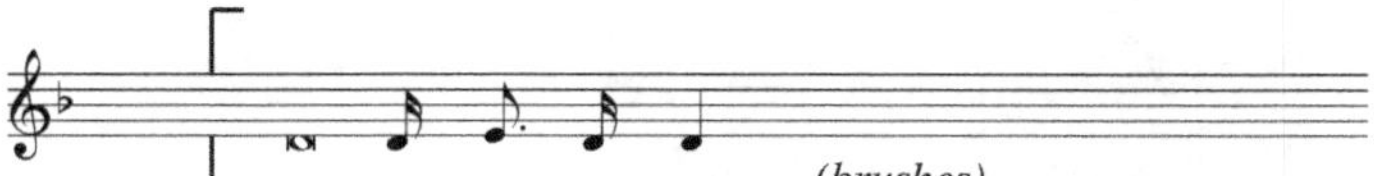

(brushes) . . . .

CHOR. 1 neát in - é - bri - ate . . . .
CALEB . . . . to down the glooms . . . .
(spoken) with a couple of drinks
and new tunes.

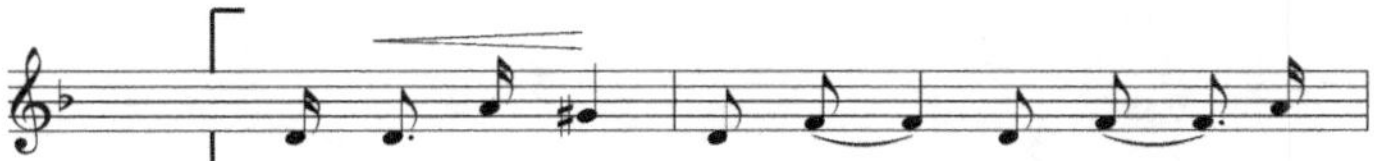

CHOR. 2 as rán-kle dránk . . . .
CHOR. 4 . . . . Jázz - rash! Jám - shyd he . .

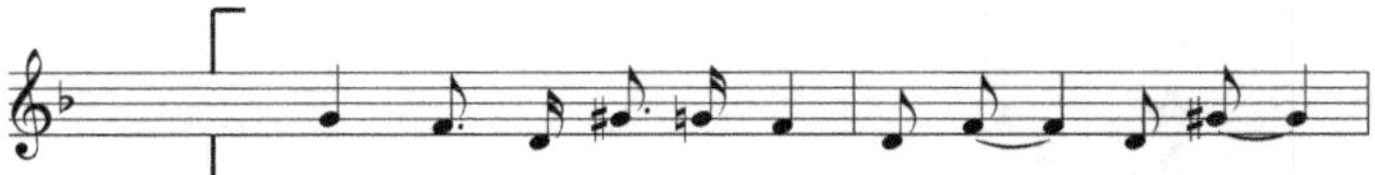

CHOR. 4 deép dránk in - é - bri - ate Jázz-rash! Jám-shyd

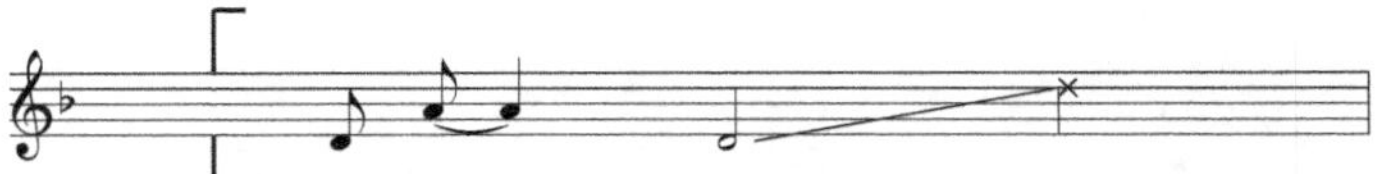

CHOR. 4 dránk deép . . . . Já - aaa - aaz - rash! . . . .

PAGE 116

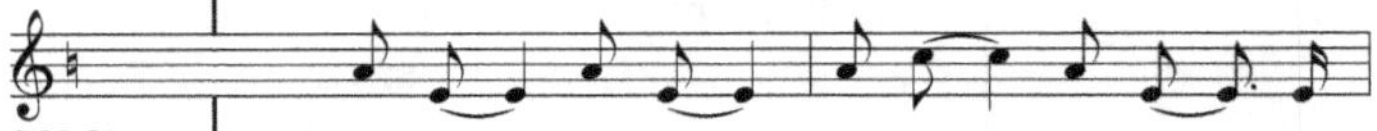

SOLO
CANTOR Thrów on Síd - rach, óld - en Mí - sach the

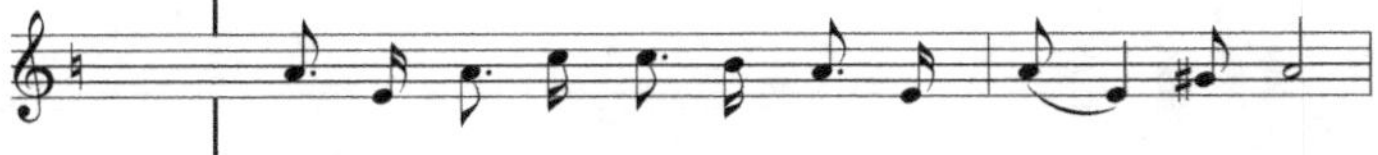

CANTOR óld-en A - bedné - go of the lóng a - go

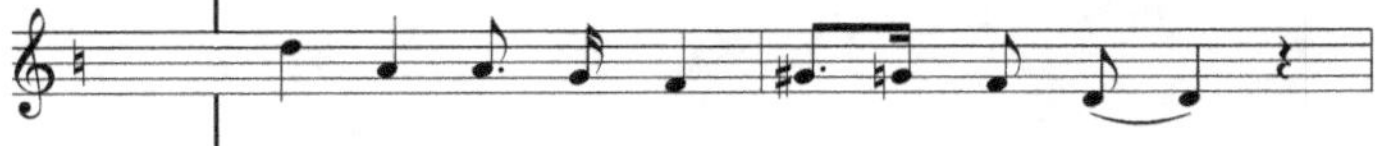

CANTOR óld embóld - en - in' Héb - rew Gód! . . . .

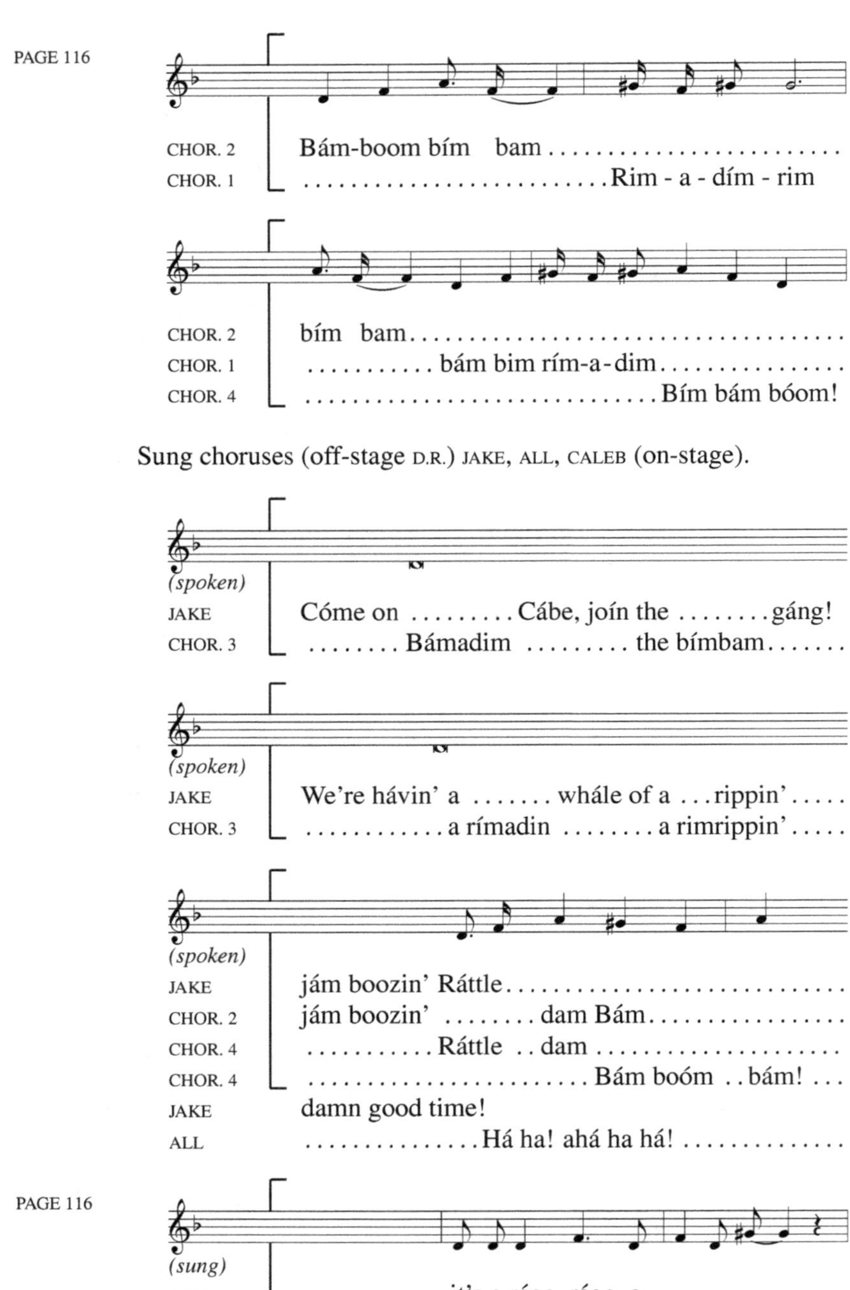

Sung choruses (off-stage D.R.) JAKE, ALL, CALEB (on-stage).

(spoken)
JAKE   Toss up a beer, Bert, come on Cabe! . . . .
CHOR. 1   . . . . Ráge, ráge, . . .
(spoken)
CALEB   Don't jolly me Jake! I'm in no mood now -
(sung)
CHOR. 2   it's a rá - gin' wréck . . . . . . and a . . . .
JAKE   . . . . (spoken) . . Héy now,
CHOR. 2   róck . . . .
JAKE   . . . . . tálk about . . . . your deád . . . .
CHOR. 3   (sung) . . . . bím bam . . . . rag . . . . .
CHOR. 1   . . . . deád . . . .
(sung)
CHOR. 3   . . . . . . and a   rá - gin' fíre! . . . .
JAKE   freéze . . . .
CHOR. 2   . . . . . . and a   rá - gin' fíre! . . . .
CHOR. 1   freéze . . . .
SANDY   . . . . (spoken) . . What gives with Cabe?
(sung)
CHOR. 1   it's a rá - gin' ráge . . . .
JAKE   . . . . (spoken) . . Oh, he's got the glooms
. . . . again - the usual.
(sung)
CHOR. 2   and a rá - gin' wráckin' . . . .
CHOR. 4   . . . . and a rá - gin' rock! . . . .

(sung)
CHOR. 1   and ráge, ráge, ...
HAGAN   (spoken) ...... That's your Theologue, ya say? ...
HAL   .... That's him.

(piano)
CHOR. 1   ráge, ráge, ... ráge, ráge,
CHOR. 2   .... it's a   rá - gin' ráge ....
(spoken)
KATY   We oughta call 'im little lovelorn Thorn!

(piano)
CHOR. 1   it's a rá - gin'   ráge, ... ráge, ráge, ...
(spoken)
SUE   He just needs t' get good 'n' stoned, that's all!

CHOR. 2   and a   rá - gin' fíre! ....
(spoken)
SANDY   What a life for the likes of a nice guy like Cabe,

CHOR. 4   a Bámbim ....
SANDY   (spoken) ... no games, no chance ....
CHOR. 2   (sung) .... a bím - bam
(spoken)
SANDY   no dice, no dance and - ....

CHOR. 3   a rím - a - dim - a - dím   bam ....
SANDY   .... (spoken) .. no dames! ....
(spoken)
ALL   Ha há ha há ahá ha há!

PAGE 118

CHOR. 4   básh, wrá-ckin' and a   rá-gin'   róck! and
(under)
CHOR. 1   ráge, ráge, ...
CALEB   (spoken) . . . All right you fellows . . . .
. . . . lay off me will you? . . . .
CHOR. 1   . . . . (sung) ráge, ráge,
(spoken)
SANDY   Oh, sure, Cabe, ... Hey Bert . . . . . .
CHOR. 1   . . . . a   rá - gin'   ráge, ... rage,
(spoken)
SANDY   nickle Blue Mona next, will ya? . . . .
CHOR. 2   . . . . (sung) . . . rá-gin' wráckin' and a
(half tone higher)
(sung)
CANTOR   Thrów on the náphtha and the búrn-in' [tów! . . .
CHOR. 4   . . . . [tów! . . .
CANTOR   Thrów on the pítch and the   tín - der [só, and
CHOR. 4   . . . . [só, and
(sung under)
(sung)
CHOR. 4   ráge, ráge, rage, ... ráge, ráge,
HAGAN   (spoken) . . . . You fellows oughta . . . .
. . . . cheer 'im up - . . . .

244

(spoken)
JAKE   ya, we oughta . . . . poor devil - . . .
CHOR. 2   . . . . . . (sung) . . . . a   rá - gin' fire! . . . . ráge,

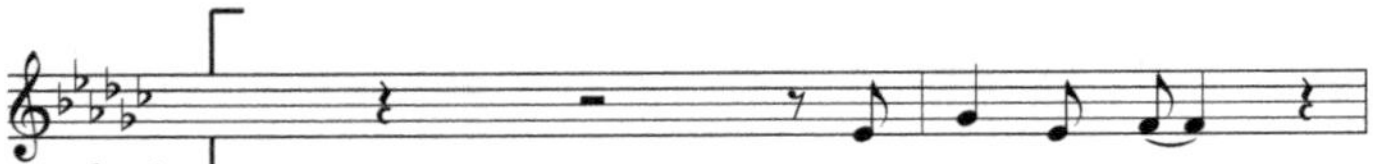

(spoken)
HAGAN   Now that I've mentioned it, ...
            whatta ya think of this? . . . .
CHOR. 1   . . . . (sung) . . . . a   rá - gin' ráge, ...

ALL   Há ha! . . . . . . a hó ho! . . . . . há! . . . hoó! . . . .
            . . . . . . hí hi hi . . . . . hi hí ha . . . ho . . . .
            . . . . ha há! . . . hoó! . . . .

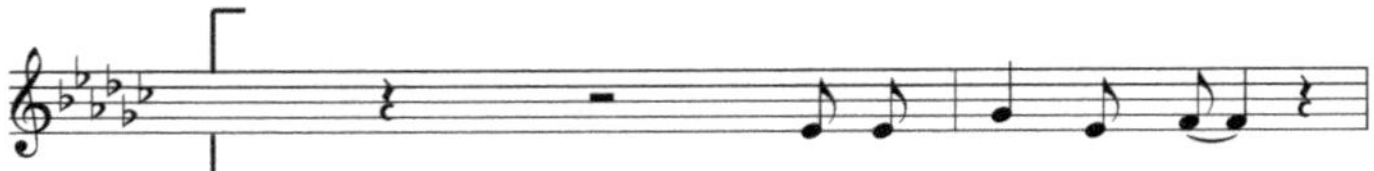

CHOR. 2   (following laughter) . . . . . . a rag   rá - gin' fire! . . .

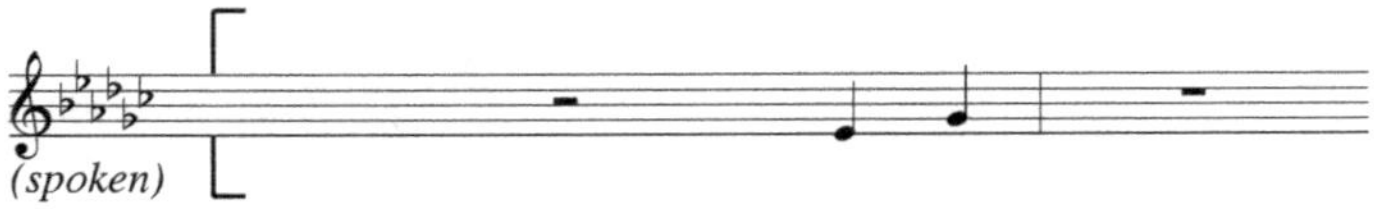

(spoken)
JAKE   Molly'll do? . . . .
            oh boy that's rich! . . . .
CHOR. 1   . . . . (sung) . . . ráge, ráge, ...
(spoken)
HAGAN   Well ya kin dare 'im but I doubts his itch.

ALL   Há ha! há ha ahá ha há!

CHOR. 2   (following laughter) . . . a rándy   stítchin' in pítch
(spoken)
HAGAN   Pretty cold fish!
ALL   Ha há! ahá ha há há!

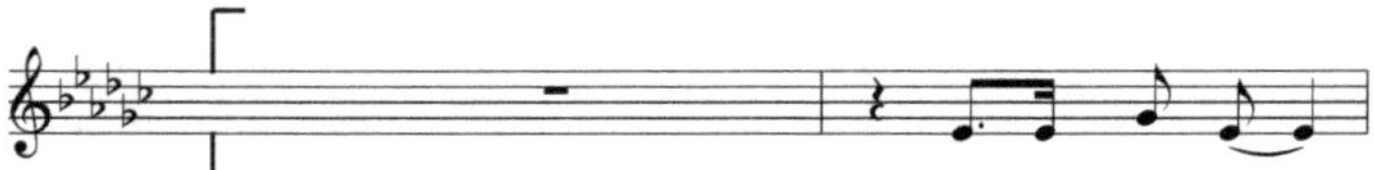

CHOR. 3   (following laughter) . . . . stítchin' in pítch

PAGE 119
(spoken)
SANDY   Hey Cabe! . . . . , come 'ere . . . .
CHOR. 3   . . . . . (sung) . . stítchin' in pítch, ...
(twice as fast)
(sung)
CHOR. 3   stitchin' in pítch, ...
CHOR. 4   . . . . and a wráckin' . . . .
PAGE 120
wréckin' and a rá - gin' róck! and . . . .
(a tempo)
SOLO
CANTOR   The ón - a gód we're gónna knów is . . . .
CANTOR   ón'y the Ná - bu - cho - dó - no - sor's Bá - by-
CANTOR   ló - ni - an mólten góld- . . . . . . en gód! . . . .
(spoken)
SANDY   so it figures - ya gotta . . . .
. . . . prove yer a man! . . . .
CHOR. 4   (sung) . . . . Bám - a - dam! . . . .
(spoken)
HAL   Lookit lady lavender . . . .
JAKE   . . . . clench 'er fists! . . . .
CHOR. 2   (sung) . . . . Rák - a - dam! . . . .

246

PAGE 120

(spoken)
HAL   Lookit 'im grow red . . . .
JAKE   cheap dud of a coward! . . . .
CHOR. 2   . . . . (sung) . . rím-a-dim bím bam

(spoken)
SANDY   Well Cabe? what's a matter? . . . .
HAGAN   . . Whatdja say, Theologue? . . . .
CHOR. 4   . . . . (sung) . . bám bim rím-a-dim

(spoken)
HAGAN   Fling it back at 'em . . . .
            . . their dare into their teeth! . . . .
CHOR. 3   . . . . (sung) . . bím bam! . . . . .

(spoken)
KATY   Mother's little coddler . . . .
SUE   Poor little pip-squeak . . . .
CHOR. 3   . . . . (sung) . . dím bam . . . .
CHOR. 2   . . . . bám bim

(spoken)
SANDY   Swear like a man . . . .
SAN. HAG.   if ya be one! Fling the . . . .
            proof back if ya can! . . . .
CHOR. 2   . . . . (sung) . . rím-a-dim . . . .
CHOR. 4   . . . . bím bam
(spoken)
ALL   Há ha! ha há ahá há! . . . .
HAGAN   . . . . If ya dare! . . . .

PAGE 121

(sung)
CHOR. 4   Bím! Bám . . . .
            . . . . Básh! . . . .

247

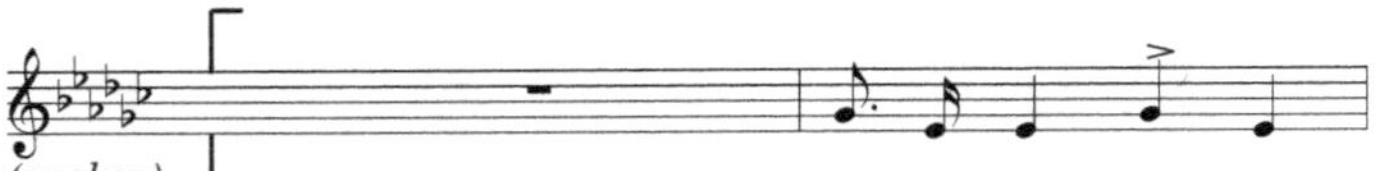

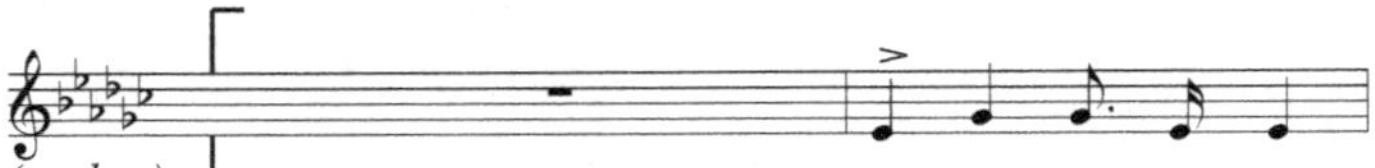

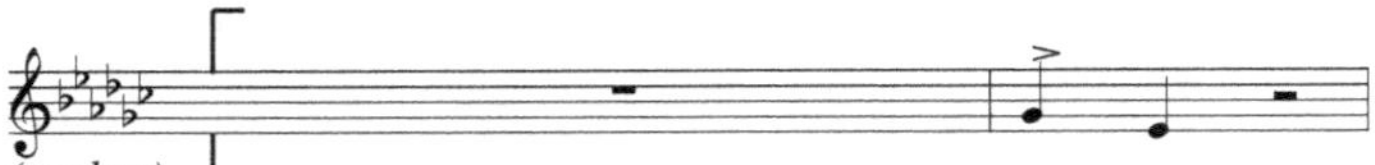

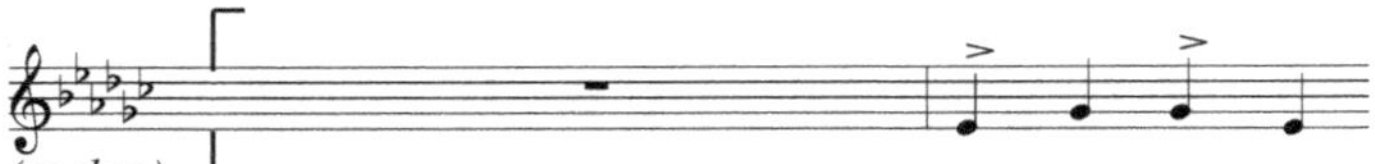

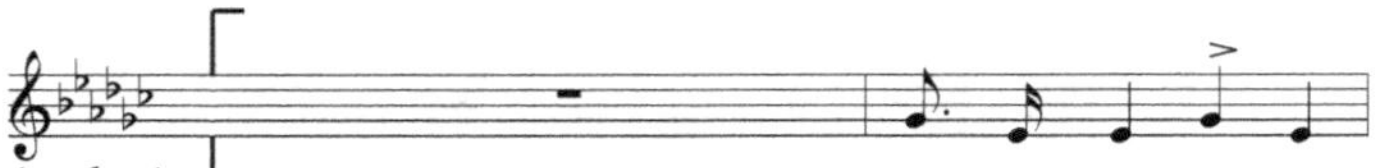

CALEB

PAGE 121

          You - you devils dare me then, do you?
          All right then I - I'll show you - I'll do it!

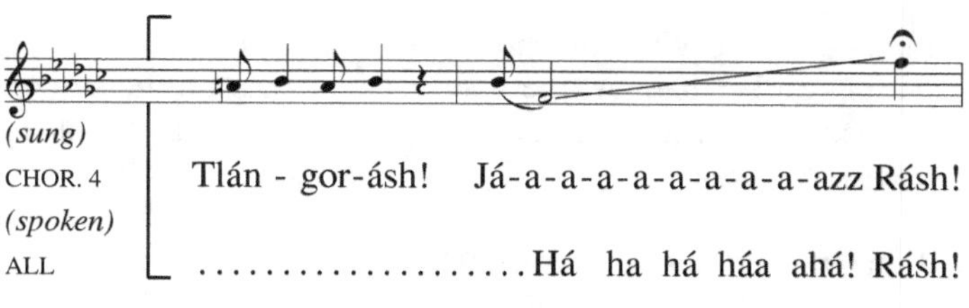

PAGE 120

PAGE 122   In his soliloquy which follows, JEROME attempts to understand his bewildering sense of kinship with the people he has seen and the voices he has heard. They seem to be clews to his own lost identity.

PAGE 123   Observed by HAGAN, CALEB enters the Bar where he sits at a table over coffee. RENAIRE also enters, hesitates for a moment, then introduces himself. During their ensuing conversation RENAIRE presents himself as a

PAGE 124
PAGE 125
PAGE 126
PAGE 127
scholar of demonic and occult science. His probing questions are unsettling to CALEB, prompting him to reveal his own inner tortured self, his duplicity, resentment and despair. RENAIRE suggests a walk by way of the quays. HAGAN, muttering to himself, relishes some of the horrors 'Eli' may recount for the edification of this callow youth.

PAGE 128   When the two of them reappear on the seawall, RENAIRE's recounting of the black rites of Satannael have profoundly shocked CALEB. He is even more shaken by RENAIRE's prediction, in parting, that the wine stain of his guilt, will remain, ineradicable in the traits of his mind.

PAGE 129   MOLLY also has been remembering how she awaited the appearance of the young nun SR. JENNIFER when she would come out on the convent porch in the morning. MOLLY needed someone to talk to who would listen. The sister comes out to shake a small carpet and MOLLY calls out to her.

PAGE 130   Reluctant at first SR. JENNIFER remains, hearing the desperation in the girl's voice as MOLLY tells her of the clerical student who visited her and of their

PAGE 131   conversation that changed her life. Urgently she asks 'what can I do? he may do himself some harm!' SR. JENNIFER counsels her to pray

PAGE 131 for him, and for herself too - that she may be a true Magdalene. The conversation ends when SR. SUPERIOR calls the young sister in.

PAGE 132 MRS. HEARTH, having overheard a part of the conversation, returns putting on her hat. At the door seeing CALEB on the steps she hurries to accost him with suggestive insinuations which she glosses with an ironic disowner.

PAGE 133 Their encounter is interrupted when WAGUARD, BRAYLORN and CARP coming down from the cathedral are denouncing the scandalous MOLLY GREEN for the parading of her questionable piety in church. MOLLY having followed PAGE 134 the others down, crosses quickly and enters McCorkeran's. MILLIE cuts short her greeting with the icy observation 'Oh, the saint! ... come along -' She introduces PROFESSOR RENAIRE who has consented to continue the account of his remarkable life. CALEB, having an appointment with DR. RENAIRE, knocks at this point, and is let in by MISS MILLIE. CALEB listens PAGE 134 with the others to ELI RENAIRE's remarkable performance; he was able PAGE 135 to sidestep the gossips' importunities with masterful adroitness, and to hold them spellbound for each new and unexpected revelation.

PAGE 136 When they have left Miss Millie's, CALEB questions RENAIRE uneasily about what he has heard - 'it seems you were ordained?' The non-PAGE 137 commital 'Of course' leaves CALEB unsatisfied - 'dispensed?' This is dismissed with '- an apostate is not dispensed' - he spells it out explic-itly. Shocked, CALEB wonders 'you feel no shame? no regret?' RENAIRE's flippant retort about 'evil roots, evil fruits' and his clincher 'I can't do good - can you Caleb Thorn?' silences the youth. Taking a new tack PAGE 138 RENAIRE slyly sounds him about MOLLY GREEN. CALEB is instantly wary. The demonologist reveals his hateful intentions and CALEB, not knowing why, defends her. But it is too late - he's already caught in the snare. RE-NAIRE tells him with tantalizing indirection that he' 'aware' ... 'aware of what?' ... 'your misfortune in 'signing the register.' It dawns on CALEB what is happening.

RENAIRE's tone is peremptory; 'You'll prevail on this 'Magdalene' pen-itent to accept my employ - If you fail', I'll send the evidence to your PAGE 139 'Rector Seminarii' - CALEB calls him back but RENAIRE adds 'Oh yes ... hack her a note, at once - immediately! ... There's no way back.' CALEB enters and runs upstairs and sitting on his bed he begins the letter saying PAGE 140 the words aloud as he does so. His light fades out as it comes up on MOLLY entering her room and reading his letter deeply disturbed. When PAGE 141 both have lain down for a troubled sleep, as darkness comes on, the PAGE 142 nightmare Sabat begins with HAGAN calling up the arrival of RENAIRE and the votaries. The incantory phrases of the blacksmith are answered by choral echoes spoken decrescendo.

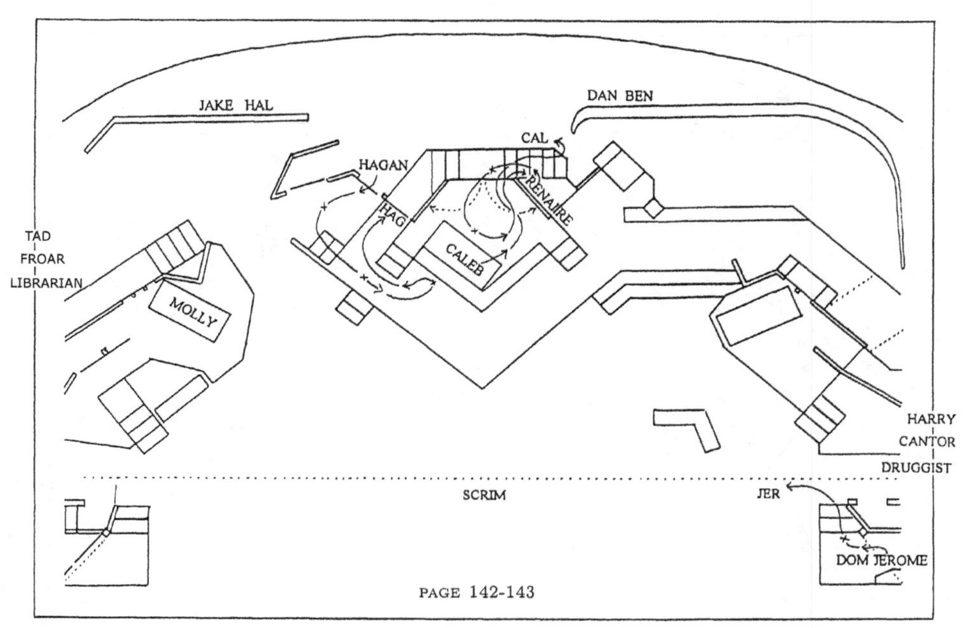

STAGE CHOREOGRAPHY FOR THE NIGHTMARE SABAT

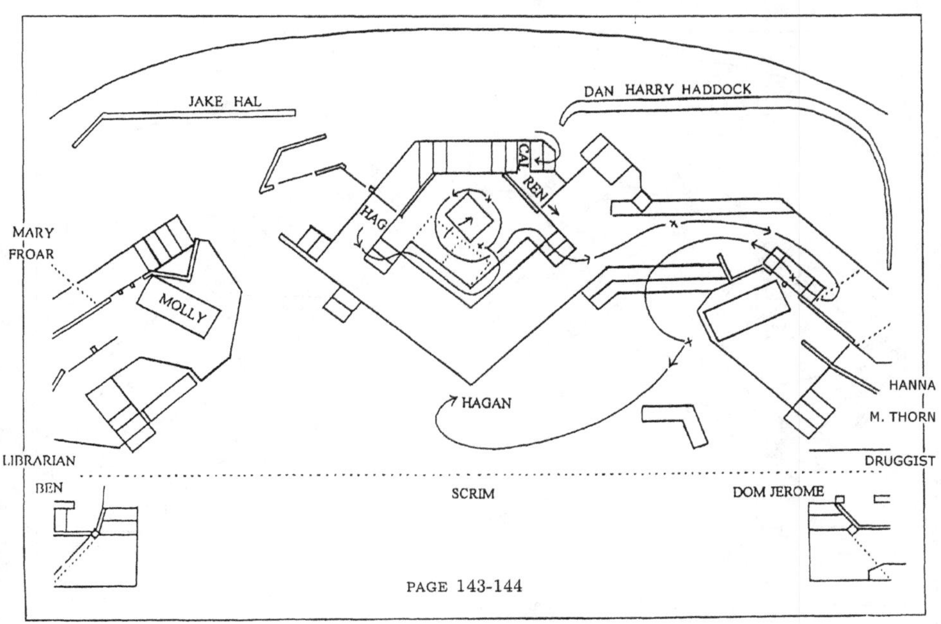

JAKE HAL
DAN HARRY HADDOCK
MILLIE
CAL
REN
CALEB
RENAIRE
MARY
FROAR
HAG
MOLLY
MCCORKERAN
HAGAN
HAG
HANNA
M. THORN
DRUGGIST
LIBRARIAN BEN
SCRIM
DOM JEROME
PAGE 144

JAKE HAL
DAN HARRY HADDOCK
HAG
MILLIE
CALEB
RENAIRE
BRAYLORN
MARY
FROAR
HAGAN
MOLLY
MIL
BRA
BRA
MIL
SANDY MCC
SUE
SAN
SAN SUE
SUE
WAG
CAR
BEN
HANNA
M. THORN
BEN
WAGUARD
CARP
LIBRARIAN
SCRIM
D. JEROME
DRUGGIST
PAGE 145-146

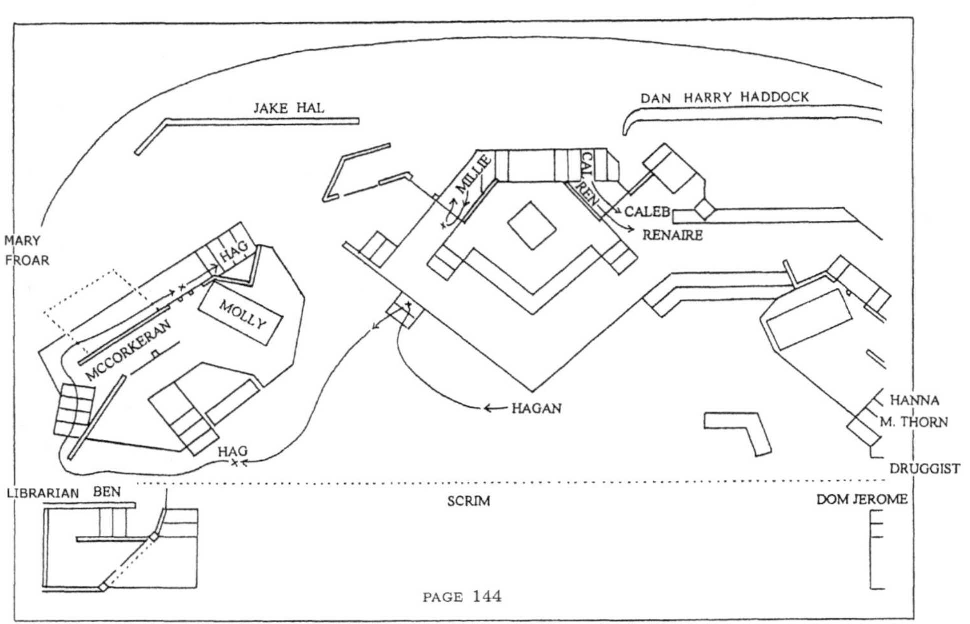

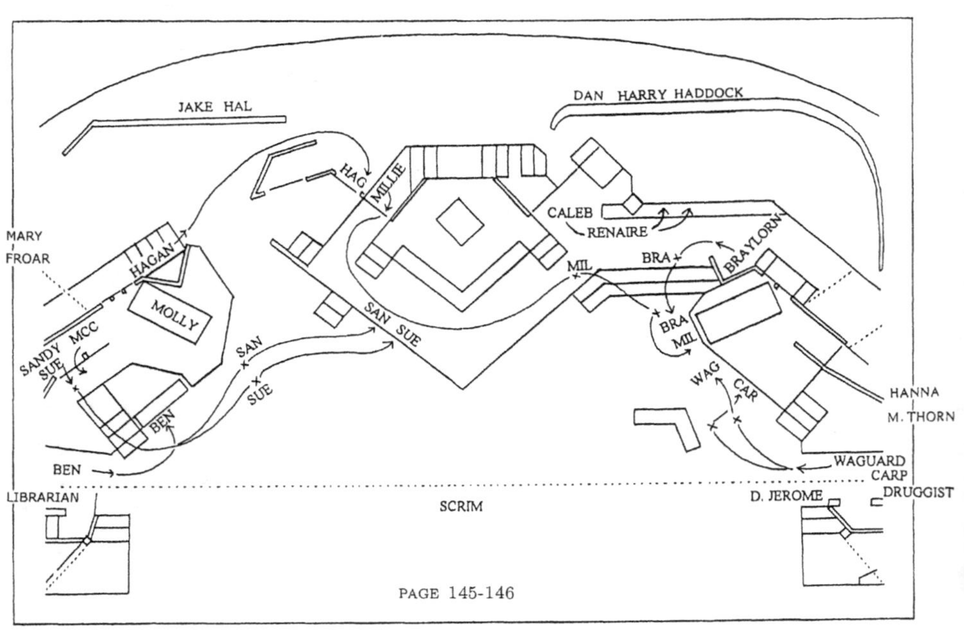

251

PAGE 141 CHOR. 1   FROAR, TAD MCFERGUSON, LIBRARIAN - *off-stage* U.R.

                2   CANTOR, HARRY IBBS, DRUGGIST - *off-stage* D.L.

PAGE 142   3   JAKE, HAL - *off-stage* U.C.

                4   DAN, BEN - *off-stage* D.R.

PAGE 143 to
PAGE 144   The bracketed choruses when taped must
                balance in volume and sound
                quality with choruses spoken live
                by the actors on stage.

CHOR. 1   ⎡ CALEB   CHOR. 2   ⎡ CALEB, DAN, BEN
            ⎢ DAN   ⎢ PADDY, DIEL, REMUS
            ⎣ BEN   ⎣ JOB, CANTOR, LIBRARIAN

PAGE 144 to
PAGE 145   A set of choruses beginning with 'Furtive'
                at the bottom of page 144 are spoken
                live by actors off-stage also in a
                decrescendo.

CHOR. 1, 2   ⎡ DRUGGIST   CHOR. 2   ⎡ HARRY, HAL *(PAGE 146)*
*(off-*S.D.L.*)* ⎢ HANNA   ⎢ HADDOCK
              ⎣ MRS. THORN   ⎣ JAKE *(off-stage* U.C.*)*

PAGE 145
CHOR. 3, 4   ⎡ LIBRARIAN   CHOR. 4   ⎡ HARRY, HAL
*(off-*S.D.R.*)* ⎢ CANTOR   ⎢ HADDOCK
              ⎣ DAN, BEN   ⎢ JAKE *(off-stage* U.C.*)*

                                          ⎢
           From chorus 4   ⎢ DRUGGIST
           spoken in a   ⎢ HANNA
           decrescendo -   ⎣ DRUGGIST *(off-stage* D.L.*)*

PAGE 146
CHOR. 5   ⎡ HARRY, HAL . . . . ⎡ LIBRARIAN
(2 brackets) ⎢ HADDOCK, ... ⎢ CANTOR
                ⎣ JAKE *(off-*S.U.C.*)* . . . . ⎣ DAN, BEN *(off-*S.D.R.*)*

CHOR. 6   ⎡ HARRY, HAL . . . . ⎡ DRUGGIST . . . . ⎡ LIBRARIAN
(3 brackets) ⎢ HADDOCK, ... ⎢ HANNA *(off-*S.D.L.*)* . . ⎢ CANTOR *(off-*S.D.R.*)*
                ⎣ JAKE *(off-*S.U.C.*)* . . . . ⎣ MRS. THORN . . . . ⎣ DAN, BEN

PAGE 143 to
PAGE 144   Spoken together in a crescendo, which builds to the entrance
                of HAGAN. More and more of the votaries enter including the
                members of the choruses as listed on the previous pages; they
                continue reciting their lines (as numbered) on stage with those
                who are still in the wings.

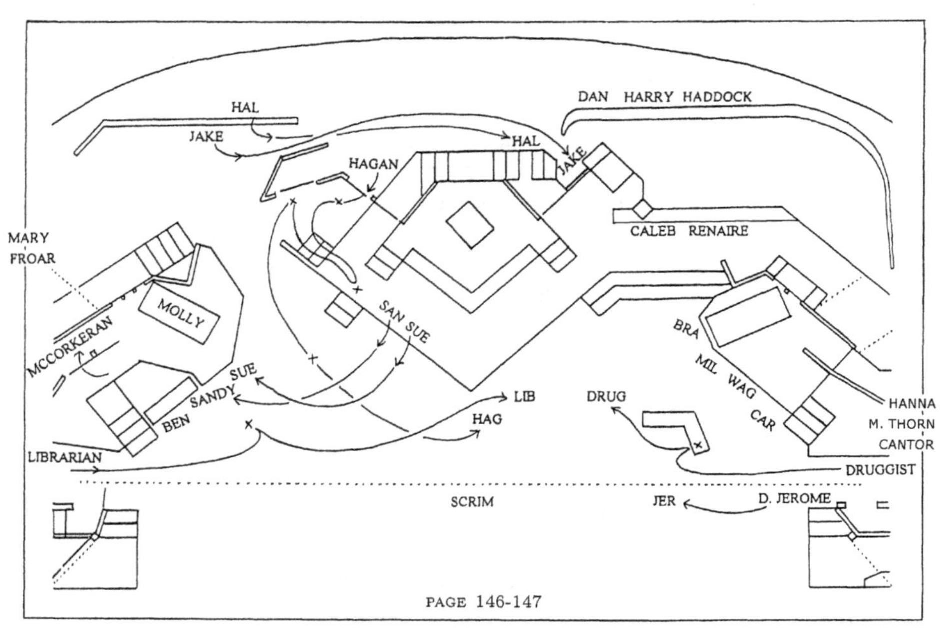

HAL
DAN   HARRY HADDOCK
JAKE
HAL
HAGAN
JAKE
MARY
FROAR
CALEB RENAIRE
MOLLY
MCCORKERAN
SAN SUE
BRA
MIL WAG CAR
SUE
BEN SANDY
LIB
DRUG
HANNA
M. THORN
CANTOR
LIBRARIAN
HAG
DRUGGIST
SCRIM
JER
D. JEROME
PAGE 146-147

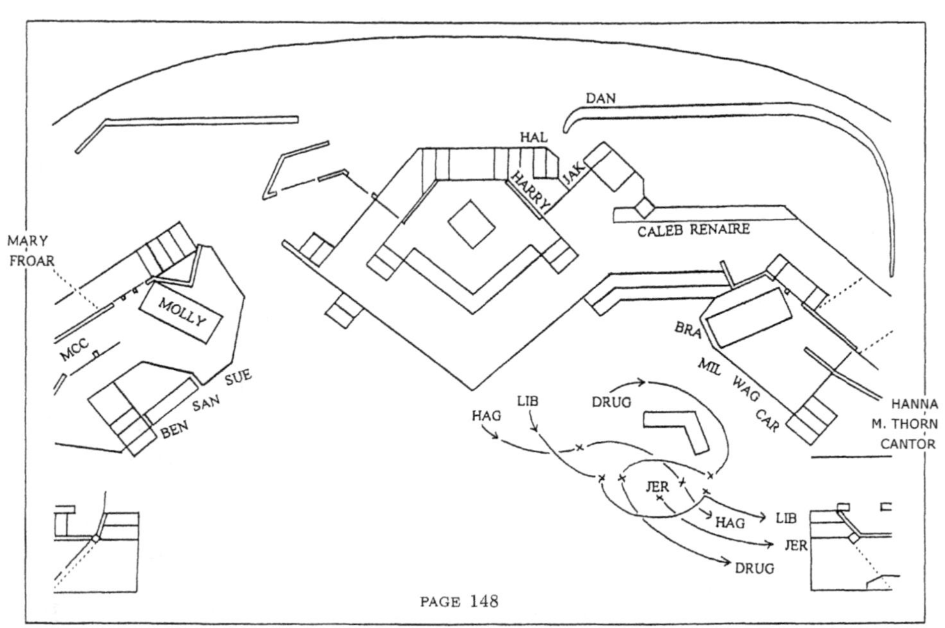

DAN
HAL
MARY
FROAR
HARRY
JAKE
CALEB RENAIRE
MOLLY
MCC
BRA
MIL WAG CAR
SAN SUE
BEN
HAG
LIB
DRUG
HANNA
M. THORN
CANTOR
JER
HAG
LIB
JER
DRUG
PAGE 148

HAL
JAK
HARRY
CALEB RENAIRE
MOLLY
MCCORKERAN
SUE
SANDY
BEN
SUE
SAN
BEN
SUE
HAG CALEB
LIB
BRA
MIL
WAG
CAR
JER
DRUG
HAG
LIB
JER
DRUG
PAGE 149-150

HAL
JAK
HAR
RENAIRE
REN
MOLLY
MCC
SUE
SAN
BEN
HAG CALEB
LIB
DRUG
JER
BRA
MIL
WAG
CAR
PAGE 150-151

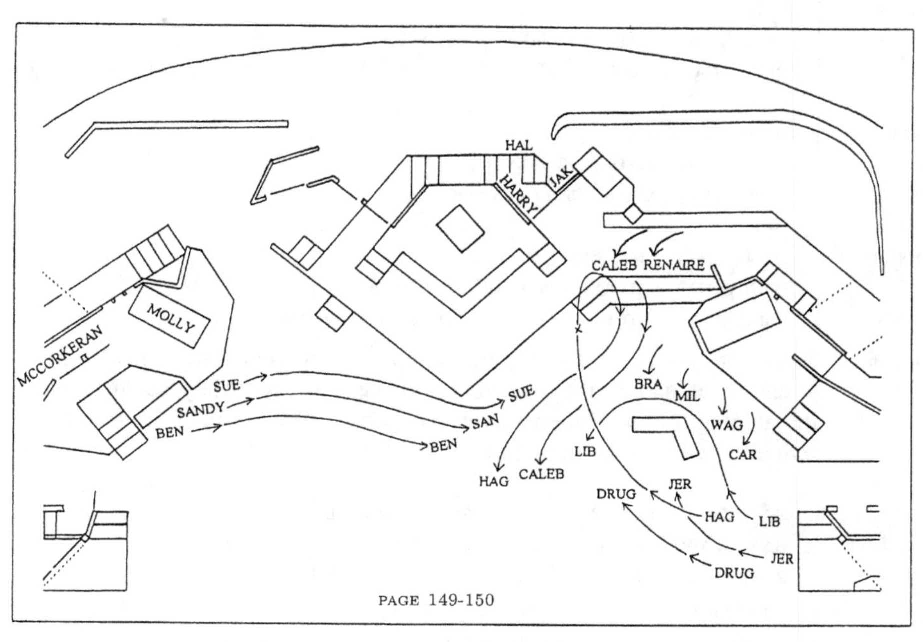

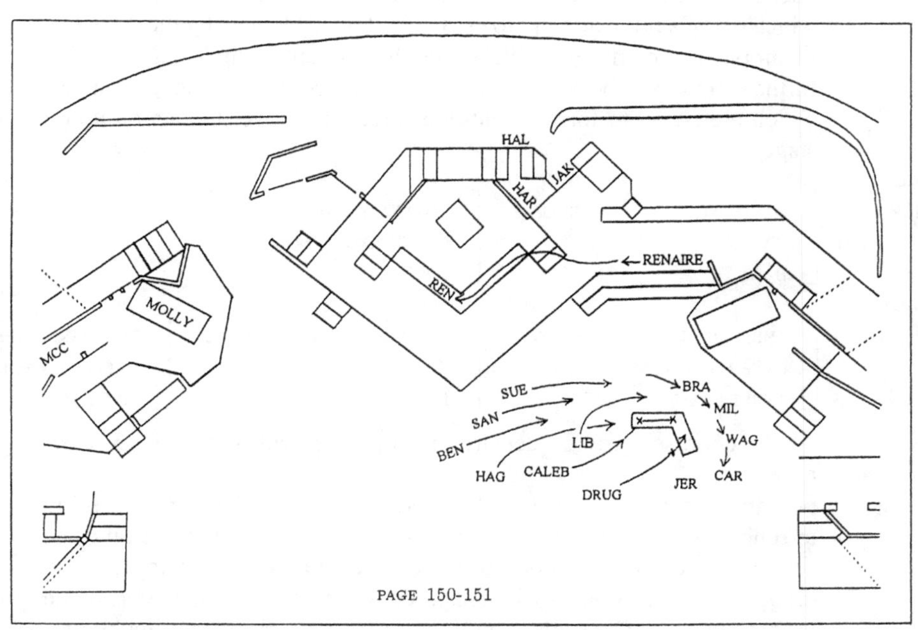

254

CHOR. 6

> HAGAN *(on-stage)*
>
> HARRY, HALS, HADDOCK, JAKE *(off-stage* U.C.*)*
>
> DRUG., HANNA, THORN *(off-*S.D.L.*)*, LIBR., CANTOR, DAN *(off-*S.D.R.*)*, BEN *(on-stage)*

CHOR. 5

> HAGAN *(on-stage)*
>
> HARRY, HALS, HADDOCK, JAKE *(off-stage* U.C.*)*
>
> LIBRARIAN., CANTOR, DAN *(off-stage*D.R.*)*, BEN *(on-stage)*

CHOR. 4

> DRUGGIST, HANNA, MRS. THORN *(off-stage* D.L.*)*
>
> HARRY, HAL, HADDOCK, JAKE *(off-stage* U.C.*)*

CHOR. 3

> LIBRARIAN, CANTOR, DAN *(off-stage* D.R.*)*, BEN *(on-stage)*

PAGE 148   As DOM JEROME enters the nightmare, he also encounters the unwelcome attention of HAGAN, the LIBRARIAN and the DRUGGIST. They seem to be threatening him with their secret knowledge. They speak in unison alternating with chorus 2, all in unison.

CHOR. 2, 1, 3
(together)

> BRAYLORN, MILLIE, WAGUARD, CARP *(on-stage* D.L.*)*
>
> HANNA, MRS. THORN . . . . *(off-stage* D.L.*)*
>
> SANDY, SUE, BEN . . . . *(on-stage* D.R.*)*
>
> CANTOR, DAN . . . . *(off-stage* D.R.*)*

PAGE 149   However at that moment their interest is diverted when RENAIRE introduces CALEB THORN to the votaries in a sinister litany of intitlement during which CALEB's futile attempt to escape is at once blocked by the three tormentors. There ensues an elaborate choreographed molestation which further terrorizes the youth. It is accompanied by five taped choruses which are paced to form a continuous recitation over the action up on stage.

PAGE 150   CHOR. 1

> BARITONE
>
> CALEB
>
> BASS

PAGE 151   CHOR. 2

> TWO BARITONES
>
> CALEB, ONE TENOR
>
> TWO BASSES

PAGE 151   CHOR. 3

> THREE BARITONES
>
> CALEB, TWO TENORS
>
> THREE BASSES

CHOR. 4

> FOUR BARITONES
>
> CALEB, 3 TENORS
>
> FOUR BASSES

CHOR. 5

> FIVE BARITONES
>
> CALEB, 4 TENORS
>
> FIVE BASSES

As the choruses grow in density they open up with spacious reverberance.

PAGE 152   DIEL and NEIL have to awaken the dead drunk HARRY. Though unwilling to touch him, at the command of HADDOCK they haul him up onto the

PAGE 153   seawall. Then MCCORKERAN rouses MOLLY with a potion, brings her out, drugged, to the votaries as gossips comment acidly about MOLLY, the

PAGE 154   'Sabat Queen'. Their attention then, turns to D. JEROME. Meanwhile RENAIRE, the superlative demagogue, stirs up the votaries, but not without irony at the expense of his own coterie. He knows his esoteric ladies will consider the barbs directed

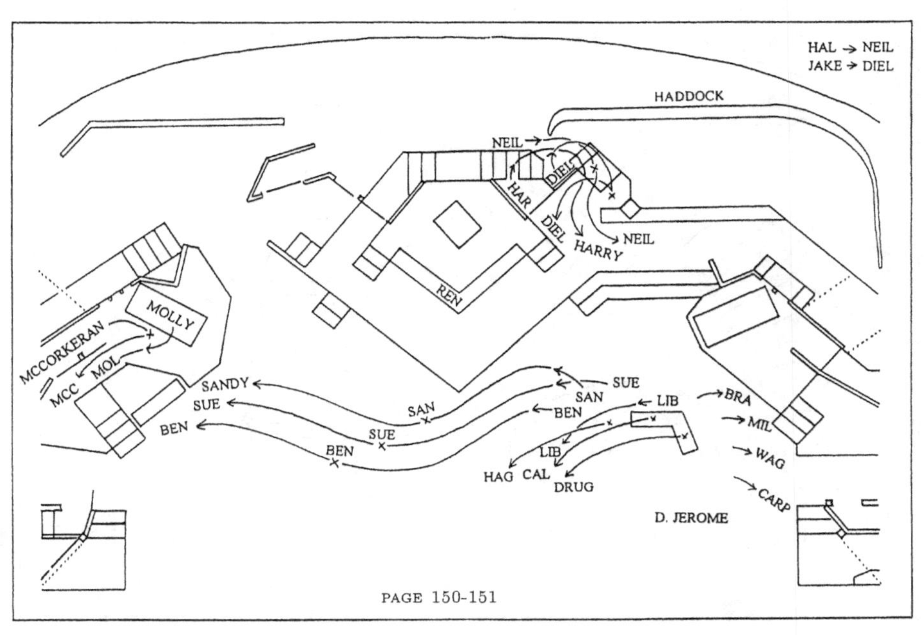

HAL → NEIL
JAKE → DIEL
HADDOCK
NEIL →
DIEL
HAR
DIEL
HARRY
NEIL
REN
MCCORKERAN
MOLLY
MCC MOL
SANDY
SUE
BEN
SAN
SUE
BEN
SUE
SUE
BEN
SAN
BEN
LIB
LIB
HAG CAL
DRUG
BRA
MIL
WAG
CARP
D. JEROME
PAGE 150-151

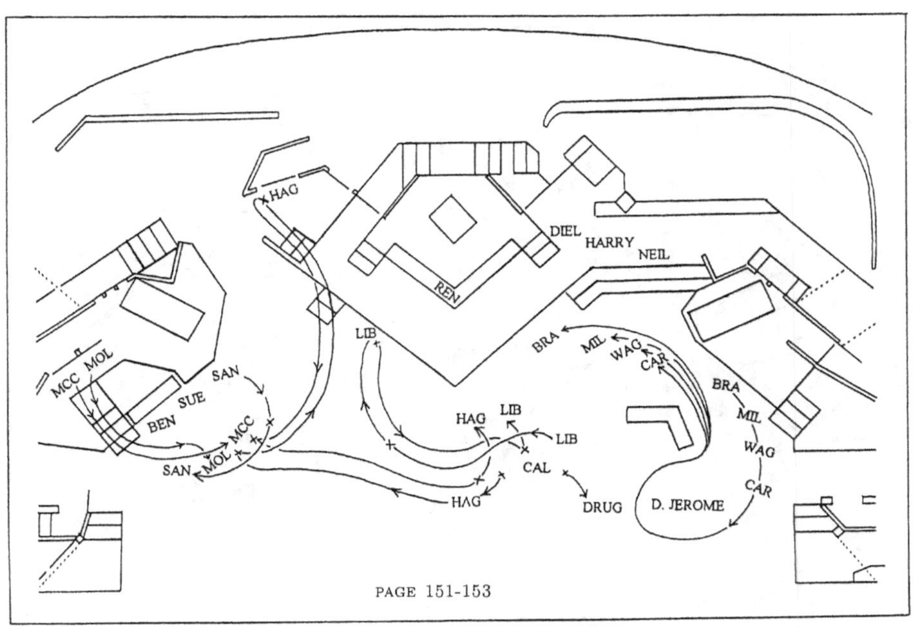

HAG
DIEL
HARRY
NEIL
REN
LIB
MCC MOL
SAN
SUE
BEN
SAN MOL MCC
HAG
LIB
LIB
CAL
HAG
DRUG
BRA
MIL
WAG
CAR
BRA
MIL
WAG
CAR
D. JEROME
PAGE 151-153

FROAR
DIEL
HARRY
NEIL
REN
REN
DIEL
BRA
MIL
WAG
CAR
HAG
NEIL
LIB
SUE
DIEL
LIB
BEN
HAR
MCC
HAG
DRUG
SAN
MOL
BEN
FRO
CAL
DRUG
D. JEROME
PAGE 153-154

BEN
FROAR
REN
BRA
MIL
WAG
CAR
(DIEL) JAKE
HAG
SUE
SUE
DIEL
NEIL
LIB
(BRAY) KATY
BEN
HAR
DRUG
MCC
SAN
MOL
CALEB
JEROME
NEIL
FRO
JER
HAR
PAGE 154-155

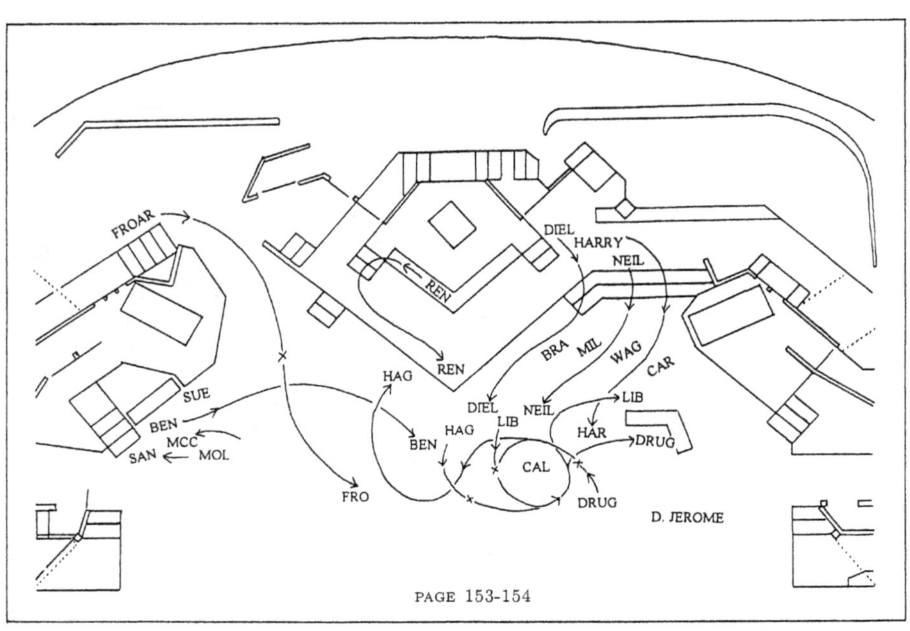

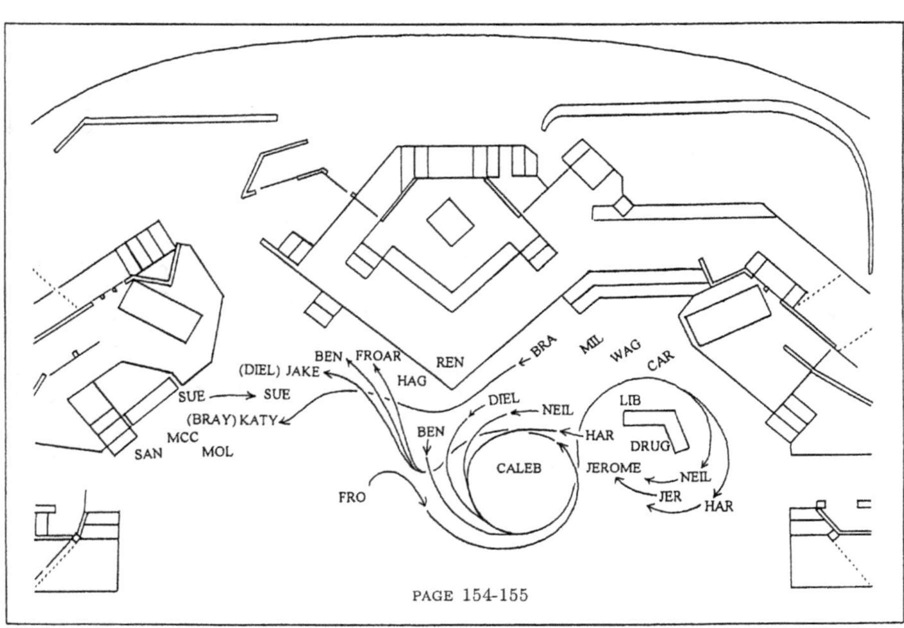

257

at the uninitiated. HAGAN, the LIBRARIAN and DRUGGIST are not averse to
enrolling the town's underworld dregs of superstitious simpletons as
the 'antients' displaying for the benefit of CALEB poisonous offertory gifts.

PAGE 155

Within these notes on the SECOND WATCH the added diagrams illus-
trate the complex choreography for the nightmare sabat. When JEROME
and CALEB meet for a brief moment before the whirlwind separates
them, their words mirror each to the other their respective weighing of
innocence or guilt.

Taped choruses accompany the violent swarming of CALEB THORN.
The stanzas meld into one recitation over the action.

CHOR. 5
> HAGAN *(on-stage)*
> HARRY, HALS, HADDOCK, JAKE *(off-stage* U.C.*)*
> LIBRARIAN., CANTOR, DAN *(off-stage*D.R.*)*, BEN *(on-stage)*

CHOR. 1
> TENOR . . . .   CHOR. 2 > TWO BARITONES . .   These choruses
> CALEB . . . .   PAGE 156 > CALEB, TENOR . . .   rise to a climax
> TENOR . . . .   > TWO BASSES . . . . .   in crescendo.

PAGE 156

CHOR. 3
> THREE BARITONES . .   CHOR. 4 > FOUR CONTRALTOS . . .
> CALEB, TWO TENORS   > CALEB, THREE TENORS
> THREE BASSES . . . . .   > FOUR BASSES . . . .

CHOR. 5
> FOUR TREBLES, FOUR SOPRANOS . . . .
> CALEB, FOUR TENORS, FOUR CONTRALTOS . . . .
> FOUR BARITONES, FOUR BASSES . . . .

CHOR. 6
> FIVE TREBLES, FIVE SOPRANOS . . . .
> CALEB, FIVE TENORS, FIVE CONTRALTOS . . . .
> FIVE BARITONES, FIVE BASSES . . . .

PAGE 157
PAGE 158
KATY, SUE, SANDY and JAKE incircling CALEB,
hurl at him once again the old taunts.

Chorus 7 is cued by HAGAN's speech(live on stage) 'Swear t' the Caprid,
Clerk . . . if ya dare!' (tape enters on 'dare!')

CHOR. 7
> HAGAN . . . *(live)* . . . .   CHOR. 8 > CALEB . . . *(live)* . . . .
> FIVE TENORS, FIVE CONTRALTOS . . . *(on tape)* . .   > FIVE TENORS, FIVE CONTRALTOS
> FIVE BARITONES, FIVE BASSES . . . . . *(on tape)* . .   > FIVE BARITONES, FIVE BASSES . .

Chorus 8 is cued by CALEB's answer (live
on stage) 'You devils have dared me!'
(tape enters on 'me!' - spoken under CALEB)

SAN
JAKE BEN
FROAR
REN
MIL WAG CAR
HAG
SUE
KATY
SAN
MCC
MOL
LIB
DRUG
WISE
CLOCK.
LIB
DRUG
LIB
HAG
CAL
CAL
HAG
CAL
JER NEIL
NEIL
HAR
HAG
CAL
DRUG
COUNTER
CLOCK-
WISE
DRUG
HAG
JER
HAR
PAGE 154-155

REN
MIL WAG CAR
MCC MOL
FRO
BEN
JAKE
DRUG
LIB
CAL
HAG
NEIL
JER
KATY
HAR
SAN SUE
PAGE 155

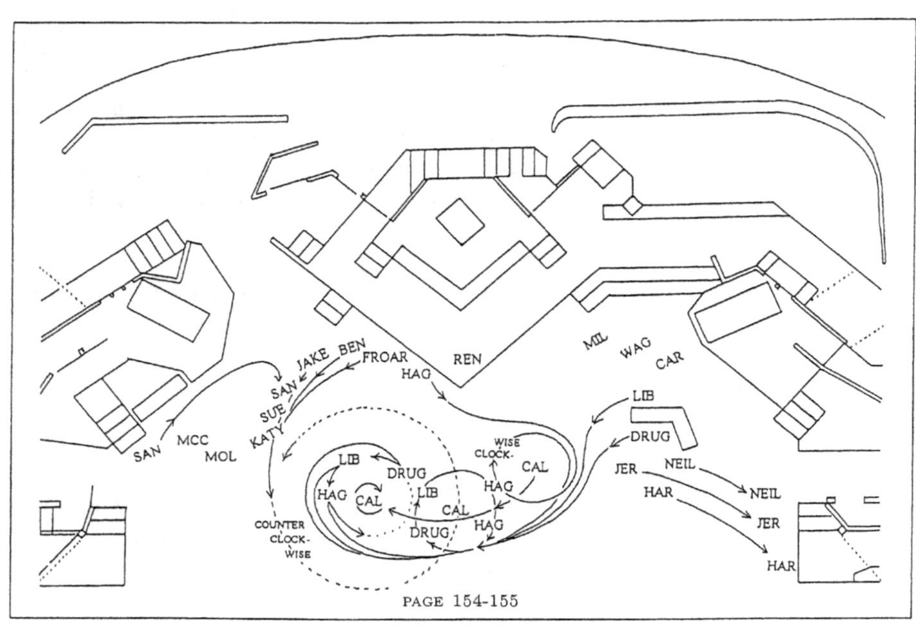

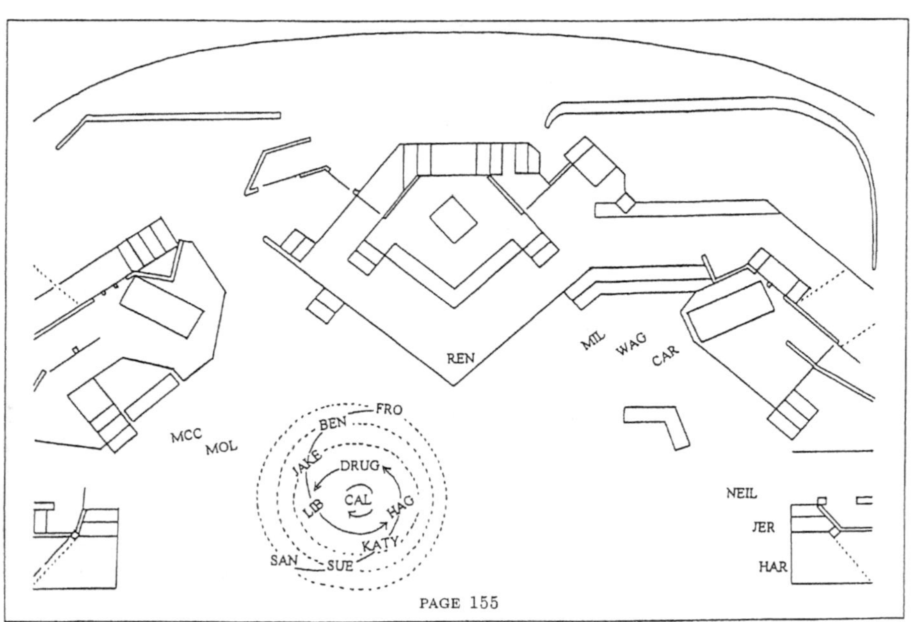

259

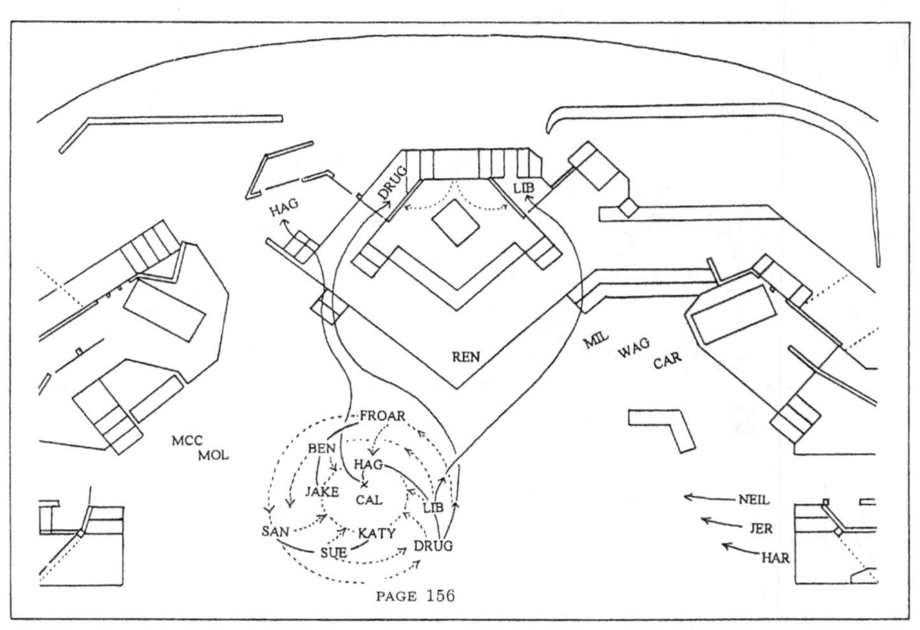

DRUG
LIB
HAG
REN
MIL
WAG
CAR
MCC
MOL
FROAR
BEN
HAG
JAKE
CAL
LIB
SAN
KATY
DRUG
SUE
NEIL
JER
HAR
PAGE 156

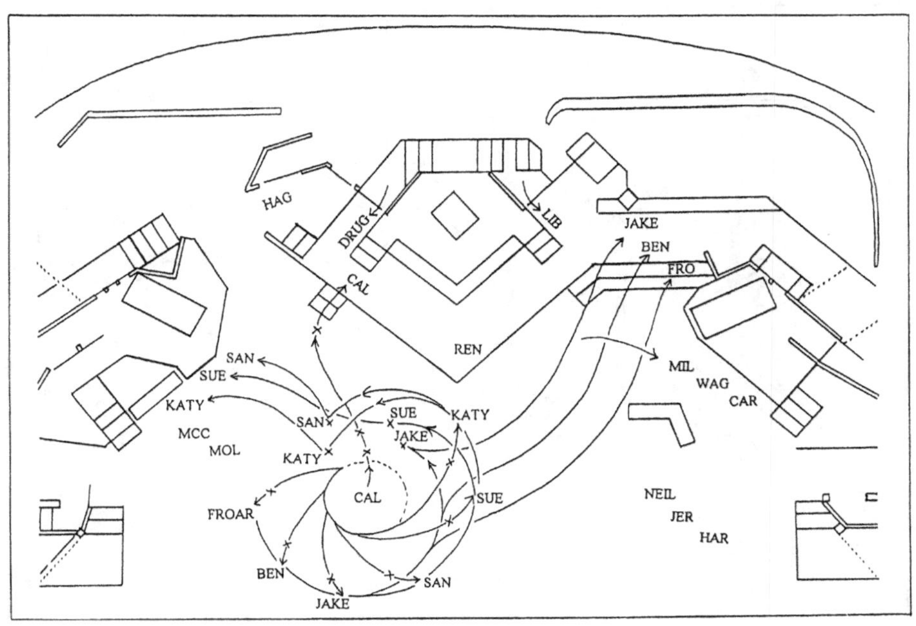

HAG
DRUG
LIB
JAKE
BEN
FRO
CAL
REN
MIL
WAG
CAR
SAN
SUE
KATY
SAN
SUE
KATY
MCC
MOL
KATY
JAKE
CAL
SUE
NEIL
JER
HAR
FROAR
BEN
SAN
JAKE
PAGE 156-157

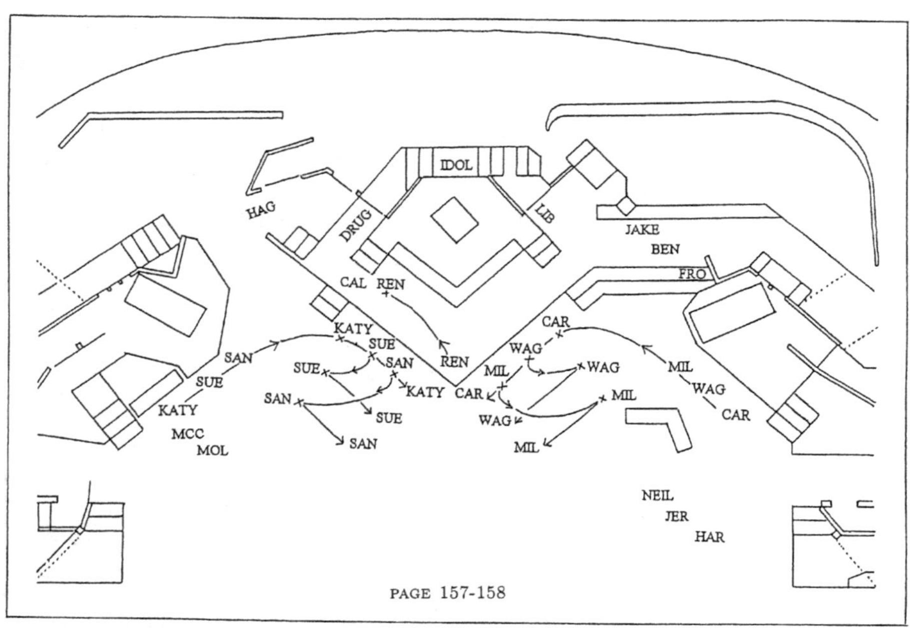

IDOL
HAG
DRUG
LIB
JAKE
BEN
FRO
CAL REN
KATY
SUE
CAR
WAG
SAN
SUE
SAN
REN
MIL
WAG
MIL
SUE
SUE
KATY
CAR
WAG
SAN
WAG
MIL
CAR
KATY
SAN
SUE
MIL
MCC
MOL
SAN
NEIL
JER
HAR
PAGE 157-158

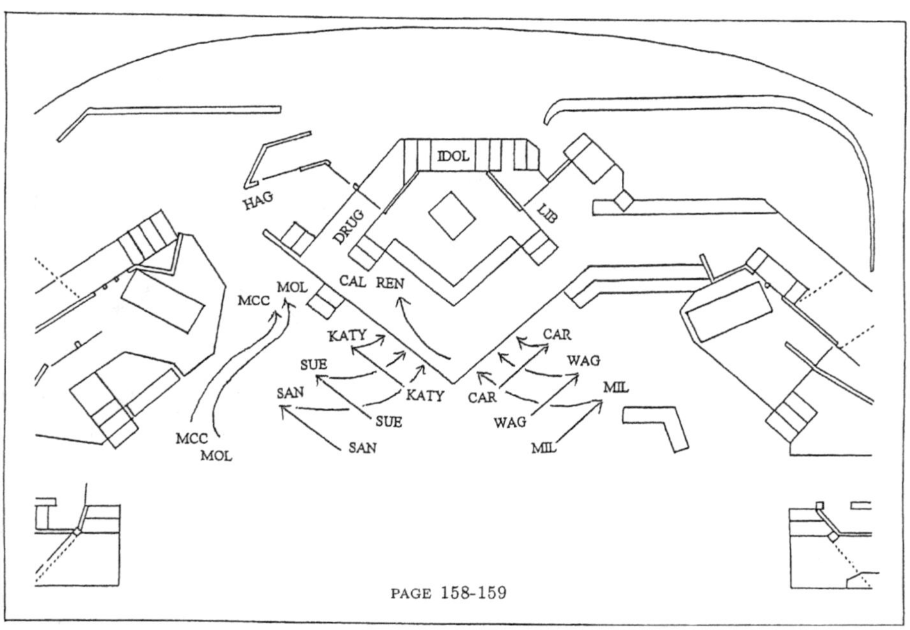

IDOL
HAG
DRUG
LIB
MOL
CAL REN
MCC
CAR
KATY
WAG
SUE
MIL
SAN
KATY
CAR
MCC
SUE
WAG
MOL
SAN
MIL
PAGE 158-159

Chorus 9 follows HAGAN's speech; choruses
9 to 13 are taped and spoken live on stage.

CHOR. 9
[FIVE SOPRANOS, FIVE CONTRALTOS, FIVE TENORS
  FIVE BARITONES, FIVE BASSES . . . .

Chorus 10 follows RENAIRE's speech.

CHOR. 10
[FIVE SOPRANOS, FIVE CONTRALTOS, FIVE TENORS . . . . *(tape and live)*
  TEN TENORS . . . . *(tape and live)*
  FIVE BARITONES, FIVE BASSES . . . . *(tape and live)*

PAGE 159

CHOR. 11
[FIVE SOPRANOS, FIVE CONTRALTOS, FIVE TENORS . . . .
  FIVE TENORS, FIVE BARITONES . . . .
  FIVE BARITONES, FIVE BASSES . . . .

CHOR. 12
[FIVE SOPRANOS, FIVE CONTRALTOS, FIVE TENORS . . . .
  FIVE TENORS, FIVE BARITONES . . . .
  FOUR BARITONES, FOUR BASSES . . . .

CHOR. 13
[FIVE SOPRANOS, FIVE CONTRALTOS, FIVE TENORS . . . .
  FIVE TENORS, FIVE BARITONES . . . .
  FOUR BARITONES, FOUR BASSES . . . .

PAGE 157
PAGE 158
During the four choruses from 10 to 13 there is a gradual accelera-
tion of tempo for dancers and choruses alike. The choreography and
choruses will need to be established before the final recording. Under
the choruses a very soft sustained cymbal surges in and out between
stanzas where it could accentuate the turning points in the dance. It
subsides under the low tympanic roll announcing the arrival of the
Caprid. When the idol lifts the severed goat's head placing it on his
headless shoulders all the votaries scatter in panic to a final surge of
PAGE 160
the cymbal. With the Caprid's darkening RENAIRE invokes the darkness
as the adversary of the Lumen Christi. When CALEB ascends to the altar he seems in a trance. Has he been drugged or hypnotized? or is it
the seeming sense of an irrational dream? He is bewildered when the
LIBRARIAN and DRUGGIST clothe him in a strange vestment and present
the 'anodyne cup' and the 'black bread of affliction', placing them
in his hands which they lift up, leaving him standing there, alone, in
PAGE 162
the presence of the demonic. Motionless, as the chorus of votaries
rises to a climax, he seems unconscious of DOM JEROME's outcry, or of
MOLLY's frantic questioning of MCCORKERAN.

CHOR. 14
[TEN TENORS . . . .
  FOUR SOPRANOS, FOUR CONTRALTOS . . . . *(together*
  FOUR CONTRALTOS, FOUR BARITONES . . . . *two timbres*
  FOUR BARITONES, FOUR BASSES . . . . *together)*
  TEN BASSES . . . .

HAG
DRUG
IDOL
LIB
JAKE
BEN
DRUG
LIB
REN
FRO
MCC
CAL
MOL
REN
MCC
CAR
KATY
WAG
MIL
SUE
MIL
WAG
SAN
SAN
CAR
SUE
KATY
NEIL
JER
HAR
PAGE 159-160

LIB
DRUG
HAG
DRUG
LIB
JAKE
MCC
BEN
CAL
REN
FRO
JER
SAN
MOL
MIL
SUE
WAG
KATY
CAR
NEIL
JER
HAR
PAGE 159-160-162

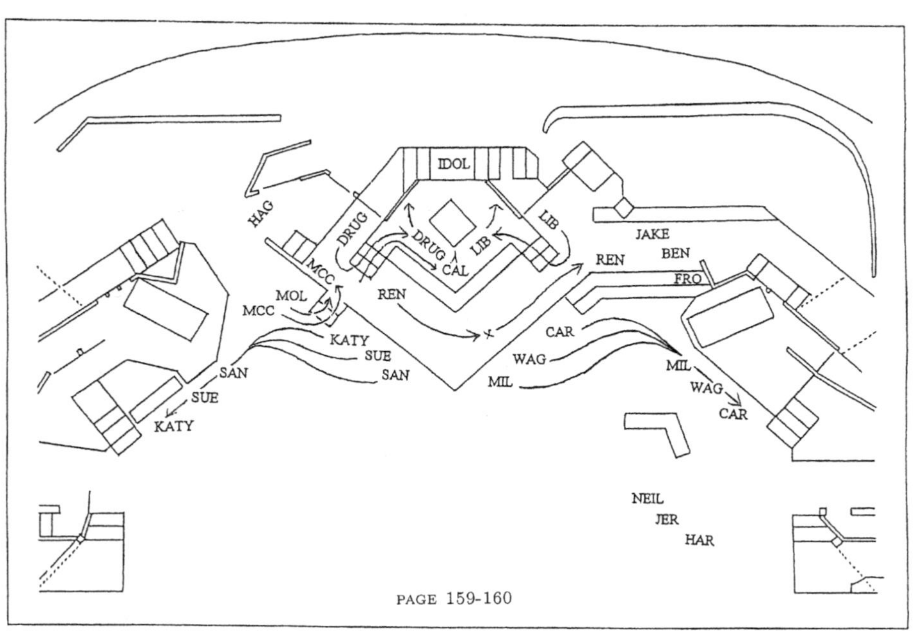

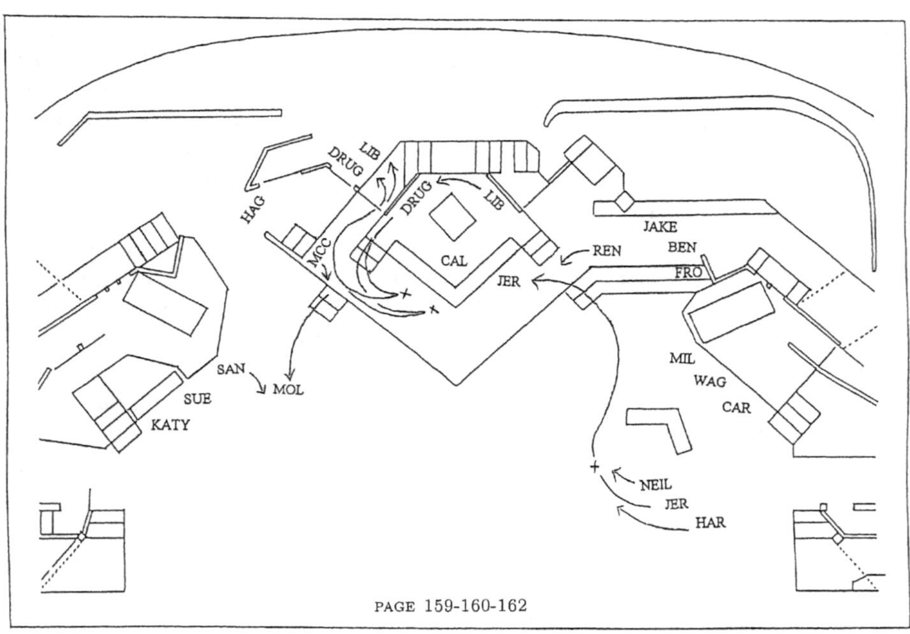

263

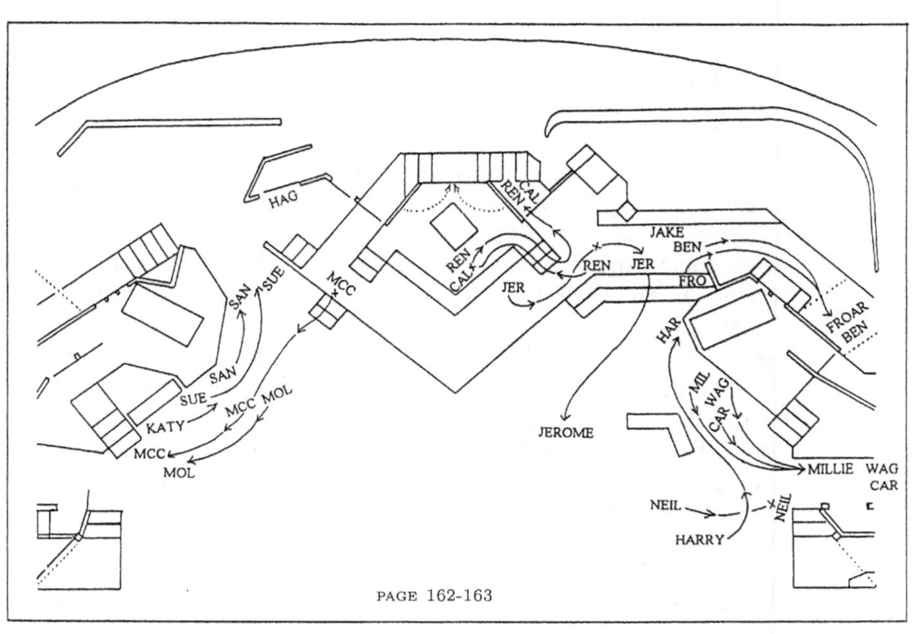

PAGE 162-163

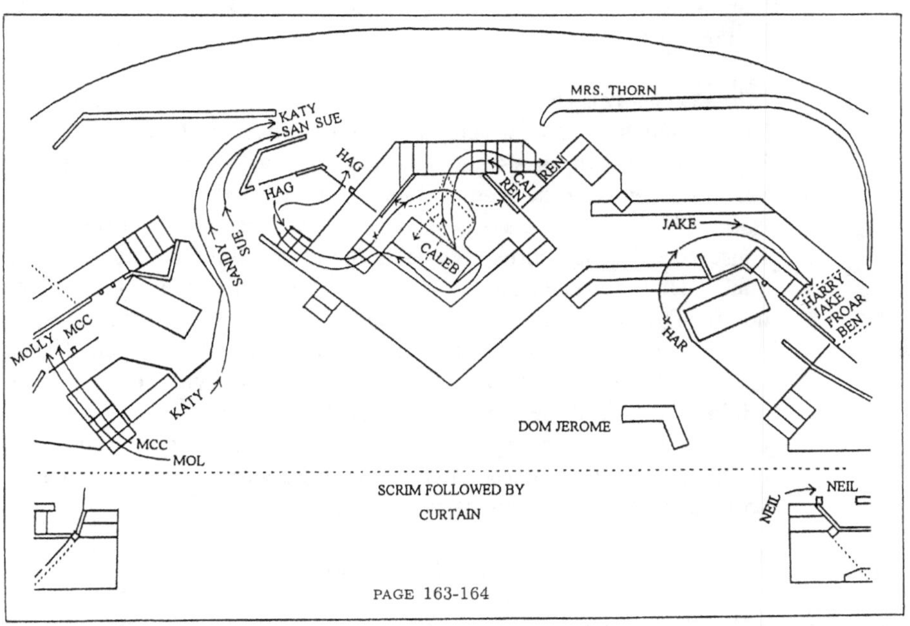

PAGE 163-164

TEN TENORS . . . .

FOUR SOPRANOS, FOUR CONTRALTOS . . . . *(together)*

[1]MCCORK., THREE CONTRALTOS, [2]MOLLY, FOUR CONTRALTOS

FOUR BARITONES, FOUR BASSES . . . . *(together)*

TEN BASSES . . . .

In chorus 14 and 15 the words 'elevation - fractio!', 'come! - execration!' are to be augmented 'live' by all on stage. DOM JEROME cries out once again, when CALEB comes to his senses and convulsed with horror, throws down the satanic cup and paten. RENAIRE intones that the prophesied 'deed is done'. In this central moment of climax, the locked doors of JEROME's memory are flung open and the light streams in - he's almost incoherent with astonishment; with words tumbling out he breaks free of his captors, runs up steps to the lower platform, where he falls to his knees reaching out to the boy exclaiming 'It is you! you are the one ... my sole self lost -' He even acknowledges 'we are one' ... He has recognized himself in the other, in the many - in Caleb, Willie, Regis, Tom. Do they not share in the same image, the same nature? Do they not have the same Father? born even of the same Mother? Overwhelmed by the words of the monk, and the magnitude of his guilt, CALEB frantically tears off the vestment. He begins to fall in a faint when RENAIRE, darting upstairs catches hold of him. At that moment a distant bell sounds. At once RENAIRE dismisses the votaries advising them that each is bearing a burden - 'a conscience he must quell!' Carrying the unconscious CALEB, RENAIRE disappears with him into the house.

While DOM JEROME stands at the top of the seawall steps, the central doors have closed and HAGAN has changed the altar into a bed. As they are leaving the votaries discuss what RENAIRE meant by 'conscience must quell'. JEROME descends the steps and still in shock, he stands motionless. MCCORK-ERAN calls the girl and MOLLY asks 'How can we quell that remorseless conscience?' The chorus completes the phrase with a whispered 'must quell!' It is repeated again and again very softly 'Conscience - must quell!' The door opens, RENAIRE enters with CALEB still unconscious, lays him on the bed, covers him and departs - the door remains open. The CHO-RUS steadily increases in volume and reverberance with voices off-stage joining the tape at the climax. At CALEB's outcry JEROME covers his ears, then listens - when the light switches on MRS. THORN calls up 'is there anything wrong, dear?' CALEB answers 'nothing wrong. Just nightmares -' DOM JEROME is still standing as CURTAIN falls.

THE THIRD WATCH

Seated in his cell, DOM JEROME questions himself about the dream - was it only a nightmare? or was it real? He cannot explain why he woke up standing in the street. Was CALEB THORN an illusory nightwalking double of himself - a doppelgänger? No, it was perhaps because he *was* real, that

JEROME recognized their human condition with but one origin, one destiny! It was that, that allowed him to remember who he was - his mother, his father. It's as if he has become a prophet, as if, in remembering times past, he is living now - what will be. As light comes up CALEB THORN is revealed seated on the bench. He is tormented in a quandary - is he going to confess visiting the whorehouse or taking part in a satanic rite? But it's urgent that he deflect RENAIRE's blackmail threat - but, procuring MOLLY? That's frightful! However after approaching MCCORKERAN's place, he hesitates but then finally knocks. MCCORKERAN answers the door with illtempered irony. When CALEB offers to pay her for the page he signed in her register, she mocks him with feigned ignorance of any such stupidity on his part - she runs 'a discreet establishment'. When MOLLY appears, MCCORKERAN is abrupt with CALEB. 'Don't come in! Talk there. Yer not a payin' customer.' In the rapid exchange between CALEB and MOLLY they touch on what was the burning question for each, the wild note, the Register, the missing page and the demonlogist's threat to denounce him - 'Molly, you've got to help me!'

He stumbles awkwardly trying to ask her, when she plainly states what he's come for - to procure her. He suggests a pretended consent, but her refusal is direct - 'no! I can't, he's a devil worshiper!' When MOLLY brings up the nightmare she had they both realize they had the same dream, but CALEB is uncertain - was it real? But for him, the blackmail, *that's* real!

Then MOLLY's persistent refusal angers him. She tells him he's got to change his life - to repent! 'Save yourself while you can - abandon theology, and set your soul straight!' CALEB reacts with outrage - 'You preach to me?' he points out she's living a lie in a whore house. Is her rumoured repentence nothing but hypocrisy? His tirade finally dies out due to MOLLY's silent acceptance of all he has said. When MOLLY admits 'It's the truth ... it's what I saw - in your face ... a merciless mirror to my life!' Her meeting with the shamefaced youth had changed her life. CALEB is dumbfounded - 'the rumours are true? Molly? - You've given up this sordid traffic?'

She tells him it is true - she's entering the convent tonight after her confession - as a Magdalene. CALEB, repentant for his unjust words, asks her forgiveness. There is nothing to forgive she says, it was his remorse that opened her eyes to the truth - no, it was the one who sent her on the street she had to forgive, her abusive father. 'But you Caleb what are you going to do?' He does not know, he cannot rid himself of the glittering eyes of his tormentor. She recalls his words of despair that night, that enlightened her - she asks him 'Why? why did you do it Caleb?'

CALEB's answer, a monologue, tries to search out his pretense of shifting the blame to his stepmother. There was a Call, but he let it die. Like a fool of a kid, he walked into his own trap - had to prove himself, he can't say why, as delinquent and wild as the rest of that crowd. MOLLY discerns his underlying loneliness and CALEB agrees, 'bereft by death and circumstance' of any 'brother, sister, father, mother.' Betraying his Lord, he failed to find his solace in the only friend he ever had.

PAGE 176

As MCCORKERAN interrupts, impatient to lock up for the night, MOLLY urges CALEB to approach the confessor, PERE BERNARD, with his trouble - he would know a way out with honour. She has convinced him, and he blurts out, 'You make me want it so!' As she turns to go in she adds - 'and

PAGE 177

pray for a Magdalene.' As penitents begin returning from the cathedral MISS PEW appears somewhat chastened by the severity of PERE BERNARD'S admonition; 'must mend my ways, uncharitable talk, antipathy to MRS. CARP -' While, unnoticed behind her, MILLIE brings her guests out to the

PAGE 178

front parlour for tea. As MISS PEW pauses to the left entrance to MILLIE's she weighs possible eventuations - when TAD MCFERGUSON enters, buoyed with hope for his pledge but aware there may yet be a struggle - MISS PEW decides to risk a surprise visit. She lets herself in to be greeted by

PAGE 179

hilarious chorusing of the gossips at her expense. She steps into the light - 'So! That's what you talk about, when I'm away!' General consternation - PEW leaves closing the door with finality. 'Oh, what a fool I've been!' Meanwhile TAD has heard the strains of a drinking carousal on the quays drifting up from below.

(Chorus begins softly.)

PAGE 180

This song having begun at a distance wafts in more distinctly on the air, then recedes again only to return in full force at the end when MISS PEW voices her warning.

MISS PEW's definitive rejection of gossipry enables her to see old TAD's humanity. There is a touch of pathos in TAD's response to MISS PEW's concern. There is also a touch of humour in her capitulation to his previously unsuspected manners - he had known better times. Now, TOM BURNS enters, reconciled and forgiven. He seems rejuvenated; his own original innocence somehow restored. Pausing to gaze at the old house from the top of the seawall, he hears again, as it were, the echo of his mother's song.

PAGE 182

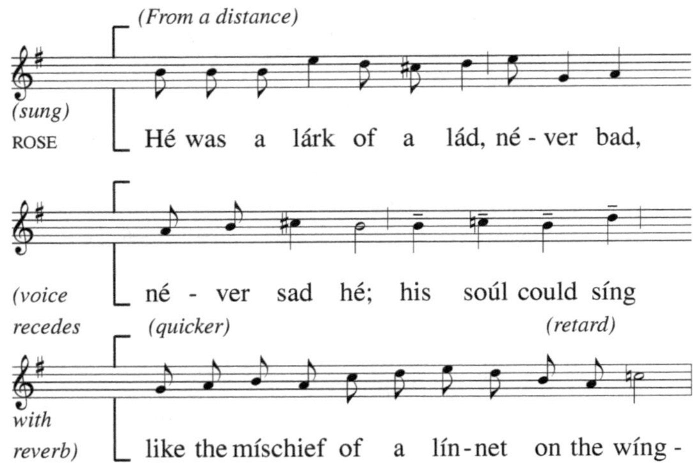

MOLLY GREEN comes out, pauses listening to the song, then goes up to the cathedral - TOM leaves on the seawall. The lower stage is dark. When the door U.C.1 opens, light spills into the darkness as RENAIRE enters. Amber light comes up revealing MILLIE seated on the bench. Their conversation PAGE 183 that follows reveals the true nature of RENAIRE, stripped of his assumed disguises, as a common but cunning thief, preying on rich but credulous women.

PAGE 184 Upstairs, he leafs through the documents with obvious satisfaction. Returning them to the briefcase he lays it on the bed. Downstairs he consults with HAGAN who asks 'how long d' ya keep us ... waitin' fer our cut?' Evasively, RENAIRE mentions the Green-Thorn caper as possibly PAGE 184 failing, he boasts of having realized substantial 'emoluments' upstairs (an incautious remark he will regret later). He waits for CALEB in the PAGE 185 Tavern. Meanwhile HAGAN's suspicions are aroused - he searches the room where RENAIRE is staying as MILLIE's house guest, discovers the briefcase, examines the contents. He substitutes folded newsprint for the documents, writes a note for MILLIE pleased that he has 'scotched that snake for awhile'.

PAGE 186 Chorus 1 with CANTOR, DAN, BEN. Chrous 2 with LIBRARIAN, DRUGGIST, both chanted off-stage U.R. The choruses precede and follow CALEB's entrance till he reaches centre stage where he stops, speaking his lines. The chorus is not loud, it represents his burdened thoughts.

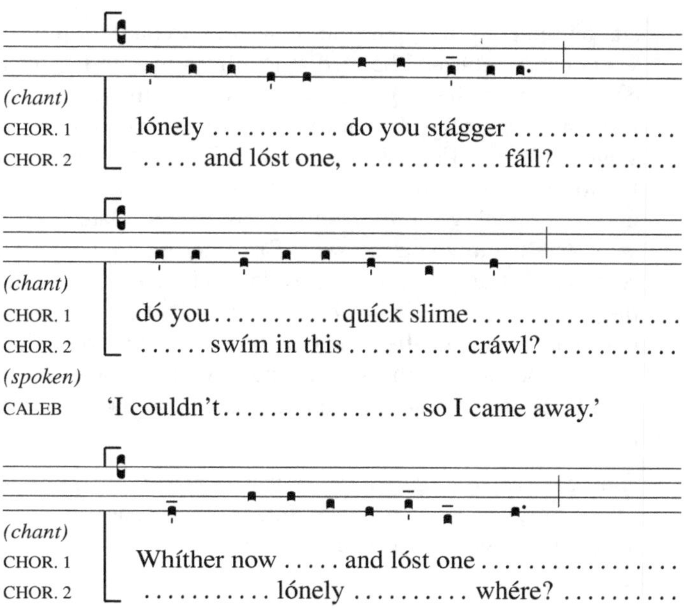

PAGE 186 Unseen by CALEB, RENAIRE approaches behind him. 'So you failed, in your commission!' CALEB is jolted out of his reverie. He swings around - PAGE 187 faces his enemy. RENAIRE informs him he has letters ready for the Rector and Jamison Thorn with the damning evidence enclosed. CALEB begs him not to send them, asking in desperation, 'is there anything I can do?' RENAIRE with a speculative gleam; 'an alternative ransom for your reputation? - yes, seventy grand with a two hour's grace.' CALEB backs away, then runs up on the seawall and lets himself in U.C.3. RENAIRE, having returned to the Tavern, sees the LIBRARIAN and the DRUGGIST entering the cellar and pausing through the door U.C.7. He is immediately suspicious, runs across and upstairs retrieving his briefcase. Returning, he disappears into MCCORK- PAGE 188 ERAN'S. CODROCKS appears, returning from the cathedral elated that the man o' God confirmed his simple belief sayin' 'Yer stone ship is surely Payter's Bark'. He rambles on about all the other little churches too. Rounding the platform he sees CALEB teetering on the parapet. COD calls out 'come down!' But CALEB has raised his arms, stepped back and fallen out of sight. COD runs up and looks over the parapet. CALEB has not fallen into the water but into the drying fishnets.

PAGE 189 COD immediately pulls in the nets and taking hold of the lad's hand, hauls him up on the seawall. 'Well, young man, what ya got t' say fer yerself?' CALEB says 'I wanted to die.' The old fisherman in his good humoured way sounds out the lad's troubles, his crimes, sins, his black ingratitude and about the criminal who found out and is blackmailing him. COD acknowledges his deep need to be forgiven and encourages him to go up there 't' the man o' God, Pere Bernard.' He quiets the boy's fears of a PAGE 190 harsh condemnation - 'He's not there fer that - he counsels an' forgives, an' he 'elps ye t' forget.' This is surely prophetic. When COD has left, CALEB sits on the bottom step of the seawall to prepare himself. At this point MOLLY GREEN returns, liberated at last from the burdens of her life. She compares it to the bright fresh morning air that time she first met SR. JENNIFER. MOLLY rings the convent bell. CALEB has risen. He comes downstage, calls to MOLLY. She runs over to him, asks if he has been to confession yet. Admitting to his inability before, he tells her he is going now. Go quickly she tells him before it is too late 'Pere Bernard is a saint - he'll show you the way. I'm entering the convent tonight. I'm so happy!' They promise to pray for each other. The light comes on in the convent porch. MOLLY runs over and is met by SR. JENNIFER. MOTHER SUPERIOR appears, and after a solemn questioning as to her intention MOLLY is welcomed among the Magdalenes. As light comes up in the Tavern, memories of that night revive. Numbered choruses sing off-stage down right.

PAGE 191

PAGE 192

CHORUS 1 - BEN, DAN. C. 2 - JAKE, HALL, HEARTH. C. 3 - BEN, DAN, SANDY, LIBRARIAN. C. 4 - BEN, DAN, SANDY, LIBRARIAN, MISS MILLIE, MISS PEW, MARY, MOLLY, KATY.

PAGE 192

271

CALEB   No! no Renaire! you'll never have it!
(spoken)   and you'll never get me!

(spoken)
RENAIRE   Wait! Come back you fool!
                                 . . . . you'll pay for it!

PAGE 193

As RENAIRE drinks, the bar lights dim, while a ruddy glow comes up in the furnace and the cellar. The LIBRARIAN and DRUGGIST enter questioning HAGAN about his suspicions. It is unlikely the blacksmith is as ignorant of legal matters as he pretends. One suspects his assumed naivety to be deeper, more devious than deception itself. When MISS MILLIE enters with a tea service for her guest, HAGAN silences the conspirators.

PAGE 194

Knocking, and receiving no answer she looks in, decides he has stepped out for a moment, goes in to set out the tea. The conspirators continue their talk about the so called 'monuments', which HAGAN says were 'just old legal forms.' which he threw in the furnace - 'there weren't no money in it! To their disbelief and outrage HAGAN asks with cunning innocence 'Ya don' mean it were worth somethin', do ya?' MISS MILLIE comes out, troubled by the sudden and unusual absence of the Professor. Then she discovers HAGAN's note, snatches it up, and reads first with disbelief, then with hysterical dismay. Rushing into the corridor she calls the Operator for the police, 'I've been robbed -' she cries, but slumps to the floor in a faint attempting to give her address. The lights fade and the doors close. The LIBRARIAN and DRUGGIST hastily leave the premises.

272

PAGE 196

RENAIRE also has heard MILLIE's outcry, and sensing something has gone wrong, he rushes off to the bank, clutching his precious briefcase stuffed with stale news. OLRIG HAGAN, alone with the furnace in his cellar, has concluded his transactions with humanity. Gloating with satisfaction, he draws the documents out of an inner pocket and flings them into the flames. His laughter is demented as if a paroxysm of long suppressed rage. Is he insane? or possesed by a devil? If it is the latter, when HAGAN crawls into the furnace he is simply doing so to incinerate his disposable accomplice.

The inhuman laughter after he had slammed shut the door of the furnace was proof enough. DOM JEROME is so shaken by HAGAN's self destruction that he flees his post in the porter's office, and goes in for a spell, to pray. The cathedral bourdon sounds as MARY SIMS enters with her son WILLIE. She is explaining how his father had abandoned ship on a life raft - he hadn't waited for the others. That's why he wasn't drowned. He blames himself for the loss of the others - WILLIE tells his mother he knew his father wasn't dead, that he was awake that night when he came home. Astonished by the candour of his admission, she tells the boy his father has become a hopeless drinker and hides himself because he's so ashamed. GRANDMOTHER OWEN has entered and calls out to her daughter, 'Is that you, Rosemary?' MARY is shocked to see her mother out at this hour. Shepherding her home, she sends WILLIE to fetch DR. MALLOY.

PAGE 199

Singing is heard as FAY, FANNY and REGIS return from the cathedral.

The children decide to visit GRANNY OWEN. MRS. SIMS cautions them, 'only for a moment, Mrs. Owen is not well -' GRANNY however greets REGIS as her grandson. MARY corrects her. 'No Mother, it's the Wicks boy', but the old woman assures her, 'every little boy I see is my grandson.' She extends her grandmaternal sway to FAY and FANNY, undoubtedly her granddaughters too!

Then GRANNY asks REGIS to run across and ask the porter, DOM JEROME, to see her. REGIS goes with FAY and FANNY trailing after. COD comes up from the quay, having spread his nets again. He speculates on a departure of the Stone Ship tonight - with a soul or two. He lights his pipe. A fog horn sounds as WILLIE returns with DR. MALLOY. COD and the doctor exchange greetings, and MARY, having been watchful for the boy and the doctor, opens to them. Thanking the doctor she says, 'it's Mother again'. Examining the old lady he chides her with 'overdoing it again'. She explains 'It's the Dedication you know' - 'I know Mrs. Owens'. He advises her after taking her pulse, to 'sleep a little more, and walk a little less'. He gives her something to take with a cup of hot tea before bed. DR. MALLOY assures MRS. SIMS 'She'll be alright tonight'. MARY worries her mother is getting senile, but the doctor allays her concern by observing 'your Mother is a very wise old lady'. The doctor is pleased MARY has told WILLIE about his father. He speaks to the boy, then takes his leave to join the Captain on the seawall for a pipe. MARY and WILLIE prepare to leave when the boy asks his grandmother, 'How can you have three grandsons, Granny?' Amused by the question, she promises him he will see when he grows up. As MARY pauses on the seawall to button WILLIE's coat, JEROME stops with the children, and says a wistful farewell to his mother and childhood as they leave on the seawall. 'They used to call me Willie', REGIS says, then confesses 'I want to be a monk - just like you!' 'You're a little young as yet' JEROME says 'but remember no matter what happens, you will be happy one day - just as I am'. Then, because it's getting late he sends them off home. They disappear on the seawall.

The monk crosses over to GRANNY OWEN's, knocks, opens the door and calls, 'Grandmother? are you sleeping?' She answers 'No, I am not asleep - come in Dom Jerome.' The old lady recalls what JEROME, after all these years remembers - his Grandmother, outside the stream of time - with whom even now he speaks; reminding him of his mother, here but a moment ago, ROSE-MARY, and NICHOLAS, his poor father, twice lost; of young WILLIE the orphan, REGIS the dreamer, TOM the tormented, distinct persons in whom he recognizes himself. JEROME acknowledges each of them as separate dreams on a dark river. His Grandmother foretells one more ghost dream … freighted with the darkest hour of your life and of CALEB's - being absolved by the confessor when a river of healing forgetfulness descended on his mind as once it did on your's. The boy is now bewildered - take care of him. 'Don't worry', JEROME tells his Grandmother, 'everything is all right now; what has happened to him, happened to me a long time ago. It's a memory - of the past - 'and that is well,' she replies. 'I'll have a little peace now - and a good night's sleep.' They wish each other good night. As GRANNY OWEN withdraws and the lights begin to fade, JEROME pauses in the doorway to whisper … 'and goodbye -'

274

PAGE 205 He exchanges greetings with COD and DR. MALLOY, with a little banter for the fisherman - that he keep an eye on the anchor, eh? When JEROME comes down the steps and crosses to Cloistergarth, COD and the DOCTOR go down to the quay. At that moment on Campus Street HANNA enters leading a dazed

PAGE 205 and bewildered CALEB. The boy's aunt is clearly distraught. She bewails the loss of his mind - 'don't even know 'is own Auntie!' JEROME calls out 'Is that you, Hanna?' 'Ah! Dom Jerome! thank the Lord ye're here!' Launching into a litany of appeals she tries to stir the boy's memory. 'Don't ye recall yer auld Aunt Hanna?' He only replies 'I can't tell' . . . 'yer Uncle Remus, surely?'. . .'I don't know'. . .'yer Grandma across the way?' 'I haven't one - no brother or sister, no father no mother . . . I've forgotten them all -' HANNA

PAGE 206 cries despairingly, 'Oh what's t' be done?' DOM JEROME manages to calm her anxiety. He promises they will take care of him in Cloistergarth, she bids

PAGE 207 goodbye to 'poor Tom' and enters Hearth's Lodge. JEROME leads CALEB to the bench where they sit. Inside the monastery we hear the CANTOR and the monks choir begin chanting for the Feast of the morrow.

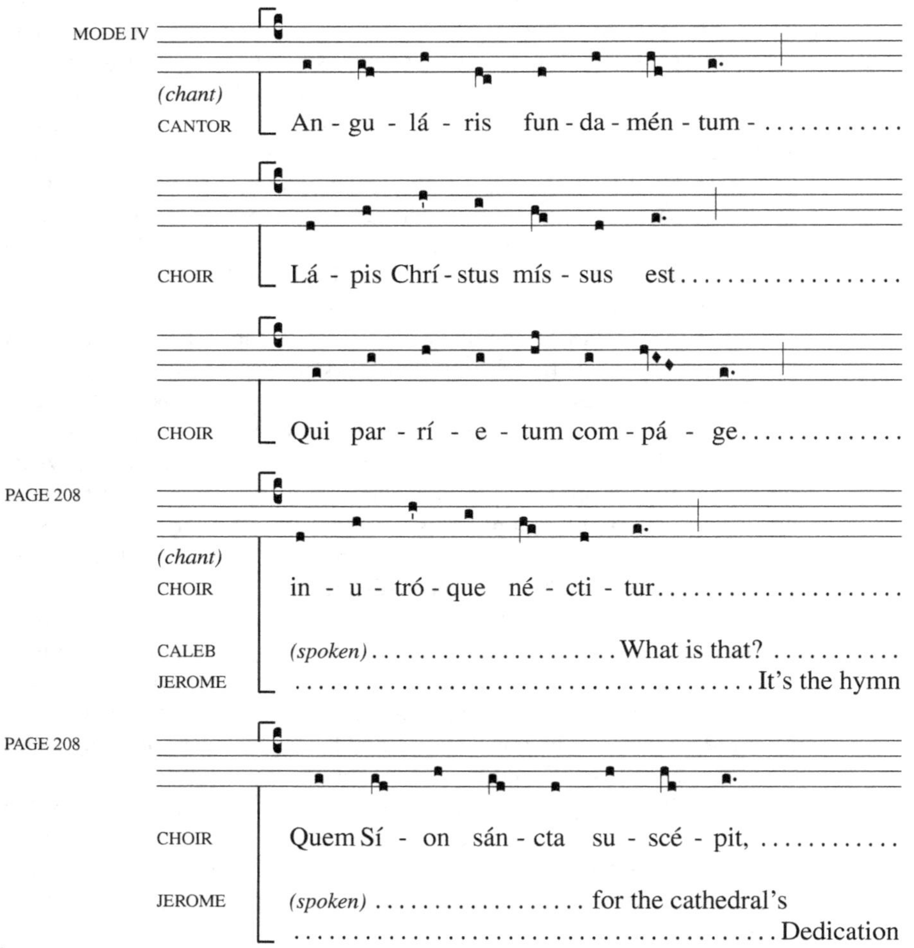

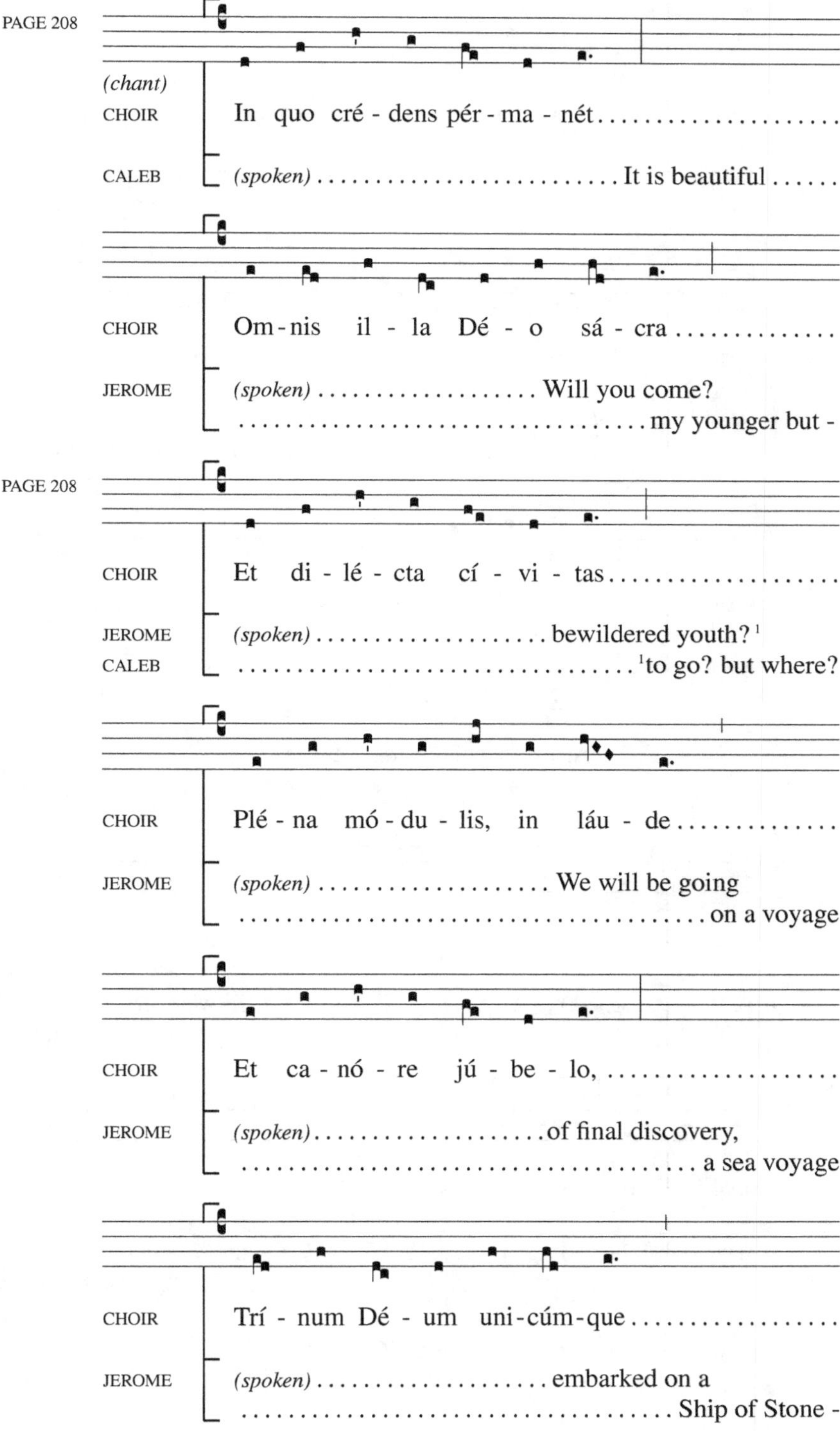

PAGE 208

(chant)
CHOIR   In quo cré - dens pér - ma - nét......................
CALEB   (spoken).........................It is beautiful......

CHOIR   Om - nis   il - la Dé - o   sá - cra..............
JEROME   (spoken)..................Will you come?
         ....my younger but -

PAGE 208

CHOIR   Et   di - lé - cta   cí - vi - tas....................
JEROME   (spoken)....................bewildered youth? [1]
CALEB   ....[1]to go? but where?

CHOIR   Plé - na mó - du - lis, in   láu - de..............
JEROME   (spoken).....................We will be going
         ....on a voyage

CHOIR   Et ca - nó - re   jú - be - lo, ...
JEROME   (spoken)...................of final discovery,
         ....a sea voyage

CHOIR   Trí - num Dé - um uni - cúm - que..................
JEROME   (spoken)...................embarked on a
         ....Ship of Stone -

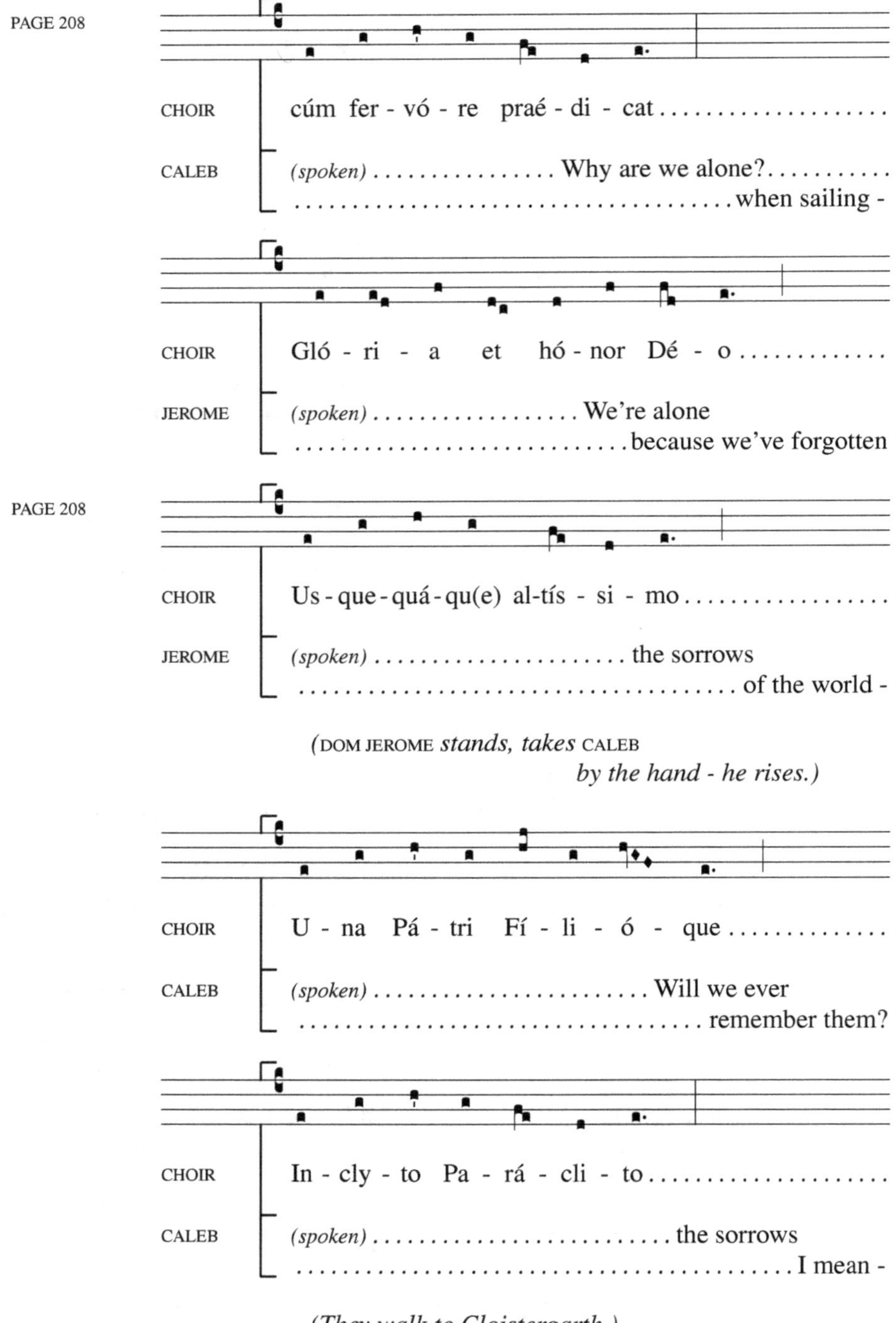
CHOIR   cúm fer - vó - re praé - di - cat . . . .
CALEB   (spoken) . . . . Why are we alone? . . . .
. . . . when sailing -
CHOIR   Gló - ri - a   et   hó - nor Dé - o . . . .
JEROME   (spoken) . . . . We're alone
. . . . because we've forgotten
CHOIR   Us - que - quá - qu(e) al -tís - si - mo . . . .
JEROME   (spoken) . . . . the sorrows
. . . . of the world -
(DOM JEROME stands, takes CALEB
by the hand - he rises.)
CHOIR   U - na Pá - tri Fí - li - ó - que . . . .
CALEB   (spoken) . . . . Will we ever
. . . . remember them?
CHOIR   In - cly - to Pa - rá - cli - to . . . .
CALEB   (spoken) . . . . the sorrows
. . . . I mean -
(They walk to Cloistergarth.)

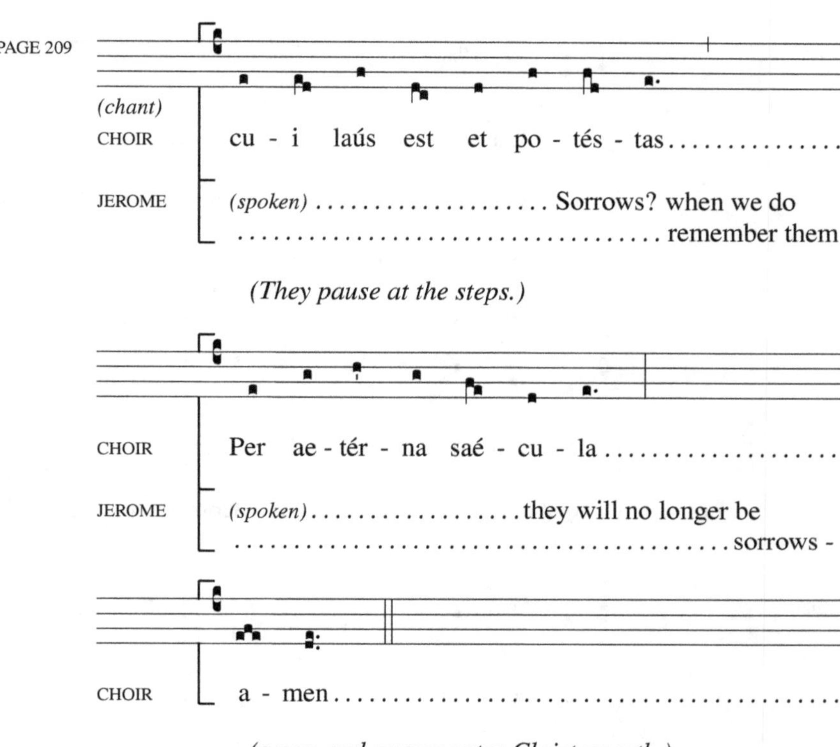

(They pause at the steps.)

(CALEB *and* JEROME *enter Cloistergarth.)*

During the chanting of the hymn above with the muted conversation of the Monk and his bewildered charge, the central doors have opened to the sky, while the ghostly cathedral unfurls her sail of rainbow gossamer, ready to slide from the slipway into the aerial ocean -

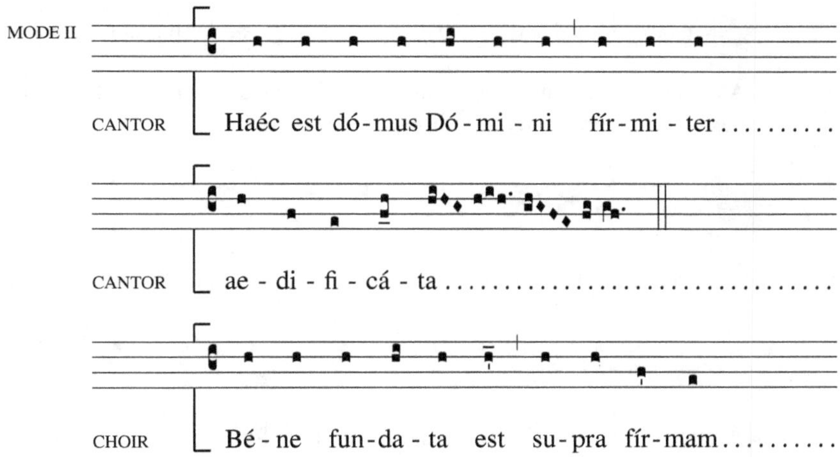

PAGE 209

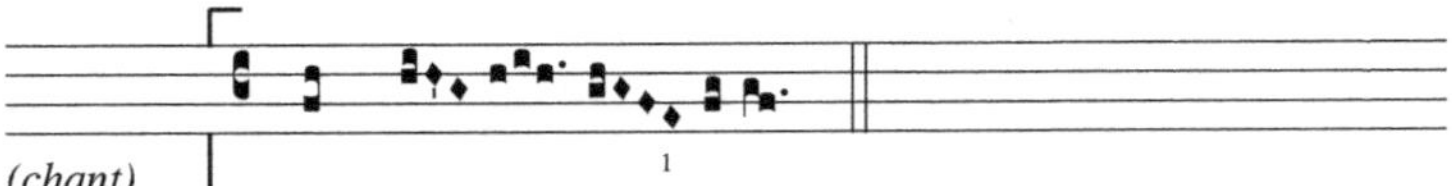

(*chant*)
CHOIR — pé - tram . . . .
(*spoken*)
COD — . . . . [1]Look! - Look up there Doctor Malloy!
(*off-stage* U.C.)

(As COD *runs up the stairs onto the seawall.)*

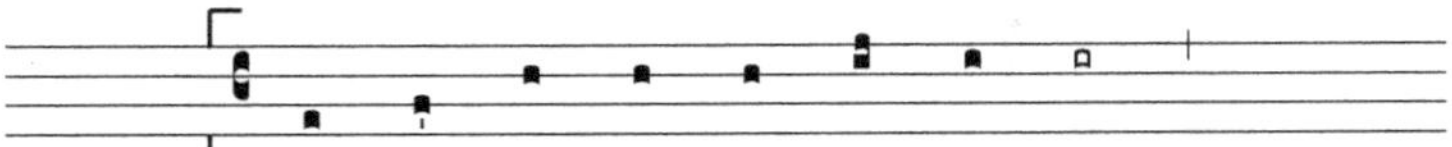

CANTOR — Dó - mum tú - am Dó - mi - ne† . . . .

COD — *(spoken)* . . . . Come up on the wall!

PAGE 209

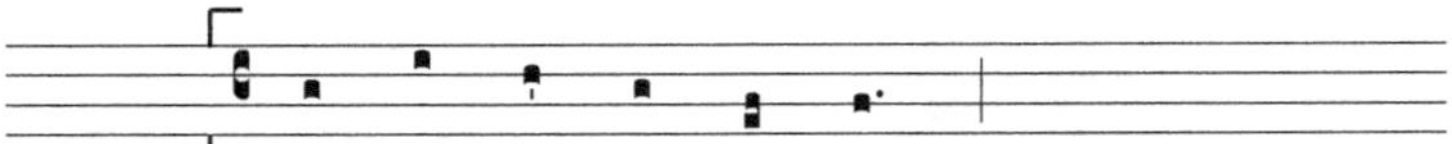

CHOIR — dé - cet sanc - ti - tú - do . . . .

MALLOY — *(off-stage* U.C. *spoken)* . . . . I'm coming . . . .

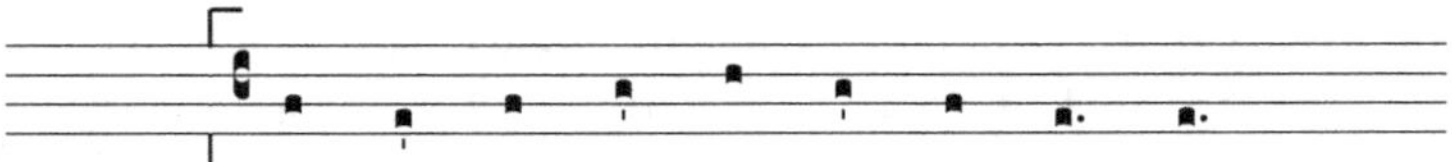

CHOIR — in lon - gi - tú - di - nem di - ér - um[1] . . . .

MALLOY — *(off-stage* U.C. *spoken)* . . . . [1]What is it Captain?

As the NOVICE intones the psalm and the CHOIR answers they fade under the dialogue gradually receding into the distance.

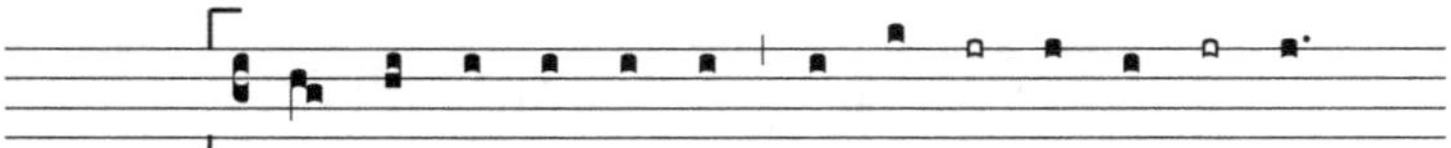

NOVICE — Dó-mi-nus regná - vit, de - có - rem in - dú - tus est† . . . .

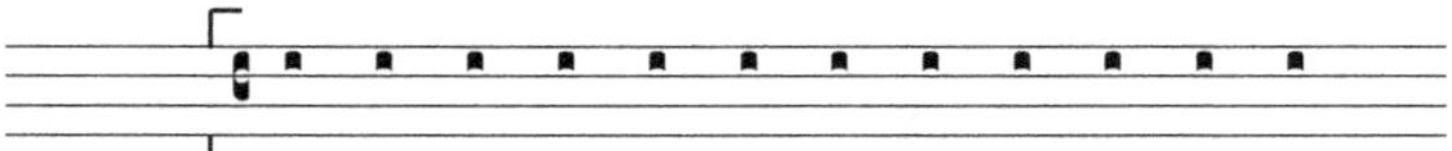

CHOIR 1 — in - dú - tus est Dó-mi-nus for - ti - tú - di - nem. . . . .

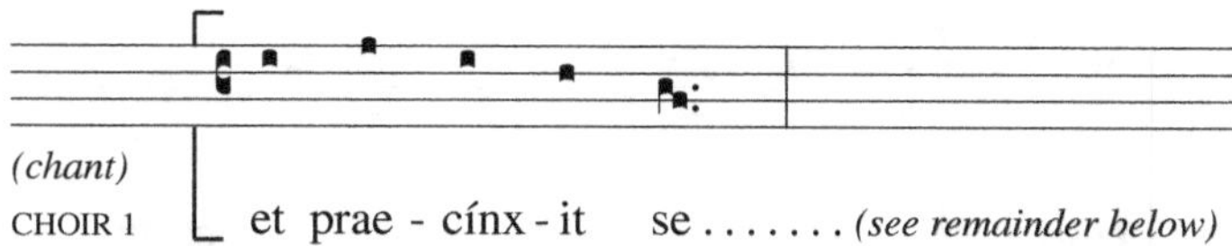

PAGE 210   Psalmody continues receding under the dialogue.

As DR. MALLOY appears, CAPTAIN COD stammers in ecstasy what he sees - he shouts, points out the sails and the spar, but the doctor admits he can't see a thing. COD's declamations grow desperate as he pleads, 'don't ya see 'er?' The doctor replies, 'You *do* see it, don't you -' COD in disbelief shouts 'ya must be plum blind - Look! The sail - the bowsprit - the wake of 'er - look man!' He runs back down to the quay where his triumphant shout echoes 'There she goes!' The doctor is left alone musing on his

PAGE 212   blindness to a beauty he cannot see - cannot believe. He departs on the seawall. DOM JEROME is the only one left on stage. He is kneeling as the ghostly ship is departing, his posture alone indicates the quiet passing of his spirit. His body remains as in prayer, sunk back on his heels, hands fallen into his lap, his head slumped forward, motionless. Then after a pause the left hand slides limply to the floor. The sound of the sea is heard as darkness engulfs the stage.

The remainder of the psalmody.

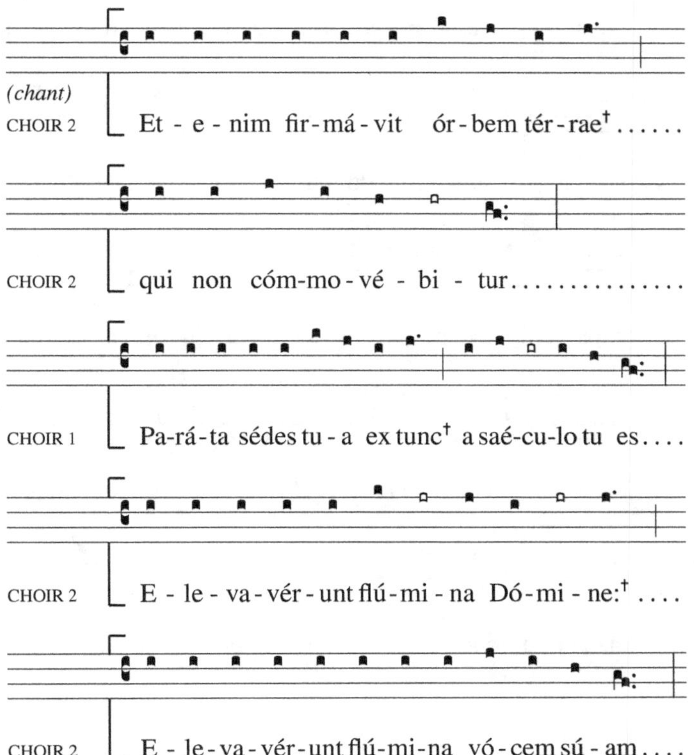

(chant)
CHOIR 1 E - le - va - vér - unt flú - mi - na flúc-tus su - os,†
CHOIR 1 a vó - ci - bus a-quá-rum mul-tá - rum . . . .
CHOIR 2 Mir-rá - bi - les e - la - ti - ó - nes má - ris:† . . . . .
CHOIR 2 mir-rá - bi - les in ál - tis Dó-mi-nus . . . .
CHOIR 1 Tes-ti-mó-ni - a tu - a cre-di - bí - li - a fác-ta . . .
CHOIR 1 sunt nímis†dó-mum tú-am dé-cet sanc-ti-tú-do . . .
CHOIR 1 Dó-mi-ne in lon-gi - tú-di-nem di - é - rum . . . . .
CHOIR 2 Gló-ri - a Pá-tri, et Fí-li-o† et Spirí-tu-i Sáncto . . . .
CHOIR 1 Síc-ut é-rat in prin-cí-pi-o et núnc, et sémper† . .

NOTES APPENDED FOR
STAGE SET, LIGHTING,
AND COSTUME.

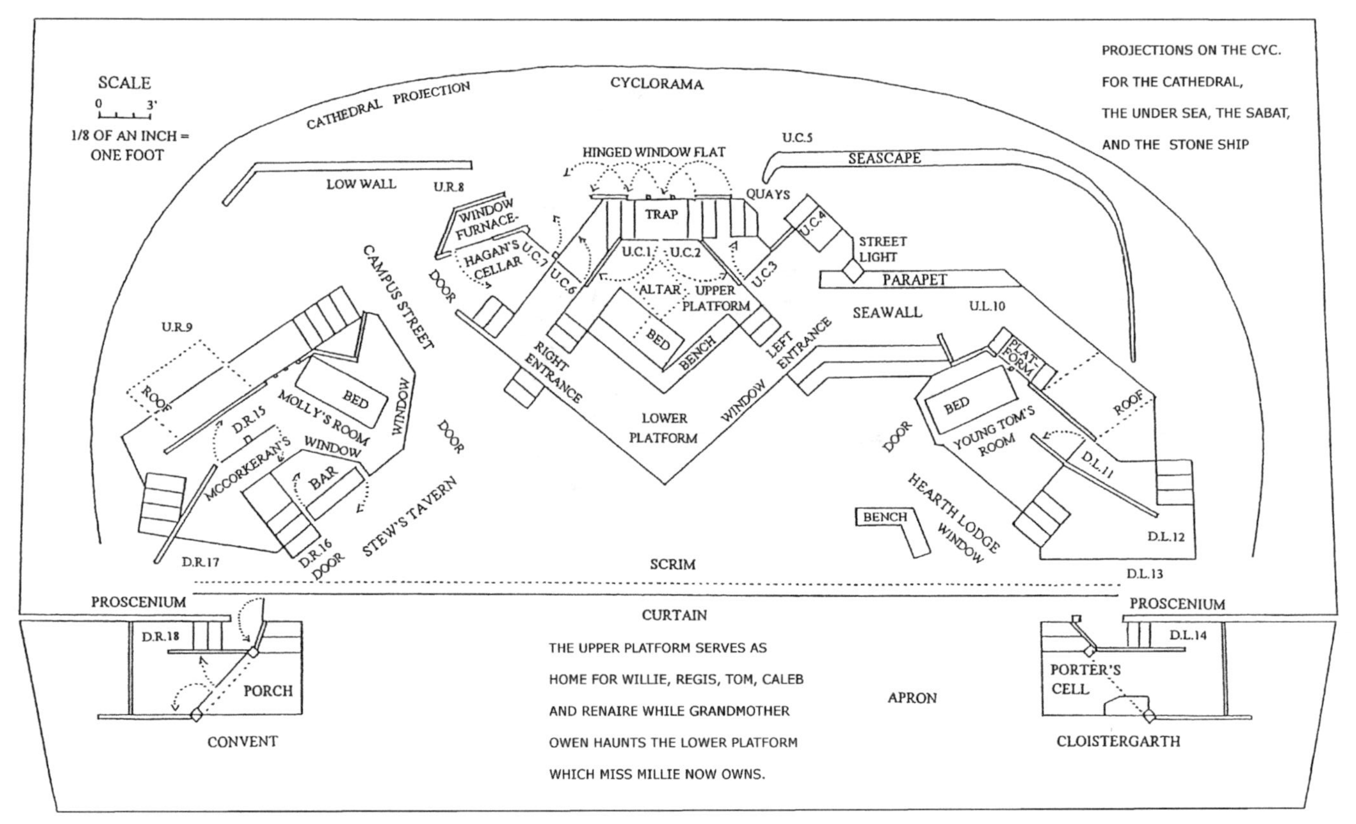

STAGE SET FOR THE STONE SHIP

STAGING

Due to the visionary and dreamlike quality of the Nocturne, the usual Proscenium-type stage with an apron in front of the curtain would be the most accommodating. The scrim enhances this dreamlike effect, suggesting fog and symbolizing the barrier of the lost memory. The cyclorama receives the various projections required.

The set is designed to allow continuous playing without interruption for scene changes. It consists of five platforms of various heights, backed by flats in the shape of house gables. The two small platforms outside the Proscenium are boxed in at the outer ends with arched openings onto the platforms, allowing the actors to come out or disappear inside. The one on the right represents the Convent porch, for Sr. Jennifer, and provides invisible access to back stage. The other, on the left, serves as the Porter's cell in Cloistergarth for Dom Jerome. His cell and the apron allow for intimate contact with the audience.

Behind the curtain and scrim are two entrances to the right and left. These should be wide enough to allow small choruses to stand in them with a view to the stage.

Adjacent to the righthand entrance there is a third platform with steps running up to a swivel door opening off-stage and into Molly's bedroom. In the bedroom there is a box-bed which is part of the cubic architecture of the platform - so the brass bedstead must be resisted, even if one is available! On the wall to the right there is a window with a blind. Other 'invisible' windows look down-stage to the Convent and up-stage to the seawall. A recessed space behind the steps on stage level serves as the bar in Stew's Tavern. It has a swivelling counter. Beyond the bedroom is Campus Street, backed by a low climbable wall, with entrances at both ends.

The fourth platform, jutting forward up-stage centre, consists of two levels. The lower has steps running up on the right and left to 'invisible' doors. Near the steps on the left are also 'invisible' windows. Real doors open off-stage in the backing flats, one on the left, the other on the right. Steps also descend into Hagan's cellar on stage level with a door up-stage, and on the right side to a flat with a furnace door which opens wide enough for Hagan to crawl through. A real furnace is not required! Instead, a removable screen is placed behind, containing lights for the fire, and a netted receptacle to catch the wood thrown into the fire. The flat is retractable to reveal another with a window, which can be slid in behind, representing Wick's garage. The cellar then serves as an office. At the down-stage end an 'invisible' door opens to the street. A low wall runs out from the platform, preventing the audience from seeing the floor of the cellar.

The upper level of the fourth platform has steps running up right and left. A bed like Molly's lies along the right side, but is hinged in the middle so that it may be folded over to form an altar. The foot of the bed has castors and a stow space. A bench on the lower platform skirting the bed serves as a runway for Hagan. Up-stage there are double doors which open onto the platform, revealing a hallway beyond with a windowed flat, the openings of the windows being lined with scrim. The flat folds back out of sight for the projections and the Sabat. Above the double doors there is a transom also lined with scrim. The double doorway is provided with a removable scrim to be used for the apparition of Rose Burns and appearance of the Satanic goat during the Sabat.

The lower level runs straight over to the left and around behind the fifth platform. This is the seawall with steps going up to it all along. A parapet guards the seaside, with a street light standing on it two feet from the righthand end. At the left end there is another entrance. Behind the seawall provision is made on stage level for a soundless fall of Caleb from the parapet. Further back a long flat representing a seascape with promontory curves around behind the fifth platform, providing an escape for actors up centre.

Down-stage on the left the fifth platform has steps running up to an entrance. Another entrance, further up-stage, opens into young Tom's bedroom. The bed is the same design as Molly's. There is a window in the wall on the left. Below on stage level is the entrance hall of Hearth Lodge, with an 'invisible' window down-stage, and an 'invisible' door up-stage. Out in front of Hearth Lodge is a stone bench.

Other furnishings for the set are a ledge in the Porter's cell for Dom Jerome's books, and a stool. There is another stool in young Tom's bedroom. Bert, the bartender, brings out two stools and a small round table from behind the counter, returning them after use. The gossips bring out two fragile, elegant tall-backed chairs and a wheeled miniature tea table with service. After use they are taken off again. For the beds there are four undersized pillows with dull off-white slips and coverlets lined with the same material, stowed out of sight on the up-stage side of the beds, and shoved there after use. Young Willie's and Caleb's are kept in the stow space under the bed. Their day clothes are put there on retiring, and the dim lantern for the Sabat is kept there.

The entire set is painted in graded tones of grey, or greyed earth colours, with due attention to atmospheric perspective. Even when the scrim is raised the pallid tones will continue to suggest the muting and veiling of the fog. The photographs in these notes are of a model designed with small figures while writing the stage business for the Nocturne.

LIGHTING

The lighting for the Nocturne is mobile, but in a slow, smooth, almost imperceptible way, flowing continuously with the acting, incoming and ebbing with flashbacks, mingling morning with evening and afternoon with midnight. Being a night watch, only those parts of the set are illuminated where Memory lights her lamp and sweeps till the lost coin is found: this bedroom, these steps, this seawall.

In the street the light is usually given a bluish cast if the scene is nocturnal, or straw-tinted for morning and warmer in the afternoon light. White light dramatizes certain climactic moments - the resurrection of Regis, for example, or Caleb during the Sabat, when the diabolic molestations surround him in a bluish haze, or when he throws down the chalice and paten, or when Jerome breaks through to his lost memory.

Light tinged with amber is used for indoor scenes - bright when the scene dominates, or fading when the scene slips into the background with mime. This is best illustrated when two scenes run concurrently, as with Annabelle and the gossips. All these changes, however, must be subtle and not draw attention to themselves. There are some exceptions, as when the light in the hallway suddenly snaps on at the end of Caleb's nightmare. There abrupt effects occur in several places. Regarding the lighting cues given in the text; they are indicative in a general way of the overall plan, but they should not be thought of as being complete.

COSTUME

Since the drama is ritualistic, in fact a re-enactment of a life almost concluded, it would be unwise to turn a pondering of destiny into a 'period piece'. Even though roughly situated in the twenties and thirties, which would make Dom Jerome a contemporary, the psychological theme, with its temporal and spacial ambiguity, the Nocturne calls for a more universal style. Certainly the play looks back to a more traditional time, when the old values were generally respected, but when the erosion of those values was already at work. Such consolidations and devastations are a recurrent theme in human history - 'the rise and fall of many'. One need not date such a stuggle as it goes on always. Therefore I wouldn't want costuming to be made up of nostalgic 'quotations', for that would allow the audience to escape (their favourite pastime), saying, 'ah - that was then ...' If a flapper appears on stage, they can say 'how silly our mothers were!', when they should be looking at their own lives, not their mother's. The costuming should be kept ambiguous as to period, and as timeless as may be - it could be anyone, anytime, anywhere.

NOR RASHLY ANOTHER JUDGE, P.40

The costumes will be described here in the order in which they are worn for the convenience of those who are doubling or tripling roles.

1 DOM JEROME wears a monastic habit consisting of a tunic, scapular and cowl, made of a dull, slightly greenish grey woolen material, which looks heavy and falls well in soft folds, with a grey leather belt about the waist under the scapular, and black shoes, not sandals.

1 TOM BURNS appears to be growing out of his clothes; a cream coloured sport shirt, open at the neck, a brown well-worn corduroy jacket, pants of a greyish tan with cuffs. His brown leather loafers with low heels distinguish his height from that of Caleb.

2 CALEB THORN wears an expensive, well-tailored suit of conservative cut of a slightly greyed and lightened navy blue, a white shirt-front and collar with black tie, like a dickey fastened at the back of the neck for easy removal, white french cuffs sewn inside the suit jacket sleeves. Under this he wears pale blue pyjamas of wrinkle-proof dacron, a little short in the arms and legs to enhance his appearance of vulnerability during the Sabat, and also to prevent their showing under the suit. With the suit he wears black socks and slip-on black shoes with slightly elevated heels.

1 ROSE BURNS looks fragile in an ivory gauze nightdress worn over a slip, with a knitted cream-coloured shawl over her shoulders. To enhance her ghost-like appearance, a slight disturbance of the gauze with a silent fan would be effective.

2 MOTHER WICKS makes her brief appearances in an ivory-coloured housedress, less severe than that worn by MARY SIMS, with a delicate canary-coloured floral pattern, and a pale blue apron worn over it.

3 MARY SIMS looks domestic in an off-white cotton housedress with prim little ivory collar and cuffs. When going to church she puts on a threadbare brown coat with a lusterless bit of rabbit fur at the neck, and a small brown hat. She wears low-heeled sensible shoes.

1 YOUNG TOM is dressed for play. His baggy grey-blue pants, ivory sport shirt with open collar and canary sweater given evidence of rough-and-tumble by their dishevelled appearance. He wears pale blue socks with old running shoes. For the night scene he is wearing pale blue pyjamas.

2 WILLIE SIMS is dressed as a poor boy, but very clean and decent. He wears an off-white cotton shirt with a narrow tan tie, a grey sweater and short brown pants. His grey ribbed stockings are pulled up to the knees and his shoes are scuffed and run-down. He has a peaked cap which has lost its shape, and a short mouse-brown overcoat which is too small for him.

1 AUNT HANNA wears a flowered print dress of pale moss green, lavender and grey with the cotton stockings of the middle-aged, and low-heeled black shoes. When she goes out, she puts on a black coat and hat.

2 MRS. THOREAU favours a frilly ivory blouse with a well-tailored suit of dusky-puce gabardine, silk stockings and black high-heeled shoes.

3 SR. SUPERIOR wears the same nun's habit as SR. JENNIFER, with the addition of a silver cross hung on a fine chain below the wimple.

1 CAPT. CODROCKS wears his old captain's hat, and what was once a navy blue woolen jacket, much tattered with its brass buttons well-tarnished, over his open-necked grey workshirt. His charcoal-coloured wool pants are tucked into rubber boots.

2 HARRY IBBS has the same charcoal-coloured pants tucked into rubber boots, and the same grey workshirt, with a thick brown wool sweater, and a rain-cape and sou'wester of olive oilskin, which have been sprayed with some streaking like green algae, and over-sprayed with a glossy medium to make them look still wet. His rubber boots are treated in the same way. For the Sabat he discards the raincape and sou'wester, replacing them with a grey-green hooded cape.

3 UNCLE REMUS wears an old smoking jacket of coppery satin, speckled black-and-grey tweed pants, a white shirt with thin pale blue stripes and a two-toned grey tie. His stockings and shoes are black.

1 REGIS WICKS wears a navy blue jacket with slim-cut grey flannels, pale blue socks and slip-on black leather shoes. His white shirt is worn with the collar open. For the play, he discards the jacket, and for the procession he dons a floor-length cape of heavy off-white material lined with ivory, which falls in soft graceful folds. It is cut like a cope - a flat sheet with a clasp in front, and the back two corners curved. The material should not be slippery, to ease its management at the resurrection. He wears a crown of vines, to be removed after his death.

COME TO THE MESA - IT'S MIDNIGHT, P.142

1 NICK, when he appears with the drunks, is dressed in rough fishing clothes
  - baggy denim pants, worn and faded, tucked into rubber gumboots; a grey
  work shirt is open at the neck with a frayed sleeveless brown sweater.

2 JOB WICKS, speaking with MR. FROAR wears a tan work shirt, blue denim over-
  alls, much faded, worn and oil-stained. He wears old workboots.

3 NICHOLAS BURNS (SIMS) for his nocturnal visit with MARY, wears a pair of dark-
  grey pants, a navy blue turtleneck sweater and brown shoes.

4 SANDY is younger and has a certain foppish decadence about him, wearing a
  dark grey pinstripe suit of modish cut, with white shirt, scarlet tie loosened
  and the collar opened. His shoes are shiny black and pointed. For the Sabat
  he has a grey-blue hooded cape.

1 FAY FLOSS wears a short blue dress with long black stockings and black shoes.
  Her wiast-length cape is rose with cream satin lining.

2 YOUNG WILLIE is wearing an off-white shirt with open collar, short pants of a
  brown-and-grey tweed, with off-white socks and scampers. Over the shirt
  he has a blue-grey windbreaker, out of which a scarlet scarf escapes.

1 FANNY FLOSS is wearing a short pale-turquoise dress, long black stockings and
  black shoes, with a moss-green cape of the same style as FAY's, with ivory
  satin lining.

2 JENNY WICKS has a lavender knee-length dress with a little flare in the skirt,
  the same black stockings and shoes as FANNY, with a turquoise kerchief large
  enough to become a veil.

1 SR. JENNIFER wears a nun's habit consisting of tunic, cloth cincture, scapular
  and veil, made of the same kind of material as DOM JEROME's habit, but off-
  white in colour. Her wimple under the veil is of white, unstarched linen.
  She wears black shoes.

2 SUE wears a tailored knee-length brown dress, silk stockings with dainty tan
  shoes to match. Over these for the Sabat, she wears her hooded floor-length
  cape of grey-puce. For the tavern scene with CALEB THORN, she changes the
  brown dress to an old-ivory chiffon party dress, with a flared skirt.

THE MYSTIC MOCKERY, P.159

1 DAN WICKS wears slim-cut brown pants, brown socks with black shoes, and a tan corduroy vest over an ivory shirt open at the neck. For the procession he puts on a short waist-length cloak of a rich old-gold material. The silver-painted wooden sword and a small hammer hang from his belt on the left, and he carries a silvered wooden spear.

2 COURIER wears a messenger boy's navy blue uniform with bicycle clips on his pant legs.

1 BEN WICKS is dressed in navy blue slim-cut pants, black socks and shoes, with a grey-blue sleeved sweater over a white shirt, open at the neck. For the procession he dons a waist-length grey cloak, with a dull silken sheen. For the Sabat he changes into grey-blue pants of ordinary cut, and a navy blue sleeved sweater over an off-white shirt with an open collar. His hooded floor-length cape is of light grey.

1 MR. FROAR wears navy pants, black sock and shoes, a grey tweed jacket over a white shirt and a scarlet bow tie and flat brimmed straw hat. For the Sabat he removes hat and tie, and dons a grey-ochre hooded cape.

2 BERT wears a bartender's outfit consisting of navy pants, black socks and shoes, a white shirt with elastic bracelets on the arms and a black bow tie.

1 MRS. WAGUARD is clad in a moss green dress, silk stockings and medium-heeled brown shoes, with a brown fur-trimmed coat. Her hat, also moss green, is trimmed with brown netting. For the Sabat she wears a greenish-grey tunic with a hooded grey-puce cape.

2 GRANNY OWEN wears a lavender-hued silk dress of old fashioned style coming just below the knees. The lapels of her collar are adorned with old lace and are fastened with a cameo brooch. She wears silk stockings and black shoes with low heels. When she goes out, she puts on a black coat and a small black hat, trimmed with a little cluster of artificial velvet violets. When walking she leans on a briar cane.

1 OLRIG HAGAN is dressed in dark brown pants and turtleneck with black stockings and shoes, the latter unpolished. Over the sweater he wears a knee-length cape of ochre tinged with grey, lined in off-white.

2 DR. MALLOY looks thoroughly professional, with a warm brown tweed suit, a white shirt with a navy blue tie, black stockings and oxfords well-polished. For the final scene he adds a short grey cape. He carries a small doctor's bag on housecalls.

GOODBY ROSEMARY, MOTHER, P.202

1 ANNABELLE PEW dons a spinterish costume of grey-blue silk, high at the neck
with old ivory lace and a cameo. Over this a black coat and matching felt hat
with a daunting gold hatpin. She wears silk stockings and black high-heel
shoes.

2 MRS. THORN is elegantly clad in an old-ivory silk dress, with a gold chain and
locket about the neck. She wears silk stockings with high-heel shoes of tan
leather.

1 MOLLY GREEN adopts an apparel which reveals a revolt of the usual vulgar-
ity of the red light sisterhood. She now wears a light brown suit of business
style cut, the skirt to the knees, with silk stockings and black medium-heeled
shoes. Her ivory-coloured blouse is plain, and she wears no jewellery. During the letter reading scene and the Sabat, she wears an old-ivory nightdress
which is feminine but modest. For the conversion with SR. JENNIFER she wears
a greyish-rose housecoat over the nightdress.

1 AMY HEARTH has no style whatever. She wears a well-bleached housedress
from which what was once a bluish flower pattern has almost faded. The
dress is well-starched. Over it she wears a no-nonsense grey apron. Her
stockings are cotton, her shoes are low-heeled and black. She peers through
black quizzical horn-rimmed glasses and when she goes out she wears a
navy blue coat and hat.

2 MCCORKERAN, slatternly and heavy: adequate padding will be necessary. A
pink fringe of nightdress is visible under a battleship-grey housecoat with
pink satin edging, and slippers with no stockings. For the Sabat she wears
a greenish-grey ankle-length tunic with a hooded cape of light grey, lined
with off-white.

1 ELI RENAIRE wears an elegantly tailored suit of charcoal-brownish wool, a
white shirt with a black tie, black shoes and stockings. For the Sabat he
dons a slightly tanned grey cape and hood with an off-white satin lining.

1 LIBRARIAN is clad in a gabardine pinstripe suit of navy blue, a white shirt with
a shot silk tie of brown and green, with black shoes and stockings. During
the Sabat, he vests in a lavender cape and hood, lined with grey satin. Over
his arm he carries the carefully folded satanic vestment of blue-grey satin,
cut like a monastic choir robe with wide sleeves falling to the elbows, and
a full-length overlapping closure in front. Panels of grey-green velvet fall
vertically to the floor, front and back, embroidered with silvered leather and
black velvet edging in geometric symbols suggesting the pentacle.

SO YOU NOW REMEMBER, P.204

1 BUB wears patched brown pants tucked in rubber boots, a tan workshirt open at the neck, a grey windbreaker, much the worse for wear, and a sou'wester.

2 DRUGGIST is dressed in a subdued brown suit with black stockings and brown shoes. His shirt is ivory-coloured with an absinthe green tie. During the Sabat he vests in a lavender cape and hood, lined in grey satin. He carries a heavy silvered chalice which will stand the battering of being thrown down, and a similar silvered paten resting on top of the chalice with a square cube of black bread upon it.

1 TAD MCFERGUSON sports a scottish tam o'shanter, an old woolen blue-green plaid jacket with leather buttons, brown tweed pants, and old scuffed work-boots. His work shirt is open-collared.

2 CAPT. HADDOCK wears brown pants tucked into rubber boots, and over the work shirt, a bulky, padded olive windbreaker.

1 MISS MILLIE, gossiprey's leading light, and definitely the haute monde's wealthiest widow, she wears fashionable black with a double string of genuine pearls, silk stockings and high-heeled black leather shoes. For the Sabat she dons a greenish-grey tunic, and a hooded grey-blue cape.

1 MISS BRAYLORN wears an old-gold brocade dress with silk stockings and black high-heeled shoes. When arriving, she has a mauvish-grey coat and very stylish black hat. For the Sabat she wears a greenish-grey tunic, with a hooded grey-rose cape.

2 KATY, for the Tavern scene with CALEB, wears a seductive, glossy black party dress, silk stockings with black leather high-heeled shoes, and a long silken scarlet scarf. For the Sabat she is wearing the same greenish-grey tunic, with a hooded grey-rose cape.

1 MRS. CARP wears a mannish brown tweed suit with an ivory blouse, grey tweed coat, a brimmed fedora-like brown hat belying her femininity, silk stockings and low-heeled brown shoes. For the Sabat she dons a greenish-grey tunic, with a hooded grey-rose cape.

1 PADDY wears olive-coloured workpants, workboots, dark grey work shirt, olive oilskin with a hood, and a bright green scarf.

2 HAL is dressed in grey flannels with black socks and brown loafers and a navy cardigan over a pale blue shirt with a grey bow tie. For the Sabat he wears the same as PADDY, replacing the oilskin and scarf with a pauper's improvised burlap rain cover and the crown of a battered felt hat.

PERHAPS I AM BLIND, P.212

3 NEIL wears the same as PADDY for the Sabat, replacing oilskin and scarf this time with a grey-tan cloak and hood.

1 DIEL appears in old black work pants, rubber galoshes, a rust-red wool work-shirt, and a grey oilskin jacket, open at the front.

2 JAKE wears a brown woolen suit with a straw-coloured sport shirt, open at the neck, grey socks with brown sandals. For the Sabat he puts on a grey-green hooded cape, closed in front while playing DIEL, with HAL.

The colours of the various costumes have been carefully selected to compliment each other, and to create ensembles harmonious with the lighting, projections and overall decor.

LEST UMBRAGE BE TAKEN

By professional producers, directors, or designers, the author's meddling in their fields of expertise was not intended to curb creativity. The hard facts are that in our time of dwindling art's funding the probability of a work of this size being preformed are slight. Clearly only a large and well established repertory company could attempt it. The work, therefore, is addressed in the first instance to armchair readers of poetic drama. They at least would be able to unfurl the sails of imagination, launching the Ship of Stone on a voyage of discovery. The elaborate notes, therefore, have been included for them, without prejudice of course to their use by any future director of the Nocturne.

9 781625 641014